About the author

I was born in Liverpool in 1934, and placed in the care of the National Children's Homes from the age of two to sixteen, living on the Isle of Man during the war, in Nottingham from VJ Day to 1949, and lastly in the NCH Hostel in Highbury. The book includes much of my early life story. I joined the Royal Air Force in 1955 as an aircraft fitter and was posted to Singapore, but received a medical discharge due to the effect of the climate on my health. On returning to civilian life, I worked mainly as an electrician. I have been married twice and have three children, four grandchildren and one great grandchild. I am now living in the Isle of Man. As well as writing, my interests include drawing portraits, learning to play the piano, and assisting young people in Tanzania through education and medical care.

OUR EM

VOLUME TWO: MAJOR EM

WILFRED SUMMERS

OUR EM

VOLUME TWO: MAJOR EM

Vanguard Press

VANGUARD PAPERBACK

© Copyright 2021
Wilfred Summers

A CIP catalogue record for this title is
available from the British Library.

ISBN 978 1 80016 190 0

Vanguard Press is an imprint of
Pegasus Elliot MacKenzie Publishers Ltd.
www.pegasuspublishers.com

First Published in 2021

Vanguard Press
Sheraton House Castle Park
Cambridge England

Printed & Bound in Great Britain

Dedication

This book is dedicated to:

All the children who were cared for in the National Children's Homes between 1869 and the late 1900s;

all the staff who cared for us when we needed them;

and all the parents who, being unable to support their children, also suffered the pain of separation and broken family life.

Acknowledgements

I would like to thank my neighbours and friends who read the manuscript in instalments as I was writing it, frequently asking 'What happens next?' to which I had to reply 'I don't know, I haven't written it yet', for their encouragement and enthusiasm which helped me to keep on writing. I would also like to thank my secretarial assistant who read each day's work through, checking especially punctuation and repetition, noting where names had mysteriously changed overnight and tracing previous references which did not fit with the latest developments. To all of them I would like to say 'Here is the book you helped to create'!

Preface

Em continues to combine the responsibilities of housekeeper at Moore Hall with her military role as long as the Americans are in residence. George/Victor uses his flexibility as a delivery driver to explore 'fresh woods and pastures new' as well as seeking to re-establish his relationship with Em. His temporary absence 'at His Majesty's pleasure' disrupts the hopes of more than one 'wife', and the fallout for Em results in considerable unplanned changes in her life as well, as she overcomes disappointments and meets both professional and personal challenges with courage and tenacity. As the story moves on, both Em and George/Victor find themselves directed as much by the wishes of others as by their own desires. Their paths cross and part again, arousing hope but denying its fulfilment. Circumstances change, as so often 'truth will out', and the scope of their story expands further in Volume Three, before drawing together into some degree of resolution before the end of the fourth and final volume.

Chapter One

"Em, do you know a Captain Joan?" Sandra asked.

"Captain what?"

"Joan, I think that's what he said."

Em shrugged. Sandra put the phone down, and continued stirring the gravy. "It's nearly ready," she said in answer to Em's glance and unvoiced enquiry.

The phone rang again. "Ignore it, we've got hungry guests and a lunch to serve." Naomi came into the kitchen. "Answer that please, Naomi," said Em, as she carried the covered silver platter that contained the roast leg of lamb towards the dining room.

"I'm sorry, but Major Summers is not here at the moment... Yes, I'll ask her to ring as soon as she is free... Who shall I say wants her? Oh... Gate Security... Captain who?... Jane?... No?... Can you spell that?... oh James... What? Joan... No? Jones... yes I've got that... I'll see she gets the message... Thank you."

James waited by the gate. "I'm sorry, sir," said the guard, "can't let you in without clearance from a senior officer, no matter who you say you are."

"Then try again, please," he asked but he might as well have not spoken. It was an hour since he'd arrived and he was still stuck outside the gate.

Getting back into his car, I'm an idiot, James thought, I should have gone from my house and along the path through the woods. Without a word to the guard, he started his engine and drove off.

The telephone rang. "Who?" asked the guard. "No," he answered, "no, he's just driven off down the road... Yes, Major."

James parked his car at the side of the road, walked round the side of the house and through the gate into a ploughed field. "Damn it," he said as his foot kept slipping into the furrow at the side of the field. "Damn it," as the brambles kept snagging his greatcoat as he made his way through the woods. There was no one available during wartime to keep footpaths clear of brambles. Arriving in the courtyard at the rear of the house, after using the long grass to wipe the soil from his shoes, and shaking pieces of foliage off his greatcoat, James opened the back door.

"You can't come in here, sir," said Naomi, barring his way.

"Tell Em it's James," he said.

"Oh, you're the man who… "She suddenly realised and stopping mid-sentence. "Em rang back but you had gone," she continued. "How did you get—? "Naomi stopped again, then called out, "Em, he's here."

"Who's here?"

"Captain whatever his name was."

James laughed, and called out, "It's me, James."

"Oh James, I thought… never mind what I thought, come in. Oh take those filthy shoes off and put a pair of kitchen shoes on. mmm, Captain… how come?"

"My platoon ran into an ambush," he said. "It's a long story, I'll tell you some other time. I could certainly kill for a hot drink."

"Put the kettle on please, Naomi," Em said, then, "Come into the office, you probably haven't eaten for a while. Sit down while I see what I can rustle up."

The ladies were in the drawing room having their after-lunch sherry. Tired of the idle chit-chat of the others, Cynthia was standing by the window watching the birds; a robin on the bird table was scattering the seeds, its mate on the ground enjoying them seemingly coming down from heaven. She chuckled as she watched the ring-necked doves also taking advantage of the ready supply. Something had disturbed the banquet; birds flew off in all directions as a lorry came round from the rear of the house.

"That's him," she shouted, pointing to the lorry as it went down the drive. "That's him," she said excitedly.

"That's who?" a chorus of voices asked.

"George," Cynthia responded, as she quickly dashed out of the room on her way to the kitchen.

Lady Jane's voice followed her. "George who?"

"I've seen him," she gasped out as she entered the kitchen.

"Seen who?" asked Sandra.

"Where's Em?" Cynthia enquired.

"She went over to see the medics. She said she'd only be half an hour. Shall I tell her—?"

Just then Em appeared. "They're going to—"

"It's him," Cynthia interrupted, "I've just seen him – George – in a lorry, going down the drive."

"Are you sure?"

"Of course I'm sure," Cynthia replied.

"No," said the store man, "the delivery man's name was Victor. You must have got him mixed up with someone else, no," he said, "no George."

"I was absolutely sure," Cynthia said as they walked back to the kitchen. "It looked awfully like him," she added, apologetically, "maybe it was his twin."

"He hasn't got a brother, let alone a twin," Em replied.

"Well? Was it... anyway, who is George?"

"I don't know," Cynthia murmured, "I was sure..." almost to herself, "I'm sure it was," then to the assembled crowd, "someone I met some time ago." Cynthia finished her drink, excused herself and went upstairs to her room.

I wonder, could he be using a different name? Both women had the same thought.

Em sat in her office. It was all too confusing. If it was George, had his injury meant that he hadn't recovered his memory, and he wouldn't know her or the boys? *That* would be bad enough, but what if it was him and he didn't want to know. The tears flowed. Oh, George, why why why, what have we done to deserve this? You can't do this to us. Sandra entered the office. "Not now, please, Sandra."

Sandra looked at Em. "Oh Em," she said, putting her arm around Em's shoulder, "what is it?"

The words flooded out. "I don't know what to think… I don't know what to do."

"I'm sure we'll think of something," Sandra said.

Em wiped away her tears and blew her nose. "Thank you, Sandra. Please finish preparing the dinner while I make a phone call," she said.

"Yes, this is Birkenhead police station. No, we don't have a Sergeant Bridges… but we have an Inspector… I don't know… Yes, it could be… Very well, he is very busy… I'll see if he is free. Who shall I say wants him? One moment, madam." A few minutes later, "I'm putting you through, madam."

"Thank you," said Em.

"Yes Mrs Summers, thank you… Whoa steady on… I'll… I'd better come and see you… Yes, are you still at…? About half to three quarters… I'm on my way." Putting the phone down, Inspector Bridges said to his colleagues, "I won't be available this afternoon, but I will phone you from a call box to check out anything urgent around five o'clock.

The phone on Em's desk rang. "Major Summers? There's a policeman asking for you, an Inspector… That's right, Inspector Bridges… Yes, ma'am… No escort? Okay, ma'am."

"What's this Major business then, Em? it sounds like it's not only me that's been promoted; more important, is there anywhere we can talk in private?"

"Have you found George?" asked Em.

"Not yet, but what is this about him coming here? Did *you* see him? No? Well sit down and tell me from the beginning," he said, getting out his notebook.

Em told him about Cynthia, also explaining how Cynthia had met George in Singapore and then later when he had stopped and helped her on the road.

"I'd like to have a word with her, please."

After a little while Em returned to the office, accompanied by Cynthia. "Please ignore my uniform, nothing formal," he said. "I'm here as a family friend, but I'd like to know what you saw the other day. Please take your time." The Inspector listened, asked very few questions, and made a few notes. "Thank you," he said, "you may well be right, but it is possible that you saw someone else of very similar appearance. Thank you for your time," he said, shaking her hand and giving a gentlemanly bow. When Cynthia had left, Inspector Bridges turned to Em. "Don't worry your pretty head," he said, "I'll make a few discreet enquiries. Now, where is the store? I need just a few more details. No, it's all right, just point me to it," and with that he was gone.

"He seemed a nice bloke for a rozzer," said Sandra.

"He is," replied Em. "If anyone can find George, he can."

"A sort of Sexton Blake."

"Well maybe," said Em, "anyway, I've every confidence in him."

There was a knock on the door. "Who was that policeman?" asked Cynthia.

"A family friend who knew George's family," answered Em. "I worked with his wife when I was living in Liscard."

"And?" asked Cynthia.

"He said he'd make a few discreet enquiries, nothing official."

***

Delilah wasn't going to allow the loss of the library for her exercises to rob her of all her fun. It had turned out that among the thirty or so American patients there were half a dozen men who professed to be budding artists, and at least that many interested in photography, although it was doubtful about how many actually had film in their cameras. She hesitated to expose what she considered would cause disapproval from her aunt, but she was quite prepared to be doing some ballet movements in slow motion in front of the cameras, and posing for the artists with lace net curtains draped over her bathing costume, while showing as much naked leg as she thought to be within the realms of

17

decency. Amusing both herself and a number of the patients during the daytime, she usually spent her evenings in the company of Charles and Harry, until Charles had to return to being a Royal Air Force Officer, then almost exclusively with Harry.

While frowning at Delilah's antics, Cynthia wasn't going to let her husband's absence rob her of male companionship. She had her sights on the more mature man both in age and rank, and was not against making discreet use of the back stairs, which meant staff had to look and listen before negotiating the staircase themselves. In the evenings, when the vast library was in semi-darkness, there were usually three or four couples, off duty nurses and patients (who were officers), making use of the large comfortable chairs.

As the year 1942 came to an end and passed into 1943, the house guests departed as they had arrived, in their ones and twos, the last to leave being Delilah driven home by Cynthia, the two sharing their petrol rations to make the round trip. Moore Hall returned to normality, a quiet country house serving as a convalescent home for the US Military.

Em and her team, nobly assisted by a heavily pregnant Naomi, were spring cleaning the rooms that had been occupied by the house guests. Naomi marvelled at the thoroughness of Sandra and Susan as they worked as a team. Every piece of upholstery, every polished surface and every square inch of carpet received the same amount of attention, each room taking about a week before the dust sheets were put into place. Spare furniture, normally stored in a room on the first floor, was moved to the Tudor suite in order for the store room to be used as a bedroom, with twin beds, for Laurence and Naomi to use up to the birth of their child.

Having experienced the loneliness that one can feel when away from one's family, especially in the later months of pregnancy, Em had one of the old loungers from the storeroom placed in her office, after the filing cabinet had been moved out to make room for it. With the door open, Naomi, who by the beginning of March was advised to rest, would be able to join in the chit-chat and companionship of the kitchen, beneficial to both as Em could keep an eye on Naomi, and Naomi could deal with any phone calls.

Chapter Two

April showers gave way to warm spring sunshine. The flower borders shone gold with daffodils and the hedgerows white with hawthorn blossom. The war seemed a long way away, the only reminders being the occasional drone of an aircraft overhead, or the military lorry making its weekly deliveries to the quartermaster's store.

Em looked across the office at Naomi lying on the lounger. "How are you feeling?" she asked, seeing her screwing up her face, then giggling.

"He doesn't half kick," she replied, not really knowing why she was calling the unborn infant 'he'. "He'll be a good placekicker for the New York Jets when he grows up."

Em smiled, but looked puzzled. "What are they?"

"One of the best soccer teams back home," said Naomi.

"That's it," Em said, putting down her pen. "Ready for a stroll in the sun?"

"You bet," replied Naomi, easing herself from the lounger and settling into the wheelchair. "Can we go to the Rose Garden, please?"

Em gently negotiated the chair through the back door and down the steps, then round to the side lawn, down the slope and into the Rose Garden, protected from the gentle breeze by the manicured hedge. With the wheelchair placed beside the south facing garden seat, they sat watching the birds and enjoying the warmth of the afternoon sun. After a while, Naomi opened her magazine and Em got out her knitting – a layette for the new baby.

The care she received from Em's 'family' and the nursing staff at Moore Hall went a long way to compensate for absence of her own family and Laurence's folk. As April drew to a close, and the first days of May approached, she became more dependent on the friendship and services of Em and her staff who, bearing in mind how slim she had been when she first arrived in the kitchen, wondered if perhaps there might be twins.

Laurence Goldstein Junior was born on a bright sunny day, a bonny baby weighing seven pounds three ounces, with District Midwife Pamela Short in attendance. Mother and baby had been moved back into a private room in the convalescent wing, to be looked after by the US Military nurses, thus releasing Em and her staff from the responsibility, although they were frequent visitors.

The presence of a new baby on the premises stirred up Em's maternal instinct. She missed the family that she had been forced through circumstances to part with, and she resolved that just as soon as she was able, no matter how long it took, she would provide a home for her two boys and make up for all the time that they had missed. Was her dream to appease her feeling of guilt, or for her own personal benefit? Whatever, seeing them last year had emphasised how much she loved and missed them. Time would tell.

***

Em put the phone down. Surely there had to be an answer, or had the Inspector just said that he would make enquiries to placate her? She didn't think so, surely he wouldn't have taken the time to call in to see her. No, she was quietly confident that he would find out if George Summers and Victor, whatever his name was, were the same person, and whether or not George had completely lost his memory. But it was frustrating. This was the third time she had phoned the police station without being able to speak to Inspector Bridges.

Police Constable Nelly Briggs shook her head. She felt sorry for the poor lady. She had been on duty the day when the Inspector had received the call that had sent him out after cancelling any appointments for the afternoon, what was that about? The Inspector had told her not to put any calls through from this poor lady. I don't know… I suppose he hasn't finished his enquiries yet, but I can't help feeling sorry for her. Well, I'd better get on with these reports. The telephone rang on the switchboard. "Birkenhead Police Station… one moment, sir." She plugged the lead in to the Inspector's line and operated the switch to ring the extension. "The Chief Super for you, sir… You are through, sir." Putting the phone back on its rest, Hmm… I wonder what he wants…

Inspector Bridges breathed a sigh of relief. The Chief Super had agreed to see him in Chester. He would need to rearrange his appointments to leave Thursday free. Taking a large envelope out from his desk drawer, he surveyed the contents and shook his head. Would he consider there was enough evidence to convict? No, he thought, he felt he needed to be able to *prove* that George had completely recovered his memory, and that he *knew* what he was doing, but what was going to be important was what the Super thought, and to start with, of course, he would need copies of both marriage certificates.

***

"I see what you mean." The Superintendent turned over the pages. "Quite a scoundrel. Nineteen twenty-four. What's this? I remember the training ships, most boys who came off those did quite well for themselves." Turning another page, "Park Prewett? How did he get away from there?"

"It seemed that he didn't need to be in a mental hospital. I helped him to get out," said the Inspector.

"More's the pity," the Super replied. "If he was still in there we wouldn't have this mess."

"If he had stayed at home helping his father he would have been all right," the Inspector said, "but he messed up and took off."

"So? Where do we go from here?"

"I'd like a few days away from normal duties to take enquiries further, sir."

"You mean?"

"Witney, sir, I think he was living there, and I've an idea that might provide another clue to the story."

"Right," said the Super, "I'll send Harris to cover for you next week, giving you enough time to obtain evidence." Smiling, the two men stood up and shook hands. "Good hunting."

"Thank you, sir," replied Inspector Bridges.

***

The old Wolseley came to a stop at the road block. "Driving licence and identity card please, sir," the police constable said. The tall man wearing a dogtooth-patterned, worsted sports jacket and a grey trilby, reached into his inside pocket, pulled out the requested documents and passed them to the constable.

"Would you pull over to the left please, sir, while we check your vehicle... I said would you..."

"I'd like a word with your sergeant, please." Inspector Bridges showed his warrant card."

"Sorry, sir... I, er, um..." stuttered the young constable, "right away, sir."

"Is there a problem, sir?" asked the police sergeant.

"Yes, I'm in a hurry, I need to get to Oxford before dark."

"Very good, sir, you're free to go."

As Inspector Bridges drove off, the constable was saying, "Honest, Sergeant, I didn't know..."

***

Mr Blake shook his visitor's hand. "Good Morning Mr... er Bridges, what can I do for you?"

"I am making a few routine enquiries, but first let me introduce myself." Inspector Bridges showed Mr Blake his warrant card. "I am Inspector Bridges of the Cheshire Constabulary and I am leading a discreet enquiry for the Ministry of Defence, let me emphasise, discreet. Just a matter of statistics, strictly hush-hush, which is why I have come straight to you, Mr Blake."

"How can I help?"

"If you could let me have a list of drivers, their addresses and their vehicle numbers, that would be of considerable assistance."

"Please excuse me for a moment," said Mr Blake as he left his office, returning a little later with a neatly typed list.

The Inspector scanned the list. "Is this *all* the drivers who deliver your goods?"

"Well, no," replied Mr Blake. "Sally," he called, "you haven't included Victor."

"He's not one of our employees, sir."

"One moment…" and he left the office once more, appearing a few minutes later with a handwritten name and address, and Victor's lorry number.

"Thank you," said the Inspector, then touching the side of his nose, "Remember, not a word," and he departed.

After a short visit to the Oxfordshire Constabulary Headquarters, Inspector Bridges, accompanied by a uniformed police sergeant, rang the doorbell at 7, Deane Close, in Ramsden. After a few minutes, a distinguished looking lady answered the door. "Hello, Brian," she said. "What brings you here?"

"May we come in, Alice?"

"I suppose you'd better," she replied. "What is it? Is it my Victor?" she asked, panic starting to sound in her voice.

"Nothing has happened to him. This is Inspector Bridges, he has a few questions, if you don't mind."

"This should only take a few minutes, Mrs Cooper—"

"I'm Mrs Bradburn," she interrupted.

Ignoring the interruption, the Inspector continued. "I'm making enquiries about George Summers who—"

Again she interrupted. "I don't know any George whatever the name was."

"I'm afraid you do, madam," he continued. "Please let me finish, then you will understand what I'm telling you." He looked at her; his eyes had a soft, gentle look in them, he felt sorry, but she had to be told.

"The man Victor Bradburn is really George Summers, already married with twin boys."

"The bastard," she burst out. "I'll kill him."

"No you won't, Alice," said Police Sergeant Clarke. "You'll tell us if you see him and let us and the court deal with him," he countered her outburst. "Can you let me see your marriage certificate please? Thank you." He glanced at it and passed it to Inspector Bridges. "We need a copy, I'll bring it back in an hour or two," he said.

The two men sat in the police car. "You've got to feel sorry for her, sir," said the police sergeant. "I went to school with her. She was, and still is beautiful, a gentle woman in every way. Fortunately she has friends; word has it that she's been seen quite frequently out with Malcolm Cooper, her brother-in-law. The former boyfriend – I nearly said husband – went off somewhere delivering, he's a lorry driver."

"I know," replied the Inspector. "It was his wife, Emily, who asked me to find him." He chuckled. "It's funny really, in fact ironic." He paused for a moment. "I went to school with George Summers' parents. He was a big disappointment to them. He had everything going for him, but somewhere he went wrong. I feel sorry for him, but he deserves a kick in the pants, and by heck he'll get it," he said. "Come on, let's get back to the station, I could murder a cuppa tea."

**

"How did you get on?" the Super asked as he shook hands with Inspector Bridges. "It only seems like you were in here a couple of days ago, won't you sit down?"

"Well, not quite, it was ten days ago, sir."

"Hm, was it? Well, yes... good work, so?" He looked up from the sheaf of papers the Inspector had given him. "They are going to take on the case, are they?"

"Well, yes, sir, I could hardly do it. I am too closely linked with the family. His parents were friends of mine, and the Oxfordshire boys will be prosecuting as the bigamous marriage was in their patch."

"And what about the Thornton Heath connection?"

"I'll pass that on when I have the proof, that is, a copy of that marriage certificate."

"Good work, just keep me informed."

The two men rose and shook hands. "Yes, sir." Inspector Bridges replaced and adjusted his hat and saluted. "Good day, sir."

***

"Em, there's a policeman to see you." It was Susan. "I hope it's not bad news," she said.

Em felt a chill go down her spine. In her experience, personal calls by policemen usually meant some kind of disaster. "Show him through, please." Em stood up to meet her visitor and was delighted when she saw the Inspector, even though she was apprehensive about what he might have to say. "Tea, Inspector?" she asked. "Susan, two teas please."

"I'm sorry I haven't been able to return your calls," he said. Just then Susan brought in the teas, and a plate of homemade biscuits. When she left, the Inspector continued. "I have been making enquiries which have taken me as far south as Oxfordshire. Hmm, these biscuits are delicious. As I was saying, the Oxfordshire police are still making enquiries, but it seems more than likely that George Summers and Victor Bradburn are one and the same person. As yet we have no definite proof and," he paused for a moment, "we do not know if he has or has not recovered his memory, but please wait and leave it until you hear from me. I will let you know, just as soon as I know."

Em breathed a sigh of relief. Overwhelmed by tears, she almost whispered, "Thank you."

Chapter Three

During the latter part of 1942, storms and high winds combined with unusually high tides caused considerable damage along the coast, while heavier rain than normal in the west and northwest caused many roads to be impassable. Strong winds meant that it would be unwise for Victor to load his lorry as high as he would have liked. Driving was hazardous due to fallen trees and other debris on the road, making journeys last late into the night before he completed his last delivery and returned to his wife and family. Deliveries to Moore Hall were few and far between, and it seemed unlikely that he would have the opportunity of finding out who the lady he had seen chatting by the back door was. Consequently when he was making a delivery shortly before Christmas, his mind was on finishing and getting back to Thornton Heath, but his presence hadn't gone unnoticed.

It was Malcolm's first Christmas, not that it had any meaning for a child of that age. Gillian and her mother drooled over him as if it bore great significance for him. Victor sat and watched, frowning in a fatherly sort of way, while Mr Woodley shrugged his shoulders and disappeared in the direction of the public bar, to sit alone in the semi-darkness, as the bar was closed over Christmas, topping his tankard up from time to time, what he called 'testing the quality',

A few days after Christmas, two regular customers came into the bar and glanced at the tree, now devoid of much of its foliage, standing in the alcove they usually occupied. "Hmph, damn nuisance," they muttered, "all that fuss over nothing," as they made their way to a table further away from the fire.

"You'd better not let the vicar hear you say that," said Mavis. "Your usual, lads?" she asked.

Victor slowed down and stopped in the queue behind two other lorries; another road block just outside Hampton Heath, the third one today. These road blocks could be annoying. They might be necessary but were still a nuisance. The front lorry driver was free to go. He had been checked and now drove off. The one in front of Victor was waved through, oh good, perhaps he would also be waved through; no such luck. Victor wound down his window. "Driving licence, ID Card, insurance and delivery papers please, sir. It's okay, you can wait in your cab, this'll only take a few moments. The policeman took the documents over to the police car, and returned a few moments later. "That will be all, thank you, sir, have a safe journey. Good day, sir." As Victor drove off, the policeman went into the conveniently situated phone kiosk. "Hello, Constable, I have a message for Inspector Bridges."

Having parked his car, the Inspector wrapped a scarf around his neck, buttoned up his plain worsted coat against the cold January wind, and walked along the road to the Red Lion. "Is Victor in?" he asked the barmaid, knowing that he was miles away, probably on his way to Witney.

"Sorry, sir, He's away at the moment, but his wife is here, I'll call her," Mavis said as she opened the door to the private quarters and called "Gillian, a man asking for Victor."

"Ask him what he wants," came the reply.

"I'm a family friend, asking about news of his mother," he said.

"Send him through."... "I'm sorry," after the Inspector went through, she said, "but he hasn't said anything to me about his mother."

"I see you're busy, how old is he?" he asked, taking hold of the baby's hand. "Hello, chubby chops, what's your name?"

"Malcolm," said Gillian.

"I'm sorry to trouble you, I'll slip out by the side entrance."

"Won't you have a drink?" she said, but the visitor didn't seem to have heard.

***

Victor wasn't sure whether there were even more military convoys than usual or whether it was his imagination, but the delays caused by them seemed longer and more frequent than in 1942. No matter how much he changed his route north or southbound, the journey was taking more time and he was arriving at his destination, or having to break his journey, later into the night. Some trunk roads, such as the A5, were notorious for delays as they led from the northwest right down to the London area, the ideal route for convoys bound for the south or southeast coast.

Trying to find alternative but quicker routes north meant using the trunk routes to the west like the A30, or to the east like the A1, both routes converging near Birmingham and other nearby industrial centres, major targets for the Luftwaffe. Eventually Victor found a clearer run using the A1 trunk road, turning off near Leicester, on towards Nottingham, then east towards Manchester, a little more mileage, but usually with fewer delays. Even then there were times that it was necessary for him to make overnight stops on the way. Like many other drivers, he was not averse to giving lifts to hitchhikers, especially those in military uniform, the womenfolk in particular, sometimes sharing overnight stops. (He felt he was helping the War Effort.)

Giving a lift could have its dangers, or at least according to some rumours that were around from time to time, of enemy agents being dropped by parachute or coming ashore on remote beaches. Victor continued giving lifts and laughed at the rumours, except on a couple of occasions after giving lifts to members of the Dutch Free Forces whose accents sounded like the guttural voices of German soldiers as depicted in films.

Almost before you could say Jack Robinson, the March winds had died down, April showers had passed and May had arrived. Malcolm would soon be having his first birthday and Mrs Woodley had started reminding Victor, "It's just three weeks…" and, "It's only another two weeks…" much to Victor's annoyance. He would retaliate with "…can't spare the time, too many deliveries for time off," which amused Gillian, but infuriated his mother-in-law, much to Victor's delight.

It was a bright sunny morning. Mrs Woodley was in the kitchen washing the breakfast dishes when Victor, dressed in his overalls, headed for the back door. "You're not going off to do deliveries today of all days, on your son's birthday are you?"

"Of course I am, I can't let the customers down," he replied as he walked out of the door.

"Oh, you men!" she said. "You've no sense of loyalty, anything for a few coppers."

He poked his head around the doorpost. "Fooled you," he said, and ducked, but not quick enough to avoid a wringing wet dish cloth in his face.

"You certainly deserved that," said Gillian, laughing.

What was there that a one-year-old child would remember about his first birthday, Victor wondered. A ride out in the sunshine in his pushchair, we mustn't have the sun on him too much, he might burn, see the big ship in the Manchester Ship Canal, careful, the sun is on him, quickly, move the shade over him… Women seem such strange creatures, thought Victor, first take baby out in the sunshine, then stop the sun from shining on him. The day had come to an end, Malcolm was tucked up in his cot. Victor relaxed in his chair, a pint tankard close by. Phew, he thought, being at home is more tiring than a day at the wheel. He sighed… He opened his eyes… The room was in darkness; where was everyone, what time was it? Two a.m., hell, why didn't they wake me?

Back on the road again, three deliveries this trip, eight bales for Dale Barracks, they must be having more recruits, maybe they're getting ready for a big bash at the Germans; two for Chester Infirmary; and, ah yes two bales for Moore Hall, a chance to find out who that woman is. With that thought in mind, he whistled as he drove. The prospect of any hold-ups didn't trouble him. The miles seemed to fly by, or maybe it was time that flew by. Arriving at the barracks by three thirty and the infirmary an hour later, he decided it would be a little late to call at Moore Hall. Never mind, he could take more time in the morning.

***

"That's right," Victor said to the American stores clerk, "just two bales, there on the delivery note it says 'Order number' whatever that number refers to, 'complete', yes I brought those in last year, okay? Good." Victor waited while the clerk signed his copy of the delivery note, then asked, " I don't suppose you can tell me who the lady in the blue housecoat over there is, could you?"

"Hold on mate," the clerk replied. "Hey, Larry, you wouldn't know..."

Lieutenant Laurence Goldstein came out of the office, a sheaf of papers in his hand. "Know what?" he asked. "Oh, she's Major Summers, her friends call her Em. I don't know what that's short for. It's no good trying, she's already married," Laurence said, a big grin on his face.

Victor sat in his driver's cab and wrote a quick note, then returned to the delivery clerk. "Can you let me have an envelope, please?" Putting the note in the envelope, he sealed it and quickly scribbled a name on the outside. "Can you get it delivered, please? Thanks, mate."

By the time he got back to the lorry, his escort had returned. Victor, with a grin on his face, was softly whistling.

"You seem happy."

"Yep," Victor replied, started the motor and drove to the gate. Once on the road, he headed off toward Helmshore Mill.

***

Em returned from the drawing room with the tray from morning tea. She had just spent an amusing half hour while the Major General had been relating happy memories of a visit to the Hawaiian Islands. "Where did this come from?" she asked, holding up an envelope.

31

"The delivery clerk brought it," came the reply.

Em split the envelope open and glanced at the paper in her hand. "What the… the flaming cheek… what does he think…" She sat down, her head in her hands. Sandra put her arm around Em's shoulder. Em looked up. "Thank you," she said and picked up the phone.

The operator answered, "Birkenhead Police Station please." Inspector Bridges just *had* to be in today.

An hour later, the telephone rang. It was the sentry at the gate. "There's a police car and the police sergeant wants to see you."

"That's fine, send him up, he won't need an escort."

"Major Summers? Did I hear the sentry correctly, miss?" asked the police Sergeant.

"Yes, Officer, as well as housekeeper, and because I am in charge of the US Army field kitchen, I hold the honorary rank of Major."

"The Inspector said that you have heard from your husband. May I see the letter?"

"It's just a rough note," Em said as she handed it to the police sergeant. "You can take it and give it to Inspector Bridges. I did say on the phone that I have *no* intention of going to meet my husband in Chester or anywhere else for that matter."

"Well, thank you, miss."

"I'll let the Inspector know if I hear any more from my husband," said Em as the policeman left.

The three of them were sitting in the office having a cup of tea. "Well, what did he say?" asked Susan.

"He said to meet him tomorrow at five on the steps at the main entrance to Chester Cathedral." Susan and Sandra waited as Em hesitated. "And then he had the cheek to say that I owed him that much."

Both girls started talking at the same time resulting in a jumble of words: "Kick 'im, throttle, kill 'im, where it 'urts…"

"Whoa, one at a time," said Em. "Anyway you won't get the chance. the Inspector said they will deal with 'im."

Unaware of the turmoil his note had caused, Victor drove on, happily looking forward to the prospect of seeing Em once more, without any thought of the consequences or how it would affect other peoples' lives, especially those of Gillian and her family.

Chapter Four

"I have to go to Chester this afternoon," Victor said. "I will probably be late back. If it looks like getting too late I might stop somewhere overnight. After breakfast I'll give the car a good clean." As he unlocked the garage doors he heard the sound of water splashing. A sly glance and he could see Mavis's dimly lit figure. Quickly withdrawing, he opened the garage doors, rolled the Hornet out into the sunlight, and without making a lot of noise went into the washhouse for a bucket and sponge and murmured, just loudly enough for Mavis to hear, "Mrs Woodley has just come out of the back door." Mavis climbed out from the copper, wrapped herself in a towel, and scurried past Victor through an adjoining door into what had been the tack room from the days of horse and carriage.

"Have you seen anything of Mavis?" Mrs Woodley asked. "I thought she was here about twenty minutes ago. If you see her, will you tell her I need her to get me some shopping before she opens the pub." Mrs Woodley disappeared back from whence she came.

"That could have proved embarrassing for both of us," Mavis said, grinning like the proverbial Cheshire Cat as she came back into the washhouse in a dress with a large round open top.

Victor kissed Gillian and patted his son, Malcolm, on the head as he was leaving. Two infant eyes, along with two loving eyes, watched as he left the room.

"Bye, love," said Gillian.

"Bye, love," replied Victor.

With a roar and a toot on the horn, Victor turned right down the London road, and right again along the road that took him through Shurlach and on into the centre of Chester. Remembering his army training, Victor had it all mapped out in his mind. By arranging to meet at five o'clock to talk over a few drinks, it would be too late for buses back to Moore Hall until the next day. He had already booked them both into the hotel and… well… 'come into my parlour…'

Victor parked his car and entered the hotel restaurant. Sirloin of beef was on the menu, but their fish was much more to his liking. Mackerel was the fish he always enjoyed and mackerel was what he ordered. It was delicious, rinsed down with a glass of white wine, nothing pretentious, but very enjoyable.

After the meal, he signed in and went up to the room. Accommodation at Ye Olde King's Head was reputed to be top notch. The view was nothing spectacular, but then he wasn't planning to spend time looking out of the window; there was still a war on and blackout was the order of the day.

"Good afternoon, sir," the doorman had said when he had entered. "Good afternoon," he said as Victor left. "Yes, sir, the cathedral is that way, sir." Victor didn't rush, but he wanted to look round the great building, learn a few salient points; he intended to impress. Shortly after half past four he took up a position to await Em's arrival, where he could observe the cathedral steps without himself being seen.

***

Nine o'clock. She looked at the hall clock and waited, listening for the hours to strike, bong one, bong two, bong three, Em counted them all, but wait a moment I only counted six, it only struck six times. She turned to face the clock then opened her eyes; she must have been dreaming. Her bedside clock showed three minutes past six, she surely had been dreaming, the Grandmother clock had been silent all the time she had worked here. Anyway, it was time to get up and start her daily duties.

Susan poured Em a piping hot cup of tea as she walked through the kitchen door; she could rely on Susan, she was one of the best. Sandra was already sitting at the table. "There'll be more toast in a minute," she said. "Susan baked another of her delicious farmhouse loaves this morning, goodness knows how long she must have been up."

"Only long enough to bake it," Susan responded. "I left it to rise overnight." Em didn't usually sit down to have breakfast, but the delicious smell of freshly baked bread gave her an appetite. A slice of buttered toast and homemade marmalade went down a treat, so much so that before she realised, she was spreading another slice. Em smiled. She had a couple of girls who got on really well. Working together the three of them made a good team. She couldn't have asked for more.

The morning went quickly, there wasn't a lot to do beyond cleaning the drawing room (if possible before her ladyship rises) 'flicking a duster around,' keeping the hallway floor clean – when will men learn to wipe their shoes on the doormat as they come in? – and freshening up the floral displays in the hallway and the part of the house not turned over to the convalescent hospital.

Lunch prepared, served, enjoyed and cleared away left everyone an hour or two to appreciate the glorious sunshine, and to spend a little while with their friend, Naomi, and baby, Laurence Junior. Em was sitting in her office going over accounts, schedules, and all those other things that form part of a housekeeper's duties. "Tea's served," said a voice from the kitchen.

"Coming," called Em, putting down her pen, and getting up from her desk.

"We thought you might be in Chester by now," joked Sandra.

"You've got to be kidding," answered Em, "and who's going to do my paperwork? Oy, where're those Welsh tea cakes you promised, Sandra? You did, didn't she, Susan?"

Sandra retaliated, "And what about him 'Waiting at the church?'" she sang, "'waiting at the church, waiting at the church'" to which Em sang in reply, "'Let him go, let him tarry'" and the others joined in, "'Let him sink or let him swim'!"

***

Victor shifted on the bench. There was a breeze and the idea of sitting in the shade in order not to be seen didn't seem quite such a good idea. The open slats on the bench were rather uncomfortable and he began to wonder whether the marks on his behind, which surely there must be by now, would be permanent. He shivered and moved to a bench in the sun at the other side of the cathedral steps, partly occupied by a middle-aged man trying to read a map, made more difficult by the breeze. Victor tried to ignore him, but with the map tending to find its way in his direction, he soon got involved.

"Thank you ever so much, I don't know what I would have done without your help. By the way, I'm Patrick, usually called Paddy, or as I usually say 'I like to be called in time for breakfast'," he said laughing, "and what do I call you?"

"Victor," he replied. Beginning to like his cheery companion, he asked "Visiting? We don't get many visitors what with the war, where are you from?"

"Burnley," came the reply. "I've always wanted to see Chester. Are you local?"

"Sort of, I come from the Wirral, little place called Liscard."

"Blimey, look at the time, I'd better run or I'll miss my train. Nice meeting you." Shaking Victor's hand, Paddy departed in the direction of the station. The cathedral clock struck half past six, Em wouldn't be coming now. Annoyed and dejected that Em had obviously stood him up, he made his way back to the hotel and headed upstairs to his room.

As Paddy walked along the west side of the cathedral, he was met by a lady. They nodded and passed each other without saying a word. Victor did not notice the lady, who entered the hotel just behind him, nor did he see her go into the manager's office.

Victor came out of his room freshened up and smartly though casually dressed, closed the door behind him, and slowly, elegantly walked down the stairs and made his way to the lounge, taking in all there was to see: a couple at the far end of the bar in deep conversation, sometimes the lady would throw her head back laughing; the young couple sitting in the seclusion of the alcove whom Victor thought would be better accommodated in their room; seats in various parts of the cosy lounge occupied by groups of three or four. But the one that interested

Victor was a lady, a slender lady, a beautiful figure which put him in mind of Alice, sitting by herself at the bar.

Victor ordered himself a Scotch, then seeing the lady's glass was empty said, "Madam, what will you have?"

Looking at him with that 'Who, me?' expression she replied, "White wine, if you please."

"I'm sure you'd be more comfortable at a table," he said, picking up the two glasses and leading her to a table away from other guests. "Forgive me, let me introduce myself, George Summers," he said, "and you?"

"My name is Joanne, but my friends call me Ann."

"What a lovely name," he said.

"What brings you here?" Ann asked. "Let me guess, you're here on business."

"Well, no not really, I was supposed to be meeting a friend, but they weren't able to come. Oh, look at the time, would you like to join me for dinner, it's already paid for and it would be such a pity to waste it," he said as he took her arm and they headed towards the restaurant.

The dinner was stupendous, the fish, delicious, the main course was unbelievable, just where did they get the venison? And the selection from the sweet trolley, it was impossible to know what to choose. After such a meal, surely Ann would keep him company overnight...

But he was disappointed. Ann apologised, saying that she had promised her old grandmother she would go round while her carer went to Midweek Mass... maybe another time.

**

"Well, how did you two get on with our friend? Let's hear from you first, Paddy," said the Inspector.

"Reasonably well. He fell for the old map trick, fortunately there was a breeze so I sat at the windward end of the bench," Paddy replied. "Told me his name was Victor and that he came from the Wirral, from Liscard to be precise. It all fitted in with the information we already have.

He and I were the only ones waiting around at the time the meeting was scheduled. It's all in my report, sir."

"That's fine," Inspector Harris said. "I just wanted Ann to know how you got on before we hear her story," then turning to Ann, "and now you, Ann."

"Summers had a booking for a double room for himself and Emily Summers for the night. The booking was made two days ago on the 17th. When he came into the lounge I was sitting alone. He bought me a drink and introduced himself as George Summers. He was very polite and charming. In different circumstances I could have easily fallen for him… don't tell my husband I said that!" she added. "He said his guest hadn't been able to come so he invited me to join him for dinner. After dinner I made my excuses and left."

"But did he invite you to his room?" the Inspector asked,

"Well… yes, sir," she answered.

"And did you go?"

"No, sir, that was when I made my excuses to leave."

***

George returned to his room, irritated at being rejected by Ann. He sat down and turned the wireless on and his mood did not improve when he heard the voice of Gracie Fields singing *Let him go, let him tarry, let him sink or let him swim.* It improved a little when *It's That Man Again*, one of his favourite programmes, came on followed by the Tommy Handley show. Their humour made listeners forget about the war and all it meant. Oh hell, just when the programme was getting really funny, the air raid siren started wailing. Grabbing his gas mask he left his room and headed down the stairs, along with the other guests making their way down into the cellars. Being among the first down he found and sat in a comfortable chair. Someone had brought a portable radio with them, so they didn't miss all of the programme.

For the rest of the evening there was dance music, with Glen Miller and his band. Eventually the music stopped, but George had already fallen into a very deep sleep. In his dream he was back in Singapore dancing with Cynthia, dancing with Alice, it didn't matter who with or where, he was dreaming, the girls were queuing to dance with him, Kathleen, Ann, Alice, Cynthia, each in turn, then there was Em… who? The music had stopped, he was awake and alone. He was the only one left in the cellar; he had heard neither the 'All clear' nor the kerfuffle as everyone else had returned to their rooms. They had all left him asleep in the damp cellar-cum-air-raid-shelter, it was already seven o'clock in the morning, and he ought to be getting back home to Thornton Heath.

Chapter Five

Victor was not in a good frame of mind as he drove out of Chester. He was tempted to go to Moore Hall but reasoned that the softly softly approach would probably be more effective. Em might not have been able to get away for some reason or other, and he wouldn't have wanted her to leave a message at the Red Lion so she had no way of letting him know. Yesterday had been a bit of a disaster, an expensive disaster, and he hadn't even had his breakfast.

"Hello, darling, have a good day?" Gillian asked as he walked in.

"Yes, thank you, dear," he smiled. "It couldn't have been better," he said, very much tongue in cheek. "Did you have an air raid?"

"Yes," she replied, "but it didn't last very long, the all clear sounded after a couple of hours." Victor swore under his breath; all night in the shelter, when he could have been sleeping in that nice comfortable bed upstairs.

"While I think of it," said Gillian, "have you any news of your mother?"

"Why do you ask?"

"There was a man asking, ooh, a couple of months ago, maybe longer."

"You didn't say anything at the time," he said, "why do you ask now?"

"I just wondered," she replied. "I forgot. When I remembered you weren't here, and when you were here I didn't remember. Perhaps we could visit her, she'd probably like to see her grandson."

Victor, feeling his tummy rumbling, remembered he hadn't had any breakfast. When he walked into the kitchen, Mrs Woodley was busy washing nappies in the kitchen sink. "Mother, dear, I'd appreciate a slice of toast," he said.

"And what did your last servant die of?" she asked. "Cut yourself a slice of bread, rake the fire and you'll find the toasting fork over there," she said, pointing in the direction of the Welsh dresser.

"And where's the butter?" he asked.

Mrs Woodley exploded. "The cow is still in the dairy being milked." Then, calming down a little, "But you should find some on the marble slab in the larder… oh, *men*!" she said slamming her hands down on the water, then reaching for a towel to wipe the suds from her face.

Somehow the bread freshly toasted in front of the fire with a smattering of butter tasted delicious, and followed by the freshly brewed cuppa, made by his mother-in-law as an apology for her impatience, compensated for missing breakfast at the hotel.

***

As Em was entering the kitchen, Susan was asking Sandra what she thought the siren was about the night before. "Was there a siren last night? I didn't hear anything," said Em. "I was in bed by eight."

"You must have been tired to have been asleep by then," said Sandra. "The siren was just after half past, and the all clear sounded a couple of hours later. Maybe it was just as well you didn't hear it." The conversation turned to the humdrum of work routines and what was on the menu.

Em returned to her office, her mind going from budget to menus and in between times her thoughts went to George and the twins. What was George up to? What did he really want? What if… wait a moment… Did he want me to…? But why?… If that's what he wants, he's got another think coming, he's not getting away with it that easily. Maybe next time I'll be ready for him'.

Life downstairs in Moore Hall continued at its own leisurely pace, the monotony broken by the frequent appearance of Laurence to discuss catering matters with Major Em and the very welcome visits of Naomi accompanied by Laurence Junior. Naomi, ever grateful for the way they had looked after her during her pregnancy, suggested that Laurence should take them all out for a drink.

"I know a nice little pub where I used to go with my husband," Sandra said. Susan declined, insisting that she should remain just in case her ladyship should require anything.

***

The showers in the spring followed by the bright, warm summer meant a bountiful harvest. In spite of having three very efficient Land Army girls working on the farm, more help was needed if all the crops were to be gathered before the weather broke. It was agreed that Mavis should go home to the farm and return when she was free. Mrs Woodley was delighted with the opportunity to look after Malcolm, so that Gillian could go back to working in the bar, and the arrangement suited everyone, including Victor, who would sit at the bar keeping an eye on any unwelcome behaviour towards his wife.

"You two sit by the fireplace while I get the drinks. Gin? Cider? right." Turning to the bar, he said, "We'll have a gin, make it a double, a cider and I'm driving so I'll have a mineral water. Have you anything to eat? A couple of packets, please."

Laurence turned to answer the man seated at the bar. "Yes, I'm stationed at the hospital at Moore Hall. No, not nurses, the housekeeper and a cook from the house. You are?"

"Victor, pleased to meet you, you're drinking? Never mind, maybe next time." Laurence took the drinks to the waiting ladies. Victor made an excuse and went through to the private quarters.

The three sat chatting for a while. "My shout," said Sandra, "same again?" She got up to order the drinks, but Gillian had brought them over before Sandra had time to gather the empties.

"Did I hear 'Victor'?" asked Em, and added, "where's the ladies, please?"

"Over on the right." She turned and indicated. "Yes, he's my husband," said Gillian. There was the sound of a car driving away. "That'll be him off on some errand," she said, picking up the empties.

An hour later they left the Red Lion, the ladies turning their coat collars up against the chill of the stiff evening breeze as they made their way to the Jeep. They had barely travelled half a mile when Laurence pointed out a Wolseley Hornet travelling in the opposite direction. "Now that's a little beauty," he said, and as it went past, "I think that was Victor." Em felt uneasy. She had only caught a quick glance, but she thought, he looks awfully like my George, surely not, Inspector Bridges said he's somewhere down south. When George came to mind, the thought of her boys was never far away.

*****

"Where have you been?" asked Gillian. "I needed some more Blue Label light ales."

"What about your dad?" Victor asked. "He could have fetched them."

"You know he's got a bad back," she replied.

"The car wasn't firing properly last time I took it out," Victor said. "A good fast run sorted it out."

"The coppers will catch you speeding one day, then where will you be if you lose your licence?"

"Never mind that, just pour me a whisky."

"Please," she reminded him.

"Please," he said reluctantly, and Gillian poured Victor his drink.

Victor was worried. He would have to be very careful when speaking to Gillian about Em's visit, that is supposing it was Em, his first and only legitimate wife. What was she doing here? Was she trying to find out where he was and hoping to make him pay maintenance, or make him pay her to keep quiet about her existence? He laughed to himself, that would be illegal. It didn't occur to him that there might be a perfectly innocent reason for Em being at the Red Lion. He would have to be very careful in case he was being followed. He sipped his whisky, truly nectar of the gods. He caught Gillian looking at him. *What is he thinking about?* she wondered.

Over the next few months business had slowed to a steady trickle, enough for a regular income but not the amount that would finance the purchase of a house, and anyway, as long as they were able to live at the Red Lion with Gillian's parents, Victor could see no sense in getting their own place.

"Christmas is coming, the geese are getting fat," Victor was singing.

"What's all that about?" asked Gillian.

"I've been asked to collect a load bound for the Chester Royal Infirmary and Moore Hall Convalescent Hospital," replied Victor. "How do you fancy a goose for Christmas?"

"I'd better ask Mother," she replied.

"Let me know when I get home tonight," he called as he went out of the door.

It was a week to the day before Christmas that Victor collected the two deliveries of geese, plus two extra birds. It was a bitterly cold day, dry but with a strong north wind, and Victor wanted to get back home in the warmth. The roads were clear and the delivery to Chester Royal Infirmary was done before eleven that morning. The only hold up was at the Moore Hall gates for an escort, even though he was known to the military personnel. Eventually he was able to unload and was free to leave, but before he did he had one more delivery to make, before he took the last goose home.

***

"We've had a positive sighting of George in Oxfordshire," Inspector Bridges said. "It is very easy to see a person of similar appearance in a passing car and think it is someone you know, especially after a long time of not seeing them, and there are a lot of men who have that look. We will investigate it anyway," he continued. "I hope that has put your mind at ease, but tell me, what took you to the Red Lion at Thornton Heath?

Ah, yes, I see. That was very nice of them. I will keep in touch," he said, and rang off.

Em put the phone down. Did it make her feel any easier? I don't know, she thought, with lorries and cars like the one Victor was driving last night, he could be living anywhere. The thought made her shiver. No, she did *not* feel at ease. Damn, she thought, George seemed to be taking over her mind. Moore Hall once more returned to its normal routine, and nothing was seen or said about either George or Victor for a month or more, although Em did wonder how long it would be before she heard anything either from the Inspector or from George himself.

Em was constantly looking forward to receiving the occasional letters from her boys, not that they ever told her much, but she would read over and over 'love from Freddie' and 'love from Walter', It was strange how it affected how she felt. Occasionally when she was feeling down, they left her feeling inadequate as a mother, that they had to be looked after by someone else, yet most times the words expressing love made her feel so warm inside. God bless them, one day, yes one day, God willing. She would sometimes look at the Isle of Man map she had on the bedroom wall… at least they were safely away from the war and the bombs.

Time seemed to be flying by. They had already prepared the rich fruit cakes and puddings for Christmas. Life this year would be quieter with fewer guests invited. More's the pity, it was good fun catering for them all and knowing that very little extra would be needed to provide for the staff. Looking down the guest list, Em could see a few of the regulars: Cynthia, when she arrives she will be wanting to hear all the latest about George, not that there's much I can tell her. Ah yes, Delilah, I thought she would be on the list, she'll need watching with all the Americans here, if she's not careful she could so easily get herself in trouble. Mrs Marjorie Dawes from Wincanton, not one I've seen before. Harry Rock, that's good, and who's this? The Very Reverend Archibald Entwhistle, Dean of Waltham Abbey. I've never heard of that one before, still if there's a dean, there must be an abbey, thought Em. We should be able to cope without any trouble and there's still plenty of time to get their rooms ready.

The phone rang. It was the quartermaster. "The geese have just flown in," he said, "well hardly flown, but they've arrived at last."

"Thank you, Sam," Em said.

There was a knock on the office door. Sandra was standing in the doorway holding a small but heavy looking sack. "It's for you, Em," she said, placing it on the floor. "It was left just outside the door."

Em looked at the label, then cut the tie. Inside there was a card and a goose. Em opened the card and swore. George had left a Christmas card in which he had written, 'Sorry I missed you, perhaps another time, Happy Christmas'.

"Damn him," said Em, "of all the cheek. I'll cook his goose for him." Sandra smiled.

Chapter Six

One by one the guests arrived at Moore Hall. Just like last year Cynthia was the first. Last year she had brought Lady Delilah with her, but this year they both travelled independently. Harry Rock, still driving his old Ford T car, arrived the next day, followed the day after by Marjorie Dawes, a rather flamboyantly dressed lady in her late forties. Last to arrive was the Very Reverend Archibald Entwhistle in an Austin Cambridge, wearing his clerical garb. As he entered the drawing room, Harry got up from his chair. "Hello, Archie, you old rogue, how are you?" he said as they shook hands and hugged each other. "I'd like you to meet Lady Jane Marbury," he said, turning. "Jane, may I present the Very Reverend Archibald Entwhistle."

"My pleasure, ma'am," he said.

"Tell me what racket you're up to this time, Archie?" Harry asked his friend, as they walked up the stairs.

"May God forgive you for such slanderous insinuation of a Man of the Cloth," Archie replied.

"Oh come off it, you old rogue," Harry said. "I wasn't born yesterday."

"Come into my room and—" The bedroom door closed, cutting off the sound of their voices.

"But," Harry was saying as he came out of the room, "leave Jane out of it."

***

"Much the same as duck only bigger," Em was telling Laurence. "Best if you look in Mrs Beeton's."

"That's a great little book," he said. "Any idea where I can get a copy?"

"You should be able to get one in Chester town centre," Sandra suggested.

"There's an old copy you can borrow in the meantime," Em offered.

"Ta, I'll look after it," Laurence said as he made off with the treasured book in his hand.

"I certainly hope he gets it right, goose isn't an easy bird to cook," commented Susan, who had many years' experience in roasting fowl. Turning her thoughts back to preparing the one in front of her, she added, "I'm glad we've only a couple of birds to do this year."

"Don't speak too soon," said Em chuckling. "I've a feeling you might be asked for to help in the field kitchen, they've had half a dozen delivered."

Harry Rock and Archie Entwhistle were often seen talking together, or driving out in one or the other's car. Quite often they were seen carrying packages, yet when the girls were cleaning the rooms the only evidence was screwed up pieces of brown paper. One morning, just before Christmas, Susan took a crumpled piece of paper out of her pocket and showed it to the other two. "Look what I found under the dean's bed," she said triumphantly, "a dollar note. Yes," she added, prompted by Em's look, "I'll put it on his dressing table in the morning."

"I don't know what mischief they might be up to, but I don't want either of you implicated," Em informed them.

Marjorie Dawes and Cynthia greeted each other like old friends. It seemed that in different years, they had both been at the same finishing school in Switzerland, and they spent a lot of time reminiscing over old times: 'Do you remember Madame... Oh yes... and no... I think she left...' occasionally breaking into French or German when staff were present, presumably so that they could not 'earwig'.

The biggest surprise was Lady Delilah. She was now a member of the Red Cross and was hoping to resume studies after the war to become a doctor. She was already reading medical course books a friend had lent to give her a good start, and spent a lot of her time helping to look after the more disabled patients in the convalescent wards, seldom joining the others at meal times.

"Have you heard anything from Nigel since last year?" Lady Jane asked Cynthia.

"Not a whisper," she answered. "I've hardly heard a word since the lily-livered imitation of a man chased off to Canada at the merest whisper of a war. Him boasting about his father being a General in the First World War and what he would do. Not worth thinking about." The others weren't sure whether she had stopped because she had run out of breath or words.

"My husband said he was going to emigrate to Australia and for me to join him later," said Marjorie. "The last I heard through a friend who visited Melbourne, he had a wife and family out there. I know I would never trust a man again."

"What if you met someone decent?" asked Cynthia.

"Decent? Huh!" replied Marjorie. "My friend, Alice, met a young fellow named Victor, I think his name was Bradburn or something like it, she thought he was decent and married him. It turned out he was already married. She only found out when the police turned up, but he had already flown."

Bradburn, Bradburn, Cynthia thought, wasn't that the name of that Victor chap I mistook as George? Bradburn. It's too much of a coincidence, anyway, he deserves to be caught and locked up, to stop him doing it again to someone else.

Cynthia was confused. She found it hard to believe that the man she knew and, she had to admit, loved, the man who had stopped and helped them after Nigel, the spineless creature, made her stand out in the freezing wind, should be masquerading as Victor, what was it Brad... Damn it! where did that come from, they shouldn't paint cars that colour, I nearly didn't see it. Now, what was it? Oh yes, Bradburn, that name, I'm sure I know it from somewhere. Oops, I'd better pay more attention to my driving or I could end up in the ditch.'

Cynthia had hoped to find out more from Em, but she didn't seem to know any more than she had last year. She felt certain there was something she had missed, something she knew but had possibly forgotten. These damn convoys were a nuisance, why can't the send their big guns? Guns! That's it! She slammed her foot down on the brake, and pulled in to the side of the road. Big guns, now what was it about big guns? Ah yes, Singapore. George had said something about his parents. Cynthia drove on until she saw a café and decided to stop for refreshments.

As Cynthia sat, a cup of tea in her hand, thinking back to her travels in the Far East, she was reliving it all over in her mind. It was at the Raffles Hotel, a day or so into the New Year. They were sitting in bed, sharing a champagne breakfast, it was so romantic, hm yes, he had said something like 'why shouldn't we, my parents didn't wait'. That was it. He had needed his birth certificate when he joined the Army. "Oh yes, miss, another pot of tea please." He had laughed as he showed her his mother's name on the birth certificate. Bradburn, yes, that was it, Bradburn. "Sorry, miss, I've got to dash. How much? There's ten shillings, keep the change."

Cynthia turned the ignition key and the engine sprang into life, quietly of course; a Rolls Royce was known as one of the quietest motors on the road. Cynthia looked at the fuel gauge; plenty enough to get her the thirty or so miles home and still have a quarter tank, but not enough to return to Cheshire and back. Her petrol ration wasn't so generous that she could afford to make unnecessary journeys. The Rolls was not an economical car fuel wise. Putting it into gear she moved off, her only question being why? Why had the man that she had admired and still loved, had so little respect for his wife, or in his case, wives? How many wives has he got? Did he keep a count like the fighter pilot who painted a swastika on his aircraft for each enemy plane he shot down?

***

Victor sat in the chair at the far side of the inglenook fireplace, sipping a large whisky, watching Mavis serving the few customers who had come in that lunchtime. There was no doubt she was a very attractive young woman, and in different circumstances he might have been tempted. That didn't stop him from looking and enjoying what he saw. Glancing across at him, Mavis saw him looking and smiled. I wonder what she's thinking, he thought. Subconsciously he smiled to himself. She must have seen it because she smiled again and brought him another glass of whisky. "Thank you, dear," he said without a thought of what 'dear' might suggest. Mavis's heart skipped a beat and she walked back with a radiant smile on her face.

"Darling," Gillian said as she snuggled up to Victor while they lay in bed on Sunday morning, whispering in his ear, "wouldn't it be nice for Malcolm to have a brother to play with as he grows up?"

"Of course, dear, whatever you say," he murmured, half asleep and not wanting to be woken up.

"I think it's on the way."

"Oh, good," he replied, not entirely taking in what she was saying. "Tell me when it arrives," he mumbled, still half asleep.

"Idiot," she said, hitting him and laughing.

"Here! What was that for?" he asked, sitting up, now wide awake.

"Idiot," she said again, "you didn't hear one word of what I said." She sat up beside her husband.

"Yes, I did," he replied, "something about a delivery, I asked you to let me know when it arrives."

Gillian roared with laughter, hitting him again. "I'm expecting a baby."

"Not yet, I hope!" Victor said, looking at her figure.

"No, not yet, silly, in six- or seven-months' time."

Gillian's mother was delighted. Having one grandchild had pleased her, but two, she was over the moon. Gillian had been an only child and as such had tended to cling; two would be company for each other. Mr Woodley wasn't quite so sure. A public house was hardly the right place for one child and certainly not two.

"I've heard your good news," Mavis said as they were sitting by the inglenook fireplace. Victor was reading his newspaper, Mavis sitting there to keep warm, at the same time watching the bar in case anyone wanted serving. "I've heard your good news," she was saying. "I think two is a perfect number, that's what I'd like, but anyone I'd want to be their father is already married," then as an afterthought, "or in the forces somewhere overseas."

Victor momentarily looked up. "Hmm, probably," shrugged and returned to his paper.

Mavis stood up, looked at Victor, then walked to the bar. "Yes, Tom, your usual?"

Victor sat reminiscing. Back in the days when he was at Larkhill there was a lot going on in the NAAFI and some great films in the camp cinema. Although he had enjoyed army life, especially after Em arrived – that was when the quality and variety of the food had improved – he was glad to be free from all the bullshit and square bashing, and now with the war the likelihood of being sent to the battlefront. There had been a lot of the poor beggars who'd never made it back in spite of Dunkirk.

Victor was finding life quiet when there was a kerfuffle at the bar. "What the—" Victor said as he looked up. A man who had already had too much to drink, and had been refused another drink, was wielding a broken bottle, threatening to use it unless Mavis served him. Victor quickly approached from behind and told him to drop it. The man unsteadily spun round. Victor grabbed his wrist, forcing him to drop the bottle, and twisting his arm up his back, frog marched him out of the door. His friend made a hasty exit, not wishing to tangle with someone as handy as Victor.

"Thank you," Mavis said as she put a double whisky on the table, "have this one on me," which usually meant on the house, and kissed him, quickly wiping the lipstick from his cheek. Victor wiped his cheek with a finger. "It's all right, dear," said Mavis, smiling, "I've got it all off. We don't want your wife to see it," she added as she walked away, chuckling.

Mavis had gone, but her scent remained. Victor's mind wandered; he was back in the… No, he thought, forget it, I must forget all about it. He quickly finished his drink and made his way through to the private lounge and his family.

"Say goodnight to Daddy," Gillian said lifting Malcolm up for Victor to kiss him. "I'll be down as soon as he settles." As she made her way up the stairs she added as an afterthought, "Maybe you'd like to tuck him in." Victor followed mother and child up the stairs.

"Early to bed tonight, dear," Victor said. "I want to get an early start for Helmshore Mill in the morning to pick up a load for Witney."

Chapter Seven

"Attention please, will Captain Kennedy-Minards report to the information desk, will Captain Kennedy-Minards report to the information desk," the loudspeakers echoed throughout Lime Street Station in Liverpool. An army officer made his way through the crowd towards the information desk. A corporal was waiting by the desk. Upon seeing the officer, he stood to attention and saluted. "Good morning, sir, I've been sent to meet you and drive you to your camp." The corporal took the cases and they headed out to the staff car standing by the station steps. While the luggage was being placed in the boot, Captain Kennedy-Minards sat in the passenger seat.

Driving through the Mersey Tunnel, the corporal explained that they would bypass Chester and head for the A5 down to just below Worcester, then across country to the camp at Middle Wallop, with a stop at Tarporley for refreshments and toilets. It was quite a pleasant drive that April afternoon. The hawthorn hedges and fruit trees were in blossom, a welcome contrast with the desert that the captain had returned from.

The tanned face made it obvious that this officer had been serving overseas, and so the café owner managed to find extras from under the counter for his customers. When they returned to their car, the corporal turned the ignition key. The engine fired, backfired and stopped. He tried again and again, but the motor didn't turn. Out came the starter handle, but try though he might, the corporal was unable to turn it. "Sorry, sir," he said, "the engine has seized. I'll have to phone the depot."

"What's the matter, boys?" a friendly voice said. "Having trouble?" They both turned and seeing an American officer, saluted.

"Yes, sir," replied the corporal, "I think the engine has seized, sir."

"Where were you heading?" asked the American. The corporal looked at his superior; should he be telling a stranger, it could be a court martial offence.

"Middle Wallop, sir," replied the captain, "I'm due there tomorrow."

"Okay," said the American. "Let me introduce myself. I'm Major General Phillips, I'll be going down to Salisbury tomorrow so I can give you a lift. In the meantime, I'm on my way to our convalescent home here in Cheshire and I can get you a bed for the night. I'm sorry, corporal, but you will need to stay with the car until your breakdown truck arrives." Then turning to Captain Kennedy-Minards, "How does that sound?"

"Thank you, sir," was the reply.

***

Em answered the door. "Good evening, Em," said Herb, "I'd like you to meet Captain Richard Kennedy-Minards. Can you find him a room for the night please?" Then, "What delicacies are on the menu tonight?" Turning to his companion, he said, "She's a marvellous cook. Let me take you to meet the loveliest lady in the land," he added as they entered the drawing room. "Richard, I'd like to introduce Lady Jane Marbury of Moore Hall, and Jane, meet Captain Richard Kennedy-Minards, recently returned from active service in North Africa."

"I'm delighted to meet you," Lady Jane said. "Pray tell me, what brought you here, and how you come to know our American friend."

"My pleasure, ma'am."

"She's called Jane," Herb prompted in a loud whisper. "I was on my way south, my car broke down, and your friend came to my rescue."

There was a knock on the door. Susan entered wheeling a tea trolley set out for three. "Em asked me to tell you, sir, your luggage is in the Edwardian suite, directly opposite the top of the stairs. Dinner will be served at eight, informal dress."

Being a stickler for punctuality, Richard came down the stairs fifteen to twenty minutes early. Having lived in a house with servants in India as a small boy, he was interested in seeing below stairs in an English

56

country house. Upon his request, Em took Richard on a brief tour around the kitchen and anterooms, where old culinary equipment was stored, many of them looking like weapons meant more for torture than preparation of food.

After the meal had been cleared, Richard sat in the kitchen with Em and the girls. Susan and Sandra were telling him about the history of Moore Hall and the village of Shurlach, and Richard enthralled the girls with his description of the North African desert campaign.

What was the sound that woke him? Richard opened his eyes. Where was he, he thought he was dreaming? A maid was opening the curtains. "Good morning, sir, shall I run the bath? There's a tea trolley over to your left... breakfast will be served at seven a.m. If there is anything more, sir, just pull on the rope to you right." With that Sandra seemed to glide across the room and out of the door. Richard pinched himself. Now he saw the room in daylight, it seemed unbelievable. He walked over to the window and looked out. The countryside stretched for miles. In the distance he could make out a church spire. It was not surprising that the poets were so lyrical.

**

The American Ford slowly glided down the drive and stopped at the gate. There was a lorry coming through. the Major General wound down the window. "Hey, Victor," he called out, "how many blankets this time?"

"Two bales, sir," said Victor. With the window wound up, the Ford glided out onto the road and quickly picked up speed.

Richard watched the changing scenery as the car sped through the country lanes and minor roads onto the A5 trunk road. Whenever they came across a convoy, the military police would take one look at the small flag being flown on the bonnet and wave them through. The flag also seemed to be recognised by the civil police, who would stop other traffic to allow the big Ford through. The car seemed to eat up the miles and by mid-afternoon they drew up outside Richard's cottage in Piddlehinton.

"Come in, meet my wife and daughter," said Richard, "stop and have a cup of tea, Pamela won't mind." Then he called out, "Put the kettle on, dear, we have visitors." As they entered his home he picked up his little girl. "Say hello to my nice lady and gentleman," and putting his arm around his wife, he kissed her. "This my wife Pamela, and our daughter Judy. Meet Major General Herbert Phillips, Herb to his friends, and his chauffeur, Captain – wait for it – Shirley Temple… not to be confused with the little girl in films… no connection. They've brought me down from Cheshire."

"Pleased to meet you, ma'am, my pleasure I assure you." Herb kissed his finger tips and touched the kiss onto Judy's forehead. The child shyly turned her head and snuggled into her father's coat.

***

Once a week Em would don her Major overall, as she called it, and accompanied by Laurence, and occasionally by Major General Phillips, would walk through the convalescent wards, listening to the patients' comments, likes and dislikes. Em's heart went out to all the young soldiers, some hardly out of their teens. They reminded her of another soldier in hospital, a few years ago, who couldn't remember and didn't recognise either or his mother or his wife.

She would return to her office, change into her housecoat and hang the Major overall on the hook on the office door. Sometimes she would sit at her desk feeling the pains of loneliness. Oh yes, she had the friendship of her girls, she had the respect of the American staff, but this was different, she missed… she needed to feel the arms and warmth of a hug from a man, any man, but preferably her husband.

Although Em was not looking forward to any approach from George, she knew it was inevitable. He was not the sort of person who gave up at a little setback. The waiting was the most trying part, in fact it had been so long since the last contact that she had almost forgotten and was taken by surprise when it did come.

Victor had begun to enjoy the time he spent at home over the weekends. As the days got warmer, the three of them would go and feed the ducks on the canal, or watch the big seagoing ships as they made their way to and from Manchester. Life had never been so much fun, made even better by the delightfully radiant smile of his young son. At last things were looking up; business was good, he had a happy family, with a beautiful wife and son, and another child on the way. What more could a man want?

Victor was reading his newspaper, seated in his usual chair in the private lounge. Over the top of the paper, he could see Gillian with her knitting. She had unravelled an old jumper with its worn out sleeves, and was using the good wool to make something for Malcolm. As he returned his attention to the paper, the date caught his eyes. It was the thirtieth of April 1944, not that the actual date had any significance, but 1944, the twins would be almost ten. He had missed, yes missed, ten years of knowing his two boys, and even more, about sixteen years of knowing his daughter and enjoying them all growing up. And he missed his first love, his Em. Victor put the newspaper down and headed to the bar, he needed a really strong drink.

Damn, there was someone sitting in his seat by the inglenook. Victor found a seat in the bay window, maybe not as comfortable but he had a better view. He could see the full length of the bar, and, if he wished he could watch the lovely Mavis, but he had other things on his mind. Would Em take him back? If and only if she did, would he be prepared to give up his present pleasant situation in order to get her back? Or would he be able to manage to keep two households, just like when he first met Gillian? Mind you, he hadn't paid for either home then. Could he afford to pay for two homes, both of them here in Cheshire? Well, he could try leaving another note for her the next time he went to Moore Hall.

"Meet me outside Chester Cathedral at four p.m.," the note had said. Em glanced at the piece of paper in her hand, yes, it definitely said four, I assume it means outside the main entrance, Em thought. She looked at her watch; a quarter to, he should be here soon. Maybe he and I...? I mustn't keep building my hopes up, it's been a long time since I last saw him.

"Hullo, Em," a voice behind her said, making her jump.

She spun round, it was him, she had been looking the other way. I'm sure he wasn't there a moment ago, she thought as she answered, "Hullo, George," not knowing what else to say.

"You look great," he said, holding out his arms, but Em didn't respond to the suggestion of an embrace. "How are... things?" he asked.

You'd damn well know if you hadn't left me with two kids, she thought. "Oh, managing," she replied.

"We must talk, let's find somewhere private," he said, and started to walk towards the High Street. Turning into Lower Bridge Street they reached and entered Ye Olde King's Head.

"We'll take dinner in the room, please, Andy," George said to the barman, and led Em towards the staircase.

"Hang on a minute," Em said.

"It's all right," George answered, "we can talk in private up there."

"Maybe, but no funny business." Not sure why she said it, Em followed George up the stairs and into a room furnished in Tudor style, with a big four poster bed, two large armchairs and a low table in front of the open fireplace.

Em sat in the chair nearest the door in case she needed a quick getaway. "Well?" she asked.

"I wanted to see you," he answered meekly, "I... I wanted to know how you and the boys were, I see you haven't brought them with you."

"I could hardly do that, they're in a children's home; I wasn't able to look after them and go out to work," Em answered.

"Oh, well, I was wondering if we could start afresh."

"What about me?" she asked. "Do I get a say in this?"

"Of course," he replied, flinching at the sharpness of her voice.

"When and why did you leave the army?" Em asked. "And how come you finished up in a coma in hospital?"

"I don't know," he answered, "there's so much I can't remember, it's all a big muddle in my head." He was almost in tears. A knock at the door brought the conversation to an abrupt stop.

"Come in," called George. The door opened and Andy came in carrying a large tray which he placed on the table. "Bon appetit," he said, as he turned and walked out through the door. They pulled their chairs closer to the table and removed the cloth that was draped over the tray, to reveal two large oval dinner plates, each with an equally large oval cover which when lifted revealed a generous helping of roast pork, roast potatoes, carrots, peas and cabbage, complete with apple sauce and walnut stuffing. Also on the tray were two glasses and a bottle of wine.

After the food, the atmosphere was more relaxed. George sent down for another bottle of wine. The evening temperature was getting cooler. A maid brought up coffee, lit the fire and removed the dinner tray. They sat talking. Yes, it would be lovely to have the twins back, a house somewhere in the countryside, they could possibly have a guest house, Em would love that, or tea rooms. On they chatted. Em looked at her watch, she needed to catch the last bus. Oh no, her watch had stopped at six o'clock, it had to be a lot later than that. What was the time? Ten? Surely not. Em had missed her bus. What now?

It was Liscard all over again, but at least this time they were married. While Em used the bathroom, George went for a shower, and returned to the room clad only in a towel. Em was sitting in the huge bed. He could see her bare shoulders as she sat against the headboard, holding the sheet up to her chest. He stretched over to kiss her as she reached out to hug him. Any thought of the past was history as they snuggled under the bedding, once more in each other's arms.

Chapter Eight

"Well?" asked Sandra, as Em walked into the kitchen.

"Yes, thank you," replied Em. She poured herself a cup of tea and disappeared into her office, wishing she could remember what they had said, wishing she could remember... oh there was so much... so confusing. She picked up her cup, eh... she did not like cold tea. I just hope that whatever I've been promised works out this time... I really must get myself a decent cup of tea.

Em returned to the kitchen. "Thank you, girls, for holding the fort in my absence, I owe you so don't let me forget."

"We won't," two voices answered in unison.

"Well?" asked Sandra, "how did you get on?"

"Okay... I think," answered Em, "only time will tell."

"And?" asked Susan. "We waited up long after the last bus."

"I wasn't on it," said Em.

"We know," they said.

"I stayed overnight at a hotel in town."

"Alone?" from Sandra.

"Well... um no... all right, I know you won't give me any peace, yes I met George, er Victor, or Victor or George, anyway... take that grin off your faces, he *is* my husband."

Sandra, being careful not to get her flour-covered hands all over Em, put her arms around her boss and hugged her. "Good for you," she said. "I hope it works out for you."

"Hear hear," joined in Susan.

Em poured herself another cup of tea.

***

"How did you get on?" asked Gillian.

"Favourably, I think," answered Victor. "You know what they're like, agreeable to your face, then back off when it comes to the crunch."

"Never mind, dear," Gillian said. "Who knows, maybe you'd be better off without them."

"Who knows?" he said "who knows?" and walked out into the yard. He could hear water running in the wash house; he quietly walked over and peeped in. Mrs Woodley was putting washing into the copper. Victor quickly withdrew.

The party for Malcolm's birthday was held in the church parish rooms. It was thought inappropriate for it to be in the public house. Apart from anything else, the private lounge was a bit too small for half a dozen parents and the children that Gillian had invited, not forgetting the space needed for the food table. Being a man who disliked a lot of squealing children, Victor had made certain that he would not arrive home until late afternoon, when the party would be over and he'd be indoors waiting when mother and son arrived home.

***

The front doorbell rang, not once, nor twice, but repeatedly; someone was hanging on the bell pull. Em made a dash through the hall. Lady Jane had come to the drawing room door by the time Em was able to open the front door and the bell stopped its clamour. The Major General burst in waving a newspaper. "Allied Troops have landed in France," he shouted excitedly. "The Normandy Invasion has begun. We're giving the Nazis a dose of their own medicine."

"Come in and sit down while you get your breath back," said her ladyship. "Em, fetch some tea... oh, and something stronger... I think Herb would welcome it."

Major General Phillips had always been a popular visitor to Moore Hall, although the purpose of his visits was normally periodical inspections of the Medical Unit. His light-hearted approach to everything was infectious, and whenever he left, that same happy atmosphere always remained. He was certainly welcome on this occasion.

Em hardly noticed how many days had slipped by since her trip to Chester, although there were times when she would be sitting in her office wondering how much more time would pass before George made contact again, or when she was lying awake in her bed remembering how warm she had felt being so close to her man, and fearing the worst, that she'd been let down once more.

***

Victor was keeping an eye open for a suitable place to house Em and the family. He eventually found a large flat in a Victorian house near the middle of Chester, with space for a lodger and still enough room for the twins to come back and live with them. It should be easy to persuade Em – she had liked the thought of having the boys back – he just needed to negotiate the rent with the landlord.

The telephone rang. Victor could hear it ringing, ringing, ringing, and ringing, was no one going to answer it? The wind blew in under the bottom of the telephone kiosk. He couldn't tell where it was coming from, but he certainly knew where it was going; he shuffled from one foot to the other, even on this day in July it was cold. Victor put the phone down and pressed button B to reclaim his two pennies. Damn it, only one appeared. He banged the button and heard the coin drop, not into the tray but into the coin box. He swore, it was no joke losing your money when the call hadn't been answered. I suppose I could go there, he thought, although I don't have a delivery at Moore Hall... no, they need paperwork at the gate. Dejected, Victor got into his lorry and drove away.

***

Em heard the telephone as she approached the kitchen, hurried into the office and reached for the phone; it stopped ringing. She rang the operator to be told it was from a kiosk in Daresbury, yes she would

64

connect her. The telephone rang and rang; Victor didn't hear it as he drove away. After a week or more, Em began to wonder whether it had been George, but if not, then who could it have been? He hadn't offered, nor had she asked, for a number, but then why should she chase around after him after all that time.

It was hardly surprising that George's arrival at the back door, asking for Em, was unexpected. Em ushered him into her office, closing the door behind them. "Well?" she asked. "I can't be long, we're very busy at the moment."

"I didn't want to call without any news," he started.

"Well?" she asked again.

"There's a nice flat in the middle of Chester, we have the first option," he said. "You can move in as soon as you like. It's ours."

"Are you crazy?" she asked. "I need to give a month's notice, that'd mean the middle of August. Will they wait that long?"

"I think so," he replied.

"Don't just think, find out, and let me know… ring me," she said, opening the door to see him out.

"Well?" asked Sandra.

"Is the gravy ready?" Em asked.

Doubt and distrust were stronger than hope in Em's mind. Could it be that the promise of the united family had been to get her to do what he wanted? But now he had called in promising a home. She didn't know what to believe.

***

Just as she had with Gillian's first pregnancy, Mrs Woodley was keeping a close eye on her daughter, almost to the point of dictating and controlling the lives of Gillian and Victor, causing a certain amount of friction, which was not good for the young mother.

Everybody knew that mothers-in-law were like that, yet men, and Victor in particular, resented them taking over when *they* decided to, without waiting to be invited. I suppose it is inevitable when you're living with the in-laws, thought Victor, sitting by the inglenook, looking into his drink. But then there was Em as well – going on at him as if he was an idiot. Well, what can I expect? Give them a bit of authority…

"A penny for 'em," a soft silky voice next to him said.

Victor looked up. Mavis was standing beside him with a replacement for his now empty glass. "Naw," he said, "you wouldn't want to know."

Mavis placed the glass on the table beside him, and sat down. "You look so glum," she said, "not your usual cheerful self. A problem shared."

"No, not now," he said, smiling. "Seeing you has made my day, love."

Victor rose early next morning; he wanted to be on his way before his mother-in-law was up. Most of the time Gillian was resting, their second child almost due, and if he stopped to see to Malcolm he probably wouldn't get away until after ten. Let mother-in-law do it, he thought as he drove out onto the London Road.

***

"Where have you been?" asked Mavis, as Victor walked into the bar. "Your ma-in-law has been asking after you; apart from expecting you back last night, Gillian has gone into labour, the midwife is up there now."

"You'd better give me a double," Victor replied. "I think I'm going to need it." He emptied the glass and went through to the private quarters, but hesitated below the stairs.

"I wouldn't go up yet if I were you," said Mr Woodley, "there's not much you can do. Wait until you hear the baby cry," he advised. There was the sound of a slap, then a wail. "Up you go, lad," said father-in-law as Victor mounted the stairs.

"Oh, darling," Gillian said, "isn't she beautiful?" as she held the new born close to her chest. "Oh, darling, we have a daughter. I hope you aren't disappointed; I know you wanted another son for Malcolm to play with."

"As long as you are well and happy, then so am I," Victor said as he bent over to kiss his wife. Turning to the midwife, "Can I have a word… " glancing round, "outside," he said, gently guiding her out onto the landing.

"Sir?" she asked, a worried expression on her face. Victor took out a pound note and put it in her hand. "But sir," she said, "you don't need…" He put his finger to her mouth. "Well, thank you, sir," she said pocketing the note.

The subject of names was obviously going to cause a fair amount of discussion. "What about your grandmother's name, Wilhelmina?" asked Gillian's mother.

"Oh no," replied Gillian. "And why not, it's my second name too!" retorted her mother.

"Can you imagine Victor's answer if someone asked if they could see his Willie?" She erupted into laughter. "Maybe as a second name, but definitely not the first." Finding it hard to stop giggling, it took a long time for the hilarity to cease.

Victor turned right from the A5 on to the A56, it would take him through Daresbury and home to Thornton Heath in a little under an hour. As he drew into Daresbury he saw a telephone kiosk just past the Red Lion public house. 'That's handy,' he thought, 'I'll give Em a quick call.'

***

"Yes, Laurence, the darker brown the sugar, the richer the flavour added to the cake mix." Em was explaining when the telephone rang. "Sandra, see who that is. If it's the stores tell them I'll ring back in half an hour." She continued her explanation. "Soaking the soft fruit. Who is it?… George?… I'll take it," she said. "Back in a minute, Laurence." Wiping her hands on her apron, she headed for the office.

"Yes?… And?… Calm down… What am I supposed to do about that?… Okay, I'll give notice in the morning, but only if… Yes… No… You'll have to call for me on the twenty fifth… No… August, not July… Yes, one month's notice… Ring me next week and we'll sort out the details… Okay… Bye… love you too." Em put the phone down and flopped into her chair. "Phew… What have I just said? I must be mad to believe him, but so long as it all works out…" she said to herself. Oh yes, I was explaining to Laurence… Em made her way back into the kitchen.

Em sat at her desk trying to think what best to say to her ladyship. Lady Jane had been so kind to her when she had been pregnant with Charlton's child. The question she must decide on was, did she trust George, or should she confide in her ladyship? That question had kept her awake most of the night.

Em wheeled the trolley through the door into the drawing room. It was time to discuss menus for the coming week, but Em needed to announce her planned departure from Moore Hall. Lady Jane looked up. She had sensed that Em wasn't quite as cheerful as usual. "Thank you, dear," she said as Em served the tea and lightly buttered teacake. "What have you got for our enjoyment next week?"

Monday… Tuesday… Wednesday, the discussion seemed to be taking so long. Thursday… Friday then Saturday, it shouldn't be long now, …Sunday?

"I can see there is something on your mind," said her ladyship, "Whatever it is, I'm sure we can sort something out… what is this?" Em handed her a sealed envelope. "I understand… Yes of course, dear… I don't want to lose you, so let me know in two weeks' time. If he hasn't kept his word I'll give the letter back to you unopened, otherwise, I will accept your notice as from today. Now shall we return to the catering for next Sunday?"

Chapter Nine

Victor sat in his usual seat by the inglenook, beside him his favourite blend of Scottish whisky, but his mind was not on the drink, the newspaper in his hand or the shapely figure of Mavis at the bar. He was wondering whether he had done the right thing in making contact with Em after such a long time. There wasn't that same sparkle in her eyes that there had been at Larkhill. She seemed reluctant to accept what he said without question. Her phrase 'and only if' suggested her readiness to dictate. He didn't like being dictated to, especially by a woman.

He hadn't seen Mavis approaching. "Goodness," she said, "it must have been important for you to forget your drink."

He looked up, she was standing holding another full glass. "Thank you, love, my mind was elsewhere for the moment," he said, smiling up at her.

"Moment? More like half an hour," she replied. "I was watching you, I thought perhaps your glass was empty, and Albert keeps asking for the paper, if you've finished with it."

Victor surrendered the paper. "I'll read it later," he said.

He had already spent more money than he had anticipated on Em's behalf. He hadn't realised quite how much accommodation was, especially when there was a war on, but then there had to be a big demand for housing bearing in mind that the bombing had destroyed large numbers of houses up and down the country. It made sense, the fewer houses available, the bigger the demand, and consequently prices had gone up. Apart from that, two nights at the hotel hadn't exactly been cheap. I certainly hope it's going to be worth it, he thought.

***

The Major General was sitting in the drawing room enjoying a traditional afternoon tea with Lady Jane. He considered it one of the highlights of his visits to Moore Hall: the pleasant conversation about the gardens. This year the Rose Garden had an exceptional display, even better when seen in the afternoon sunshine.

When all the usual subjects had been exhausted, her ladyship picked up her paper. "I was glancing through the obituaries in *The Times* to see which of my friends have passed on when I saw this about a young officer…"

"I know," he said, "yes, it is the one who was here a few months ago. Tragic. That's what brought me here ahead of my scheduled visit. With your permission, I'll go and tell Em and the girls."

"On the third of August, Captain Kennedy-Minards was piloting an Auster aircraft," the Major General read out, omitting one or two minor details, "on an exercise to practise forced landings near Stonehenge." Em and the girls already knew what was coming. "While he was flying into the sun in hazy conditions," he continued reading, "the aircraft hit high tension cables and crashed in flames." He put the newspaper down and continued. He leaves a wife, Pamela, and a lovely baby daughter, Judy, I know because I met them when I took him home. I'll leave the paper here so that you can read the whole obituary for yourselves." He gave each of the girls a hug. "He must have been a very brave man to have been awarded the Military Cross," he said, "and I know how much you liked him. Now if you will forgive me, I have to get back to my office."

Em and the girls looked at each other in bewilderment. They knew about men being killed at the warfront, but this was here in England. How could it be that after fighting out in North Africa, where you expect men to be killed, he died in a training accident, away from all the fighting.

Em tried to keep the mood in the kitchen as light and happy as possible, and the normal cheerful atmosphere returned within about a week or so. Not suggesting that Richard was forgotten, each of them at times remembered the happy young army officer who had stayed at Moore Hall for such a short while, and told them so much about North Africa.

"Yes, dear… It's ours from the twentieth… Yes, dear… I'll be along to collect you and your belongings at around ten… Okay, I'll make it eleven… Yes I know, the twenty-fifth… I'll come round the back." George put the phone back on its rest and tried button B. There's no harm in trying. I certainly hope all Em's stuff will fit in the Hornet, he thought as he headed back to his lorry.

Driving up and down the country, Victor had plenty of time to think. It was not going to be easy with his two wives living in the same county. It would have been better with one somewhere down south. He didn't want to leave Gillian, but deep down he still had feelings for Em and the boys, even though he had never known them. He felt that he had let them all down, and come to think of it, there was their first kiddie. What was her name? I can't remember. She must be sixteen by now. probably a smasher like her mum. The boys are ten. I don't know. Kids seem to grow up so quickly these days.

It had been a long day and Victor had had enough, loading bales of yarn at Helmshore Mill, running into three convoys as he headed south, and the kerfuffle at Witney trying to get unloaded; then managing to load the bales of blankets just before the factory closed, meant that he was feeling tired before he arrived at Maid Moreton. Climbing out of his lorry, he took out his overnight bag and locked the cab door. A quick check to make certain that the tarpaulins were securely fastened, and he walked into the bar of the Wheatsheaf. "Scotch, please," he said to the barmaid. "What's on the menu tonight? Sounds good… Yes please… And a room for tonight… And early breakfast… Ah yes," he said handing over his identity card. "Yes that's right… Your name? Hi Linda… Call me Victor… Yes, I'll be over there." He pointed to the table in the bay window.

***

"I've called you all together," Lady Jane said, "so that I can let you know what changes are going to be made." She continued. "Both Em and I have been aware that except on occasions like Christmas, we are overstaffed, but neither of us wanted to part with either of you, and the situation has now changed. Em will be leaving us in a couple of weeks' time, so neither of you will need to go." Her ladyship went on, "When Em leaves I would like Susan to resume the position she held before Em joined the staff, that of housekeeper. That will be all."

Back in the kitchen they all seemed to be talking at the same time, congratulating Susan and excitedly asking Em about what she was doing. "That is no slight on your capabilities," Em was saying to Sandra. "When I arrived Susan was running the whole caboodle on her own, including visitors, so please don't be disappointed, you really are appreciated here."

Em set out to make the transition as painless as possible, for herself and Susan, but especially for Sandra; all three had to adjust to a change in leadership in the kitchen as Em gradually handed over the everyday routine. It wouldn't be easy for Susan and Sandra, but as long as they continued to work as a team and remained good friends, Em thought all would be well.

"I have been instructed by her ladyship to make up a package of bedding for you to take with you tomorrow," Susan informed Em.

"But…" About to deny the need, Em was almost in tears. Hugging Susan she replied, "I don't know what to say." She knew how much it could have cost her, in money and in more clothing coupons than she possessed.

***

"Be a good boy for Mummy," Victor said to Malcolm, "and help to look after your baby sister," then turning to Gillian, "The conference is over two days, so with one day at each end for travel, I should be back before the weekend. Sorry, dear. You'd be bored and it would be difficult for you with two small children. I know. It's only four days." Victor kissed his wife, and ignoring the glare from his mother-in-law, made his way out to his car. Four days? Would that really be enough to set up a second home? To satisfy Em? Anyway the die was cast. He would have to play it by ear.

Ten o'clock; the Hornet drew up outside the gate of Moore Hall and waited. "Hi, Victor, what brings you here today?" asked Joe, "where's your truck?"

His colleague was looking closely at the identity card. "Hey, Joe, what's this 'hi Victor' about? His ID shows George, George Summers. I think we'd better ring the lieutenant. Get him to move his car clear of the gates, will you?"

As George moved his car out of the way, the big grey Ford of Major General Phillips came through the gates and stopped. Winding down his window he asked, "What's the hold-up?" A jumble of words came from the two American soldiers. The Major General stepped out of his car. "Run that by me again." It still sounded a little confusing so he asked Joe to bring the driver into the office. By this time the lieutenant arrived and after smartly saluting the Major General, both officers retired into the inner office, to be shortly followed by George, escorted by an armed sentry.

The lieutenant patted his side arms (the pistol hanging from his belt). "It's all right, Harris," he said to the sentry, "you can go back to the gate." Harris, making a great show of military discipline, saluted, turned about and left the office. Major General Phillips crossed his arms and sat quietly watching. "Name?" asked the lieutenant. There was a long silence while George tried to think of any way out of his predicament. The lieutenant looked up "Name?" he repeated.

A frown spread across the Major General's face as he waited in silence, remembering what he had once told Em: 'Victor would be better for you than your no-good husband'. Was this Victor? he wondered, or was this George? Or were they both the same man?

The explanation came as a confused muddle. "Stop," said the Major General, and turning to the lieutenant, he said, "Just for the record, *the matter was handed...*" he dictated "*... that's right,*" he said, "*to the*

Commanding Officer… now sign it… and I'll countersign it… thank you, Lieutenant."

"Thank you, sir," replied the lieutenant as he swiftly left the room.

"You realise I could hand you over to the civilian police," said Major General Phillips, "so how about the truth, Victor," then glancing at the identity card on the desk, "or is it George?"

***

"Where's Em?" asked the Major General as he walked into the kitchen, using the back door.

"She's in with her ladyship," replied Susan.

"It's all right, I'll make my own way through," he said, as he walked through to the hall.

Lady Jane sat down at her desk and once more started to write in her journal. "Today I bid 'Farewell' to the best housekeeper and cook I have known in the last ten years. Mrs Summers, affectionately known as Em, left with her husband in the hope of being reunited with her twin boys at present in care. I shall miss her." Putting her pen down, her ladyship rose and walked over to where Major General Phillips was standing by the window; they watched as the car made its way down the drive.

"According to her husband," Major General Phillips was saying, "he was apparently attacked and knocked out. He woke up in hospital but couldn't remember anything, not who he was, nor that he was married with a family, and that it's taken all this time – all of eight years – to find out about Em and the boys."

"And you believe him?" asked her ladyship.

"I'm not sure," came the reply. "There're one or two things that don't add up."

"Like what?" she asked.

"I'm not sure," he repeated, shaking his head. "I just hope she hasn't made a big mistake."

Chapter Ten

Forty Lower Bridge Street, Chester, was a typical double-fronted, four-storey Victorian building with shops at ground level, and a central door leading through a short hall to a stairway that wound up through the centre of the building to a landing at each level, until it reached the uppermost rooms. Apart from the rooms that were to be occupied by Em and her family, the rest were usually occupied by students at the university.

George opened the door, and with a case in each hand climbed the stairs to the first floor. Holding his hand to his mouth to represent a trumpet, "Ta ra rara," he went and, ceremoniously presenting Em with the key said, "Welcome to our new home."

Em opened the door and walked through the small hallway into the front room; it was spacious, the few pieces of furniture seemed to emphasise the hugeness of the room.

"I thought we'd go down the road for a celebratory lunch before we unpack," George said. "Come on, love, let's go" – heading towards the landing – "I could eat a horse."

By down the road George had obviously meant Ye Olde King's Head to which they went. "Hello George… and who's this beautiful…?" Andy asked, eyeing Em up and down.

"Come off it, Andy," said George, "I told you last time we were in, this is my wife, Em."

"Would you like a table by the window, sir, madam?" Andy asked as he led them through the restaurant. He held the chair for Em, asking, "Something to drink while you wait?"

It didn't matter how ingenious the chef was, what herbs and spices, or sauces were used, nor what fancy foreign names you gave it, whale meat was still whale meat; nevertheless, for Em, when someone else had done all the hard work, it was delicious both in presentation and flavour.

Em had made an excursion to the 'powder room' and when she returned, George and Andy were deep in conversation. "Don't forget," Andy was saying as he cleared the dishes from the table, "I'm looking for somewhere if you're going to take a lodger."

Back at the flat it was obvious that although George had bought some furniture, his idea of necessities was sadly lacking. The bedroom had a big double bed but nowhere to put your clothes. The living room had a table and chairs, but nowhere to relax in comfort, coal for the fire but no wood, paper or matches, and the kitchen… Well, what could you expect? He was a man. Fortunately, with the bedding and linen, and provisions that Herb had contributed, they were able to spend their first night in comparative comfort.

A trip to the local market the following morning equipped the kitchen with pots and pans and cooking utensils, while a visit to a second-hand shop saw the delivery during the afternoon of a comfortable three piece suite and a carpet for the living room. Em looked round their new home, thinking, I'll turn this into *my* home, all in good time.

Em swept and scrubbed, dusted and tidied until the place was as she wanted, while George had made himself scarce. His vision of domestic bliss didn't include him helping with any of the chores. That was woman's work, his dad hadn't, so why should he. George had forgotten that his father, as breadwinner for his family, had spent all his time in his workshop turning heavy marble slabs into gravestones.

Em had just set the table for their evening meal when there was a knock on the door. Andy was standing there carrying a small case and a large bag. "George said you had a spare room if I needed it. I need it, so here I am," he said, with a sheepish grin on his handsome face.

That evening they were sitting quietly, listening to the music on the wireless, when George put his newspaper down on his lap. "Early night tonight, dear," he said. "I've an early start in the morning, I'll need to pick up my lorry from the depot and collect a load from Helmshore for Witney."

"Don't mind me," said Andy. "I'm enjoying the music." Em glared at him. "On second thoughts, it's nice out, so I think I'd like a walk before I settle." He stood up. "Good night, folks," and he disappeared out of the door.

***

As George drove into Thornton Heath, London Road was already busy: a queue at the bakery for the warm freshly baked bread; the butcher's shop with a display of rabbit and game, discreetly supplied from local sources; a few cars and bicycles at the side of the road, and pedestrians crossing from one side or the other. George hardly noticed the black Wolseley police car a few doors away before he turned in beside the Red Lion, nor did he see the two officers slowly get out of their car. Driving carefully, he manoeuvred the Hornet past his lorry and backed it into the garage, patted the bonnet as he walked out, closed and locked the door and headed in through the kitchen.

"I'm home," he called out as he entered the bar and poured himself a drink. There was a loud banging on the door. "We're closed," he called out, "come back later." Then thinking it might be the brewery he called out, "Who is it?"

"The police," came the reply, "open up."

The banging had brought Mr and Mrs Woodley and Mavis into the bar; Mavis picked up the keys and opened the door. "You'd better come inside," she said, hastily closing the door behind them.

The Police Sergeant reached into his tunic pocket, looking directly at George. "George Summers—"

"No, he's Victor Bradburn, he's my husband," said Gillian, who had also entered the bar. "No, there must be some mistake," she cried, tears streaming from her eyes.

"I'm sorry, miss, he *is* George Summers," then turning his attention to George, "George Summers, I have a warrant for your arrest on a count of bigamy."

"I'll kill him," said Mrs Woodley, holding her arms around her weeping daughter. "I'll kill him."

"No, Mummy," wept Gillian, "I love 'im and I'll need 'im when he comes out of prison, whatever he's done."

"Would you take him out the back way, please?" Mr Woodley asked the policemen. "I don't want everybody gossiping, we've got a good name here and I don't want it spoilt."

***

Em knew that if she was going to have any chance of getting the boys back she would need the backing of the local Methodist Church, and so with George and Andy away from the house she made her way to the St John's Street Wesleyan Chapel, where there were activities that she might be able to join, to take note of the times of the Sunday Worship. Moore Hall had been a long way from any church, the nearest being the parish church in Shurlach, a pleasant but long way to walk even in fine weather, and not to be recommended when wet. Em's visits to any church since her wedding had consequently been few and far between.

Em was standing looking at the noticeboard as a steady stream of women of varying ages went past. Her eyes sometimes followed them, but as she stood there watching, the numbers reduced until a last few hurried past.

"Are you coming in?" a gentle voice beside her asked. Em turned to see who had spoken; a lady was standing beside her. "I'm sure you'll find it interesting."

"Come on, Hilda, they're about to start," a poker-faced lady called from the doorway.

"Coming," Hilda called back in reply.

Em followed her into the building. She found a seat at the back of the crowded hall, trying to see past heads and hats: tall hats, short hats, and hats with feathers; Em was unable to see all the four or five ladies seated on the stage at the front. The meeting started with a hymn and prayer and then 'poker-face' stood up and in a strange-high pitched voice announced, "We have great pleasure this afternoon," she turned to face the guest speaker for a moment, making what she was saying less audible to those at the back of the hall, "to welcome Sister," turning back to the hall, "Mabel Stanton of the National Children's Home and Orphanage." Em's blood froze, especially when she heard, "And this afternoon I want to tell you…" Em hardly heard what was being said, "…home in the Isle of Man…" Em couldn't listen to any more; she fled. Hilda quickly followed her, but when she reached the steps there was no sign of Em. Hilda shook her head and went back into the hall.

Em sat on the bench by the cathedral steps. Why had she run away? What had she been afraid of? She didn't know, she had panicked, but why?

Even before she climbed the stairs, she could hear the wireless. Em turned the key and opened the door; the noise was deafening. She walked across the room and turned the wireless off.

"Ah, you're back," said Andy.

"Get your feet off my settee, and if you want to have a wireless blasting like that, you can take yourself out from here, the further and the sooner the better."

"Oh, Em," he said in a whining voice, "I'm sorry." He put his hands forward to hold her shoulders.

"Shove off," she replied, pushing his hands away, "and go to work."

No matter how busy Em tried to keep herself, she missed the companionship she had known in the kitchen at Moore Hall. She missed seeing the others and the banter. Never mind, she thought, it'll be worth it when I get the boys back.

Andy didn't get back until the following morning. When Em asked him about it he just answered with a broad sheepish grin. It was quite obvious that he wasn't going to give her an explanation, so she told him to let her know if he wasn't going to be in overnight, to save her waiting up.

After a lunch of hotpot using whale meat, although one wouldn't have guessed, and which Andy praised as being the best he had ever tasted, Em went into town for one or two what she called 'what-nots' while Andy said he was going for a walk by the river before going to work, and might be late back, as the hotel bar closed about ten. Em assumed that meant he might not be back until next day, Sunday.

Sunday? Oh, goodness, thought Em, nervous about her reception if she went to church after her exit during the meeting only a few days earlier. Oh well, she thought, if I'm going to seek their help with the boys, here goes. Dressed modestly, and with her hair neatly permed and wearing a plain blue hat that matched her coat, she set out for church. The service was the normal Wesleyan format led by the Reverend Norman Pike, a severe looking gentleman who, standing in the pulpit, appeared to be looking down his nose at the congregation, unless, of course, you were sitting in the balcony. Standing by the door after the service, he greeted members of the congregation, "Good morning, Mrs Clitheroe, nice to see you – Good morning, Mrs Brown – Ah, Mr Fellowes, tell me…"

"Ah, I was hoping to see you." Em turned and faced the lady speaking to her; it was Hilda. Someone said something to Hilda to which she replied, "Oh yes, I'll see you on Tuesday about that," then turning back to Em gently guided her into a side room away from the rest. "I was hoping to see you again," she repeated, "you were obviously upset about something the other day, perhaps it might help to talk about it?" Em looked at her, uncertain what to say. "Was it something to do with Sister Mabel and her talk about the Isle of Man?"

A head came round the door. "Your husband is asking where you are."

"Tell him I'm busy, I'll be along shortly."

"But…"

The second time Hilda answered more firmly. "Tell the Reverend gentleman his lady is busy."

Em looked at her with surprise. "You mean… you're…?"

"Yes, dear, I'm Mrs Hilda Pike, the minister's wife for my sins. Now we were discussing what made you leave in such a hurry."

Em walked home, grateful that she had been able to tell Hilda about her boys being in the home in the Isle of Man, how she was hoping to get them back and seeing Sister Mabel had confused her; also relieved because apparently no one else had noticed her departure, and everybody had enjoyed a most informative talk about the homes, for there were two homes in the Isle of Man.

Once indoors she made herself a cup of tea and sat in the easy chair that gave her a view out of the window. Across the other side of the road she could see into a room much the same as the one she was in; she could see two children playing together. Em smiled and closed her eyes; she drifted off to sleep, and dreamt that her twins were playing on the floor in front of her.

Chapter Eleven

"Who am I speaking to...? Yes... He was arrested on the twenty-ninth of August... We've sent the necessary paperwork for his transfer... When...? oh, I see... I'll see if Inspector Harris can be spared although it shouldn't need an Inspector... No, bigamy... That should be sufficient to prosecute. The third wife? That's right, three... Thank you... What was that...? Oh Cartwright... Yes... These telephone lines... We'll be in touch." Inspector Bridges pressed the bar on his telephone. "Harry, can you spare a moment?"

Police Sergeant Harry Jones came into the office. "Yes, sir?"

"It looks like we're stuck with Summers until Monday. The Oxford boys are expecting trouble over the weekend, so please arrange for meals for him, we don't want to be accused of starving the poor beggar."

"What about his transfer to Oxford, sir?"

"It seems that will be down to us," said the Inspector, "but I'll have a word with Oxford to decide which day. I'll also speak to Summers," then after a quick look at his watch, he added, "I'll see him in the interview room, er... give me about ten minutes."

Had it been anyone else, things might have been different. George had known the Inspector ever since he was a lad, he had always been a friend of the family, and even though he had frequently crossed the line between bad and acceptable behaviour, Inspector Bridges had always been ready to help him, even after being sent to the Training Ship when he was a teenager. The offer of a quicker, more comfortable journey from Birkenhead to Oxford was typical of the caring nature of the man responsible for his arrest and transfer.

An early breakfast saw George seated in the back of the police car, accompanied by a policeman. With Inspector Bridges and a driver in the front, they headed south towards Chester and beyond, eventually joining the A5 trunk road on its way to Oxford. Convoys and traffic congestion were no obstruction, giving way to the flashing headlights accompanied by the urgent ringing of the bell, and the skilful driving of the officer at the wheel.

The journey broken only by a refreshment stop at the Birmingham Police Headquarters meant they arrived shortly after noon, and after being shown into a cell and given a meal, George was interviewed by a solicitor who would represent him in the magistrates' court the following morning.

***

"No, Mother, I'll stand by him," Gillian insisted. "I love him. He loves me too," she muttered defiantly. "I know he does; he always came home to me…" fighting back her tears. "It's some spiteful woman trying to get her own back 'cos she couldn't keep him."

"All right, dear," replied her mother, "we'll see what happens when they release him," not sure herself whether she would want him back, although he was the father of her grandchildren.

"Gillian, will you keep an eye on the bar," asked Mavis, "while I get some light ales from the cellar?"

"Can't Mr Woodley fetch them? That's his job," said Mrs Woodley as Mavis headed towards the cellar door, and Gillian to the bar.

"I know, but I don't know where he is," Mavis replied as she negotiated the wooden steps and turned the corner. "Mrs Woodley," she called. "It's Mr Woodley. He's lying on the floor."

"He's probably drunk again, let him sleep it off!"

"I don't think so," came the reply from the cellar.

"Harry, Bert," Gillian said, "go down and fetch 'im up, quickly." The two men hurried down into the cellar, brought Mr Woodley up and sat him in a seat by the inglenook.

Mavis came up from the cellar with the crate of light ales. "How is he?" she asked.

"I don't know," answered Gillian.

"He's drunk," sneered Mrs Woodley. "He spends all day down there sampling the goods, he's drunk."

Gillian smelled his breath. "No, Mother, he's not drunk, he's ill. Mavis," she called out, "ring for the doctor."

Mrs Bailey, the district nurse, who had been in the bar with her husband, came over and sniffed Mr Woodley's breath. "Quickly, fetch some sugar," she ordered Mavis, "he's diabetic."

"Where's the patient?" Doctor Bates asked as he entered the bar. "Ah there you are," he said as he put his Gladstone bag on the table. "Hello, Ethel," he said turning to Mrs Bailey, "it's a good job you were in here... hmm... yes." Reaching into his bag, taking out a syringe and a small glass phial, he gave Mr Woodley an injection, waiting with one hand holding the patient's wrist, his pocket watch in the other. After a little while, he nodded, closed his bag, and rose. "Mrs Woodley," he said, "may I have a word with you," and they walked through to the back.

***

Em looked at the clock, it was already six in the evening. George had been away two days more than he had said. She had grown used to one day rolling on after another, and this expecting someone home in the evening wasn't something she was familiar with, but then she remembered that he had said he expected to be back by Monday. She was getting worried, where was he? What had delayed him? A breakdown maybe? Extra deliveries? Or an accident? Or maybe... no, it couldn't be that he'd left her again, not so soon after getting back together, no that can't be it, how could I even think it, she scolded herself, we've been so happy getting the flat ready together, he'll be back, she told herself, yes he'll be coming in any moment now.

Another hour passed, then another, before there was a knock on the door. Here he is, Em thought, the silly idiot's forgotten his key. Em opened the door and stepped back, frightened; two police officers stood in the doorway. "Is it George?" she asked.

"May we come in, Em?" asked the gentle voice of Inspector Bridges. A dazed, confused Em led the way into the living room, closely followed by a uniformed police woman. "Hilary," said the Inspector, "see if you can find your way to making a cup of tea." Hilary headed towards the kitchen.

Em looked at the face of the man who had always been a friend. "I am so sorry to have to tell you – no, he's quite all right," he said. "Apparently George married a lady in Oxfordshire, and has been arrested for bigamy. It's been suggested that he married her before he regained his memory, and it's hoped the court will be lenient with him in the circumstances."

While he was speaking, Hilary brought in a cup of tea for Em. "Sugar, dear?" she asked.

"I'll let you know when the hearing will be," said the inspector, as he stood up. "If there's anything I can…"

"Thank you," said Em.

Inspector Bridges placed a card with a phone number on the table. "This number comes direct into my office," he said. "If there's anything I can do… as a friend…" The door closed behind them.

Em was sitting in the dark when Andy got home. "I thought you'd be in bed," he said, turning on the light, then rushing over to close the blackout before any one saw the lit windows and reported them. Seeing Em's tearstained face he asked, "What is it? What's happened?" He picked up the card, and asked, "The police… is it George?" He sat down on the settee beside her.

"Yes," she replied, "he's been…" She was sobbing. "He's been arrested…" The tears started to fall. "How could he… he's been arrested for bigamy." Andy held his arm around her, her head was on his shoulder as he comforted her.

Em woke to the sound of the curtains being opened; Susan or Sandra? she wondered. She opened her eyes; neither, it was Andy. He turned and walked towards the door. "There's a cuppa on the bedside table," he said as he left the room. Em didn't remember coming to bed or how she got there; had Andy spent the night with her? Surely not. She looked at the other side of the bed, relieved to see that it hadn't been slept in. She dismissed the thought from her mind.

Em was spreading butter on a slice of lightly toasted bread. "There's homemade marmalade on the Welsh dresser, if you'd like some," she said as she reached for the grill pan and another piece of toasted bread.

"Did you make it?" asked Andy.

"No," replied Em, "Susan did – one of the girls at Moore Hall."

"Hmm… delicious," he said as he took another bite of the toast. "I thought you…" munching noisily.

"I have made it," Em said, "but not this time."

There was a loud banging on the door. "I'll go," said Andy, getting up from his breakfast to answer the door and returning a few minutes later. "It's Higginbottom, the landlord, asking for the rent."

"I thought George said he had bought this place."

"No," said Andy, "he says George owes him rent for the whole of August, and one week in September, twelve pound ten shillings, in all."

"Who carries that much around with them? I don't," said Em, almost in tears.

"It's okay," replied Andy, "I'll sort it."

Ten minutes later Andy sat down once more, to continue his breakfast. "Thank you," she said, "Oh thank you, I don't know what I would have done without you." Getting up from her chair, she walked over to him and kissed him on the cheek, then laughed as he blushed and tried to rub the lipstick from his face.

"I'm working in the restaurant lunch-time," Andy said. "I'll see if I can get something special to bring home, there's usually plenty left over."

"Be careful," Em answered, "I wouldn't want you to fall foul of the law… I've already lost George."

"Don't worry, pet," he assured her. "I won't do anything illegal, they usually let me have a meal at work, I think they'll let me bring it home," he said, showing Em a large sandwich box he was putting into his bag. Andy walked over to where she was sitting, bent down and kissed her, saying, "See you later, love," as he left.

Em's eyes followed him as he went out of the door. 'Hmm,' she thought and smiled, 'I suppose I could do a lot worse.'

Em spent the rest of the morning window-shopping, she particularly liked looking in the pawnbroker's window at the things that had gone past their redemption date, or items that had just plainly been sold to raise money to meet some urgent need like a doctor's bill, or even to buy food. Em wasn't looking with any intention of purchasing anything extravagant, it was just a pleasant way of passing time. Mind you, there was always the possibility of finding a real bargain, and selling it on for a good profit. There was money to be made if you were lucky.

"Do you know anything about geysers," asked Em when Andy arrived in from work.

"Who are you talking about?" Andy asked, laughing,

"The one over the bath, silly," answered Em laughing.

"It's not your birthday, is it?" Andy asked.

"You cheeky beggar," Em retorted.

"I'll have a look after lunch," he pacified her, taking the sandwich tin out of his bag. "Let's get this while it's still hot." Em quickly got out two plates and cutlery, and they sat down to a lunch of roast chicken.

"Oh, while I think of it," said Andy while they were eating, "have you done any waiting? Silver Service? That's handy. Alexandra, one of the waitresses is leaving at the weekend. You'd be working two or three nights a week, and on special functions at the weekends. You game for it? Good, I'll have a word with Claude, the maitre d'... now what's this about some old geyser?"

It took Andy only a few minutes to light the geyser and have hot water running into the bath. Em wasn't going to miss the opportunity of a hot soak, it was a luxury she had missed since moving to Chester.

"I've got to get back, see you later," he said as he made for the door. "Enjoy your bath, dear."

"And who's going to scrub my back for me?" Em called out.

"Maybe another time," he answered as the door closed behind him. Em turned the key in the door, she didn't intend anyone to disturb her leisurely bath.

The curtains were drawn, the room was in semi darkness, soft relaxing orchestral music flowed from the wireless. Em was spread out on the chaise longue, her hand gently swaying in time with the melody as if conducting the invisible musicians, a scene only disturbed by the sound of the key in the lock as Andy entered the flat. He stood in the hallway for a moment, absorbing the atmosphere before he quietly entered the room and sitting beside Em, bent over to kiss her on her lips.

Chapter Twelve

Andy slipped out of bed and into the bathrobe. Easing the door open so as not to waken Em, he made his way to the kitchen to put the kettle on the stove, then stood in the bedroom doorway watching Em gently breathing as she lay between the sheets.

Em stirred, reaching out across the empty space that had so recently been occupied. She sat up, pulling the sheet up to her chest. Andy walked across the room and sat on the side of the bed, spreading his arms around her, drew her close and they kissed. The sound of the kettle whistling reminded him that he had been about to make some tea. He kissed Em again and returned to the kitchen.

From where he was standing in the kitchen, Andy could hear Em singing along to the music on the wireless: '...my dreams are getting better all the time...' Smiling to himself, he carried the tray into the living room; mine are too, he thought.

After a relaxed breakfast, Andy cleared the table before setting off to the hotel. Today he would be working right through from ten in the morning until nine in the evening, in order to allow Muriel, his colleague, to visit her mother in Southport once a week. Muriel would return the favour from time to time, an arrangement that suited them both.

With Andy out of the way, Em spent the morning sweeping, dusting and generally tidying up, something which she didn't consider to be a chore. In fact one might call her houseproud, not that she ever went to extremes, she liked the tidy but lived in appearance that made visitors feel comfortable.

Several days later, after finishing her chores and enjoying a light lunch, Em headed to the St John's Street Wesleyan Chapel, hoping to join in with the activities of the Women's Institute. Today there was to be a talk by someone from the Food Ministry about *Jam Making by the*

W.I. and how valuable it was for the nation. Em had heard mention of it, and wondered where it was being done and whether she might be able to help. She found the talk interesting; when she gave her name she was told that they had more volunteers than there was room for in the hall, but they would add her name to the list. The meeting finished with the rendering of *Jerusalem* and a prayer. It was a long time before the hall emptied, due to the general chatter of women who seldom saw their friends away from the midweek meetings or on a Sunday, when they usually had to dash home to do the Sunday lunch.

There were times this late in the day in September that a cool or even chill breeze blew up the River Dee, and having come out in a summer frock, Em wasted no time in getting home out of the wind. Once indoors, she put on a warm cardigan and lit the fire in the living room, then made herself a hot cup of cocoa, which she drank sitting by the fire, listening to the wireless.

Seated in front of the fire, with the wireless playing the music of the Glenn Miller orchestra, tunes like *Moonlight Serenade* and *A String of Pearls*, Em closed her eyes as she listened, the soft seductive rhythm steadily drawing her into sleep, and dreams of that first time in Liscard, the thrill, the pleasure when the heart becomes enveloped in the sound of beautiful relaxing music.

Not knowing how long she had slept, Em woke to find the room was in darkness, the fire was little more than a glow. She went to the window and closed the black-out, switched on the standard lamp and returned to the fireplace; a couple of sticks of wood, two pieces of coal, a gentle poke and a spark turned into a flame.

Em glanced at the clock; it was almost eight thirty, Andy could be home shortly after nine, she must be ready for him. Would he have eaten or would he expect a meal? Or maybe after such a long day, he might just want to go to bed. Em went into the bedroom and turned the bed sheet down, just like she had for the visitors at Moore Hall. It's amazing how one falls into a routine after such a short time, she thought, never mind, there's no harm in it.

Em heard the key in the door. Andy came in, put his coat on the hook in the hall and flopped into an easy chair. Em bent over and kissed him; she could smell alcohol on his breath. "Tea, dear?" she asked.

"No thanks," he answered and made a grab for her. Em quickly sidestepped, narrowly avoiding being pulled down on his lap.

"If you want..." she was saying, but stopped. Andy's head had dropped down to his chest and he was already snoring loudly. Em kissed him on the head, switched off the standard lamp, and leaving the light on in the hall, undressed and climbed into bed.

*****

Em was puzzled. She hadn't eaten anything unusual, yet she didn't feel very well, not that she was actually sick but... She looked at the calendar, she wasn't usually late... And then it hit her, six days late, she must be pregnant. But whose? George's or Andy's?

Andy was in the kitchen making toast. "Butter?" he asked, "marmalade?"

"No thanks, dear," she answered, "just dry."

"Dry toast, are you all right, love?" He looked at Em suspiciously. "You're not, are you?"

"Yes, dear, I think I am."

"Wow, that's great!" he said, putting his arms around Em, lifting her off the ground and swinging her round. "That's fantastic."

"Stop it," she said, "you'll burn the toast," struggling to get out from his arms.

Andy had already gone off to work. Em had been busy making the bed, cleaning and tidying up in the kitchen, after which she sat down by the window with a cup of Oxo, trying to make up her mind, not who the father was, although she had wondered about that from time to time. Em was trying to decide whether she really wanted another child at the moment. Andy was delighted so maybe it would be a positive step towards a stable family for her boys to come home to.

There was a knock at the door. Em opened it to Inspector Bridges and the young police woman, Hilary. "Come in," she said, trying not to show any nervousness. "Would you like a cup of tea?" As they entered Hilary offered to make it while the inspector explained the purpose of their visit.

"My wife would never forgive me," Inspector Bridges said, "if I just sent you a formal letter, but you can read it at your leisure." He passed Em a sealed envelope. "George has been sentenced to twelve months for the bigamous marriage to Alice Cooper in Ramsden in Oxfordshire using the name of Bradburn. He has asked for another offence to be taken into consideration, that of bigamously marrying a Miss Gillian Woodley of Warrington. There are two children with Miss Woodley." Em swore under her breath, what did he think he was up to, how could he do this to her? If she had known she would never, not ever have left Moore Hall. He could rot in jail so far as she was concerned.

After the departure of the inspector and policewoman, Em tore open the envelope, glanced at the letter, screwed it up and threw it in the bin, but after thinking for a short while, she retrieved the letter, carefully smoothed it out, folded it and put it on the mantelpiece.

Having made up her mind that she wanted the baby, there was the question of what they, she and Andy were going to need, apart from clothing the baby, she had better start knitting. It might also be a good idea to join the Young Wives Club at the church. Getting involved with such activities, she thought, would give her the opportunity to make friends; being a newcomer to the area there were times when Em felt quite lonely.

The Young Wives Club was on Tuesdays at two o'clock in the afternoon, timed to enable those with children to meet them as they came out of school. Em made certain she arrived at the church hall in good time, and Hilda greeted her as she entered the hall. "I'm so pleased to see you," she said, "I was going to suggest you coming on a Tuesday, but I didn't want you to feel pressured. Find yourself a cup of tea, and I'll introduce you to some of the other girls. Sarah," she called, as she disappeared through a doorway at the other side of the hall.

"Tea? Milk? Sugar?"

"Milk, no sugar, thank you," Em replied.

"You new here? I think I saw you in the market," said the young woman pouring the tea. "I'm Jennifer. You are?"

"Emily," she replied, "my friends call me Em."

"You'll enjoy it here," said Jennifer, "they're a nice friendly bunch."

"I'm sorry I had to dash off just then," Hilda said as she reappeared, "but I needed to see someone about tomorrow's W.I. meeting. I see you've met Jenny. Tea please, Jenny."

The talk and demonstration were on 'Etiquette' by Thomas Whatmore, the former butler of Speke Hall in Liverpool. Em found the talk, which narrated the development of British etiquette over the ages, very interesting. It finished with a challenge to spot the mistakes on a table layout at the front of the hall. She was the only person to recognise that the fish knives and forks were missing from the layout, something she had learnt early on in her time at Moore Hall.

When she arrived home Em found Andy waiting for her. "If we go now," he said, "Mr Braithwaite will still be in his office; he's agreed to see you about the Silver Service vacancy."

Mr Braithwaite was a distinguished looking man in his middle to late fifties. After a short discussion, he took Em into the dining room and asked her to set a table for six. "Excuse me, sir, I need to see the menu," Em said.

"A standard setting for six courses," Mr Braithwaite replied.

After a few minutes Em once more turned to Mr Braithwaite. "Excuse me, sir, shouldn't there be finger bowls?"

"Where did you set for Silver Service?" he asked.

"At Moore Hall," Em answered, "for Lady Marbury."

Em walked home while Andy stayed on at the hotel to finish his shift. She hadn't wanted to name drop but when the question was asked it was impossible not to answer. Ah well, Em thought, it was worth a try, even if I don't get the job. But she still felt discouraged.

Em always liked to drive disappointments out of her system by working hard, so after a quick snack she started giving her flat a thorough clean, and she was so busy when Andy came home she didn't hear him come in.

"What on earth are you doing?" he asked, as her took hold of her.

"Oh dear," she exclaimed, "is that the time? Sit down," she said, "I'll make you a cuppa tea."

"No," he replied. "You sit down, while I tell you what the boss said."

"Must you?" Em asked. "I'm not in the mood for criticism."

"Shush…" he said, "the boss was so impressed he phoned your Lady Whatshername – Marbury – so…" he paused for a moment, "the job's yours if you want it."

Em threw her arms around his neck. "Oh, darling," she cried, "and I thought I'd muffed it! Now you sit down, and I'll open a bottle to celebrate."

"And by the way," he said, reaching into his pocket, "here's the letter offering you the job. You'll need to sign it to say you'll take it."

Em took to waitressing as if she had been born to it. At first she was a little uncertain about the short skirt which she thought showed too much leg, but after a couple of weeks she accepted the French waitress style as being the usual outfit for the job, and learnt to ignore the looks and comments from some of the men, and occasionally their companions.

The months leading up to Christmas were a busy period, and although the wages and tips were not exceptional, Em thought that with care, after she'd had the baby, she and Andy would be able to have her boys home here in Chester during the summer, in time to start secondary school in September. That would certainly be wonderful for her, but what would Andy think, would he want to take on two eleven year old boys? Did he love her enough for that?

Chapter Thirteen

Christmas 1944 and the start of 1945 had been a busy period for the staff of Ye Olde King's Head in Chester. In spite of the war, rationing and shortages, people still took advantage of any plausible reason and opportunity for special celebrations, and the Silver Service catering was busy, even to a less extravagant standard. Mr Braithwaite had been quick to take advantage of Em's capability and very often left her to organise the functions.

As the year progressed, although Em enjoyed the work, she was beginning to find it tiring, and so gave it up half way through March, one or two weeks later than she had intended. Upon her insistence, Andy had moved the chaise longue so that Em could sit or lie in the sunshine during her afternoon rest; she would often read her penny dreadfuls, or watch life from her vantage point as it went by. If she stood by the window watching people on the other side of the road, sometimes someone would look up at the window and she would give them a friendly wave; quite often the person would wave back. After a short while a 'distance' friendship developed between her and families with small children, and they would be watching out for each other.

As her child developed and became more active, Em would enjoy lying in the sunshine, feeling the movement and kicks with her hand. Often she would doze, to be woken when Andy came home after work.

On one such day in May, Em had drifted into a restful sleep when Andy dashed in. "Em, Em," he shouted, "have you heard the news?" Then realizing he had abruptly woken Em from sleep, he toned down his voice. "They've capitulated, they've surrendered, the Germans have surrendered, we've won the war."

Somewhere in the distance a church bell started to ring, then another and another. Em marvelled. She had heard that church bells had been taken down and melted to make weapons; obviously some had been left. Equally amazing was how quickly flags and bunting appeared. She was fascinated as she watched from her vantage point by the window. Andy had gone back to the hotel, it was going to be a busy night as revellers drank to the health of just anyone they could think of as an excuse for a drink, which kept staff in hostelries up and down the country busy long into the night.

The next day, 8th May, was declared as the official Victory in Europe Day, VE Day as it became known. Em suddenly realised that 7th May had been the twins' eleventh birthday; how had she forgotten that?

As Em woke she realised that whatever time Andy had arrived home he had not shared her bed. For a moment she panicked. Had he deserted her like George had done? The sound of the key in the door calmed her fears. "Sorry, dear," he said, "we finished so late it didn't seem worth coming home, anyway I would probably have disturbed you, so I slept in a chair in the hotel lounge." Those clothes don't look slept in, thought Em, then instantly dismissed the idea from her mind. Andy kissed her. "I'll make a brew. What d'you fancy for breakfast?" he asked.

'They must have busy baking all morning' Em thought as she watched the preparations for the street party from her vantage point. Tables started to appear, dining tables, trestle tables, and even wrought iron tables from someone's conservatory, covered with tablecloths and linen bedsheets, plates and cups of all colours, in a line along the far side of the road.

A knock on the door drew Em away from her window; two ladies were standing in there, one in Red Cross Uniform. "We've come to take you down," one of them said, "we're not leaving you out of the celebrations."

"But…" Em started to say.

"When's the baby due? That's okay, we'll look after you and see that you're all right." As they reached the street Em could see two men struggling to bring a piano out of a doorway, chairs and benches were now around the tables, even an armchair had been brought out for Em to use.

There were cheese sandwiches, fish paste, meat paste, spam and ham, corned beef and jam, even egg sandwiches. There were cakes of all sorts, cream sponges (no one asked where they got the cream from), jam sponges, chocolate cakes, the list of food and drinks seemed unending. Em marvelled at the resourcefulness and ingenuity of everyone. After the food came the singing and the knees-up. Too tiring and noisy for Em in her present condition, so the two ladies who had brought her down gently and carefully saw her back to the safety and comfort of her flat. Em looked down at the party, grateful that she had not been left out. She made herself comfortable on the chaise longue, and while listening to the happy sound she drifted off to sleep.

***

The cinema in Ramsey was packed full of all the people who had taken part in the victory parade. The place was buzzing; the war with Germany was over and patriotic songs were sung, followed by speeches, singers and comedians, even a raffle by seat number. Freddie was disappointed he didn't win, but when he saw it was a doll—well, what would a boy do with a doll? The show finished with the national anthem, followed by the Manx national anthem, (O Land of our Birth) then a parade back through Parliament Square.

After the euphoria of the celebrations, within a few days everything was back to normal. School during the week, the beach if the weather was fine, and so May turned into a radiant June.

***

Em's child was born in Chester Royal Infirmary at eleven a.m. on 2nd June 1945, weighing in at seven pounds and six ounces. As Em and Andy hadn't discussed names, they called their daughter Annabel, after the midwife who assisted at the birth. Em had been able to buy things she needed for Annabel, and still had quite a good amount saved for when the twins came home.

Annabel was beautiful, everyone said so, which made Andy very proud, and happy to take her out in her Silver Cross perambulator. "Oh she's so pretty. She's so like her father," some would say, while for others it would be "You're such a sweetie, so much like your mummy."

It's all so very different from when I had the boys, Em was thinking. It was hardly George's fault, he was in the army, far away in Larkhill, or even worse, in Singapore and I saw so little of him and he saw even less of the twins, but now what? Now he's in prison, he's hardly likely to be any help getting the boys back from the orphanage, they would not consider him to be a good example for his children. On the other hand Andy would make the perfect father, the way he's taken to Annabel, if only I didn't chicken out of talking to him about the twins, but somehow it never seems the right time. Em looked at the young child as she was feeding her, with that lovely feeling mothers have when the child is held so close, those gorgeous eyes looking up at them, making all the months of waiting and tiredness, and all that they went through to bring that bundle of love into the world, well worthwhile. I'd go through it all again, she thought, yes I'd probably go through it all over again.

Andy walked into the living room and seeing his darling daughter was being fed, quietly slipped out of the room and into the kitchen to make them both a pot of tea. He loved to see the bond between mother and child and tried to be home for what he called a heart-warming vision even though he was sometimes given the job of changing Annabel's nappy, not always the most pleasant of tasks, but he was always happy to oblige. Em would watch Andy with a feeling of admiration and love.

***

It was July. The atmosphere in Ramsey was buzzing, the King and Queen would be coming through the town on their way back to Douglas, after their visit to the Royal Air Force Station at Jurby in the north-west of the island. Bunting started to appear strung across Parliament Square and roads nearby, Union Jacks and other flags along with all sorts of decorations that had been on lamp posts and public buildings for VE day celebrations reappeared, with VE symbols hastily replaced by printed pictures of the King and Queen. Barriers were put up in the square to hold back the crowds, with school children in the front all dressed in their Sunday best, or the uniform of whatever organisation they were members of: Cubs and Scouts, Brownies and Guides, or school uniforms. Each group was in its allocated area, with mothers and preschool children at the front on the other side of the square. Dignitaries in all their regalia and anyone who was anyone, from the Deemster (Judge) to the Postmaster, were assembled waiting for the arrival of the Royal Party, while the town band kept them entertained by playing a mixture of popular forties tunes.

The time steadily ticked away, parents with young children and teachers began to worry about their charges getting fidgety. Somewhere an infant wailed and two or three more joined in. A solitary car drove through the square, and a half-hearted cheer started and died away. Excitement built up at the sight of a Police motorcyclist coming into view and stopping, blocking the road across from the Town Hall, and cheers broke out as the Royal Entourage came to a stop and the Royal Party alighted. The town band led the crowd in their rendering of the National Anthem, promptly followed by the Manx National Anthem, to which a few of the crowd also attempted to sing the words. A posy was presented to the Queen by the small daughter of one of the personages waiting, and while the dignitaries were being presented to the royal couple, the band played various patriotic tunes including *Rule Britannia, Land of Hope and Glory* and the Manx *Ellan Vannin*. There were renewed cheers and clapping of hands as King George VI and Queen Elizabeth walked along greeting the crowds. Walter and Freddie waved their Union Jacks and cheered as the Royal Couple came past and walked back along the other side of Parliament Square, then upon reaching the Town Hall turned around and waved to the crowd before disappearing through the massive doors. The ranks of children were directed out of the square, dismissed by their teachers and thus free to go home and enjoy the rest of the day off. The rest of the crowd also dispersed, apart from a few who waited patiently for the royal party to finish their banquet, reappear and enter their limousine; the entourage was then driven off at speed towards the Mountain Road on their way to Douglas.

***

It was not unusual for a boy to feign illness to avoid school especially on a day when there was a subject they did not like, but today was not a school day. In fact it was August and the boys were on their summer holiday, and it looked like being fine, warm and sunny, the sort of day for a beach picnic, definitely not a day to be stuck in bed, but this boy seemed more susceptible to childish ailments, and with over twenty boys in the Children's Home one had to be careful.

"Open your mouth and lift your tongue… that's right." Sister shook the thermometer and put the mildly antiseptic tasting thing under Freddie's tongue. "Now close your mouth …gently …don't bite." She watched the second hand on her watch, then sliding the thermometer out quickly glanced at the reading and disappeared downstairs. Freddie turned over and dozed off only to be woken up. He didn't want to get up, but where were they taking him? Oh yes, the isolation room. He felt tired, his face felt puffy and sore, he just wanted them to leave him alone and to go to sleep.

"Say ah. Has he been sick? There's no doubt it's mumps. Yes, Sister," the doctor said. "Keep a close eye on the other boys. Open the window and give him plenty of fresh air. I'll call back in a couple of days to see how he is."

"Thank you, Doctor."

"Oh, Sister," he was saying as he left the room, "it would probably be wisest if only one member of staff attends to the boy, to reduce risk of spreading the infection."

"Wakey wakey, we must keep your strength up." Freddie sat up. His throat felt sore, even the well soaked bread and milk was difficult enough to swallow, but what's that? Red jelly? Mm, that almost makes it worth being unwell.

Freddie lay back in bed. Sister had brought him up some comics and a couple of Biggles books, but even reading those could get tiring after a while. He could hear the gate just below his window slam, not once or twice but several times as the other boys were going out. In the smatterings of chatter he could hear something about the park, then all was quiet. The room had been warmed by the morning sun and he dozed a little until strains of music wafted in on the breeze. He climbed out of bed and stuck his head out the window. The sound was clearer: he thought he could hear a lady singing. Then he remembered, Deanna Durbin was in the Mooragh Park, singing the title song of her film *Can't Help Singing*, and here he was, stuck in isolation. Of all the rotten luck, he had been looking forward to it so much! The boys had seen the film itself; the chance to meet a real live film star was a once-in-a-childhood experience, and Freddie had missed it.

***

Em had received a letter from the Children's Home with the news that whilst Walter had passed the eleven plus exam, Freddie had not, and they would be moved to Nottingham, as the home only catered for boys up to eleven-years-old.

August was the month when the twins crossed the Irish Sea on the Isle of Man ferry, *King Orry*, from Douglas to Liverpool, where they were met and taken by train from Lime Street Station to Nottingham Central; a day that went into the annals of history, not because of the boys being transferred to Nottingham, but because Victory had been declared in the war with Japan; it was August the eighth, VJ Day, and the country went mad once more with celebrations.

The happy times that Andy and Em were having together with Annabel, coupled with the Victory celebrations, meant that before Em realised, August had passed and September was upon them and she still hadn't said anything to Andy about the boys.

***

Nobody said it was going to be easy. While George was doing time in Walton Prison for bigamy, he had plenty of time to think over his options. Should he go back to Em and the boys? It was going to be difficult to forge a relationship with Em after a break of eight or more years and especially as she would now know about his other wives. She probably wouldn't welcome him back. Anyway his intention before his arrest had been to use it as a pleasant relief away from Gillian's parents. As for the boys, he just didn't know them, and would they take to him?

Alice, she was of a different class, and he hadn't felt comfortable as a toff, living off her money, always at her beck and call. Not that she would be likely to welcome him back either.

Now Gillian, she was the sort of woman for him, and Malcolm? He adored the lad and he felt really comfortable with those two. He wasn't too sure about Gillian's parents, her mother seemed to want to take over, and poor Mr Woodley, well, he was gutless. George enjoyed living at the pub, but run it? No thank you; a seven-day twenty-four-hour job working for the brewery, no way.

To sum it up, George decided to keep on being Victor Bradburn and go back to Gillian and Malcolm.

Once news got around about George's/Victor's imprisonment, Mr Bradshore at Helmshore Mill had taken the opportunity to claim the ownership of the transport company, but without Victor's drive and management it soon went bust. The one consolation for Victor was that he still owned his own lorry; he had paid for it, and it was registered in his name.

By October 1945, Victor had been out of prison three months and he was back at the Red Lion. The downside was that Mr Woodley was an old man by the time he was fifty, a bad back and testing too many barrels meant he was no longer fit enough for the heavy cellar work, and needed a younger, healthier man to help him. Mrs Woodley's attitude towards Victor, in spite of his reassurance that he was now a reformed man, and had chosen to come back to Gillian, hadn't changed and was threatening to break up their relationship.

Victor suggested to Gillian that he should move to somewhere in the Midlands, perhaps to Nottingham, get a house or flat for the four of them, and then come back and collect his family. While he was looking for somewhere, he would be doing deliveries, and be back for the weekends, just like he had been doing, then they would move as a family. Gillian was reluctant to leave her parents and her friends, but when Victor explained that Mrs Woodley's attitude to him, and his dislike of working in the dark and dingy cellar, were getting him down, and how much the situation was threatening their relationship, she agreed provided they kept in touch with her family.

Monday morning and Victor was happy back in the cab of his lorry, a world where he was in control. He was king of the road with all the freedom of the open countryside as he headed east, first to Derby then turning north to Nottingham, the home of legendary Robin Hood. Upon arrival in the city he drove along Castle Boulevard and stopped outside Ye Olde Trip to Jerusalem for refreshments, and to make enquiries about board and lodgings in town. The Victoria Station Hotel was suggested to him as suitable place to stay while looking for somewhere more permanent.

Victor parked his lorry on open ground in Huntingdon Street, walked the short distance to the hotel and booked in, asking for a room overlooking the road; whilst he wasn't too keen on the view, he considered it better than all the smoke that rooms facing the station were likely to receive, as well as the noise of the huge railway engines.

His was a pleasant enough room on the second floor, not as spacious as the ones on the first floor but those were almost twice the price. Having unpacked, Victor went down to the station café for a quick cup of tea and a cheese roll. "Sorry, sir," said the lady serving at the counter, "no cheese; I can do corned beef or spam," looking at him, anticipating a quick answer, and moving her weight to the other leg. "Or perhaps tomato?" She glanced at the display case on the counter. "Perhaps I can serve this young lady while you decide. Yes, love?" she said, turning to the ATS girl next in the queue, "Tomato roll and tea? Milk? Sugar? Thank you, dear," as she took the money and gave her the change. "I'm sorry, sir, the ATS girls had the last tomato rolls."

Chapter Fourteen

Victor sat down at a table and took a bite of the corned beef roll. Where he sat gave him a good view across the width of the café and he was able to watch the group of four ATS girls. Three privates and a corporal, all good lookers, probably ranging around early twenties, maybe a bit young but he was only… hmm… thirty-four but so what, he didn't look it. From their accents they were from different parts, the one he was interested in, maybe from London, but definitely somewhere down south.

Sitting where he was, he could hear them reasonably well. They had come into Nottingham on forty-eight hour passes and had booked rooms in the same hotel as Victor. "Perhaps you ladies would like to join me for a drink in the bar next door," he said.

Four heads turned to see who was speaking. "All four?" asked the corporal in amusement. "You mean…?"

"Sure, why not?" he replied, "by the way, I'm Victor."

"You think you can manage all four of us?" she asked.

"I'm only inviting you for a drink."

"What do you say girls? Okay you're on. What time? Eight? Oh yes, I'm Sharon, this is Charlotte, Shirley and Liz. We'll see you later then." With that they got up and left the café.

Victor had been in the bar for half an hour when he heard a nervous voice behind him. "Hello."

He spun round on the stool, expecting to see the four standing there, not just one. "Where are the others?" he asked.

"We forgot," she said, "we had already got tickets for the Theatre Royal, the Ivor Novello play, *Bitter Sweet*.

"The others?"

"They've gone."

Holding her by the shoulders, he said, "Go and get your coat, be down here in five minutes."

Ten minutes later Victor and Liz were in a taxi heading the short distance to the theatre. The FULL HOUSE board stood outside the door. They made their way past the board, but the doorman barred their way. "Sorry sir, the theatre is full."

"I bet you there's at least one empty box. We'll take it."

Liz looked at him in amazement. "Really?"

"Yes," he replied as they were led from the ticket office to a box level with the stage.

There was no doubt that Noel Coward was able to write intriguing yet humorous plays, making it an absolute pleasure watching him on the stage. At the interval a waiter brought a selection of drinks to their seats, "With the compliments of the management," saving them from the crush at the bar and enabling them to enjoy their refreshments at leisure.

The final curtain, and a taxi back to the hotel meant Victor and Liz were seated in the bar waiting for the others to return. "You seem very quiet, Liz," he said, as she sat quietly sipping her drink. "Penny for them."

Liz looking up, avoided his eyes and answered, "Taxi, theatre and all you've spent," blushing, "you'll be expecting—"

"No, Liz," he said interrupting, "I've enjoyed your company. That was enough."

"Really?" she asked, smiling.

"Yes, dear, really." Liz leaned over and kissed him.

The bar door opened and three ladies entered. "Over here," Liz called out. Victor asked what drinks they would have, and went to the bar.

All three started to talk at once. "Oh, it was marvellous," they said, "You should have come, you would have loved it. We were in the circle so we couldn't see very well what was happening, but at the end of the play the leading lady gave a rose out of her bouquet to the leading man to give a couple in the box near the stage. Oh, so romantic."

Liz blushed. Charlotte looked at her. "You? No surely..." then seeing the rose on the table, "but..."

"The commissionaire jumped to the wrong conclusion, but yes, it was Victor and me in the box."

It was almost half past ten as all five climbed the stairs to the second floor. "I thought you ladies would be on the first floor," Victor jibed.

"What, on our pay?" asked Sharon. "You're on the top floor as well?"

"Room 204, next to the bathroom," he replied, "but I'll be a gentleman and let you ladies go first. Sweet dreams, ladies." He disappeared into his room. Waiting what he thought was a reasonable amount of time, Victor slipped into a dressing gown and went out into the corridor. Sharon was just coming out of the bathroom. Looking him up and down, she said, "It's all yours," and went into her room.

Victor was tired, and was soon fast asleep. It was *Bitter Sweet* re-enacted, only unlike in the play he was wrestling the ghost-like figure, at least it seemed like wrestling, and then he was awake or was he dreaming? He was no longer alone. "Who is it?" he started to ask.

"Shhh," a voice whispered, a finger being held to his lips. He must be dreaming, so he relaxed back into the dream. Something woke him, his bedroom door was open, silhouetted against the corridor light, a shadowy figure was leaving the room; it looked like Corporal Sharon.

Women in uniform have an attractiveness, the four ATS girls certainly had that certain je ne sais quoi, but Victor had to admit he much preferred the visions of beauty they had portrayed the previous evening. "Good morning, ladies. You're leaving us so soon?" he asked, as if he represented all men.

"Yes," they replied in chorus. "It will take quite a while getting back to camp, and I'm due on duty this evening," said Sharon as they were walking into the restaurant for breakfast.

"I'd offer you a lift," Victor said, "but I've got an open back lorry. It should stay dry until late afternoon."

Sharon looked at the other three for agreement. "That'll do fine as long as it's not dirty."

"Where are you stationed, Chilwell?"

"Yes," answered Shirley, "do you know it?"

"Yes, I've delivered blankets there," Victor replied.

Sharon, as the corporal, climbed into the passenger seat in the cab, insisting that to avoid favouritism the others would all travel in the back. Victor spread the cleanest of his tarpaulins out for the girls to put their bags on, and they sat on their bags, protected from the wind by the driving cab.

"You slept well?" Victor asked Sharon as they drove along, seeing the twinkle in her eyes as she answered.

"Yes, thank you, and you?"

Hm yes, I bet you did, he thought. "Very well, thank you," he replied.

They had been driving for about fifteen minutes when Sharon asked Victor to stop at the side of the road just a short distance from the barracks, she didn't want her colleagues to see them climbing out of a lorry. Victor helped the three girls down from the back and quickly but quietly asked Liz for a date. "Meet here, six thirty on Friday," she whispered and dashed off to join her friends. Victor stood and watched and as they reached the gate, Liz turned, waved, threw a kiss and disappeared inside.

Friday? Friday? he thought, 'I was going to see Gillian on Friday! Victor climbed into the cab, started the motor and drove back to the hotel. By the time he had parked his vehicle in Huntingdon Street he had changed his plans.

***

It was still dark when the train left Victoria Station and Nottingham soon became a memory, a happy memory. He closed his eyes to avoid the soul-searching stare of the old lady in Salvation Army uniform seated on the opposite side of the compartment, and to visualise more clearly the happenings of the last few days. With the gentle swaying of the train, and the regular chunk-t-chunk of the wheels on the track, Victor was very soon asleep, reliving those happy memories, once again seeing the gentle smile in Liz's eyes.

"Tickets, please, your ticket, please, Sleeping Beauty!" Victor woke with a start. "Sorry to wake you, sir," the guard said as Victor gave him his ticket. "Er Warrington? You'll need to change in Manchester." The guard clipped his ticket. "We should be there in about ninety minutes, sweet dreams," he said as he slid the door closed. There were now no other passengers in the compartment, the Salvation Army lady must have got off in Derby or gone to another compartment. Victor looked out of the window at the rain and shrugged, then opened a magazine he had bought before boarding the train.

Manchester Piccadilly Station was busy. The platform teemed with soldiers travelling, north, east, south or west, it was impossible to tell where, but Victor almost had to fight his way off the train, only to hear, "The train now standing at platform three," the train he had just got off, "will be stopping at Warrington Central, Widnes and ..." he didn't wait to hear the rest, he joined the fight, this time, to get *on* the train he had just left, and stood in the corridor the rest of the way to Warrington.

Buses from Warrington to Thornton Heath were few and far between. There was only a light breeze, and when the sun condescended to show its face it was quite warm, so Victor decided to walk the couple of miles to the Red Lion. As he walked into the public bar, Mavis was busy vigorously rubbing the sticky residue from a table. His eyes were instantly drawn, along with others' eyes, to the low-cut neckline of her blouse.

"Hello, love," she said as she stood up, "I didn't think you'd be back before the weekend. I think they're just about to serve lunch. If you're quick." She turned her head towards the door to the living quarters.

"Make mine a double please," he said as he sank into his favourite seat by the inglenook. "I'll go through later."

Gillian threw her arms around him and kissed him. "That was quick." There was a look of expectancy in her eyes.

Victor ignored Mrs Woodley's mumbling about a 'bad penny'. "No, sorry, dear," he said, "there's a problem with the lorry, so I need the car.

I've got a couple of appointments to keep, drumming up business. I'll er, oh, blow it, they'll have to wait until tomorrow." Putting his arms around his wife, he kissed her. "Now tell me what you and Malcolm have been up to."

Next day Victor was getting the Hornet ready for his journey to Nottingham when he heard the sound of someone in the washroom pouring water into the copper, and the now familiar voice of Mavis gently singing. Quietly easing the door from the garage open, he watched as she slipped out of her dress and climbed over the side into the heated water and started to wash. As she stood in the water only her lower part was hidden, and as she combed the water out of her hair she turned, until she was facing Victor's direction. Mavis was smiling; why? Had she heard him? Had she seen him? Victor crouched down and went back into the garage, hoping that she hadn't.

As he went indoors, Mrs Woodley was busy in the kitchen rinsing the hand washing, which she called smalls, and he referred to as larges, but not within earshot. "Where's Gillian?" he asked. Mrs Woodley moved her head twice as if pointing in the direction of the living room. "Ta, Ma," he said, trying unsuccessfully to dodge the flick of cold water as he headed through to find Gillian.

"I'm just off to Helmshore Mill to see Mr Bradshore, hopefully back in time for lunch and the afternoon and night here at home, okay?" Victor asked.

"Yes, but what about the weekend?"

"If the lorry is ready," he answered, "I'll need to be making up the time I'm losing now."

The Hornet's exhaust seemed to voice the car's delight as it took once more to the road. Driving to Rossendale in the lorry was one thing but there was no comparison to making the same journey in the Hornet.

"You're back, which is it?" Mr Bradshore asked, "Victor or...?"

"Victor," he replied. "What's this I hear about you taking over everything?"

"It was my money," Mr Bradshore answered, "and the business wasn't earning while you were... er... away, so I thought I'd run it until you got back, and now you're back."

"And have you take it away again when it suits you? No, I'm working on my own now, thank you. But I am prepared to help to shift your backlog, at a price. I'll be back with *my* lorry on Monday, my terms are *cash*." Victor walked out of the office. "See you Monday," he said to the dispatch clerk, went to his car and drove home.

The table was set for five, Mr Woodley, Mrs Woodley, Malcolm, Gillian and Victor. Gillian was feeding Molly in the lounge so Mrs Woodley put her dinner in the oven to keep warm. Mr Woodley wanted a larger helping than his wife had served. "You'll eat what you're given," snapped his wife, and handed a similar serving to Victor. He watched as she also served herself a small helping then proceeded to feed Malcolm from the same plate. Ah well, thought Victor, there'll be fewer dishes to wash. Mrs Woodley might be frugal with the servings but at least she made sure they never went short. After a pleasant afternoon, and when the children were settled, Gillian cuddled up to Victor in the lounge listening to the music on the wireless. "I want to get an early start in the morning," he said, "so it's cocoa and bed in a short time."

Gillian's eyes lit up. "Ooh, yes please," she said.

Chapter Fifteen

Em looked at the display of children's books in the shop window: *The Adventures of Sherlock Holmes*, a selection of Biggles books, two or three Romany nature books, *Swallows and Amazons* by Arthur Ransome, and many more. It was hard to decide what to give two eleven-year-old boys for Christmas, especially when they lived halfway across the other side of England. Entering the shop, she had made up her mind. "A copy of *Swallows and Amazons* please, and er, *Out with Romany by Meadow and Stream*, ooh and wrapping paper. This one please. Sorry I've only got a ten shilling note, I don't like splitting those, the change disappears before you know it. Thank you."

Em sat in front of the fire carefully wrapping the books and writing cards to the boys. Which one for Walter...? Or was it... What does it matter, they're bound to swap, you know what boys are like... But I wish... Stop it, girl you'll set yourself off again, and then what will you tell Andy. Em wrapped the two books separately with their cards, being sure to label them well, then wrapped them as one parcel ready to send addressed to the governor at the Children's Home in Nottingham.

"What are you doing?" Andy asked as he arrived home from work.

"I'm wrapping a Christmas present to a child in a home," she answered.

He bent down and kissed her. "Your kindness is only surpassed by your personal beauty," he said, and kissed her once more.

***

'Dear Mother'. Freddie sat with pen in hand. After lunch on Sundays, even on 23rd December, the boys in the Children's Home had to write letters to their parents. Freddie looked across at Walter, who seemed to be busy writing, then down at the sheet of paper in front of him. 'Dear Mother', he wrote, 'I hope you are keeping well, I am although I have chilblains again this year on the same fingers and toes as I had last year. Sister says it's because I don't keep warm enough but we have to have the windows in the bedroom open a bit because there are six of us in the same room. We went to a Christmas party at the church in Hucknall yesterday and watched Laurel and Hardy and *Snow White* films, then we had some sandwiches with fish paste or meat paste, and trifle and ice cream, then jam tarts and fairy cakes and fruit cake, then Father Christmas came in and we sang carols then he gave us presents. I had a box of crayons and a mouth organ, but Sister won't let me play the mouth organ indoors and it is very cold outside. We will be going to Carlton Methodist Church next Saturday for another party, I hope they don't have fish paste sandwiches because I don't like them. I hope you have a nice Christmas. Love from Freddie'.

Freddie gave his letter, the pen and the writing pad to Sister Gladys and looked across at his brother who was still writing. He took the *Adventure Stories for Boys* book he had received on his eleventh birthday from his locker, sat down in the alcove, and started to read his favourite Biggles story for the umpteenth time.

***

With a healthy roar the Hornet once more expressed its love for the open road as it headed towards Nottingham with Victor at the wheel. By taking the road to Knutsford and the A537 to Macclesfield and Buxton, Victor was able to enjoy the beautiful autumn countryside as he drove through the Peak District and the towns of Baslow and Chesterfield, arriving at Nottingham, his final destination, before the daylight turned to dusk.

That evening, Victor scanned the local papers hoping to find something that would give Liz an evening that she would enjoy, but there didn't seem to be much choice. The cinema was showing The Woman in Green as the feature film, with Sherlock Holmes played by Basil Rathbone, and *Ivan the Terrible, Part 1*, as the supporting film.

Alternatively there was the play, *Devil's Disciple* at the YMCA. He put the paper back on the rack, finished his drink and went up to his room.

Victor must have been more tired than he realised. It was already eight o'clock when he woke up next morning. If he was going to be making enquiries when the house agents opened at nine, he would need to hurry, but then… why hurry? He had all day before he was due to meet Liz.

Rent or buy? Victor reasoned that if he rented he might finish up paying more over twenty years than if he bought outright, but at least he wouldn't have to dig too deep into his savings. He could do a lot with four hundred pounds, whereas if he bought, his savings would be depleted, and he might have difficulty selling if he wanted to move.

A few discreet enquiries from members of the hotel staff sent Victor on his way to estate agents in Carlton, a pleasant residential area bordering the northeast of the city, with a frequent bus and train service. The agents in Burton Road were able to direct him to addresses where he might find temporary accommodation while he searched for a three bedroom family house to rent close to the shops, and near the River Trent, a good place for walks in fine weather.

The day had started out rather dull with only the occasional break in the clouds, until shortly after eleven when the sun broke through, tempting Victor to walk along the river embankment. Looking across the river he could see the Trent Bridge Cricket Grounds, soon to welcome cricketers from far and wide, and a short distance further away, the Nottingham City Football Club premises, then the Trent Bridge itself. From there he walked along Arkwright Street towards the city centre with its magnificent Town Hall building.

Victor made his way to Ye Olde Trip to Jerusalem, where he had a locally brewed ale and a fruit bun, his usual sort of midday meal when working. Whilst the atmosphere was pleasant, the bar was compact, and even at this time of day it was both crowded and noisy. No, he thought, not where I would take a lady on a date.

Victor sat in his car, a short distance away from the gate. Determined not to be late he had arrived a few minutes after quarter past six and sat carefully watching as each person came out from the barracks, many of them on bicycles. He glanced at his watch; six twenty-five, it won't be long now. Ah! There she is, Victor flashed his headlights and slowly moved forward, stopped, then got out of the car and walked up to her. "Hello, Liz." Liz turned and smiled. "Your carriage awaits, ma'm'selle," he said, opening the passenger door. Liz eased herself into the seat and Victor closed the door. It was too dark and too late to visit places like the Arboretum, so Victor drove to the Victoria Station Hotel, where he had booked a table for two in the restaurant, but first they had drinks in the lounge bar, chatted and got to know each other better.

"Tonight," said Victor, "chef's speciality is roast chicken and I have ordered it especially for us."

As he eased her chair forward to the table, the waiter asked, "Would you like to order drinks, sir?"

Victor looked at Liz, then replied, "White wine, please." The waiter returned, and poured a small amount into the glass for Victor to taste; he nodded and the waiter poured the wine and stood the bottle on the table. From then on everything went as well as Victor had hoped, and after they had finished their coffee Victor suggested it was time he took her back to the barracks.

"Another time dear, and maybe daytime so we could visit some of the sites?"

"I'd love that," she answered.

"When will you next be free?" he asked.

"I don't know yet," she answered, then writing a number on the page of a notebook, which she tore off and gave him. "Ring me on this number on Thursday," she said, kissed him and walked through the gate. Victor watched her go, then got back into the Hornet.

It was seven o'clock on Saturday morning and Victor was already on the A1, many miles south of Derby. There was very little traffic on the road at that time of day and he had been able to make good progress as he headed towards London with the intention of turning off well before Barnet and driving through Oxford to arrive in Witney sometime in the early afternoon.

Victor arrived at the Witney Blanket Factory a little later than he had hoped; there had been masses of cyclists in Oxford town centre and it had been necessary to find a way past the congestion, costing him valuable minutes and resulting in his arrival at the factory just thirty minutes before work was due to finish until Monday. The store men unloaded the bales of yarn and loaded an urgently wanted consignment of blankets for the Chilwell Barracks. Driving late into the evening, Victor stopped outside the Wheatsheaf Inn at Maid Moreton where he checked in for the night, and was able to order an evening meal shortly before the kitchen closed.

Sunday morning saw Victor breakfasted and on the road by seven; he was in Leicester before eleven and arrived at Chilwell Barracks just after twelve. After waiting half an hour for the quartermaster sergeant to be located, Victor's lorry was unloaded and he drove out of the gate, heading west up and over the hills of Derbyshire as he made his way towards Thornton Heath.

Gillian was standing by the bedroom door watching the two children as they lay sleeping. Malcolm was already asleep when she picked Molly up from her cot to feed and change her ready for the night. She had tended to sleep through the night from a very early age. At first Gillian had been worried, but both the midwife and health visitor, and also her mother, had told her not worry, rather be grateful that she was able to have an undisturbed night herself.

In spite of that, Gillian was unhappy. Her father's continual complaining about Victor not showing an interest in taking over the running of the Red Lion, and having to pay someone to do the heavy cellar work, was irritating, and the comments her mother kept making about Victor's 'liking for wedding cake', as she put it, were getting her down.

Gillian sat in her favourite chair by the fire, picked up her knitting and looked at the pattern; now that three-ply yarn was available it made knitting woollies much quicker, and larger when using a pattern for two-ply. Knit four, slip two stitches onto a cable needle, pass slip stitches... front or back? Oh well, back, knit two, slip stitches off cable needle...

no that doesn't look right; take it back, undo those two stitches, then cable needles round the front, that's better knit two…

"Where's your mother?" asked Victor as he came through the door, bent over and kissed his wife.

"Hello, dear," Gillian said. "I think she said something about almshouses, she's probably thinking of applying for one now that father is having to pay a cellar man. Let me get you something to eat," she offered as she got up from her chair.

"While you're doing that," he replied, "I'll get us something from the bar."

Victor walked into the bar just in time to see Mavis bending down to pick up some broken glass. "Let me do that," he volunteered.

"No… it's all right, dear, I've almost finished," she said, sweeping the last piece onto the dustpan and tipping it into a pail. "I thought you weren't expected this weekend." She said it almost as a question.

Victor carried the glasses back into the lounge and sat in the chair opposite his wife. On the small table beside him was a plate of sandwiches. He picked up the local paper, "Hm… not much in it," he murmured. Finishing the sandwiches Gillian had prepared for him, he glanced at the mantle clock, then downing his drink said, "I've a pick-up at Helmshore in the morning, so I'm going up to bed. Come on, love."

Chapter Sixteen

Victor arrived at Helmshore Mill at seven, while it was still dark. Leaving Thornton Heath early meant very few vehicles on the road and consequently no traffic hold-ups in Warrington or anywhere else on the way north. It was obvious from the amount of yarn stacked under cover outside in the yard that the mill had not been able to get sufficient transport to move it. After the way he had been treated when incarcerated, Victor was determined to make Mr Bradshore pay dearly. He had the store men load his lorry with a double load and insisted that unless Mr Bradshore was prepared to pay the price that he wanted, he would have the lorry unloaded and leave with it empty. It was only when he gave the order to unload the bales from his lorry that Mr Bradshore agreed to meet him half way. He hadn't got quite the price he'd asked for, but he had forced Mr Bradshore to pay a higher rate per bale than he had previously paid.

The lengthy negotiations had delayed his departure, which meant breaking his journey to Witney with an overnight stop half way. There was no sense in gaining on the deal but losing by paying for accommodation when he could stop overnight at home in Thornton Heath.

"What brought you back so soon?" asked Mrs Woodley, as he walked in the back door.

"Your magnetic personality," Victor replied. "Tell me, Mother dear," he continued, "how did you get on with the almshouse people?"

"All in good time," she replied, "all in good time".

"Hello," said Gillian, as Victor entered the lounge, "I thought it was you. What brings you home so soon, dear? Perhaps you could look after Malcolm while I am seeing to Molly."

"There was a hold up at the mill which upset my schedule. Come on, little 'un," he said, squatting down to pick up his son, "let's go and feed the ducks."

***

"Who saw this load of blankets in?" asked Sharon.

"It must have been the QM, Sergeant Howes," replied Shirley. "We were all in the Mess. Why?"

"Have you seen who the driver was? On the consignment note it says V. Bradburn, there surely can't be more than one of 'em delivering blankets."

"Don't tell Liz," said Shirley, "she'll be heartbroken to have missed him." They both laughed.

"Never mind," chuckled Sharon. "I don't doubt he'll be around again someday soon."

"Where is Liz?"

"Oh, I sent her to the orderly office with a load of dockets that need countersigning by Captain Mason," said Sharon.

***

Em watched as the excited children from the orphanage in Frodsham filed out of the charabanc and into the Wesleyan Chapel hall. They made her think of what her two boys had written in the letters she had received that morning, obviously sent before her parcel was given to them on Christmas Day. She had no idea what the organisers had planned for the Frodsham children, but with the amount of food that members of the Young Wives and others had brought, there was plenty for them all to enjoy.

Em headed back to the flat with Annabel, warmly wrapped against the cold wind, sleeping inside the pram. It would soon be time for her feed, and Em would prefer the privacy of her flat to a cold side room at the chapel.

***

Victor was sitting in his usual place by the inglenook when Mr Woodley came into the bar. "Over here," Victor called. Mr Woodley turned, then seeing where Victor was, walked over and sat in a chair beside him. "How are you feeling, Dad?" asked Victor.

"Hmm, so-so," came the reply. "I'm glad you're here, away from the girls," and looking round in case one of their wives was within earshot, he murmured, "What's this about almshouses?"

"I'm not sure," answered Victor, "but as long as one of you is old enough..." he paused and went on, "It sounds ideal, self-contained cottage with small garden to sit out in when it's warm, modest rent and no maintenance charge. It seems a good idea to me, I hope I can get one when I'm your age."

"Go on, they put you up to try and persuade me."

"No, they haven't 'cos they know I'd refuse to do their dirty work. I'm telling you what I think."

"Thanks, son," Mr Woodley said as he got up and headed towards the living quarters.

"What did he want?" asked Mavis.

"I think he wanted an independent opinion," answered Victor.

"Silly old fool," said Mavis.

"No," corrected Victor, "just a tired old man who needed someone else's guidance."

Time is a peculiar commodity, it tends to be gone in a flash when one is busy, yet drags when one is kicking one's heels; that was how it was for Victor. It got him wondering whether he had made the wrong choice in staying at home with his family, not that he was with his family, they were in the lounge whilst he was sitting in the bar. He picked up the paper and put it down again, there was no more in it that interested him after the second or third time. He was bored, perhaps if he went for a walk... No, it was raining. He looked across at the bar, the towel was draped over the pumps meaning the bar was closed until the evening.

Victor got up, went out to his lorry and sat in the cab thumbing through his delivery documents; time was still dragging its heels.

Eager to get going, Victor was up early next morning and drove out onto the London Road while it was still dark, knowing there were likely to be one or more army convoys even during peacetime. He was lucky today, following the A5 as far down as Leamington Spa onto the A429, a quick and easy route he had used many times before on his trips up and down the country for deliveries to places west of the Pennines, or through Buckingham and Leicester for those to the east. By careful selection Victor made his deliveries and was back in Nottingham by Wednesday evening. He once more parked his lorry on the waste ground in Huntingdon Street, walked into the Victoria Station Hotel and checked in. The receptionist handed him an envelope addressed to him. Sitting in the bar he read the letter carefully, then finishing his drink drove to the barracks and waited. Promptly at six Liz appeared carrying a suitcase. Victor flashed his headlights and got out of the car to meet her, put the case in the back and as soon as they were both safely in the car drove back to the hotel.

Over a drink, Liz explained that she was on a forty-eight-hour pass, to be back in camp before it was in effect closed over the Christmas period. She and others who had been nominated, or like her had volunteered to remain on camp while the rest were on leave, would be able to take their leave at a later date. Her forty-eight-hour pass was a gift from Sharon for volunteering. Victor asked Liz to check in separately as he did not want her thinking that his intentions were dishonourable. "That's all right, dear," she said laughing, "my father told me what to do if they were, and anyway we could have a bolster down the middle of the bed." After a few minutes absence Liz returned. "My room," she informed him, "is at the other end of the landing."

Victor carried the case as they went up the stairs to the second floor, Liz's room held a single bed with just enough furniture for a one or two night stay, obviously a room meant just for sleeping. Victor's room had a large double bed and was furnished to a higher standard. Obviously it cost more to rent but was more suited to guests staying for a longer period.

They had booked a table in the restaurant, both choosing rabbit stew with a good helping of meat. The stew was superb, followed by fruit salad which mainly consisted of home-grown apples and pears in homemade syrup with a sprinkling of desiccated coconut, topped with a glacé cherry. After dinner Victor suggested taking drinks up to the room. With the exception of the bedside lamps, he turned the lights off, and tuned the wireless into a foreign station that was playing soft relaxing music. They sat quietly chatting until they found each other's company sufficient, no longer needing words, then falling asleep, fully dressed lying in each other's arms.

Victor stirred, what was that whispering noise, shhh it went. It was the wireless, the station had shut down and the music had stopped. It was almost half past one in the morning. Victor gently slid his arm from under Liz, being careful not to wake her. He turned the wireless off and the shhing stopped. The temperature in the room had started to drop, so he covered Liz with a blanket then wrapped the counterpane around himself, lay down and slept.

Victor woke to the sound of traffic in the street. He was alone; the blanket he had used to cover Liz was neatly folded on the other side of the bed. Victor struggled to extract himself from the counterpane as the bedroom door opened and Liz came in carrying a well-laden tray. "Good morning, darling," she said as she gently put the tray down on the bedside table and kissed him. "You really are a gentleman," then kissing him a second time, "Thank you."

"What for?" he asked, "I didn't do anything."

"Precisely," she answered.

It was a glorious day. It had started with a dull, cloudy sky, but by the time Liz and Victor had finished breakfast the sun had broken through and was warm for the time of year; even the cool breeze didn't spoil the day.

The receptionist lent them an old map, and following her directions they found the end of Robin Hood's Chase, a long avenue of trees that led from St Ann's Well Road, across Abbotsford Drive and Woodborough Road up to a large circle of horse-chestnut trees, then turned down to Mansfield Road junction with Huntingdon Street. "Amazing," said Liz as she looked round at the trees, "it must look gorgeous when they're in bloom."

"Yes," Victor agreed, "but it wasn't like this in Robin Hood's day."

As they walked along Mansfield Road towards the town centre, "Look," Liz said pointing to a fish and chip shop and looking up at Victor, "I fancy some fish and chips please. I think I saw a park on the map, there... in Bath Street, St Mary's." They crossed the road to the shop.

"Two plaice and chips please... No plaice? Oh... What do you have then?" Turning to Liz: "Hake or squid? Okay two hake and chips, please... Thank you... Salt and vinegar too, please."

Finding a seat in St Mary's Gardens, they tucked into their fish and chips, breaking off small pieces of chips to throw down to the pigeons that had appeared almost as soon as they sat down. To Liz hake had never tasted as nice as it did sitting here with Victor. And to Victor? It was lovely being here with Liz; fish and chips were much the same anywhere. He opened the map; if they were to make their way to the city centre, they would be just a short distance from Ye Olde Trip to Jerusalem where they could pop in for a drink before visiting the castle.

Unfortunately the castle was closed, the sign said 'for renovation', whatever that would be. Rather than looking disappointed, Liz seemed relieved. "Let's take a walk by the river," she said, with a hint of excitement in her voice. Following the map, they made their way over the Nottingham Canal and down to the Victoria Embankment, where arm-in-arm they strolled round the long U-bend, watching the ducks and swans on the river, and the sparrows, wagtails and other birds. They stopped for a while by the weir while Victor explained how it helped the flow of water, and added oxygen into the river, freshening the water and making it habitable for fish and other creatures, and how without the weirs the river would virtually die. Liz looked admiringly at Victor, not only was he gentlemanly and kind, he was knowledgeable... and handsome.

By the time they reached Trent Bridge the light was starting to fade and the temperature was dropping, so they quickly made their way back to their hotel and the warmth of the restaurant, where they enjoyed baked potatoes with baked beans, and a pot of tea, before going to the cinema where *The Bells of St Mary's* starring Bing Crosby and Ingrid Bergman was showing. Arm-in-arm they walked back from the cinema, Liz singing *Ding Dong* while Victor softly crooned the words to the song, laughing together as they ambled along. When they arrived at the hotel Victor purchased drinks, taking them upstairs while Liz retrieved her belongings and joined Victor in his room, eventually snuggling up together beneath the blankets.

Chapter Seventeen

The trouble with forty-eight-hour passes is they only last forty-eight hours and in the end one has to return to camp, no matter how much one may be enjoying oneself, and so it was for Liz and Victor.

Victor opened his eyes. Apart from the street lights casting a faint glow in the room, it was still dark. Liz was asleep and he could feel her body against his own, yet he had not taken nor was he going to take any advantage of her closeness or trust, he loved her too much. For the first time in his life he loved, without lust. Of course he wanted to make love with her, any man would, but she was lovely, delicate, she was special, she was... He lay marvelling at this feeling, so new to him, and drifted off to sleep.

He woke abruptly, Liz was shaking him. "What is it with you? Did you not want to?"

"Yes, dear... er... no dear, I love you so much I just couldn't take advantage," he replied.

"Oh darling," she said as she kissed him.

Breakfast seemed a solemn affair, porridge followed by toast and marmalade. "I'll run you back to the barracks after we've eaten," he said, "then I'll be making last minute deliveries up to the twenty-fourth, I promised my cousins I'd be with them for Christmas." Liz looked disappointed. "But I should be back sometime on the twenty sixth. Can I ring you on that number?" he asked, reciting the number. He ran Liz back to the barracks in the lorry and after they had kissed outside the gate drove off, down as far as Derby then headed toward Thornton Heath.

***

Sister sat all the boys on the floor. One group had sheets of coloured crepe paper which they cut into lengths one inch wide and glued end to end, making long strips to hang up as streamers around the room and across from the corners to the lights. Freddie and Walter were in the group that had been given sheets of dark blue paper and pieces of corrugated cardboard shaped like swallows, to cut as many as they could and hang them on the streamers using strips of sticky paper. It looked very nice, and as a treat there was jelly and cakes for tea.

On the landing of the first floor there was a large open square to the ground floor with beautiful big oak carvings, and the Christmas tree that was usually given to the Children's Home was often tall enough to reach right up into the square. Mr Bilby, the gardener, helped to get it through the front door and stand it in a huge tub in the hall. This year it was just too tall to fit under the ceiling of the hall, so they stood it in the centre of the square. It was decorated in the evening after all the boys were in bed, so they didn't see it fully dressed until the morning. It looked fantastic, especially when Mr Smith, the governor, turned the lights on.

When any parcels for the boys arrived they were put around the tub until after Christmas Day lunch, so it was wise to behave or you might have to wait till last to get your presents. The parcels were mixed up, one or more family presents and at least one from the home. Those who didn't get any family present always had extra from the home. There were often presents received from church groups, so there was always a big pile under the tree by Christmas.

Christmas Eve, and the house was full of excitement, there were so many parcels that some had to be stacked in a pile each side of the porch. After tea of sandwiches and homemade mince pies, the boys all sat around the floor and sang Christmas carols. Halfway through the evening Mr Smith recited a comic monologue about Mr and Mrs Ramsbottom and their son Albert going to the zoo. What made it funnier was he spoke in a strange accent and everybody laughed so much, it took a while until they were able to sing another carol before Sister Millicent sent the boys to bed.

**

Victor drove along the London Road and turned into the yard at the back of the Red Lion. He heard the noise above the sound of the engine as he was passing the front of the public house. As he walked into the bar he was confronted by a crowd shouting and cheering; in the centre of the room there were two big men arm-wrestling. "Quiet!" Victor yelled, pushing his way into the middle. "There are two young children upstairs," he said, moderating his voice, "so please tone it down. What's this about?" he asked.

"It's Audrey's birthday, and they both fancy her," someone answered; there was a ripple of laughter.

"Why doesn't she decide herself?"

"She doesn't know yet. It's best man wins," another voice said amid the laughter. "Oi, why don't you try?"

The volume of laughter increased. Someone else called out, "Go on, take on the winner!"

Another voice, "He wouldn't dare, his mother-in-law would kill 'im." The place erupted, and Victor retreated, having once more asked them to consider the children.

"Hullo, love," said Gillian, as Victor walked into the lounge and gave his wife a kiss, "what's going on in there?"

"Bill and Harry are arm-wrestling to decide who's going to take Audrey out for her birthday," he answered.

"Does she know?"

"Apparently not, nobody has thought of asking her."

"Poor kid," said Gillian.

"I've got an engine for Malcolm," said Victor, pushing a smart looking locomotive along the floor with it emitting, "Whooaoo," as it went along, "and a teddy bear for Molly."

"Oh darling, how wonderful, you're so thoughtful," Gillian replied. Mrs Woodley entered the room.

"See what I've bought for Molly," she said taking a teddy out from her bag. "Oh," she continued, rather deflated, "you've got…"

"It's all right, Mother," replied Gillian, "she can have twins."

Victor immediately thought of his twin boys, trying unsuccessfully to dismiss the thought from his mind. He returned to the bar to collect drinks for the family. "Who won?" he asked.

"Harry," replied Mavis, "but the funny side? Audrey came in on Gary's arm," she said laughing.

"Talk about laugh," Victor chuckled "I bought Molly a teddy for Christmas; guess what Mrs Woodley bought."

Mavis grinned, and carefully hid the teddy she had purchased in a bag under the counter. "Don't forget," she said, "you were going to run me home so that I can have Christmas with my parents."

"Oh, yes," he said, "I'll get Gillian to take over in here."

It only took thirty minutes in the lorry to reach Mavis's family's farm. "Have a nice Christmas—" he was saying. She grabbed his head with both hands, pulling him towards her and kissing him aggressively, squarely on the lips. His hands went forward to fend her off, but came in contact with the softness of her upper body and he snatched them back, and wrestled himself free. "Don't you want to?" she asked.

"I do... but I mustn't," he said, "it wouldn't be right, and certainly not here and now."

Kissing him gently, "Gillian is so lucky," she said as she opened the door and got down from the lorry. "Happy Christmas," she called out as she ran towards the house.

***

Em opened her cards. Her eyes filled with tears, Wiping away the droplets from her cheeks with her handkerchief she opened the first card, a robin on a sprig of holly, beautifully drawn and coloured by – she opened the card to see, another hand drawn picture, this time a fir tree – from Walter. The second card was from Freddie with a hand drawn snow scene on the outside, and holly and mistletoe inside, so carefully done, the handkerchief came out again.

Looking around her she wanted somewhere where Andy wouldn't find them but she would be able to look at them when he wasn't in. Her note book seemed as good a place as any, after all, she kept it with other private papers hidden away under her twinsets and stockings, not a place she would expect anyone to find them.

Apart from a box of chocolates and the almost transparent blouse that she was hardly likely to wear in public except possibly under a twin set, that Andy had given her, Em found Christmas day a bit of a disappointment. Andy was working, so the thought of cooking just for herself… no, soup and a cheese sandwich would do, except that Andy had eaten what cheese there had been left of the week's ration for breakfast, so she made herself some porridge, a far cry from what she had served at Christmas over the last few years.

Em sat down and cried. Damn George, she thought, why did I listen to him, him and all his big ideas and tall stories. Well I suppose I've only got myself to blame. Picking up little loveable Annabel, she held her close and cuddling her sat down by the fire and fed her, and her spirits rose as she nursed the young child. By the time she had finished seeing to her daughter, her porridge had gone cold, so she heated some milk and stirring it into the porridge made it more palatable.

With Annabel settled, Em made herself a hot drink. Listening to the dance music on the wireless and closing her eyes, she was once more dreaming of dancing round and round in the arms of… in the arms of… whose arms? She was trying to see… It was not George, not Charlton, nor Andy, it was… Was it Herb? No, surely not… Yes it was Herbie; but why? Em woke with a start; it was already dark outside, so she turned on the light, closed the curtains and went into the kitchen to make a cup of tea.

She had just lit the gas when she heard the key in the door. "Happy Christmas, I know it's kind of late but I've brought some Christmas food for you." Andy was carrying a box which he put down on the kitchen worktop. "I've got to get back. I'll be late even if I can get back at all tonight, so probably see you in the morning. Oh, there's some bloke in uniform down there asking after you, said his name was Phillips. Shall I tell him where you are?"

"I suppose so. Send him up. Try not to wake Annabel or me when you come in."

Andy kissed her. "Okay," he said, "if I'm very late I'll sleep in the other room," and he went out.

"Merry Christmas, Em, may I come in?"

"Of course you can, Herbie," Em said, throwing her arms around him and kissing him. "Of course you can. What would you like…? Tea or coffee… Camp coffee… with milk… I've no cream, and only white sugar not the brown that you like…"

"Hush, woman! I came to see you, not some high falootin' hostess! Lady Jane and the girls send their love, you're missed terribly and the girls want to know when you'll be going back… oh I've got some cards for you," he said as he reached into his briefcase and took out half a dozen cards, and a couple of small parcels. "How are you and whatsisname? George or Victor, whatever his name is…" Then seeing Em's smile disappear to be replaced with one or two tears, he drew her close. "What is it? Now what's he done?"

Trying to hold back the tears, Em told Herbie how George had been arrested and jailed for bigamy, and how he had disappeared after coming out of prison, leaving her with a little girl, and how she had only been able to stay in the flat by taking in a lodger.

Herbie listened intently. "You don't deserve to be treated like that," he said. "I think it's time we thought about something for you to eat," walking into the kitchen as he spoke. "What have you got in the box? Hmm it smells – and looks – delicious," he said as he took out the canteens of food. "Still hot enough, so sit down and I'll wait on you for a change."

What Andy had brought for one was plenty enough even when shared between two, so they sat, ate and chatted about old times, once more enjoying each other's company. "Y' know," he said in his broad southern accent, "I haven't enjoyed a meal so much since you were at the Hall. Perhaps we should do this more often…" He hesitated for a moment, "Y' know, you could join me back home in Houston, or better still come back with me when I leave in two months' time." Seeing Em's quizzical look, he added, "As my wife. I'd take care of you, and your kids. We'd make a great team. I'm not rushing you. Take your time an' please say yes. You'll think about it?"

"Give me a couple'a days and I'll think, honest I will, although I don't see how I can. I'm still married, I know it might sound daft but I've been brought up to believe in 'Marriage is for Life'. Oh, Herbie, you are such a lovely man and I love you dearly. I wish I knew what to do. I'd love to go with you, but I've got to think of my boys. What if the home won't give them back, then what will I do?" Em burst into tears of confusion. Herbie held her close, whispering soothingly until Em looked up and kissed him. "Thank you, Herbie, you're a darling," and she kissed him again. "Yep, arl think abart it," she said trying to speak in a deep southern accent, causing Herbie to burst out laughing.

Please, dear," she begged, "stay with me tonight. There's room for two in my bed."

Laughing, he said, "Arl think abart it, darling."

Chapter Eighteen

It was customary for the children to hang up one of their socks at the end of their beds for Father Christmas to fill when he came round during the night, and although one or two of the boys had tried to stay awake and listen for him, they had fallen asleep by the time he arrived. When they awoke in the morning the socks had been filled and were bulging.

Freddie got out of bed and stood for a moment on the cold lino. It was chilly in the bedroom up on the top floor, so he quickly dressed and looked out of the window. There had been a heavy frost leaving a white coat on the lawn and on the tennis court. Brrr, he thought, it's going to be cold going to church.

The other five boys in the dormitory were still sitting in bed in their pyjamas emptying tangerines, packets of sweets, crayons and Dinky cars out of their socks onto their beds. Freddie was now dressed apart from the one sock, which he emptied as he sat on the bed and put on before looking to see what had been in it.

Like any efficient organisation, the routine jobs around the home were allocated on a rota, according to age and capability, and on school days taking into account the amount of homework any boy had. Today might be Christmas, but making beds and tidying bedrooms before breakfast was the rule of the day, as was cleaning shoes. Breakfast usually consisted of porridge followed by bread and marmalade, accompanied by a cup of tea; Christmas day was no exception. Washing the dishes after meals was also included in the rota.

Thirty boys in groups of five or six made their way to the Methodist Church in Mansfield Road like they did every Sunday. But there was a shorter service with plenty of singing Christmas carols, a short talk instead of the long sermon, and then going home earlier, to the Christmas lunch of turkey, stuffing and vegetables, followed by yummy Christmas pudding and mince pies. There was also Cherryade, or Freddie's favourite Dandelion and Burdock.

After the tables were cleared and the washing up was finished, everybody waited while their names were called out two or three times as Mr Smith, the governor, waded through the pile of parcels. Every boy had at least two. The piles of discarded wrapping paper grew rapidly, some eagerly torn apart, while some was carefully taken off, folded and put away for reuse.

Walter opened his presents, delighted to have received a book from his mother, not sure what to expect from the title, *Swallows and Amazons* but Sister looking at what he was holding said "Oh, you'll enjoy that..." starting to tell him what it was about, until she was distracted by James who had cut himself on a piece of brown paper.

Walter looked to see what book his brother Freddie had received: *Out with Romany by Meadow and Stream* looked much more interesting than *Swallows and Amazons*. As the oldest he considered he should have the right to choose which book he received, but Freddie had already written his name in his book, as Sister had told them to do, so he had to make do with what he had, but he would make sure he got to read Freddie's book as well.

"Hurry up, boys," said Sister Millicent, "put your toys away and tidy up if you want your tea." There was a flurry of movement as toys and books were stowed in or on lockers, scraps of paper were hastily collected and put into the wastepaper bin, and the tables set and decorated ready for a Christmas treat, a meal of sandwiches, jelly and fruit trifle, mince pies and fairy cakes, followed by a huge Christmas cake which had been donated by the Theatre Royal. The boys weren't too interested in who had provided it, as long as it was for them.

After the meal had been cleared away, all the boys sat on the floor and they sang a few seasonal songs, then much to the delight of boys and staff, Mr Smith, using a variety of accents, recited two hilarious monologues: *Three ha'pence a Foot* followed by *The Return of Albert*, the sequel to *Albert and the Lion*. To quieten the hilarity, they sang a couple more songs and then said prayers. The younger boys went to bed at seven o'clock, older ones had a special treat of staying up an extra half hour past their usual bedtime of half past seven.

**

The Red Lion was closed, the only times it was closed since the death of King George the Fifth in 1936, being on Christmas Days. Victor lit a fire in the inglenook so that he and Mr Woodley could escape their womenfolk and any chores. Christmas is a holiday, they would say, without any thought of it also being one for their spouses, or of helping even with trivialities that women took in their stride, like washing dishes or keeping children amused and away from under their wives' feet, especially Malcolm with his engine going 'whooaoo' around the floor.

For the menfolk there was the added advantage of an endless supply of drink, out of the ladies' sight but within easy reach; needless to say the temptation was greater than their resistance and both men were getting inebriated, especially Mr Woodley, even though being diabetic he had been advised to keep a watch on his drinking.

"Bless 'em," said Mrs Woodley, "it seems a pity to wake them."

"What?" asked Gillian, "you mean go and have lunch without them? Mind you, it would serve 'em right for leaving us to do all the work."

As they turned to go back to the kitchen Victor stirred. "Dinner ready? Ah, good," he said, going over to where his father-in-law lay.

"Leave 'im, let 'im sleep it off."

"But you can't…" Victor said.

"We can and we will," answered Mrs Woodley.

"He's been told about drinking too much. I sometimes wonder whether he knows what he's doing," Mrs Woodley was saying to her daughter. "Is he trying to make me a widow? Mind you, someone told me widder women get priority at the almshouses."

"Oh Mother," Gillian said, "you mustn't think things like that."

"I don't know what we'll do if he loses his licence, the brewery could close us, then where would we be."

"Victor could become the licensee, couldn't you, love," Gillian said, as she looked up at him while hanging onto his arm."

"Er what? Er, yes, dear," said Victor, with his mind on other things.

Mr Woodley slept on, eventually waking shortly after four p.m. On the table beside him was a plate of sandwiches with thinly cut meat from the Christmas goose, with a smearing of Women's Institute pickle, purchased earlier in the year, accompanied by a slice of Christmas pudding, and a cup of dandelion root 'coffee', after which he asked, "What happened to the cake icing?"

Victor had been playing on the lounge floor with Malcolm and his engine when Mrs Woodley came in pushing a tea trolley. "Come on, you two," she said, "it's time for tea and for 'Whooaoo', to go to bed."

Malcolm jumped up. "Can I have a cake?"

"Sandwiches first, just like Daddy," she answered, offering Victor a sandwich, with a look that dared him not to take one.

Victor took a bite. "Ooh, yummy," he said, looking up at Gillian. Malcolm sat down on the floor beside Victor, holding a sandwich and looking up to his father for approval.

That evening Mr and Mrs Woodley occupied the chairs by the fire. Victor was sitting on the settee with Gillian sprawled out, her head on his lap, dance music softly playing on the wireless, only interrupted by the steady snoring of Mr Woodley, and the occasional giggle from Gillian, in answer to Victor's whispers.

"Come on, dear," he said, "I need an early start tomorrow if I'm going to collect Mavis, and drive across to Nottingham tomorrow."

"But it's only ni—" Gillian felt a dig from Victor, that stopped her in mid sentence. "Good night, Mummy," she said, "say good night to Daddy for me," and kissed her.

Victor followed suit. "Good night, Mother dear," and bending to kiss her, getting a friendly slap on his ear, and mimicking crying, laughing as they headed for the stairs.

***

Mavis came running out of the farmhouse door just as Victor drew up outside the gate, and climbed into the passenger seat. "Drive on," she said, "Mummy will be watching," turning to wave at the unseen figure, real or imaginary. Driving along the farm track, a long way out of sight of the house, she asked him to stop, then moving closer, leaned over and kissed him.

"We'd better get back," he said. "I told them I wouldn't be long."

"Then perhaps you would like to wash my back," she replied. The vision in the copper wash tub instantly came to mind. Victor tried to concentrate on driving along the twisting track as they made their way to the road.

***

It was still early when Em stirred, looked in admiration at Herbie's handsome face and slid her hand across his chest. His free arm came over and pulled her closer, she could feel his muscular body against her and just relaxed, determined to enjoy every moment of his closeness while she could.

Em kissed him. "Tea or Camp Coffee?" she asked.

"Er... your English tea, please," he answered. She slipped out of bed, into her dressing gown and headed for the kitchen. "Is it okay if I take a shower?" he asked poking his head round the kitchen door.

"Yes, of course," turning as she answered, "but wait while I light the geyser."

"That's okay, I've got a degree in those things."

"Really?"

"No, not really," he said, laughing. "Hey, stand still, you look real handsome in that thing."

"In England," she corrected him, "it's men who are handsome. Ladies are—"

"I know, beautiful and that's what you are, really beautiful."

"Flatterer, hurry up or your tea will be cold."

There was the sound of a key in the lock. Andy came into the lounge. The gas fire was burning, Herbie and Em were sitting on opposite sides facing each other, Herbie was bouncing Annabel on his knee. "Has he been here all night?"

"Yes," Em answered, "And you? Where were you sleeping?" Andy's face coloured a little as he turned and went to the kitchen. "Two teas please, Andy," Em called out, with a smirk on her lips. Andy muttered something indistinguishable. Five minutes later he brought in a tray with two teas and a plate of biscuits.

***

Walter was sitting in the alcove reading a book. He looked up when he thought he could hear his brother's voice, quickly made a mental note of the page number and slid the book up the back of his pullover. Freddie came far enough into the room to see into the alcove. "Finished already?" Walter asked.

"I'll be another five minutes," Freddie answered.

"Freddie," a voice called from the direction of the kitchen, "there's still two more pans."

"Coming, Sister," he answered as he disappeared.

Walter quickly took the book and put it back in Freddie's locker. Bother, he thought, it was just getting interesting.

***

Liz slipped out of bed, put on her dressing gown and picking up her toilet kit and the nice big towel her mother had given her, made her way into the communal bathroom. She liked to have a cold shower to start the day, it always seemed to fully liven her up and give her that extra zing. Breakfast was usually cereal bran, followed by toast, with honey when available, the same being applicable to an apple, or whatever was left when she reached the mess. With the barracks manned by a skeleton staff—the description amused her thinking on the size of the ATS officer,

Captain Peggy Smythe—there was more than sufficient fruit for those who liked it.

Sitting at her desk in the orderly room, Liz gradually worked her way through the pile of paperwork that had been left for her by her colleagues, stopping mid-morning for a cup of tea when the NAAFI trolley came past. Leaning back in her chair, cup in hand, she chuckled remembering a couple of incidents from Christmas Day, the first being at lunch, when the officers were waiting on the junior ranks in the mess; the CO, offering her a box of dates, had asked if she 'would like a date' to which she had replied, 'Oh sir, what would your wife say?' Later on, waiting at the dinner table in the officer's mess, some of the officers had prompted her to give the CO a dish containing hazelnuts and chestnuts and say, "Your nuts, sir," much to everyone's delight.

Looking at the telephone on her desk from time to time, she was willing it to ring; it had only been a few days since she had seen Victor, but to a young girl, for that in life's experience was what she was, to a young adult even, a day can be a very long time, and a week an eternity.

The telephone rang; its shrill tone made her jump. For a moment she let it ring, she mustn't seem too eager. She reached out her hand and raising the handset, held it to her ear. "Hello; orderly room," she said.

Chapter Nineteen

Mrs Weston in flat one having offered to take care of Annabel, Em and Herbie were sitting in the bar at Ye Olde King's Head, enjoying a drink before going to the restaurant. With a late booking, their table wasn't ready and they had been asked to wait in the bar; perhaps they would like an aperitif before lunch. Andy was busy clearing and cleaning tables and putting the furniture straight. A waitress came into the bar and spoke to Andy. Em thought she could hear them discussing arrangements being made for when they finished work, and Andy kept glancing round, presumably to see if they had been heard. Em had been able to piece together enough of the conversation to be aware that Andy was likely to be out all night.

"Sir, madam, would you come this way," the waitress said, after finishing her conversation with Andy. "A window table?" escorting them to a table overlooking the garden, which even at that time of year looked lovely with the different colour foliages.

"Muriel," said Em, reading the badge attached to the apron bib, "are you local?"

"No miss, I'm from Essex."

"Ahem, when you two ladies ..."

"Of course, sir," she said, as she left to fetch the menus.

"Sorry sir, most things are finished," she said. "We have fish pie, turkey pie or gammon."

"I think I'd like gammon," Em said.

"That'll be two gammon steaks please," Herbie ordered, "glazed with honey."

"Yes, sir, madam, anything to drink?"

"When the gammon is ready," he replied, "then I'll order."

As the waitress disappeared Herbie asked why Em seemed so interested in the waitress. Em told him it was just a woman's intuition, and to ignore it. Herbie shrugged his shoulders, saying he'd never understand it, men's logic was more in his line, even that was not always easy.

Collecting Annabel from Mrs Weston after the meal, they returned to the flat. Em was eager to feed and change her daughter, but unsure about the feeding while Herbie was in the room. "Relax," he said, "and ignore me if you don't mind me being in the room. What you will be doing is the most natural and beautiful thing in the world, it's better for your child and it's better for you."

They were quietly relaxing on the chaise longue; the music was soft and romantic, Em turned to look at his handsome face. "You know, dear," she started saying, "it would be wonderful, but—"

He put a finger to her lips. "Shh... not just now." The clock struck four; Herbie sat up. "I'm neglecting my duties," he said, "I must go... I've a desk full of paperwork that must be done."

"Darling, must you?"

"Yes, dear, I must, but I will be back, I promise." Putting on his coat and picking up his briefcase, he bent down and kissed her.

"Thank the girls for me, dearest," she said as he slipped out of the door, closing it as quietly as he could so as to not waken Annabel. Em went to the window, watching as he got in his big staff car and drove away.

I love him, she thought, truly love him.

***

"Hullo, can I speak to Liz please... Liz Norman... Yes... Thank you... Hullo, Liz? How are... It's Victor... Yes, Victor... Yes, dear... I'm in Derby... I should be there in about an hour... Outside the gate?... Okay, seven outside the gate, see you then." He blew a kiss into the telephone. Just five or ten minutes outside the gate is better than nothing, I suppose, Victor thought. I'd better hurry if I'm going to be there in time.

Victor left the kiosk and got back in his lorry. He had rung from a telephone on the outskirts to avoid the noise of passing traffic, but on Boxing Day there had been very little traffic about, especially that late in the day, and in the dark, for at six it was very dark driving out of town, even with headlights on main beam vision was limited so you had to drive carefully.

Victor arrived outside the Chilwell Barracks with fifteen minutes to spare and sat waiting, watching for what seemed an eternity. Pencil and pad in hand, he was making a few notes of "must do's" when he dropped his pencil; he was bending down to retrieve it when a there was a knock on the window, in the confusion he hadn't seen Liz come out of the gate.

"I'll sign you in and we can go to the NAAFI," she said. At the gate he was asked for his Identity Card and Driving Licence, and was informed that the gate would be locked at ten, that would give them less than three hours together. In his hurry to get to Chilwell before seven, Victor hadn't stopped for any food, so he welcomed the suggestion of going to the NAAFI where they would be together, and he would be able to have something to eat. Not being a 'resident' he was not allowed to pay, and had to accept Liz's insistence on paying.

It is and always will be, an anomaly that when waiting, time passes slowly, yet when enjoying yourself or with the one you love, it passes in a flash; and so it was that evening. In no time Victor found himself outside the gate looking in and bidding his love, "Good night."

***

"What was that, Em?... You mean?... Where?... Houston? Where's that?... Texas? Oh, Em... yes, I know what mother would say... Don't worry about what she thinks, go if you *really* want to, but what about Walter and Freddie?... I'm due a weekend off at the end of the month, I'll see you then and we can talk about it, tarraa, sis." Flo put the phone down.

"Trouble, Nurse?" asked Sister Monica, the ward sister. "I'm sure if you ask around, one of the other nurses wouldn't mind changing their weekend with you in the circumstances."

"Thank you, Sister," Flo said and went back into the ward to carry on looking after the patients.

***

When Andy arrived back at the flat in Lower Bridge Street, Em was sitting on the floor in the lounge, changing Annabel, who after having been fed was happily waving her arms and legs in the air. "Is that you Andy? Be a darling and make a brew please," Em called out.

"Why, who else did you think it might be?"

"I wasn't sure," she answered. "You're a lot earlier than usual this morning and I just wondered—"

"You mean you thought George—"

"No, I think we've seen the last of him," said Em. "Where were you last night, at Muriel's?"

"Yes," he replied, "she went off after lunch yesterday, she's gone to Southport again to see her kids. They're in a home there, when she's away I use her room, it saves paying to use the spare room."

Hmm, very convenient, thought Em.

"Can I do you some breakfast?" he asked. "Toast or something?"

"Thank you, dear, toast and marmalade would be nice, that's if there's any marmalade left."

"If your boyfriend left any, you mean."

"He's a colleague, someone I worked alongside at Moore Hall," Em answered, "the CO at the convalescent hospital."

"You worked for the Americans?"

"No," Em answered, "I was the housekeeper; I worked for Lady Marbury, but during the war I held the rank of major and he was my CO."

Andy glanced at the clock as he brought a tray into the lounge. "Table or chair?" he asked.

"Table, please," Em answered, as she was putting Annabel into the bouncy swing Andy had bought her for Christmas. "It's so much easier than juggling cups and plates while sitting in the armchair."

"I'm due back at work at ten," he said. "Can I bring you anything? I've a break at three, then late shift from five. You'll be okay on your own tonight?" he asked, a statement rather than a question.

"Yes, of course, Annabel'l look after me, won't you, my poppet?" she said.

Em spent the rest of the morning with tidying and dusting, but without a man around there was only a minimal amount to be done, apart from keeping up with the washing of nappies and other baby things and her own personal washing, followed by a quick snack, before attending to Annabel and settling her down for her afternoon sleep. Pulling an armchair over by the window, she sat watching fathers and mothers with their sons and daughters gliding along the pavement on their scooters, some younger ones, first timers on two wheels struggling to control the presents that Father Christmas had left them. The afternoon passed slowly, soft classical music on the wireless, until she woke up with a sudden jerk in the semi-darkness, having fallen asleep. The wireless was now playing the more rhythmic music of Edmundo Ros's Rhumba band.

Em turned on the lights and closed the curtains. If Andy had been in, he certainly hadn't woken her. She went into the kitchen to make herself a drink; there was a box on the table, and a note which said 'For sleeping beauty with love. your prince x'. A feast of thinly sliced ham sandwiches, mince pies and cupcakes. I hope he had permission to bring these out, she thought. I'd hate him to lose his job on account of me.

***

"Good afternoon, miss, is there any mail for me?" Victor asked. "Ah, thank you." He looked at the neat handwriting while walking towards the bar, and nearly colliding with a lady coming out. "I'm sorry, miss," he said, only briefly taking his eyes off the envelope he was attempting to open. He had barely sat down when a waiter approached. "My usual, please," he said without looking up.

"I'm sorry sir, I am not familiar with your regular," said the waiter.

Victor looked at him. "Where's Harris?" he asked.

"Regrettably he is unwell, sir. What can I get you?"

"A Scotch, please, make it a double, room 202." Victor was about to read the letter as the waiter returned.

"Your drink, sir, and if you'd be so kind." Victor signed for the drink. "Thank you, sir."

The note from Liz told of a dance on New Year's Eve in the NAAFI, and that he was invited; she would meet him at the gate at nineteen hundred hours, and whilst he would be able to remain on the camp past midnight, he must leave before two a.m. In the meantime, she hoped to see him on Friday, usual time, usual place.

Monday evening, at a quarter to seven, a smartly dressed Victor was sitting in his car, carefully watching. At seven he walked up to the gate. "ID please, sign in here, sir. Methinks the lady approaches," the sentry said, with a smirk on his face.

"Ah good, thanks, Bert. Hullo, love, who's this posh looking guy?" Liz asked, laughing, reaching up and kissing Victor.

"And who's this gorgeous—"

"Hush, Bert," she said, "I'll tell Glenys."

The evening went well, no shortage of drink, ample food, and lots of dancing, which gave Victor the opportunity of holding Liz closely, and as the floor got more crowded, he was obliged to hold her closer still, not that he was complaining. Just before midnight the band leader started the countdown: ten, nine, eight... A myriad of voices joined in: six, five... The sound grew into a crescendo: two, one... Everyone shouted "Happy New Year" as the chimes of Big Ben sounded through the loudspeakers. After the national anthem, dancing resumed, only to be broken by someone starting a conga chain weaving in and out of the dancers while the band played along until almost everyone joined in. Liz and Victor joined the tail, then slipped into an adjoining room where they could have a little time alone. Just after one-thirty a.m. on Tuesday, January 1st 1946, Victor and Liz kissed goodnight at the gate, having made arrangements for their next meeting at five-thirty on Friday.

Chapter Twenty

Mrs Woodley was quite adamant. "If Victor *is* going to take over as licensee," she said, "he really needs to see the magistrate before someone at the brewery finds out about your father."

"Why, what's wrong with Daddy?" asked Gillian. "He hasn't had any more passing-out fits, has he?"

"No, but he's in no fit state to run a pub, and if the licensing people find out, we could be out of house and home as well as losing the business, then where would we be?" Pausing for a moment to think, she added, "Now if Victor took on the licence, perhaps with Mavis as barmaid and Colin as cellar man, you could run it as the manager, which would give you little more responsibility than what you already have, virtually running it for your father, and, listen, and get paid doing it, how does that sound?" asked Mrs Woodley. "Think what you could do with the money."

Gillian turned the idea over in her mind. Hmm, she thought, hmm.

***

Liz had decided to travel light; well, for her travelling light was two small cases instead of one larger more bulky case, two small cases being easier to handle. She wrote a label for each case and carefully tied them on the handles, called out, "Cheerio girls, see you when I get back" to the other occupants of the Nissen hut, and headed for the door.

Victor got out of the car and went to greet Liz as she came out of the gate. They kissed, then with Victor taking the cases, headed back to the car. "How about we drive back to the hotel and discuss plans over a drink," he suggested.

"That sounds good to me," she answered as she sat back and thought of ten days away from ATS routines, and what they could do if she hadn't promised her sister a trip to a London theatre. They entered the hotel and Liz, wearing Victor's raincoat over her uniform, went up to his room to change into mufti, then joined him in the bar. Victor had thought of going out to eat, but it had started raining so he suggested a meal in the privacy of their room. Liz said she would rather eat in the restaurant, after which they could go up to their room and talk in private, so after a meal of liver and bacon with baked potato and mixed vegetables, followed by creamed rice with spiced apple, they retired upstairs.

Liz was on leave for ten days, which included two weekends, returning to camp the following Monday. She had worked out that if she travelled to her home in Chingford on the Monday and back on the Friday, with her fourteen-year-old sister still being at school, it would not be practical for them to visit the theatre during the week, so she would put that off until she, Liz, was demobbed later in the year, when there would be something apart from pantomimes, which her sister thought too infantile for someone of her age.

Victor suggested driving down to London for the weekend, then he would drop her off in Chingford and return, do a couple of days' deliveries, pick her up on the Friday, and have a leisurely drive back to Nottingham. "Maybe stopping somewhere en route overnight as the mood takes us," he suggested, "but getting you back to camp in good time, at the end of your leave."

"Can you do that?" she asked.

"Of course, dear," he answered, "I'm my own boss."

Next morning they were up early, had breakfasted and were clear of the outskirts of Nottingham before it was fully light. With very little traffic on the main A1 trunk road the Hornet was making good speed, while driver and passenger were laughing and joking as they journeyed south. "How about going to Southend?" asked Liz.

"Or Broadstairs?" suggested Victor.

"Oh, yes, please," begged Liz, "I've never been to Broadstairs."

"Okay, but we might need to stay overnight on the way there," he said.

It was almost dark as they crossed Tower Bridge and headed toward the Elephant and Castle, where they joined the A2 bound for Dartford, Rochester and Broadstairs.

All was well until they arrived at Star Hill in Rochester, where an army lorry was causing an obstruction. While they were waiting Victor was chatting to the driver, and explained that he had during military service driven similar vehicles, so he knew a few 'wrinkles' that might work. "Naa, not these motors," said the driver, but he let Victor rummage through the tool box; after a few minutes Victor told the driver to turn the motor then a short while later to switch on and press the starter. After a few muffled attempts the engine fired and ran with a roar. Victor's 'wrinkle' had worked.

"What the…"

"A small drop of this," said Victor holding up a small bottle of ether he had found in the tool box, "usually works, but only use a very small drop."

"Thanks, mate," replied the soldier, and drove steadily up the hill.

Stopping at a small café for a quick meal before driving on through the Kentish countryside, aided by the moonlight, they passed Whitstable and Herne Bay, reached the square at Birchington on Sea and turned left towards the railway station, stopping outside the Seaview Hotel in Station Road, where they checked in for the night.

Waking up in a strange bed is one thing, but being woken by the sound of horses as they clip-clopped on the tarmac a short distance from your bedroom window was something neither Liz nor Victor had experienced before.

What the… thought Victor as he tried to work out what the noise was that woke him.

Where? What? Who? Questions invaded Liz's mind as she woke up in a strange bed, roused by an unfamiliar noise, and in bed with a man. Of course, Victor, she thought, smiling happily, but what was that noise?

Victor looked out of the window; across the other side of the road, in the dim light he could see someone harnessing a horse to a milk float.

"It's all right dear, we're quite near a dairy and they're getting ready to deliver the milk," Victor said as he got back in bed and Liz snuggled up close to him.

The church bells rang calling the early morning worshippers to church, the bells, also telling Victor and Liz that it was time to rise for a hearty breakfast before they headed out to explore the sights of Broadstairs, and enjoy the fresh invigorating air of the seaside.

Over breakfast they decided to drive round as near to the seafront as they could, going through Margate and Cliftonville on the way to Broadstairs, spend the afternoon there, then continue to Ramsgate and back to the Seaview Hotel for another night before making their way back to London and Chingford. Breakfast over, they drove down to the Birchington seafront at Minnis Bay, after having been told a little of the local history by the licensee. In front of them lay an open expanse devoid of the arcades of gaming machines which formed a blot on the landscape of so many coastal towns.

Winding their way through a maze of turnings, they managed to find the route back onto the suitably named Cliff Road, leading down to Westgate and past the once grand Nayland Rock Hotel, which stood as a sentry at the western end of Margate's seafront and promenade. Driving along the 'prom' past the Dreamland Cinema and Amusement Park, closed at that time of year, they continued along the harbour, stopping to look through the gates at Margate Pier where paddle steamers, like the Medway Queen, which did such astounding work at Dunkirk, brought Londoners to Margate for the day.

Victor was amazed to find himself driving along a promenade. He stopped the car so that they could stand by the railings and look out to the horizon. There was a cold easterly wind blowing from the sea. For a moment they watched the seagulls, then, "Brr," said Victor, "phew I didn't realise—"

"Just how cold it would be," Liz said, finishing Victor's sentence. "Let's find somewhere for a hot drink."

Driving as close as they could to the seafront, after a short distance they found themselves heading along Victoria Parade overlooking Viking Bay, and stopped in front of a likely looking public house, The Charles Dickens. After a piping hot cup of coffee, wrapped up warm against the wind, they walked through York Gate, built in 1540, passing the Tartan Frigate, the oldest flint public house in the whole of Kent. With the wind bringing spray over the harbour wall they retreated as far as the harbour master's office—the building provided some protection from both the wind and the spray—before returning to the Tartan Frigate's restaurant to enjoy lunch selected from the large and varied seafood menu.

Guided by the waitress in the restaurant, Victor found his way from Broadstairs on to the seafront road high above the promenade, from which on a fine clear day the coast of France could be clearly seen, especially from the road which ran above the Ramsgate Harbour Railway Station. Victor then drove down the hill to the harbour where they stopped to see the fishing boats and other small craft moored up to the quayside. It was almost dark by the time they arrived back in Birchington, so after enjoying a light meal and a few drinks by the fire in the bar they retired to their room and a quiet night.

"We'll keep a welcome in the hillside," a strong Welsh tenor voice was singing.

"Shurrup, Taffy, you'll wake 'em up in Seaview an' they won't like that," a voice bellowed.

"We'll keep a welcome in the dales ..." Taffy sang on. Victor got out of bed to close the slightly open window.

"Leave it please, dear," said Liz, "it's nice to be woken by someone singing, and he's got such a lovely voice."

"You wouldn't say that if I started." The clip-clop of hooves on tarmac heralded the other noises of the dairy at the start of the day's business.

**

They reached Tower Bridge shortly before midday. Having started their journey early, they encountered very little traffic until New Cross, not that it delayed them there very much, and after Elephant and Castle the roads were clearer. Once north of the Thames crossing, by avoiding Commercial Road and other roads linking with the docks in east London and Tilbury, Victor was soon driving towards Chingford. "Let me drop you at the station," suggested Victor.

"No thanks, dear," answered Liz, "I've told my parents about you, so as we're already here, you might as well meet them."

"But I'd planned…" he was saying, "well… okay then, but I can't stay long."

"I'm home, Mummy," Liz called out as she opened the door. "Just leave the cases here," she said to Victor as she hung her coat up on a hook in the hall.

"I'm in the parlour, dear," came the sound of a woman's voice. "Who's that you're talking to?"

"Come through," Liz was saying. "Victor," she called back, "he's driven me home."

As they entered the parlour Mrs Norman was seated at a sewing machine. "I know it's awfully rude of me but I won't get up," she said. "If I do I might spoil this blouse I'm making for your sister."

"Mummy, this is Victor," Liz replied. "He's brought me all the way down from Nottingham."

"I'm very pleased to meet you," said Victor.

"Can he sleep here tonight please, Mummy?" Liz asked. "We can't expect him to drive all the way back tonight."

"Yes, of course, dear," answered her mother. "I'll ask Father to open the put-u-up for him; you can use that tonight," she added, addressing Victor. "Perhaps you'd like to go down to Murphy's café and see if you can get some pie and chips?" asked Mrs Norman. "And while you're at it, get some for Father and Dinah, you can put theirs in the oven."

"Come on, dear," Liz said to Victor, "we'll take my cases up then go, I want to show you off. We don't need the car, it's only just round the corner."

"I met the ten past three train, but she wasn't on it," called Mr Norman as he came in through the front door.

"I know, dear," answered his wife, "they arrived half an hour ago."

"What do you mean, they?" he asked.

"Liz and her boyfriend," she replied. "He drove her down from Nottingham… that's his car out front."

"I wondered whose it was," he said.

The front door opened. "Hot dinners for five," Liz called out. "Oh! Hullo, Dad, didn't know you were back, this is Victor."

"Pleased to meet you, sir," said Victor, trying not to drop the parcel of food while holding out his hand.

"You're welcome, lad, but put it down first," replied Mr Norman. "That's a nice little motor you've got," he said, "but it'll not be big enough for more than two kids."

"Dad, really, must you? What are you suggesting? We're not even married. I don't know, Mummy, what can we do with him?"

"What am I supposed to have suggested?" asked Mr Norman. "I only said—"

"We know," replied his wife, laughing, "you only said. Oh, and while I think of it, would you get the put-u-up in the front room ready, Victor is stopping tonight."

"And no shenanigans," said Mr Norman.

"There he goes again," his wife said, this time they were all laughing.

"What?" he asked, a puzzled look on his face.

Chapter Twenty-one

"But, Mummy," Gillian said, almost in tears, "he wouldn't do that to me, would he? He loves the children, look how he dotes on them."

"Then why wasn't he here over the New Year?" asked Mrs Woodley. "Surely no one would be having deliveries then, and that was over a week ago."

"But Mummy—"

"Don't interrupt me when I'm talking. Where's your manners, girl? Oh, what was it I was saying?" Mrs Woodley stopped when she heard a lorry backing into the yard. "About time too," she said.

Victor felt the tension as he walked into the room. "Wha'... What have I done now?" he asked.

"Mummy says—" Gillian saw her mother's glare and stopped mid-sentence. "Mummy says we need to go to the magistrate's office for you to become licensee before Daddy's licence expires."

"Why me?" Victor asked.

"Because there's some silly notion about women licensees," said Mrs Woodley. "If you're licensee, Gillian could be manager while you're still driving your lorry; after all, she's been virtually running the business these last couple of years."

Signed, settled and sealed, Victor Bradburn was now the licensee of the Red Lion. "Oh, darling," Gillian threw her arms around his neck and kissed him firmly on the lips.

"Ahem, not in here, please," the clerk said, looking over his spectacles. "I've other people to see."

"Come on, dear," said Victor, "let's get back and celebrate."

"Don't forget these, sir," the clerk said, handing Victor a large envelope full of papers.

Back at the Red Lion, a small group were meeting in the bar, there was still a little while before opening time and both old and new staff celebrated the hand-over to the new management. Colin wasn't quite sure about Victor being the licensee until he heard that Gillian was going to be the manager. He considered that cellar work was a man's domain, and there would now be no risk of him losing his job. As for Mavis, the thought of Victor being around pleased her, although she was a little unsure about Gillian, there was no knowing what she would be like as the official boss, but they were good friends and that should mean a lot.

Lunchtime the following day saw Victor's lorry heading across the Pennines. Arriving in Derby at dusk in squally rain, he could have parked up for the night; but for the need to collect his car and drive down to pick up Liz, he would have done so, but his determination to be in Chingford by Friday evening spurred him on, arriving back in Nottingham shortly after eight-thirty.

***

There was a knock on the door. Em laid Annabel down in her cot as the caller knocked again. Em hurried through the hall, she didn't want anyone to wake her daughter, fumbled with the door catch, and thinking, I must get Andy to fix that, she opened the door and was confronted by a large bunch of flowers.

"What …" Em uttered as the familiar face of Herbie appeared.

"Good morning, dear lady," he said, "may I come in?"

"Of course, kind sir," she replied, stepping aside and curtseying.

"What brings you here so early?"

"I happened to be passing and wondered who these beautiful flowers reminded me of."

"Flatterer, but they are lovely, and thank you," she said, kissing him.

"Well actually, I'm just on my way to Brigade Headquarters, and wondered if you had come to any decision about my proposal. I'm not trying to rush you…" he said.

"Well… I'd love to, but there's the boys to consider and… I just don't know what to do…"

"I understand," he replied. "I'm due to fly home in about six weeks so I… I need to know fairly soon. Don't leave it too long. I'll try to pop in again before I leave."

Em stood in the doorway watching as Herbie went down the stairs, she blew him a kiss and stepped indoors, quietly closing the door behind her.

Andy came in at the end of his shift. "Hello dear," he said, bending over to kiss Em, then catching sight of the flowers in vases each end of the sideboard, "Where… Who…" pointing a finger at the blooms.

"I can see you're jealous, darling. Well, there's no need to be. It was the American officer's goodbye present, he's on his way back to the States."

***

Victor loved his car; he got a great deal of pleasure driving his Bedford lorry, but that was business, that was work. His real love was the Hornet, from the moment he sat in the driver's seat it became part of him and he of it. With a snort of delight the car pulled out, picking up speed as they passed the lumbering tank transporter; oh yes, there were still cumbersome military convoys to overtake, even in peacetime, but to the Hornet, just another obstacle to zip past.

As Victor headed south, he was wondering whether to drive straight to Liz's house where her parents might feel obliged to offer him accommodation, or find somewhere to stop for the night and collect her on Saturday morning, ready for the journey back to Nottingham. Victor decided the more diplomatic approach would be the second option.

Victor had a liking for the older public houses and being guided by the building style, location and name chose the King's Head on King's Head Hill, Chingford Green. Nor was he disappointed; the accommodation was dated but comfortable, and although quite noisy, what Victor would call lively, it was Friday so what could you expect.

The bar snacks were a bit sparse but he had eaten just north of Barnet and it was almost nine when he had arrived, so a quick drink and up to his room on the second floor where it was quiet and peaceful.

Victor woke with no idea of how long he had slept, or what time it was. His room was at the back of the building with no street lighting, which made it necessary for him to get out of bed in the cold room to turn on the light in order to look at his watch… a quarter before five. Hm, thought Victor, a bit early to get up, but if I get back in bed, I might oversleep… brrr …it's a bit chilly. So he got back in bed… The next he knew, it was sevenish; a quick shave and down to breakfast, a good fried plateful with plenty of toast, maybe they could have allowed a bit more butter, but it was still rationed, good value for what he'd paid, a handy pub when making deliveries this way.

At half-past-eight Victor stopped outside 17 Northend Road, a house typical of the area, modest, well built and worth the three or four hundred pounds that he had seen advertised while looking around Nottingham; but why was he thinking of Nottingham when he was here to collect Liz and take her back to her barracks, though not until after the weekend.

No sooner had Victor pressed the bell push than the door opened. Liz's fourteen-year-old sister stood in the doorway. "Oh, it's you, is it? Sis' is still upstairs tarting herself up."

"Dinah," her mother called out, "you shouldn't be talking about your sister like that. You should show more respect when talking to visitors. Ask him in."

Dinah held the door open and Victor stepped inside. "Good Morning, Mrs Norman," he said as he walked into the living room. "It's a bit on the cold side today."

"Humph," said Dinah, "typical. The first fing he talks about is the wever."

"Children…" Mrs Norman was saying as Liz came in the room, "I don't know what the world is coming to."

"No need to talk posh 'cos he's here," declared Dinah. Liz and her mother laughed.

"You'll not get anyone decent if you speak like that," said Liz.

"What makes you think he's decent?" Dinah retaliated.

"Dinah, that is enough," said her mother," it's time you were on your way to hockey practice."

Victor smiled; he liked her. She's got spirit, he thought, watching her swing her coat around her shoulders and slipping her arms into her sleeves, nice figure for her age.

"Are you going anywhere near Chingford Plain?" asked Dinah. "If so you can give me a lift in your car."

"Are we?" Victor asked Liz. "We'll be going through Potters Bar."

"That's okay, love. If you take Manor Road, onto Ranger's Road, we can drop Dinah off at the park," replied Liz, "then go over King's Head Hill to Enfield, and Potters Bar is quite near."

"Thanks, sis'," Dinah said. "Come on or you'll make me late."

"The cheek of it. *Extractum digitalis* then," said Liz, giving her sister a shove.

Driving up through Enfield and Potters Bar, Victor avoided the worst of London traffic, then going across country, reached Hatfield. After having a short refreshment stop they joined the A1 trunk road and headed north. Although the idea had started in 1913, it wasn't until 1919, after the First World War had ended, that the classification of roads connecting highly populated areas started to appear, and it was another four years before numbers started to appear on the roads and maps, and they became known as trunk roads. The number one set out from London towards the north east; the numbering went clockwise, so that number six was heading north, numbers seven and eight being north of the border in Scotland.

One of the problems of driving long distances in January was how early the daylight faded into darkness. At dusk, when it was neither light nor dark, it became difficult to see and it was prudent either to take a meal break and continue after dark, or stop overnight at a local hostelry. Among the nearby inns in the High Street in Stamford was the George Hotel, a thousand year old coaching inn, which they decided would admirably suit their needs.

The modest meal of Spam fritters, chipped potatoes and vegetables, and a dessert of homemade apple pie and custard, served in the almost empty restaurant, was followed by a drink or two in the bar before they headed upstairs to a room dominated by a beautiful big four poster bed.

Next morning, as they were driving along the A1 towards Grantham, Liz asked if they were anywhere near Lincoln, and said, "I would simply love to see Lincoln Cathedral while we're up this way."

"Your wish is my command," replied Victor.

"Oh darling!" she said, putting her arms around him and trying to kiss him.

"Steady on! Not while I'm driving. You could have had us in the ditch!" Victor expostulated as he sought to keep the car on the road.

"Sorry, dear," Liz murmured, sitting back in her seat.

Arriving a little while before the morning service ended, they found a cosy café to pass the time and have some refreshments while watching for the congregation to leave, then joined a group of tourists waiting to enter the magnificent building.

Lincoln Cathedral, once reputed to be the tallest building in the world, certainly the tallest in England, stood on a mound overlooking the city; its spire pointing high into the sky seemed to be trying to reach up to Heaven. As Victor and Liz entered the great doorway, they were amazed at the beautifully carved archway over the entrance, and awestruck with the size of the pillars that supported the lofty roof.

Following the other visitors who were on a guided tour, they heard the history, not only of the building but the various features like the Dean's Eye Window in the north transept, the Lincoln Imp in the eastern end of the choir stalls, Eleanor of Castile's tomb and St Hugh's shrine, and many features that made the cathedral such an interesting place to visit.

Two hours later Victor and Liz emerged out into the winter sunshine; the streets were wet, evidence that it had rained while they were inside the cathedral. The damp brought a freshness to the air and even though the sun was shining it was still quite cold. "Let's get back home to Nottingham," Victor said, "with luck, we should be there before dark."

The Hornet was at the peak of its performance as it roared along the A46 towards Newark on Trent and Nottingham, eventually turning off at Bingham and crossing Trent Bridge just as darkness was falling. With a sigh of relief Victor and Liz mounted the steps up to the hotel foyer, checked in and went to their room to freshen up before heading towards the restaurant. They were sitting quietly with their coffees after dinner, listening to the soft background music that was playing next door in the bar, when Liz turned in her seat to listen. "I know that voice," she said. "That's got to be Charlotte or I'm a monkey."

"The best looking monkey in the zoo," Victor replied. "Shall we go in and join them?"

"Must we?" asked Liz. "We could slip upstairs. I'll be seeing them tomorrow anyway."

Chapter Twenty-two

Em was sitting on the chaise longue, looking out of the window. Annabel was bouncing up and down in her sling in the doorway. Em was listening to her daughter's happy chuckling and trying to imagine what it would be like to have her two boys home. It was now part way through the month of January, only six or seven weeks and it would be Easter. She wished she could have them stay over the holidays but she was frightened to tell Andy about them, or even tell them about Andy, and what was more important, about Annabel, their sister.

The letter slot flap rattled, and an envelope floated to the floor. Em bent down to pick it up and glancing at it recognised the neat script handwriting of her former employer, Lady Jane. Em's mind flashed back to the pleasant companionship of the kitchen; the thought made her more aware of the isolation and solitude that motherhood had brought, not that she regretted having Annabel, she loved her dearly but... Em reached for the paperknife and slit the envelope open. There was a neatly worded letter and an invitation card.

Em glanced at the invitation dated for sometime mid-June. So Charles was getting married... to... oh! So Lady Delilah had hooked her man, hmm... that could be interesting, no doubt Lady Jane's letter would give more information about the proposed marriage. Putting the invitation down on the table Em picked up the letter and started to read it. That was nice, typical of her ladyship sympathising with me over George leaving me in the lurch after all his promises... she was so right about being careful, never mind, it's too late now to have regrets.

So, they are having problems with staff and her ladyship would like me back. Hmm, I'm not sure. Sandra has left over some disagreement, I thought Susan and Sandra would be all right together, and now Susan has got herself pregnant, probably with one of the American staff. Ah well, you can never tell what may happen. Em put the letter aside while she made herself a cup of tea, then sitting down on the chaise longue picked it up again. Charles and Delilah must have been meeting away from home for her baby to be due in December. I wouldn't be surprised if she still wears white. Hmm it should be an interesting match. I hope it works out for them both.

I don't know about going back, it's kind of Lady Jane to invite me, and I'll be quite happy to do the cake, that would definitely be easier in their kitchen, maybe I could go for a visit and bake it then.

***

Liz awoke to the sound of rain beating against the window. Only a few hours left before she was due back at Chilwell barracks, a wet day was disappointing. Victor stirred. "What is it, dear?" he asked.

"It's raining," she answered.

"What's the time?"

"Time we were out of bed and dressed if there's going to be any breakfast left for us."

"So," he asked again, "what is the time?"

"Half-eight," she replied. "Race you."

"Not like that, you'd better get something on before you go downstairs."

Over breakfast they discussed the places available for them to visit. The rain had stopped but it was expected again later in the morning, so they decided to visit Wollaton Hall, Gardens and Deer Park on the western outskirts of the city. After loading Liz's cases in the car they drove past the castle and along University Boulevard, where they stopped to admire the beautiful view of the university across the lake and Tottle brook, before driving into Woodside Road and making their way to the gates of Wollaton Hall. Unfortunately it was closed for the winter but they could see the spectacular sixteenth century Elizabethan mansion in the distance, somewhere for them to visit later in the warmer months of the year. The rain had not returned, resulting in a pleasant drive, so after stopping for some refreshments in a small café they headed to Chilwell, and parted at the gates of the barracks having made arrangements to meet again.

***

Em looked out of the window, watching the police car as it drove away; she really must find time to write to her boys. The front door opened. "What did those two coppers want?" Andy asked.

"They didn't come here," Em lied, worried in case he had been downstairs and seen them as they left. Damn, she thought, that would have been a good opportunity to tell him about the boys.

"That's good," he said, "we don't want them sniffing round here, it could get us a bad name. Cuppa tea? Oh, you've got one." Em picked up her now cold cuppa and sipped. "I'm due back soon, I'm on late this week covering for Muriel, remember her kids are in Southport, so I'll stay over."

"But you haven't been here for almost three weeks."

"I know, dear, but with staff off sick and you know what, I'll be home as soon as Muriel gets back."

Andy had only been out of the flat fifteen minutes when Em sat down and started to write. 'Dear Walter, I hope you are keeping well. I'm sorry I haven't written for a while but I haven't been well and was unable to go to the Post Office…'

***

"Em's not Irish, is she?" asked Muriel.

"No," Andy answered, "why do you ask?"

"Because I was told I was wanted on the phone, but it was an Irish woman asking for a Muriel O'Connor, not for me."

Andy shrugged his shoulders. "Never mind love, come here my little cockney sparra," he said throwing his arms around her as he pushed the bedroom door shut.

Gillian looked up from her paperwork as she heard Victor's lorry back into the yard. "Mummy," she called out, "can you ask Victor to bring his drink into the lounge, oh, and one for me please."

Ten minutes later Victor walked in carrying two drinks. "Yes, dear?" he asked.

"Would you cast your eyes on these please, dear?"

Victor looked at the figures. "They seem all right to me," he said. "Is there something wrong?"

"There must be, but I can't... wait a moment; yes, I see... there was a crate of Light Ale breakages, but they haven't credited us for it. I'll phone the brewery in the morning." she said triumphantly.

Mavis came into the lounge. "Ready to open, boss," she said, smiling as she spoke. "I saw Colin going down the cellar, I think he wants to speak with you about something."

"I'll have a word with him," said Victor.

"Ahem," Gillian interrupted. "As manager, I think it might be better coming from me, otherwise he might doubt my authority."

"Okay, sorry, love," Victor answered, "you're right, I wasn't thinking."

Gillian came back into the room. "I didn't remember it was so dark down there," she remarked, referring to the cellar. "I've arranged with Colin to work as assistant barman alongside Mavis provided that he still does the cellar work when needed," she said. "I've had a word with Mavis, I think she's okay with that, it'll also mean any time she's away he can help me in the bar."

***

"And he was the perfect gentleman..." Liz was saying.

"Hmm, boring," Sharon murmured.

"You're only jealous," said Shirley.

"Insubordination," Sharon answered.

"I didn't say a thing, did I Charlotte?" asked Shirley, as the friends all chuckled.

Ignoring the comment, Liz continued. "We stopped at a place called Birchington on Sea, in Kent, somewhere near Margate. We stayed in a hotel next to a dairy. No, there were no cows, just horses and milk floats, where they deliver milk from. Then on Sunday we drove along the coast to Broadstairs, it was beautiful... Yes, where Charles Dickens lived... Bleak House, overlooking the harbour; it was very windy and the spray was coming right over the pier... watch out... tell you later." Liz picked up her telephone, as though in conversation, " ...yes, sir, very good, sir."

Regimental Sergeant Major Mitchell had entered the orderly office and approached Sharon's desk. "Which of you young ladies," the RSM looked at the papers in his hand, "is Private Norman? Ah, yes, report to the orderly office... of course you're in the orderly office... Hmm... I'll see you in my office in fifteen minutes," he said, and turning around marched out of the office, leaving four personnel attempting to stifle laughter.

Liz knocked on the door. "Come in and shut the door. Ah, yes," said the RSM, "the Daily Routine Orders." He spoke as he stood up. "I know I normally just put them in the tray, but I also wanted to give you this..." He handed Liz a Stores Requisition Form. "And congratulations, Lance Corporal."

"What... me? But..."

"Yes, you... good girl... now run along."

"Yes, sir, thank you."

Sharon read the paper that Liz had given her. "Congratulations," she said, as the others crowded round to shake Liz's hand. Envious? Yes, but not jealous.

"I suppose the drinks are on you tonight," said Shirley, always quick to accept a drink, but invariably slow coming forward when it was her round.

***

Annabel looked so cosy, so warm as Em laid her in her pram ready for their walk to St John's Street. It wasn't that Em wanted to attend the W.I. meeting on this afternoon; she needed to speak to someone and she thought that Hilda, the minister's wife, who had been so understanding before, would be the best person to speak to. Em gently eased the pram out of the front door, down the steps and turning right, was briskly pushing the pram along the pavement when she saw a familiar looking car heading towards her.

The black and yellow Rolls Royce slowed and stopped beside her. The uniformed chauffeur stepped out and came round the car. "Good afternoon, Em," he said as he opened the passenger door. "Her ladyship would like a word."

"But..."

"Come on inside out of the cold," Lady Jane called, "and bring your daughter with you. James can secure the perambulator on the back." For a moment Em hesitated, then she lifted Annabel out from the pram and carried her into the car; after a short while the Rolls glided away.

***

Herbie was looking out of the library window as he waited for the return of Lady Marbury, who had gone out shortly after lunch. Major General Herbert Phillips's flight back to the States had been brought forward by a month and he had to report at Upminster the day after tomorrow. He considered it would be improper for him to leave without thanking her ladyship for her hospitality. His staff car was standing in the courtyard at the rear of the house ready for him and he was eager to leave before dark. He hadn't heard from Em since his proposal; he had begun to wonder if it had been appropriate, indeed he doubted whether he would hear from her or ever get the chance to speak to her again.

The Rolls glided to a stop beside the step at the front of the house. James opened the passenger door and assisted Lady Jane as she alighted. The major general waited in the hall as Susan opened the door for her ladyship. "Tea for two please, no, make it three," she said as she made her way into the drawing room, followed by Herbie.

James unstrapped the pram and followed Em as she entered the kitchen through the rear entrance. "Oh Em," cried Susan, "how lovely to see you, and she's so beautiful," she added, indicating the child asleep in her mother's arms.

Em gently laid Annabel in the pram, and gave Susan a hug. "You'd better take Lady Jane's tea to her," she said.

***

Freddie sat in the alcove. Walter had been sitting at the table struggling with his homework for almost an hour. Freddie was glad that he didn't have homework, but in a strange way he would have liked it if he had, because it would mean he went to the grammar school like his brother. Secondary modern was okay, he enjoyed doing art and singing, but there was nothing special, not like learning languages and things.

Freddie looked round at the other boys, Derek and Maurice, playing on the floor with their Dinky cars. It was amazing how the pattern on the carpet could be used as roads. I bet the makers never considered that, thought Freddie. Maurice is lucky, he often gets letters and postal orders from his mother, he's even had two letters so far this month, it isn't fair.

At last Walter had finished his homework, and while he put his books back in his satchel, Freddie put his treasured atlas away in his locker. Everything had to be put away before bedtime, and on school days that was seven o'clock for anyone under thirteen years of age.

Grammar school boys' school uniform consisted of white shirts, grey shorts, jerseys and socks, school ties and navy blue blazers and caps. The boys that went to Huntingdon Street School also wore white shirts, grey shorts and socks—more a home boy's uniform, although there wasn't meant to be one—and although there was a green school blazer and cap, it was not compulsory so they never wore them. It was worse for those in the Gordon Boys' Home (founded by General Gordon of Khartoum); they wore a military style uniform and had to march to and from their school, whereas the home boys walked to school in ones and twos.

Huntingdon Street Secondary Modern School, not that there was anything modern about the building, was about a mile from the children's home, a fair distance to walk but not far enough to need a bus ride. Sixpence pocket money didn't go far with a half-penny bus fare to or from school.

For PE the secondary school used the gym in the YMCA. Not one of Freddie's favourite lessons. It was all right for some kids, they seemed to enjoy the exercises and games. He didn't much like football or cricket either; sports meant going by bus to the university sports ground, and either changing at the sports field or, in the winter, travelling there already dressed in football gear. Freddie always found himself standing out on the wing while the ball was being chased around in the middle of the football field, and he was usually the last to be chosen for anyone's team. Mind you, he didn't like what he had heard about rugby, played at the grammar school, it sounded a lot rougher than football.

Chapter Twenty-three

The two of them were sitting in the office with a cup of tea. "It was just a misunderstanding," Susan said, "and Sandra blew her top. She stormed in to her ladyship and was gone. I was left on my own to do everything."

"And when is your baby due?" asked Em.

"I'm not sure," came the reply, "it could be July... or August..." Susan started counting on her fingers, "or maybe September."

"And the father? do you know who he is?"

Susan shrugged her shoulders and burst into tears. "Major Clarkson I think. He's gone back to America, he said he'd take me with him," she replied, almost in tears, "and my dad said I can't go home until I've got rid of it."

Em knocked on the door of the drawing room, and entered, but when she saw Major General Phillips, thinking she had interrupted a private conversation, she hesitated.

"Come in, Em," said Lady Jane, "you two already know each other," then turning to Herbie, "You've met baby Annabel?"

"Oh yes, ma'am, I met her about a month ago." looking at his watch, he continued, "If you ladies will excuse me, I'm due in Salisbury at nineteen hundred hours." He made his way to the door.

Em watched from the window as the grey staff car disappeared down the drive. I don't think I'll ever hear from him again, she thought. What is it about me that drives men away?

"Pour yourself a cup of tea," said her ladyship, "and I'll have another cup while you're at it."

"Would you like a buttered scone?" Em asked as she passed Lady Jane her tea.

"No thank you, dear," she replied. "I don't suppose he propositioned you like he did Sandra?" her ladyship asked. "Mind you, he did tell me a little while ago that he was looking forward to getting back to his farm and his wife and children."

***

Walter glanced at Freddie, who was looking at his blank sheet of writing paper. He was just as fed up as Freddie was. Almost every Sunday they were made to sit down and write to their mother, but why should they? They hadn't heard anything from her apart from a card and a measly book at Christmas. The other boys got better presents from their mums and dads, Peter Baronowitz had that super Meccano set. And what about Dad? Where was he? We've never heard from him. Perhaps the home don't post our letters. Whatever, it will be Easter soon.

"Come on boys," said Sister, "put your things away. Simon, it's your turn to set the tables."

There was a scurry to put pens and writing pads away before Sister realised they hadn't written their letters. Simon scowled. "I only did it… mm, I suppose it's right." He tried to remember the last time he had laid the tables. "My turn seems to come around so quickly," he said as he disappeared into the scullery to collect the tablecloths, cutlery and crockery, while the other boys sat down quietly reading books and comics.

Freddie picked up his *Atlas of the British Isles*. It had cost him a *Dandy Annual*, but he preferred the atlas. He liked maps; he would look to see where explorers and missionaries were from, and he often looked at Chester to see where his mother lived, almost willing her to travel the short distance to Nottingham. On paper it looked so near.

Without any real understanding of time or distance, he would sometimes sit and plan imaginary journeys. On one such occasion Freddie worked out that if he was going to look for his mother, it would be assumed that he would head direct across country going east to west, but to travel north from Nottingham to Barnsley, crossing the Pennines on the A625 Manchester road, he might get all the way without being stopped. If he didn't hear from her soon, he might… well, maybe.

Em was thinking about Lady Jane's request as James drove her back to the flat. The prospect of returning to Moore Hall definitely was attractive, although it would mean any thought of having her boys home would have to wait. The Rolls slowed and stopped outside number forty-one. James carried the pram up the steps and placed it in the hall. "It's been a pleasure seeing you again," he said. "I hope it won't be long before we meet again. Goodnight, miss."

"Where've you been?" came a voice from upstairs, "and who's Roller was that?"

"Wouldn't you like to know? You're jealous," Em teased as she climbed the stairs carrying Annabel. "How is Muriel?"

"Muriel?" came the guarded question.

"Yes," answered Em, "the lady you stand in for while she visits her children in Southport."

"Oh her…" replied Andy.

"Why, are there others?"

"Er… no," Andy answered, shaking his head. "How is our little darling Annabel?" he asked, hastily changing the subject.

"Fine, just fine, aren't you poppet? Fine but hungry, let's get you fed, bathed and into bed. Not you, Andy," she said laughing.

***

The children's home in Nottingham had been a stately home in Alexandra Park called Springfield, a magnificent house once owned by Sir Arthur Black, and donated to the National Children's Home by him in 1935. The house stood in extensive grounds that included huge vegetable gardens, an orchard and a large field, a tennis court, lawns with a formal garden, and a modest open air swimming pool.

Three or four times a year the boys at Huntingdon Street School stayed for school dinners, usually when some charitable organisation visited and stayed for light refreshments. It was on one such occasion that after dinner, instead of remaining in the school premises, Freddie decided it was a good opportunity to go and see if he could find his mother. The weather was fine and dry as he set out at a brisk walking pace, through Carlton and along the road that led to the village of Burton Joyce. Freddie could see that all the turnings on one side of the main road led down to the river, so he left the village and walked along beside the river. Bearing in mind that it was still winter, the footpath was muddy and slippery with puddles in places, as well as uneven ridged areas where motor vehicles had been. Freddie was hurrying; he wanted to be a long way off before anyone realised he was missing, that is assuming the school thought he had gone home.

Trying to hurry meant Freddie wasn't taking care where he put his feet, not that he was running, but even walking with any kind of speed along the footpath made it hazardous. Slipping on the mud and tripping over brambles and clumps of grass brought the risk of falling sideways down the side of the river bank onto the mud or even into the water, which was likely to be extremely cold, even if it was shallow, but that was something that Freddie hadn't even thought about in his hurry to put distance between him and Nottingham.

Making his way carefully past places where the riverbank had collapsed, and keeping his eye on the twists and turns of the river, he could see where the deepest and shallowest sections were, so when he heard any vehicle passing on the nearby road, fearing it might be a police car looking for him, he knew where he could hide behind the river bank without getting wet, or when to lie down in the long grass, hoping not to be spotted.

Freddie had left his raincoat in the school cloakroom, and although the day had started mild and dry, the afternoon gradually turned duller. What had started as a gentle breeze became a cold wind which penetrated the woollen jersey Freddie was wearing. Somehow walking along the river bank started to lose its appeal, and as the daylight started to fade there was more risk of falling into the water. In the near distance Freddie could see a bridge across the river and street lights. He was cold, he was hungry, and it was starting to drizzle. Perhaps if he asked, someone would give him a hot drink, and just maybe, something to eat.

Freddie followed the path under the bridge and up the slope to the road junction. He hurried across the road and around to the back door of the nearest building, nervously reached up, pressed his thumb on the bell push and waited. After what seemed an eternity he pressed the bell push again, this time for a bit longer. Suddenly a light above his head came on, and he heard the sound of a key in the lock. The door opened and a silhouetted figure of a woman stood in the doorway. "Yes? What do you want?" the voice asked.

Freddie almost wanted to run away from the cold harsh voice, but plucking up courage, at the same time unsuccessfully trying to speak without his teeth chattering, he said, "Ppplease miss... cccan I have a dddrink?"

***

Victor had parked his lorry at the side of the road in Huntingdon Street. The waste ground had been fenced off and foundations were being laid ready for workshops for the local secondary school about two hundred yards up the road. February was almost at an end, and he needed to find somewhere to see Liz on her own before she was demobbed and returned home. Victor was driving around looking at potential places, but although there were plenty of pubs and hotels they all seemed quite ordinary, he wanted somewhere special.

Victor looked at his list. 'Mm... the Unicorn at Gunthorpe, I'll give that a try, then call it a day.' Parking his car on open land, he crossed the road and entered the bar. While ordering a drink he realised he hadn't eaten in the last four or five hours; a quick word with the barmaid and he was soon tucking into a ham and cheese sandwich. Pleased with the friendly service, and as it was already quite late and he was in no hurry to return to Nottingham, he booked a room for the night.

While he was reading a copy of the local newspaper, Victor could hear the chatter in the bar. One conversation in particular intrigued him, so he took his drink up to the bar and listened. "I'm puzzled," the barmaid was saying, "It didn't make any sense, just all came out in a jumbled mixture of words." Victor's curiosity was raised. "He said something about going to Chester," the barmaid continued, "but I think he's going the wrong way, I don't know, he was in a right state. I couldn't leave him out there in this weather." She broke off to serve another customer.

When she returned Victor asked, "Where is he now?"

"Upstairs in bed, in the room next to yours," came the reply.

"Where is he from?"

"According to the police he's from the children's home in Alexandra Park—a house called Springfield, I think he said—anyway, I said I'd take him back in the morning, but I forgot, Clive and his missus are taking a coach load of school kids to Lincoln Cathedral tomorrow so I need to be here for the brewery delivery."

"I'll take him back if you like, I've got to get back to Nottingham tomorrow."

"Oh would you? Thanks a bunch. Have another, on the house."

"What's the kid's name?"

"I'm not sure, either Freddie or Teddy, he mumbled it in the middle of a jumble of words and I didn't have the heart to ask him again. He was soaked, shivering and covered in mud, so I put him in the bath and gave him a pair of knickers and a dressing gown while I put his clothes in the washing machine. Er, excuse me one moment." Then she rang the bell. "Time, gentlemen, please!" she called out. "You're in room five," she said, handing him the key. "It overlooks the river. Goodnight, sir, sleep well."

Chapter Twenty-four

"What's your name, kid?"

"I'm not a kid, that's a goat, I'm a boy, and my name is Freddie," came the reply.

"Okay, Freddie, what is your surname?" asked Victor, as he settled into the driver's seat and turned on the ignition.

"Summers," answered Freddie, continuing, somewhat to Victor's surprise. "My father is an engineer and my mother lives in Chester." Then, turning to face Victor he asked, "Can this car go fast?"

"Yes, it can do more than sixty miles an hour," Victor replied.

"Cor, but I bet it can't go as fast as the Bluebird."

"Well, no," replied Victor, "the Bluebird was specially designed for speed."

As they drove out of the car park, instead of turning right to Lowdham, the shortest route to Nottingham, Victor turned the car left and crossed the bridge, driving past East Bridgford to join the Fosse Way, the A 46. "Would you like a treat, Freddie?" Victor asked.

Freddie looked puzzled. "Well, yes," he answered, almost a question of but what?

"Then hold tight," said Victor as he changed gear then gently but firmly pressed his right foot down on the accelerator pedal. The Hornet rapidly picked up speed with a roar of delight, thirty, forty, the needle climbed, fifty then sixty as the little car ate up the miles. Victor eased the pressure on the pedal as the speedometer climbed up past sixty five and stayed for a short while on seventy, then gently slowed the car down to forty miles per hour before he turned it round and returned to driving within the speed limit.

Driving back down Fosse Way and passing the junction to Lowdham, they continued until they reached Saxondale where Victor turned off and drove past the Trent Bridge Cricket Ground, over the bridge and through the centre of the city, eventually arriving at the children's home just before eleven. Before they got out of the car Victor reached into his pocket and took out a florin. "I want you to share that with your twin Walter," he said, "and if you're good, with no more running away, I'll take you for a drive to somewhere nice next year when I'm in Nottingham."

"How did you know I had a twin?" Freddie asked, just as Sister opened the door.

"Go and change out of your school things," she said to Freddie; then turning to Victor, "Thank you for bringing him back. Would you like to come in, I'm sure Mr Smith would like to thank you personally, and please join us for a cup of tea. That's the least we can offer you, Mr... er?"

"Bradburn, Sister, but please call me Victor."

***

In 1946 the weather at the start of March bore no resemblance to the old folklore adage that says 'When March comes in like a lion it goes out like a lamb'. If anything it seemed confusing, rain and sunshine, strong winds and gentle breezes making it hard to decide lion or lamb, but what March did bring was masses of paperwork for the ATS girls in the orderly office, especially discharge papers for servicemen coming back from overseas.

"It's no good moaning about it, Shirley," said Sharon, "the War Office doesn't operate a ladies first principle when it comes to the question of demobs."

"Anyway Shirley ain't no lady" murmured Charlotte. Shirley gave Charlotte such a glare that if looks could kill, Sharon and Liz would have lost a friend and colleague.

"Pack it up, you two," Sharon rapped out, "we've got all these discharge papers to finish before twelve and another batch this afternoon."

The office door opened with a bang against the wall. "What the..." Sharon had looked up and stopped mid sentence. Captain Smythe was standing in the doorway, supported by two crutches. "Charlotte, a chair for the captain," said Sharon. "Liz, rustle up a cuppa tea please."

"Thank you," the officer said as she settled down beside a desk near the door, "and two sugars please, Lance Corporal."

"Yes, Captain," Liz replied.

"What I've come for is a travel pass, the MO has okayed me going on sick leave. Oh yes, and a leave pass, Sharon, if someone would take it and get the MO to sign it."

There was a knock on the door and two soldiers entered the office. "Excuse me ma'am," the first one said, "I was told to go to the orderly office and collect..."

Before he finished, Captain Smythe, momentarily thinking she was in her own office, interrupted him, "The orderly office is two blocks down on the right."

The two men hesitated, then left looking slightly puzzled, only to come back ten minutes later. "But on the door it says..."

"Sorry, lads," said the captain, "I thought I was still in my own office."

The requisition book duly signed, Sharon handed over the package addressed to the RSM and the two men left. Almost as soon as the door was closed Captain Smythe and the four ATS other ranks looked at each other and fell about laughing. "Sh, not too loud," said Sharon.

***

Em lay in her bed. She could hear the wind rattling her window and at this time of year, it was terribly cold in the mornings until the living room fire was lit, something that Andy had usually done before Em got up, but he hadn't spent a night in the flat since just before Christmas, almost three months ago. His excuses, for she felt they were excuses, had seemed reasonable at first, but were wearing a bit thin. Not only did she feel cold, she felt lonely, maybe even deserted. Lady Jane's offer had grown more tempting as the days passed, but then, what to do with the flat, or with the furniture?

The front door opened. "I'm home," a cheery voice called out. "What, still in bed? Brrr it's cold in here, I'll light the fire and make you a hot drink. Toast and marmalade?" the voice continued over the sound of fire making. "I know what you need, a nice hot bowl of porridge."

Tears formed in Em's eyes. You just don't understand, she thought, what I need is company. George, or if not, then anyone who really cares. She wiped her tears away on the bed sheet because it was nearer than her hanky and she didn't want Andy to see her crying.

Em got out of bed, dressed quickly and lit the gas ring to warm some baby food for Annabel. Lifting her daughter out from the cot, she wrapped her in a blanket to keep her warm while she held her close, sat in front of the fire and fed her. "Thank you, dear," she said to Andy when he brought her the promised cup of tea. "I'll make myself some toast when I've dealt with Annabel."

"It's all right, love," he replied, "just say when, and I'll have it ready in no time."

"How was work?" Em asked.

"Hmm, not too bad," he replied. "They're allowing late shift to sleep at the hotel after we've finished."

"But what about me?" asked Em. "I need you here."

"But—"

"It's lonely here without you. Oh, I know you think I'm moaning but at Moore Hall I had company, it was always warm."

"If that's all you want—"

"You don't understand—"

"No," he said as he made towards the door.

"Very well then," she said, "I'll tell the landlord I'm leaving."

"You can't," he countered, "what about me?"

"What's stopping you moving into the hotel with Muriel?" Em burst out, almost regretting saying it.

"Okay," he said more calmly. "If you decide to go back to Moore Hall, let me take on the flat."

"And the furniture? It cost me over sixty pounds."

Andy nodded. "No problem".

"I'll have to think about it," Em said.

"Stay where you are and I'll do you some tea and toast," he said, disappearing into the kitchen.

***

Retirement accommodation was in very short supply due to the amount of damage experienced in Manchester and Warrington during the bombing in the earlier years of the war. The Red Lion being under new ownership, and the accommodation required by the new owners, Mr Bradburn and his family, meant that Mr and Mrs Woodley, the former licensees, needed somewhere to live and so, on March the first, with the help of Victor and his lorry, not forgetting the assistance of Colin the cellar man, they moved into number 6 Vicarage Gardens, a two bedroom cottage just a quarter of a mile from the Red Lion and three doors past the church. The back garden had a small well cultivated vegetable plot, with onions and spring greens planted during the autumn ready for use middle to late spring, and cloche pots upturned over rhubarb roots, with the promise of a good crop later in the year. While the others were occupied with the business of moving and placing the furniture where Mrs Woodley wanted it, then moving it again each time she changed her mind, Mr Woodley sat in the bar beside the inglenook, enjoying the warmth of the fire and being waited on by Mavis.

***

"Private who? There is a Lance Corporal Norman in the camp, Elizabeth Norman." Sharon tried not to laugh as she was pretending not to recognize the voice at the other end of the line. "I'm sorry, she appears to be absent from her desk... I'll ask her to call when she returns... Maybe five or ten minutes... What number? Thank you." Sharon put the receiver down and smiled as she turned her mind back to the pile of forms on her desk.

Damn, thought Victor, I suppose I'd better stay in the kiosk to stop anyone else in case it's in use when she tries to phone.

Dring dring, dring dring. The phone made Victor jump, the sound surprised him, he had been daydreaming about a pleasant few days beside the River Trent.

"Hello... Yes, is that you, Liz? I was told... Well, congratulations, Lance Corporal. Anyway, when can you get away? Week on Friday... See you then... Oh, okay *this* Saturday evening at the Railway Hotel, see you about... seven... okay... Love you too, byeee." Victor held the kiosk open for a lady who had been waiting a short while to use the telephone, joyfully anticipating those pleasant few days with Liz.

***

For the last fortnight Andy had shown more consideration and paid a lot more attention to Em and Annabel, helping in the home, being around more when he wasn't working and bringing home the occasional small treat. One afternoon however, Em had left to attend a Women's Institute meeting at the Wesleyan Chapel, but upon arriving there realised she had got the date mixed up and the premises were closed. Disappointed, she returned home to find Muriel looking around the flat. Andy said that Muriel had offered to do the cleaning and she wanted to see how big the flat was. He may have thought he was fooling Em, but the implication that she was not keeping the flat clean was quite insulting, and increased her inclination to follow up on the offer from Lady Jane, while lessening her willingness to allow Andy and Muriel to take over the flat.

Em spent many hours sitting on the chaise longue gazing out of the window watching the world go by, or reading stories like *Pride and Prejudice*, *Wuthering Heights*, *Little Women* and *Great Expectations*; she found books by Dickens were more difficult to read than the Bronte sisters, Jane Austen and Louisa Alcott. Sometimes she thought about Herbie Phillips and his proposal. Over the time she had known him, she had trusted him as an honest and upright man, forgetting Lady Jane's last words about a farm and family, and believing that he had only approached Sandra because Em hadn't accepted his offer to join him in America straight away. She knew she would jump at the chance if he asked again. It would therefore make sense to accept Lady Jane's offer, get rid of the flat and furniture and be free to join Herbie in Texas at a moment's notice.

"I've had a word with Mr Higginbottom, he's agreed to let you take over the tenancy, but he wants a month's rent in advance as a deposit… good luck."

Andy hesitated, then almost begrudgingly handed Em six large white five pound notes and thirty scruffy looking one pound notes for the furniture, and she handed over her keys. "I'm ready now, James," she said as she followed her ladyship's chauffeur down the stairs.

Chapter Twenty-five

"What on earth are you on about?" asked Victor. "It might be my name over the door, but you are the Manager."

"It's the tax man," Gillian replied. "They want a list of staff and wages, and they want tax forms for everyone who has worked for us in the last six years."

"That's easy, we have only been employers since I took over the licence," he answered, "so it's just you three."

"What about you?" she asked. "As licensee they would expect you to be on the payroll."

"But I'm only the licensee by name."

Gillian shook her head in frustration. "Okay," she said. "Leave it with me. You always do. I'll sort something out. Oh, and while we're about it, I could do with some help around the house." Gillian looked up; there was no sign of his lordship. I suppose I could employ a nanny. "Ah, Mavis," Gillian called out, "keep an eye on the children for me while I go to the paper shop. On second thoughts, do you know of any girl who would make a good nanny?"

"Hmm, no, but there's Mrs Fisher, she used to be a school teacher, she was great with the kids, would you like me to nip out and ask 'er? It'd only take a coupla minutes."

***

"Are you all right about it, Susan?" asked Em. "The last thing I want you to think is that I'm pushing you out."

"It's okay," Susan replied, "I'm finding it difficult to cope these days, and I'm glad to have company with someone who must know how I feel. Goodness knows how you managed when you were expecting."

"Well, I had you two to do all the heavy stuff, whereas you've had it all to do on your own."

"Let me welcome you back with a cup of your favourite tea," Susan said, "oh yes, a dash of milk but no sugar."

Whilst Susan was boiling the water, Em put two chairs in the office.

"Two chairs?" asked Susan.

"Yes," replied Em, "in this kitchen we are both chief cooks, you're boss today, tomorrow it'll be my turn." They raised and touched their cups together with a slight 'chink.'

"As you wish, Boss," said Susan and they both laughed.

***

"Happy birthday to you, happy birth..." the girls were singing.

"Sh..." interrupted Sharon, "I don't want anyone to hear, or I'll be expected to stand drinks for *all* the corporal's mess."

"It'll cost ya," muttered Shirley.

"Come off it, Shirl'," said Charlotte, "she's taking us out on Saturday."

"Oops, I forgot, I've made arrangements," Liz was saying.

"Oohoo," chorused the others.

"Never mind, bring him along," said Sharon, "the more the merrier."

"So long as it's not all the corporals," Shirley chipped in. "Anyway what's so special about your birthday?"

"It'll mean I've only got another six months before I'm demobbed."

"Six months?" joked Charlotte. "Do you mean...?"

"Her?" Shirley broke in. "Who would ...?"

"Watch it, Private," said Sharon.

"Yes, Corporal," Shirley replied laughing. The sound of typewriters once more filled the air as the four ATS girls turned back to the paperwork awaiting their attention.

Sharon pushed her typewriter away from her. Discharge, she thought, discharge... I wonder... Walking into Second Lieutenant Carver's empty office and taking the keys from the desk, she unlocked and opened the personnel file. 'Let me see… ah, ATS… Charlotte Cooper… not yet; Shirley Morrison… August; Elizabeth Norman… interesting, hmm… she must have joined up earlier than I thought.' Sharon quickly put the files back in the drawer and without forgetting to lock it, returned the keys to the desk drawer then went back to her desk.

The hour hand on the wall clock was almost pointing to five, and finally moved there as the minute hand reached twelve. Chairs scraped on the floor as the occupants stood up to head through the office door. Three voices in unison whispered, "Happy birthday, Sharon."

"Oh, Liz," said Sharon, "can you spare a minute?"

"I'll catch you up," Liz told the others.

"How old are you?" Sharon asked.

"Why?"

"Because I've a feeling it'll be your birthday soon," she answered.

"May the first," said Liz, "the original May blossom. I think I know what you're thinking, I must have said I was eighteen when I joined up, 'cos I'm due for discharge this May, when I'm twenty."

***

"I don't feel I can stay here after Bradshore took the Warrington depot," Victor was saying. "If I can get a place more central, like Derby or Nottingham, I won't have to drive past my old depot."

"But dear, we've only just got going here, and wherever it is you want to settle is going to be a long way from my mummy and daddy, and you know how much she likes to see the kids."

"How often does she see them now, once or twice a month? We won't be that far away from them, maybe a couple of hours in the car."

"I suppose you know what you're doing, but I wouldn't say anything to them yet."

"Say what to them yet?" Mrs Woodley asked, coming in the door. "What are you two planning?"

"We thought you might like a dog," said Victor, thinking fast. "It might help get Dad back on his feet."

"Naw, he'd need a stick o' dynamite to get 'im out of 'is chair," retorted Mrs Woodley. "Anyway a young dog would wee and poo all over the place, and guess who would have to clean up after it, no thanks!"

Victor could see the look of relief on his wife's face, her mother had obviously not heard what they were talking about. "Well, Mummy, what brings you here?" she asked.

"Can't I come and see my daughter and grandchildren? Or do I need an appointment?"

"Of course you're always welcome, Mother dear," said Victor.

Mrs Woodley gave him her stern if-looks-could-kill glare. "That's enough of your cheek, young man," she said.

"Now what have I said?" he asked as he walked towards the door.

"Don't forget to phone me tonight," Gillian called out.

"Trunk calls aren't cheap," he replied.

"They are for elephants," he heard his mother-in-law say.

Now where did she get that from? he wondered, repeating her words. Hmm, probably from the *Dandy* or *Beano*.

***

Class 1d filed up the stairs to the second floor where Mr McClennan's classroom was. It was the last lesson that day, and being Friday, the last lesson of the week. Music was Freddie's favourite lesson, he enjoyed singing. At Huntingdon Street School there were two music teachers, Mr Keys, the assistant head whose liking was classical music, and Mr McClennan who, being Irish, liked traditional music. Although Mr Keys was the 1d form teacher, on Fridays he took 2a for music while Mr McClennan took 1d. The lesson always commenced with singing the scale. Mr McClennan would say, "The tune might not be much, but the words are easy, sing 'La la la'." After about ten minutes, they opened up the Community Song Books, and started what Freddie liked best, the singing. *Down yonder green valley... (The Ash Grove)* then *Annie Laurie, Sweet Lass of Richmond Hill* and *The Lincolnshire Poacher*. For Freddie the lesson was finished all too soon, with the rendering of Mr

McClennan's favourite, the *Londonderry Air*, the same tune as *Danny Boy* but different words. He was only satisfied if the class hit the top note loud and clear, then and only then would he dismiss them.

***

"All right, ladies," said Victor. "Name your poison."

"I'll have a…" Shirley was saying.

"Yes miss?" asked the waiter.

"…a pint," she continued.

"And six straws," chipped in Charlotte.

"Six? There's only five of us, who's the sixth?" asked Sharon.

"The gorgeous waiter, of course. Don't tell me you don't fancy him, you've had your eye on him ever since we started coming here," answered Charlotte.

"Shh…" said Sharon.

"Ladies, please, can I have your orders," the waiter said, "there are others waiting."

"Serve the others while they make up their minds," Victor suggested.

Finally, with drinks ordered, the talk turned to what they might do over the Easter weekend in two weeks' time. Sharon suggested the four ATS girls might book in together somewhere for the Saturday and Sunday nights. Shirley and Charlotte agreed. Liz however remarked that she would already be on leave. When Sharon had showed no signs of surprise the other two girls looked at her, then at Victor. "You knew?"

Sharon nodded, while Victor said, "No… it's news to me."

"In that case, Liz," said Shirley, "the next round is on you."

"No," Victor put in valiantly, "I'll cover Liz's turn," as he summoned the waiter. While the others were chatting Victor leaned over to Liz and whispered, "Are you free tonight?" When she said that she was free until Sunday night, he suggested they went off somewhere else.

"See you, girls," said Liz as they were leaving.

"Where are you two off to?" asked Shirley.

"Don't be nosey," said Sharon as Victor and Liz made their getaway.

"I've nothing with me," Liz said.

"You don't need anything, not where we're going, I've got enough toiletries in my overnight case," he replied, as he reached into the cab of the lorry.

"We're not going in that, are we?"

"No, I just wanted the case," he answered as they headed towards the car.

Ten minutes of driving and they headed out from the city into a dark country lane, finally drawing up outside a public house. "Where are we?" Liz asked.

"A little place well off the beaten track," he said. "Somewhere I happened to come across. I thought you'd like it." He opened the passenger door. "Come on, let's go in."

They mounted the steps and entered the public bar. "Oh, hullo," said the barmaid.

"Have you a room at the front please?" Victor asked.

"Yes," she answered, "how many nights?"

"Just the one, room at the front, please, thank you, oh, menu please."

"Sorry, sir, the kitchen is closed, but I could rustle you up something. Egg and chips okay, sir, madam? Drinks?"

"This is all very nice, but," Liz asked, "where are we?"

"Gunthorpe," Victor answered, "just a stone's throw out of town."

"I thought I heard water when we arrived."

"Yes, dear," he said, "we're near the river."

Conversation stopped for a moment while the barmaid served two steaming plates of fish and chips. "I've saved the eggs for breakfast, I hope you don't mind. It's locally caught trout," she said.

"Hmm, it looks almost too nice to eat," Victor replied as he squeezed the lemon slices over the fish.

"Excuse me, but aren't you the man who took that boy back to the Children's Home? How did you get on? The poor lad was soaked and frozen," the barmaid said, more to Liz than Victor.

"Yes, he told me," Liz answered.

"It was freezing that night, he could have died if he hadn't knocked on the door. He didn't say much when he arrived."

"Oh yes," Victor said, "he was okay once he was in the car. He'd reckoned on walking to Chester to find his mother, it seems he's got a twin brother. Yes, the home seems a very nice place, he was just welcomed back, I don't know whether he was punished, but the staff seemed very kind."

Chatter, food and drinks finished, the tired couple climbed the stairs and went to their room. Victor handed Liz the key. "After you, my dear," he said. Liz put the key in the lock, turned it and slowly opened the door, switched on the light and peeping round the door, turned round and kissed him.

"Oh, darling, it's beautiful," she said.

As they entered the room, he headed towards the ensuite bathroom. "I could do with a shower."

"Why don't we share a bath, that'd be more fun," Liz suggested, "just don't make it too hot."

Chapter Twenty-six

Em woke up with a start. She was back in her old room in Moore Hall. She lay looking up at the ceiling; had she dreamt that she had lived in Chester, or was this all a dream, it seemed so real yet so confusing. She heard a young child cry; wearing only her nightdress, she went out onto the landing and followed the sound into the next room. "Come to Mummy, my cherub," she said as she picked up her daughter, and holding her close returned to her bedroom, where she laid Annabel on her bed while she got dressed.

Em knew it was not going to be easy working and looking after a nine-month-old toddler at the same time, but she was determined to keep Annabel with her. Lady Jane had said she would get a nanny for Delilah's baby and Annabel, but as Delilah's baby was not yet due, a nanny had not been taken on.

"Thank you, but I have asked Taylors to provide everything for the wedding reception," her ladyship was saying, "including the marquee, furniture and catering. They will also provide the waitresses, so I've asked their Mrs White to liaise with you. She should be phoning you to arrange a meeting. Where is your daughter, Annabel?"

"I've asked Agnes if she would have Annabel for a short while in the mornings after she's finished her cleaning."

"Perhaps you might like to use the nursery?" Lady Jane asked.

"Thank you," said Em. "It's going to need reorganizing anyway. I'll ask Agnes and James to look at what will be needed."

James and Agnes seemed an odd couple. He was in his mid to late thirties, and she about twenty or so years older. Widowed in 1916, her only child, a daughter, and her husband, having served with the army in Singapore, now lived in Lincoln. The relationship between James and

Agnes was more like mother and son than husband and wife, which resulted in occasional periods of friction.

The removal of things like the toy fort and lead soldiers, the rocking horse and the pedal car, then the washing of walls, floor and furniture took almost two days, during which time either Agnes or Susan would be looking after Annabel in the lounge. From time to time James would appear for the inevitable cup of tea, but any attempt by Em to enter the nursery during the two days was strongly repelled. Eventually she was invited to make an inspection and to approve the nursery as ready for occupancy.

Lady Jane mounted the stairs, followed by Em carrying Annabel. James handed the nursery door key to her ladyship, who in turn passed it to Em. Shaking her head, Em said that Lady Jane should be the one and gave the key back to Lady Jane, who opened the door and the group entered the room. The walls were all painted with characters from *Snow White and the Seven Dwarfs*, with birds and animals on all four walls, and there were cushions and soft furnishing everywhere in the room. "It's beautiful," exclaimed Em, "absolutely beautiful."

"He may not be a Michelangelo, but he certainly can paint," Agnes said.

"Thank you, James and Agnes," said Lady Jane.

***

"Two large cases, a box of books, a kitbag and a shoulder bag, anything else?" asked Victor looking round expectantly.

"That's all, darling," Liz said.

"Just as well," replied Victor, "otherwise you'd be sitting in my lap in the car."

"Ooh, yes please," Liz answered.

"Not while I'm driving," he said, laughing.

"Where to?" Victor asked, as he started up the car. "Home? Or holiday?"

"I think I'd like to go home and get rid of all this luggage," Liz replied, "then perhaps a few days away, but you still have a business to run, and we, er, you can't afford to let that go."

Maybe Victor hadn't heard Liz's reference to 'we'. If he had, he didn't say anything, his mind was on his driving and where they could spend a few days somewhere quiet, where they could relax in solitude. Perhaps they could buy a tent. No, not very comfortable, anyway they'd need a lot of other equipment as well. Or hire a caravan… or stay on a farm… "Do you like cows?" he asked.

"Cowes, you mean on the Isle of Wight? That would be nice. Can we?" Liz answered excitedly. That settled it, overnight at Chingford then off in the morning to the Isle of Wight.

***

Em gently laid the cake onto the board on the kitchen table alongside the other layer. Without the surplus stores left behind when the Americans had closed the convalescent home, there would hardly have been enough to bake one decent sized cake, let alone a second tier. Susan carefully measured out the ingredients ready to make the thin layer of marzipan, sufficient to cover the two cakes, making them ready for Em to work her wizardry with the royal icing, not that she would be doing it all. Susan had shown her own skill in making beautiful arches and miniature roses which were to be used to decorate the cake.

The bell on the wall rang. Em glanced at the board, quickly wiped the flour from her hands and headed for the door, she didn't want to keep Lady Jane waiting. The doorbell echoed through the hall. "Answer that please, Susan," Em called out as she crossed the hall and entered the drawing room.

"Who's that at the door?" asked her ladyship.

Before Em had time to turn, the Reverend Mudford burst through the door. "You can't let your niece marry some idiot just because he's a military officer and wears a medal…"

"*Sit down,* Gerald." Lady Jane was furious. "How dare you burst in on a private conversation between my staff and myself."

"But—"

"No buts. Just go and wait in—"

There was a knock on the door and Susan entered. "His Grace the Right Reverend Douglas Crick, Bishop of Chester," she announced, then retreated.

Reverend Mudford looked confused and almost embarrassed as Em took his arm and guided him past the bishop and out into the hall. Em nodded courteously to His Grace as she passed, then turning to her ladyship, asked, "Tea, madam?"

"Who the... He..." Reverend Mudford spluttered as he sat down. Em went into the kitchen; if she knew, she wasn't going to say.

"Jane," the bishop said as he crossed the room.

"Your Grace," Lady Jane replied as she took his hand.

"Come now," he said "you've known me long enough to call me Douglas. Let me see, it was in the days of the Liverpool Seamen's Mission. Hmm, that was a long time ago when I took over the chaplaincy."

A knock on the door and Em wheeled in a well laden tea trolley. "Would you please, Em?" asked her ladyship.

"How would you like your tea or coffee, Your Grace?"

"Coffee? Real coffee?"

"Yes, sir."

"With cream?" he asked hopefully.

"Yes, sir," Em answered as she poured from the cafetiere. "Madam," Em said as she served her ladyship with her tea, then curtsied and left the room.

***

Gillian crossed another day off the calendar, it was now two weeks since Victor had mentioned the idea of moving to Derby, or was it Nottingham? He always managed to bring something up when she was busiest and not able to give it full attention. It was not surprising that she hadn't understood what the garage in Warrington had to do with him wanting to move away, but she was prepared to move to the other end of the world so long as it kept the family together. Well, maybe not quite that far, as she would like to be near enough to visit her mother and father from time to time. She sat at the table with the account books spread out in front of her. She had grown up in the pub; her dad had been the landlord since she was a four year old. He had often sat there, with paperwork strewn over the table, when she would climb on his lap to give him a good night kiss. Now as she sat in the same chair she dreamt of the day when she would be sitting in a sunlit garden in front of a little cottage somewhere in the country… Then, seeing the paperwork in front of her, she would say, "Dream on," as she picked up her pen, hoping that Victor really was planning to share that dream.

***

Susan looked up at Em. "Are you expecting a delivery? I think there's someone at the door," she said as she wiped her hands on her apron and headed for the back door. There were two ladies standing there.

"Good morning, is Mrs Summers available, please?" the older lady asked.

"Come in, please. Who shall I say?"

"Mrs White of Taylor's Catering."

"Visitors for you, Em," Susan said as she walked into the kitchen, followed by the two ladies.

"Tea or coffee, ladies?" Em asked, as she led them into her office.

"Tea would be very nice, thank you, Mrs Summers. I'm Marjorie White of Taylor's Catering, and this is Miss Baker, my right hand, er, girl," the older lady continued. "Her ladyship asked me to contact you prior to the wedding."

"I'm pleased to meet you," said Em, proffering her hand. "Please call me Em."

"Thank you," replied Mrs White, "you can call me Marjorie, and this is Veronica."

Em hesitated for a moment. Veronica Baker? No… surely not… it couldn't be. She dismissed the thought from her mind, as Susan entered the office carrying the tea tray which she set down on the desk. "Oh, would you see to her ladyship's morning tea, please, Susan," Em said. After a few more preliminaries, they started discussing arrangements for the forthcoming wedding.

From time to time while preparing the lunch, Susan would glance up at the three in conference, particularly Veronica; she looked kind of familiar, but Susan couldn't think where she had seen her before.

"You will join us for lunch, ladies?" asked Em.

"We would be delighted," replied Marjorie, glancing at her colleague who nodded in agreement.

"In the meantime," said Em, "I'll take you to meet her ladyship. We won't be long, Susan."

Susan looked up as they walked past. That face, she thought, Veronica could easily be Em's daughter.

"Oh, Em, is the Reverend Mudford still waiting?" asked Lady Jane. "I so enjoyed talking to Bishop Douglas that I had completely forgotten about him, poor fellow."

"I'm sorry, but I haven't seen him," replied Em, "I think he must have left while you were talking to the bishop."

"Maybe it's just as well. He hasn't been invited, anyway, and he's made himself unpopular down in Portsmouth with unjustified criticism of Bishop Lovett's schools, as well as his womanising," Lady Jane replied, then turning to Marjorie, "You are evidently acquainted with my housekeeper? Good, then it's just a matter of the formalities," her ladyship continued. "If you liaise with Em and work with members of my ground staff, I'm sure we'll have a successful and enjoyable day."

***

Victor looked at the notice, then at Liz. "Oh well," he said, "I suppose we should have booked, but then we didn't expect one of the ferries to be undergoing major repairs during what must be one of their busiest periods! Never mind, let's find a café and get something to eat, then we'll look at the map and decide where next."

Liz had proved to be a good navigator, and her skills came in useful as they wound their way westward out from Southampton, then into the outskirts of Lymington and along the seafront. "How about there?" Liz asked. "The Mayflower looks quite a nice place, and it is overlooking the beach."

"Okay, let's try them," Victor replied, pulling up outside the hotel.

"Yes, sir," said the receptionist, "we have a room available until Saturday, then we are fully booked… Yes, it is at the front… overlooking the beach, you should be able to see some of the yachts practising for the Round the Island Race in August – it will be the first one since the war. What name, sir? If you would just sign here, thank you. It's room three," she said as she handed him the keys. "Dinner is at seven, have a pleasant stay."

Chapter Twenty-seven

Life at Moore Hall was getting busy. Em had taken on three extra staff to help with the preparation for expected visitors for whom accommodation was being provided. The three girls, Esther, Ruth and Rebecca, were seated at the kitchen table getting to know each other over afternoon tea.

"I've had a word with Lady Violet," Lady Jane was saying. "Delilah and her bridesmaids will be staying at Daresbury Hall on the night prior to the wedding, but the girls will be sleeping here after the reception. I believe there will be six of them, although knowing Delilah..." Em and Susan were sitting in the drawing room, discussing the guest list with her ladyship.

"I'll put them in three rooms in the west wing," said Em. "We've three or four folding beds left behind by the Americans, if needs be we can set them up. I'm sure they won't mind sharing. Come to think of it, we can always use the nursery for one or two nights."

With the lists of overnight guests, those invited to stay longer and dietary plans, Em and Susan made their way to the kitchen. Esther and Rebecca were sitting at the table, looking through Em's cookery books, while Ruth could be heard busy in the scullery. "Tonight," said Em, "get a good night's sleep, because tomorrow we start getting the rooms ready for the guests, so an early start in the morning, with a good breakfast at seven. After dinner we will have a chinwag about how we will work together."

With just four days left before the house guests were expected to arrive, it was all hands on deck. Working with Em in pairs, three rooms were cleaned and ready on the first day, which meant that all eight rooms should be ready with time to spare, even with Em breaking off from time to time to help Susan with the preparation of meals in the kitchen, and occasionally looking in on Annabel, who was spending the days in the nursery with Agnes.

"Hmm, your muscles feel really tense," said Agnes. "Sit still, let me see if I can…" she was saying as her fingers started to move gently but firmly around Em's shoulders.

"Ooh, that's lovely," Em said, "I could do with that more often."

"I don't know," replied Agnes. "James is the one with magic hands, he would make a really good masseur. I'll send him round."

"Oh, I'm not sure…" said Em.

"Oh, he's all right, he won't mind."

Harry Rock in his old Ford car was the first to arrive, greeting Em like an old friend. A day ahead of schedule but with most of the rooms ready it was no problem. Charlton was not far behind. He seemed surprised to receive Em's usual polite and friendly welcome. Then some of the other guests seemed to arrive in quick succession. Cynthia had again come without Nigel. "I haven't seen or heard anything of him since the lily-livered toad went to Canada," she announced. William and Brenda Pilkington and Marjorie Dawes all appeared later that evening, having been met at Warrington Station by James.

Next morning, the day before the wedding, Charles arrived, driven by his batman, Alfred, just ten minutes ahead of the Bishop of Chester driving himself in a little Morris Eight. After taking Charles's luggage up to his room, Alfred offered to take the bishop's case up. "It is very kind of you," the bishop said as Ruth showed them up to the Stuart suite.

Sitting in her office, Em glanced at the list. Good, she thought, everyone accounted for. The telephone rang. "Answer that please, Susan."

"It's Reverend Mudford," Susan said, holding her hand over the receiver. "He's asking for Em."

"Ask him what he wants."

"He's insisting on speaking to Em."

Em took the telephone from Susan. "Mrs Summers speaking, who am I speaking to? Ah, Reverend Mudford… you wouldn't want me to call you Gerald, so please don't call me Em. As housekeeper I am Mrs

Summers, just as you like to be respectfully addressed as Reverend Mudford, and I expect my colleagues to be treated with respect too, *not* just brushed aside as a nothing. Apology accepted, now what can I do for you? No, that is not possible without her ladyship's instruction, and anyway all the rooms have been allocated and occupied. No, I'm sorry, sir, that is outside my jurisdiction, only those invited will be welcome at the ceremony, and at the reception." When Em finished speaking she put the receiver on the rest.

"Em," said Susan, "you were amazing."

***

Em stirred as a gentle breeze momentarily parted the bedroom curtains and a slender beam of sunlight flashed across the room. A perfect day for the wedding, she thought. Suddenly she was awake; she gave the clock the shortest of looks, there would be a lot that still needed her attention. Dressed and reaching for a clean house coat, she was surprised by a knock on the door. Susan had brought an early morning cup of tea. "Oh, thank you, dear," said Em, "I was just coming down. As you've brought it up, I'll be down after I've drunk it." From her window she could see the big marquee, almost ready for the reception. The organisers had gone to a lot of trouble to ensure an enjoyable day for the happy couple and their guests.

Her ladyship had breakfast in her room as usual. Breakfast buffet style for eight guests in the dining room wasn't a problem, nor was providing refreshments for the few workmen finishing the preparations in the marquee. Alfred, Charles's batman, would be eating with the staff in the kitchen. Although Em preferred the staff to eat together, the practical aspect of getting the bedrooms done so that the girls would be free to attend the wedding, meant staggering the workload, attending to rooms being vacated as soon as they were free, and the others later in the day. Lunch was again served buffet style, unusual for the household where all meals, except breakfast, were normally served at the table. Today there was a selection of cold meats and salad.

"James will take His Grace and myself to the church," Lady Jane was saying to Charles, "and if Charlton drives you to the church in the Wolseley, he will be able to bring the bridesmaids and any of Delilah's friends that need a lift back afterwards."

"What about Harry, he's got to be there in good time if he's giving Delilah away."

"He'll be using his car."

"But," Charles replied, "he's got a problem, the generator or something has packed up."

"Then he can travel with you and Charlton."

"Alfred has offered to take anyone who would like to go to the service, and bring you back afterwards," Em said. "He will be taking me, Susan has offered to hold the fort, so let me know, and be ready by two."

The bell on the wall rang, the indicator panel lit up for Charles's room. Em quickly ascended the stairs, knocked on the door and entered. Charles was bending over, watching Charlton who was on his knees rummaging around under the edge of the bed, with his rear end towards the door.

Em thought, what a target, almost begging for a boot, smiling to herself. "Yes, sir?" she asked.

"We've lost a collar stud, or rather Charlton has," replied Charles.

Em walked across to the dressing table and opening a box from the top drawer gave Charles another stud. Quietly chuckling she headed back to the kitchen. "Men!" she said, shaking her head.

One by one the cars left for the church, Charlton driving the Wolseley carrying Charles and Harry Rock, James in the Rolls with Lady Jane and the bishop; Cynthia followed in her car shortly after with Marjorie, Brenda and William, while Alfred drove the staff car carrying Em and the three girls. Susan stayed with Agnes and Annabel.

Word that His Grace the Bishop of Chester was taking the service had drawn quite a large crowd from the neighbouring villages, and the pews not allocated to the wedding party were already filled by the time Em and the girls arrived, whilst outside there were quite a few onlookers.

Click, click, click, the official photographer was having to move members of the public and guests aside, as they were trying to get snapshots with their own cameras of the happy couple with the bishop standing in the church doorway. Eventually the photographer felt he had enough photographs of the wedding party and family at the church, and loading his equipment into his car, headed back to Moore Hall while the public dispersed. The bride and groom led the way in the Rolls Royce, and their guests followed them back to Moore Hall ready for the reception.

"Tea, Em?" asked Susan.

"Yes, please," Em replied as she and the three girls entered the kitchen through the back door.

"Tea for—fancy a cup, Alfred? Make it five."

"I hope you'll excuse me, but while the tea is brewing I'll be loading the car ready to take the boss back to Wittering in the morning," Alfred said.

"Let me help," volunteered Ruth.

"It's all right miss, it's only a couple of cases. I've got to leave them enough for tonight."

"I shouldn't think they'll need much for tonight," commented Em, making them all laugh. In the distance they could hear the band in the marquee. "Ruth, I'm leaving you in charge while Susan and I are at the reception," said Em. "I'll ask Mrs White if she would send some goodies over so you shouldn't need to prepare anything for yourselves unless you want to. There are the extras we had prepared for lunch if you need them. We should be back in about an hour. Ready, Susan? I think it's time we joined them."

The inside of the marquee looked smaller than Em had expected. The tables were laid out like a large letter E, a small table on which the cake was displayed formed the middle stub while seating and tables for the wedding party and guests filled the remaining three parts of the letter. A screen had been placed behind the wedding party. Mrs White invited Em to tour a smaller marquee that contained a field kitchen and larder, making it possible to provide for the reception without using the kitchen in the house and disturbing the normal running of the household. Em showed interest as Mrs White explained some of the planning that goes on in functions. While Em was listening, she was also watching the waitresses who were busy preparing the dishes. "You know," Marjorie was saying, "you and Veronica look so much alike, if I weren't friends with her parents I would have said you must be related."

The young couple looked radiant; Charles in his R.A.F uniform and Delilah in a beautiful white wedding dress, of nineteen twenties elegance, first used by her aunt, Lady Jane, the train having been removed just prior to the reception. The guests were now seated. Em and Susan, at Em's request, had been placed at the end of one of the tables. The service was quick and efficient, the food and drinks plentiful, and the band playing quietly in the background was loud enough to be heard and enjoyed, but not to interfere with conversations. A thank you and applause to Em and Susan was followed by the cutting of the beautifully decorated cake. Speeches, though numerous, were amusing. The toasts followed, first to the king and royal family, then to the bride and groom, Lady Jane and so many other personages that glasses needed several refills.

Charles and Delilah led the dancing with a Viennese waltz; they swayed to the tune of *The Blue Danube*, much to the delight and applause of those watching. Suddenly the music and tempo changed. Delilah lifted the hem of the dress and the couple started to jive. "I can't dance in this dress," she said after about five minutes. "I must get changed," and they headed towards the house. Charles scooped Delilah up as Em, who had already returned to the house, opened the door and smiled as she watched them running up the stairs, Delilah holding up the beautiful dress to avoid tripping or treading on it.

Fifteen to twenty minutes later, they crept down the backstairs, into the library and out through the French windows. Harry Rock was already waiting in his car with the engine running. The sound of the music coming from the marquee drowned out the noise of the old Ford T as it made its way down the gravel driveway and out onto the road.

It was more than an hour before Charlton realised that the couple hadn't returned. Looking around but not seeing Harry either, he went to the house to ask Em, who was in the kitchen enjoying a drink with Alfred.

"Don't ask me," Alfred said, shrugging. "I'm due to be taking them back to camp at Wittering in the morning, so they told me to enjoy the evening and not bother them."

"Have you seen Harry?" Charlton asked. "He's also vanished."

"No," answered Em, "but I know he was hoping to leave in the morning."

"How can he?" asked Alfred. "His generator is kaput," he added, using the German expression.

"Maybe he's working on it," said Charlton as he headed out of the back door, followed by Alfred. "No Harry, now no car."

"He's probably giving it a trial run," suggested Alfred.

"Oh well, he's missing all the fun; you coming?"

"No, thanks," answered Alfred. "We've got an early start in the morning."

"Okay," said Charlton, "tell him I'll set up a drink for him when he gets back. Hmm, I don't blame Charles being in a hurry, lucky fellow."

Alfred grinned as he walked back into the kitchen. Em gave him that knowing look. "Don't worry," she said, "I won't ask."

Chapter Twenty-eight

Gillian looked at the letter from Birkenhead Breweries in disbelief. If only Victor was here, he would know what to do… or maybe not, after all he was expecting her to run the pub. Raising the rent was one thing and then increasing the pension fund charges, that would eat into what little profit they made after paying the staff, pension fund, electricity and gas, but redecorating, and making improvements, well that was out of the question. Gillian looked down the list of suggested improvements, juke box? What the hell is a juke box? This is supposed to be an English country public house not some American cocktail bar.

"Malcolm, put that down." Oh dear, she thought, it looks like mother won't be round today, I'll have to see if I can get Malcolm into day care. I can't cope with the paperwork while trying to keep an eye on a four-year-old.

***

The car drew into the driveway of Knoll House. "The house is in darkness, it looks empty," said Delilah looking out of the window. "Are you sure you've got the right place?"

"Trust me," replied Harry. "Wait there a moment, I'll be back shortly," he said as he got out of his seat and walked round the back of the building.

A light came on in the hall and the door opened. Harry emerged followed closely by a younger man. "Welcome to Knoll House. Any friend of Harry is a friend of mine. Call me Chris," he said as he helped Delilah down from the car. "I hope you had a good journey. We're not officially open until July, so feel free to stay as long as you like." Harry helped Chris with the cases, "You'll stay for a drink, Harry? In fact Poppy's made a room up for you."

"Thanks," said Harry, "to be honest I wasn't expecting to be back so soon so I've got nothing in."

"Anything you want you only have to ask," Chris was saying. "Ah, here comes my wife with the drinks, you'll love Poppy, she's the brains behind the joint."

"You must be Delilah," said Poppy. "Harry has told me all about you."

"Only good stuff I hope," Delilah replied.

"Of course dear, Harry is the perfect gentleman," she said, laughing at Delilah's frown. "Do make yourselves at home. Dinner will be ready in half an hour. Harry darling, there are one or two things..." Their conversation fadied out as they disappeared through the doorway.

***

It was a week after the wedding before James came to see Em. "Agnes said—"

"I know," replied Em, "but I'm busy right now."

"When will you be free?"

"About four."

"Okay, four o'clock in the library."

"We can't do anything..."

"No, silly... we'll decide where then," he said laughing.

Four o'clock was a long way away, and time seemed to be passing so slowly. Em was looking forward with mixed feelings, she had no idea what to expect. If it was a repeat of what Agnes had done, why was she feeling so nervous? But what if James showed interest in anything more? Em tried to shut any thought like that out of her mind, but... what if?

"It's four o'clock, Em," Susan said. "I'll do that if you like."

"Thank you," said Em as she washed her hands and slipped out of her apron, then made her way to the library.

James was waiting. "Shall we go up to the Tudor suite?" he suggested. "We could quite reasonably be going there to inspect the work I've been doing there." Em hesitated for a moment. "It's all right Em, I won't get up to anything, or try to take advantage," he said as they made their way to the back stairs.

"Thank you, that feels a lot better," Em said, as she eased her housecoat back over her shoulders.

"You've a lot of tension in your back," James said. "I can ease that if you will let me." Em looked hesitant again. "I've already promised you…"

"Will I need…"

"Well, yes…"

"But I'm not wearing a…"

"It's all right," he assured her, "you'll be lying on you tummy," and he laid a large towel on the dust sheet that was over the bed.

"Okay, but turn your back," she said, having forgotten the mirror on the dressing table. Em lay down as instructed, and James proceeded to massage her back. After half an hour or so he gently wiped the remaining oil from her back and laid the housecoat over her.

"How was that?" he asked.

"So relaxing," she replied, "I was almost asleep."

James chuckled. "I think you were at one point."

"Did I snore?"

"No," he said, "just breathed deeply."

Em pulled her vest up over her shoulders, slid her arms into the housecoat and fastened the buttons on the front. "Thank you," she said again, as she wriggled her shoulders and twisted her body. "That feels wonderful. Another time maybe?" she asked.

"My pleasure," came the reply, "just say when."

Em thought for a moment. "Maybe sometime next week," she said.

***

"That was fantastic, darling," said Liz, "I always thought that the New Forest was a large area of trees, I never visualised large open spaces, with ponies grazing in them. It was beautiful, really beautiful," she said as she leaned over to kiss him. "I think we should get home to Chingford, and you can get back to work."

Victor smiled as he turned on to the A3 and headed towards London. "It's been lovely," he said. But he was thinking, I suppose I ought to make an appearance at the Red Lion.

***

"Where's Gillian?" Victor asked as he came outside from the kitchen. Mavis was hanging her towel out on the line, "Where's my wife?" he asked.

"Oh," Mavis replied, "she said something about taking Malcolm to the church hall to day nursery. She'll be back shortly."

"When you've finished chatting up the staff..." a voice said behind him.

"What's this about a day nursery? I thought you said your mother–"

"She can't come," Gillian said. "Dad's worse now and needs her to look after him all the time, and I can't keep an eye on Malcolm when I'm doing my paperwork."

"I'll be in in just a minute," he said. "I've got one or two things I want to do."

As Gillian disappeared indoors, Victor gave Mavis a look. "Cheeky," Mavis murmured.

"What's a juke box?" asked Gillian.

"What are you on about?" asked Victor.

"They want us to have a juke box," she answered.

"Who do?" he asked, getting a little impatient.

"The brewery," she replied. "They are saying we should have a juke box."

"What for?" he asked.

"I don't know, I don't even know what it is."

"It's a sort of electric gramophone with lots of records." Gillian looked at him quizzically. "You choose which one you want and you put a coin in to play it."

"Oh, I don't like the sound of that, and I don't think our regulars would either," she said.

"Anyway, what gave you that idea?"

"Read this," she said thrusting the brewery letter into his hand.

After a long pause Victor shook his head. "We haven't got that sort of money."

"As it is," Gillian said, "the staff are getting more than I should be, but we're not making enough profit to pay me as well."

"It looks like we should give up and get out while we can, dear."

Gillian wiped a tear from her eyes, "But—"

"I know, dear—" he was saying.

"No you don't, how can you understand?" she demanded, sobbing. "This has always been my home. I was born here. I went to school from here... I, I, I ..."

Victor took her in his arms, took out a handkerchief and wiped away the tears. "We'll find somewhere nice to bring up the children in," he said.

"What about Mum and Dad?" she asked.

"Let's find somewhere for ourselves first."

***

"This is the part of this job I'm not too keen on." Em was talking to the three girls, Ruth, Rebecca and Esther. "I took you on to help out while we had house guests. Unfortunately I now have to lose you. If you wish I will keep you in mind for next time, but don't stop accepting work you may be offered."

Esther looked at the others, they both nodded. "Yes," she said, "please keep us in mind."

"That leads me onto the next item. As you will have realised, Susan will soon be leaving. I would like Ruth to stay and learn the trade. No favouritism, just selection out of a hat. Rebecca and Esther, see me in the office after lunch, I'll have ready your written references and pay to the end of the week, and you will be free to leave. I've arranged with James to take you to Daresbury.

"I've had a word with her ladyship," Em was saying to Susan. "You're due to leave us at the end of the month, you can leave as soon as you wish. Don't worry, I'll see that you are paid to the end of the month anyway. If you stay, I would like you to show Ruth how to make some of Lady Jane's favourite dishes." Susan hesitated. "No hurry, dear," said Em. "Just let me know what you have decided when you are ready."

James appeared at the office door. Em looked up. "Is it that time already?" she asked.

"As you wish, Em."

"Can we leave it until four?"

"It is four."

"Give me fifteen minutes."

"Okay," he said. "Tudor suite, see you later."

"Susan, have you..." Em called.

"Twenty minutes ago," came the answer. "It's all right, Ruth pushed the trolley."

James faced away as Em lay on her stomach. She could feel the pressure of his hands and fingers ease away the tension in her back... so relaxing... so...

"Turn over," he said,

"But..."

"It's okay, I won't get up to mischief," he said, laying a towel over her bosom as she turned over. Gently but firmly his hands and fingers eased from her abdomen to below her chest. Em found it so relaxing. Almost before she realised he had finished.

Em sat up and wiped the oil away with the towel, eased her vest up over her shoulders, then James helped her into her housecoat. "Thank you dear," she said. "That was lovely. Same again next week?"

***

A slight touch of the brakes and adjustment of the steering wheel, Victor narrowly avoided driving into the ditch at that corner. Stopping at the side of the road he poured himself a drink of tea from his flask. I must concentrate more on my driving, he thought, sitting quietly for a while until he was able to think more clearly. He would rent a place for the family in Carlton on the outskirts of Nottingham, and while he was calling on Liz, stay at a nearby bed and breakfast on a regular basis (partially to avoid commitment but also to preserve his savings), alternating between Nottingham and Chingford, while he decided what he was going to do. Having worked out a plan of action, if you could call it that, Victor started the engine and drove on with his load of yarn to Witney.

The need for delivery of blankets to military bases and hospitals had been greatly reduced since the end of the war, and replaced mainly with transportation of bales of blankets to Southampton and Liverpool docks. The demand for yarn continued, although other companies were now competing for the business, making it necessary for Victor to reduce his prices, and look for other customers.

Over the past twelve months Victor had visited the estate agents in Burton Road, Carlton on several occasions. In the meantime, he was living in bed and breakfast accommodation, staying at one address on a regular basis. Private rented accommodation was in short supply, and was expensive. "Why don't you try the council?" he had been asked several times. "Having two children, you should soon get a place."

"What do we want a council house for? This is *our* home," Gillian was adamant.

"But dear—"

"If you want to live in a council house, go on your own and live in a council house," she said, regretting her words almost before she had finished.

"What would you do if I did? How would you pay the bills? Remember we're living in a rented house, only for as long as we work for the brewery, and the rent is going up. What then?"

Gillian started to cry, she loved the place, but she knew that they couldn't afford to stay on in the pub, there wasn't enough money coming in.

"What I suggest," he said, "is that we tell the brewery that we will be closing the pub two days before the rent increase. They'll want us out so that they can have someone take over, that means we're being evicted."

"But, dear—"

"Hush, love, don't worry, we'll go into digs in Nottingham. In the meantime, I'll apply to the council, then you won't be working for nothing and you'll be able to have the kids at home with you, and who knows, we might even get a place with a garden." Gillian's eyes lit up at the prospect. "Come on," Victor said, "I'll draw up a notice and we'll tell the staff we're closing."

Chapter Twenty-nine

Mavis pinned the notice up on the board beside the Darts' League programme.

"What's this? The brewery can't just close us!" Harry exclaimed.

"The old fella probably drank all the profits," answered Joseph.

"Mmhmm," grunted Fred, "I don't remember when I last saw him sober. You could sail the Queen Mary on what he drank."

"Hey, Mavis," Joseph called, "what's it about?"

"The boss can hardly be expected to bring up two kids on what you lot drink," she answered.

"I suppose not," said Joseph. "Come on, Harry, it's your shout."

***

"Yes, that seems fine, Mr Bradburn," the clerk said. "We will let you know in due course." Victor stood up and was about to leave. "Don't worry, Mr Bradburn," she said, "I feel sure you should soon hear something favourable."

"Thank you," Victor said, leaving the office. I'll believe that when it happens, he thought as he stood at the top of the steps, looking out over the city centre. He was feeling despondent. Did it really need that much form filling, just to see if they had a house available? he thought. It could be ages before I hear anything. He might even be forced into buying, which he did *not* want to do, it would mean dipping deep into his savings. Stepping into Ye Olde Oake Tree public house, he ordered a double whisky, shortly followed by a second.

***

"You shouldn't be driving at all in your condition, young lady, even less so in a tiny sports car."

"But Auntie, or should I call you Mummy?" asked Delilah.

"Mama yes, Mummy definitely *not*," answered her ladyship, "and don't think you can avoid the issue, I forbid you to use that thing, at least until after your confinement, even then it is totally unsuitable for someone with a family."

"But Mummy—"

"Mama," snapped Lady Jane, "perhaps it would be better if you continued to call me Auntie."

"All right, Mama," Delilah answered.

"As Charles's wife you may decide to use his rooms, although I think it might be more practical to continue using your old suite. Give the bell pull a little tug, gently dear, it's not a church bell you're ringing."

"Ah, Em, please ask James to take Delilah's cases up to her rooms and park the car in the garage. Give Em the keys, Delilah."

Em received the car keys. "Thank you, miss, er sorry, I meant ma'am."

"Oh Em," Delilah said, "would you arrange for the library floor to be cleared, I'd like to continue my ballet exercises." Em looked toward her ladyship, who nodded.

***

Victor parked his lorry on the waste land, just round the corner from Mrs Rudley's Bed and Breakfast, and let himself in the front door. "Is that you, Victor?" came his landlady's voice. "There's a letter for you on the hall stand. It's from the council. I hope it's good news" she said.

Victor tore the envelope open, "It is, and it isn't," he replied.

"Don't talk in riddles, lad. What do you mean?"

"It is for me," he said, "but maybe not for you. I've been offered a house in Warwick Street."

"Jammy beggar," she said. "They're on the new estate just off Carlton Way. They've only been up eighteen months. When do you move in?"

"Er…" He searched through the letter. "The first of the month."

"Then get round sharp, first thing in the morning, or you could lose it," Mrs Rudley said.

***

Em was delighted to hear from Susan. A few days after she had left Moore Hall, Em had redirected an airmail letter that had arrived from America. Major Clarkson, Susan told her, would be flying over in February, giving her enough time to get a passport for her and baby Harold, named after her father, much to the delight of the child's grandfather, making it possible to return home while they waited for the child's father to arrive from Chicago.

Life at Moore Hall had its ups and downs. Ruth proved to be a capable and quick learner, and Em had no qualms about leaving her to take over when necessary, like on a Thursday afternoon when Em was not only receiving, but was being taught the art of massaging. Her subject was, of course, her tutor, James. The downside being when Agnes, twenty years senior to both James and Em, was absent from the nursery, due, she said, to some obscure internal disorder. On this occasion Em and James were taking a selection of homemade biscuits to Agnes. As they were approaching the cottage, James stopped Em and they moved back out of sight in the cover of the trees. They stood and watched a man's figure at the bedroom window. A few minutes later the man left by the back door and quickly disappeared towards the village. "That be Jimmy Cleghorne," James murmured. "He's got a reputation as a womaniser. Come on, let's get back to the hall."

***

At the start of the new school year Walter, who had found it hard keeping up with the work at the grammar school, joined his brother at Huntingdon Street. Mr Smith, the governor at the children's home, was slightly bemused; the twin at the grammar school hadn't come up to expectations, while his brother appeared to be exceeding them. Perhaps being separated from Freddie had unsettled Walter. Hopefully he would be happier back with his brother, and would prove more capable with the work at the secondary school.

Once Walter had settled in he seemed to be doing better. Freddie, after a year in the secondary modern school, was also doing reasonably well; the more relaxed perspective they had acquired in the Isle of Man had probably resulted in a more thorough approach to the subjects they were studying, with the exception of history and English. In the Isle of Man, history dealt with the Nordic connection with the island, which meant that to the twins, English history was virtually a new subject and the list of kings and dates tended to be tedious and boring.

Each of the boys had their own reason for disliking English, apart from the teacher who always seemed to be picking on the twins. Apparently he had a dislike for grammar schools, and not knowing which one had been there, picked on them both to show the rest of the class how poorly educated grammar school kids were. For Freddie, the main reason was that although nouns and verbs were easy enough, pronouns, apostrophes and semi-colons were not. Why do I need to know those? he thought. I'm not going to write a book.

***

"Doctor Williams has asked me to call," the lady dressed in nurse's uniform said as she stood at the front door, "I believe you have a Lady Delilah... er," looking at the papers in her hand. "Oh, I'm terribly sorry," she said, "I should have introduced myself, I'm Sister Bethany, call me Beth, O'Donnell, I'm the midwife. I'm new to this area. Oh, there I go, a right chatterbox when I'm nervous."

"That's all right," said Em. "The ladies are having afternoon tea, come through to the kitchen. I'm sure you'll enjoy a nice cup of tea."

"I t'ank yer, there's nothing like a cup to calm yer nerves."

"Ah, Ruth," Em said as they entered the kitchen, "a cup for, was it Beth?"

"To be sure," Beth replied, and glancing at Ruth. "I'm sure she won't want my services."

Ruth frowned and Em laughed. "Beth is a midwife, to see Lady Delilah," she explained.

Em knocked on the drawing room door, opened it and entered followed by Sister O'Donnell. Em introduced her, and the midwife explained the purpose of her visit. Lady Jane and a reluctant Delilah arranged a programme of appointments, with Em to be in attendance to assist in any regular exercises that Beth wanted her patient to learn and practice, with special emphasis on breathing. As the expected arrival drew closer, it would involve more of Em's time and make it more difficult for her to fit in sessions spent under the calming, soothing hands of James.

Aware that James needed to be available to drive Delilah, or to tidy up any paintwork that showed signs of damage, so that he would be spending more time at the hall, Agnes seemed more frequently to suffer the odd cold, sore throat, or strangely, for someone previously in exceptionally good health, the occasional migraine, but needing neither doctor nor nurse, only a visit from Jim Cleghorne.

***

"We can't take it all, dear," Victor said. "If I leave enough for you and the children, I'll just take the spare beds. I'll put a table in here from the bar while I take this one. The same with the chairs. You can stay with Mrs Rudley, you'll love her, while I come back for the rest of the things and deal with the hand-over."

Within a week most of the furniture they would need, the furnishings and personal belongings had been transferred to number nineteen

Warwick Street. Mrs Rudley was delighted to be playing grandmother to the little ones, fussing over Malcolm who took to her immediately, leaving Gillian free to give Molly all the attention she needed and making it possible for Victor to carry on with his deliveries while keeping an eye on the running of the Red Lion. Strangely business had seemed to improve in the last two weeks, maybe it was a matter of people just being inquisitive, or hoping that the new people taking over would be doing a special night of 'on the house'.

Victor managed to be at the Red Lion most nights, using what had been Mr and Mrs Woodley's room, as most of the things from the other rooms were already in Nottingham. The absence of children's voices and empty rooms gave a feeling of dereliction about the place. Although at times Victor found the silence disconcerting, more often than not the quietness and solitude was relaxing.

Victor bade the last customer goodnight as he closed, locked and bolted the door, shuttered the windows, and took the cash tray out of the till, normally part of what Mavis did at the end of the day. She had obviously left in a hurry, unusual, but then...

"Goodnight, boss," said Colin as he left from the side door.

Victor stood for a moment and looked out at the moonlit night, even with a clear sky and a full moon all was still and surprisingly warm for an evening in October.

He closed the door, locked and bolted it. I'll do the till in the morning, he murmured as he walked into the lounge. Strange, he thought, I don't remember opening the bed settee. There were no curtains to block out the moonlight now, but it didn't worry him as he let his clothes fall in a heap on the floor. There was a slight sound behind him; he turned and saw Mavis, as naked as the day she was born.

Chapter Thirty

Gillian turned the key as Victor gave the door a gentle shove with his foot, whisking her off her feet he carried her over the threshold, almost colliding with Malcolm as the older child tried to push past. "Mind your head, dear," he said as he manoeuvred past the door post and placed Gillian on her feet inside the hall. Phew, he thought, I won't try that again in a hurry.

Molly, still on the outside, let out a wail. "Look what you've done," said Gillian, "you've upset Molly."

"Maybe I should have lifted her over the threshold instead," he remarked, then "Ooo, that hurt," holding his arm where she had laughingly swiped him.

"Idiot".

Having not consulted his wife when placing the furniture around, it was inevitable that Gillian would have other ideas where everything should go. "Why have you put the table at the front and the easy chairs at the back nearer the kitchen?"

"'Cos that's to the south and we'll be sitting in the sunshine."

"I would rather sit by the fireplace in the evening, especially in the winter," replied Gillian.

"I'll change it all around. You grab hold of that end of the table. Hang on, I'll take the flaps off first. Which side of the fire do you… If it's this side you can watch… Okay, near enough? Good, shall we leave upstairs until after lunch?"

Room by room they sorted out the positioning of the furniture, either until Gillian had it put how she wanted, or a compromise, until Victor had unwittingly moved everything round to where his wife had wanted it in the first place.

"Now we're in," said Victor, "I suppose I had better go off in the morning to earn a few shekels, or we'll have nothing for the rent man."

Surely, thought Gillian, we're not that skint. "Well, before you go, I'll need some money for housekeeping."

"Will five be enough?" he asked counting out five crumpled pound notes. "Oh, and a couple in case the coal man calls round, I've already had some coal and kindling put in the coalhouse."

"I bet you didn't think of getting light bulbs? I thought not," said Gillian. "And while you're down the hardware shop, we need some pegs, matches and curtain hooks."

"There are hooks in the curtains."

"Yes, but some are so old they're already rusty."

"When rationing finishes we'll be able to get new curtains."

Gillian's eyes lit up at the thought of being able to choose and buy brand new curtains instead of using her mother's hand-me-downs.

***

Ruth had turned out to be a good learner, and Em felt very confident in her ability to take over during the times she was in attendance with Beth the midwife, and once Delilah started taking afternoon naps, Em would go to the nursery and chat with Agnes while Annabel was resting.

As Em was finding that she was spending more time away from the kitchen, with her ladyship's approval she was able to employ extra staff earlier than usual for the Christmas period. Esther and Rebecca were available and made a welcome return. Em was not only attending to Delilah but also to Annabel in the frequent absence of Agnes.

There was a knock on the back door. "See who it is please, Esther," said Em.

"It's…" Esther was saying as the now familiar sight appeared in the kitchen.

"Ah, I know I'm early but…" looking round, "do I detect that wonderful aroma of tea?" Bethany asked.

"While you're on your feet, Esther, see if you can squeeze a cup out for our friendly midwife please," Em said, "and one for James," she added, seeing him come through the door.

"Agnes says she's got a headache," he said, "so she won't be in today."

"I'll look after Annabel for you if you like," offered Rebecca. "I've cousins her age."

Annabel took to Rebecca instantly; 'Becca' as Annabel called her, seemed to have that natural aura about her that children love.

I'll see how things go, Em thought. We might have found our nanny already.' She left the nursery and went to join Beth in Delilah's room.

"Why do I need to do all these breathing exercises?"

"Believe me," Beth answered, "it will help you."

"How do you know? You've not had any—"

"I have," interrupted Em, "and I can assure you it helps."

"But it—"

"Helps," said Em. "It certainly helps."

"T'ank yer," said Beth, as they were sitting in the kitchen enjoying a cup of tea. "How many children have yer?"

"Annabel, as you know," Em answered, "and twin boys... oh, Esther," she said, turning away for a moment, "would you take a tea tray up to Rebecca, please."

"Well then," Beth said, "sure and yer'll know how important breathing exercises were."

***

The rain was falling as Victor kissed Gillian goodbye. Having dawdled over a delicious breakfast he once more took to the road, the rain was not heavy but persistent. He had intended to pick up a load of yarn from Helmshore Mill, but he should have left home just after six to stand any chance of delivering it before the Witney factory closed. He decided it would be unsafe to leave a loaded lorry standing over the weekend, so he headed south without a load.

Top of the list this week was to establish a base near Liz's parents which he could use to operate from in the south. More importantly it would be a private place he could call home, somewhere he could take Liz. While he was having a cup of tea in the Corner Café in the High Street, an advertisement in the Chingford Chronicle caught his eye; a three-bedroom flat over a shop in Monkhams Lane, with views across the park, seemed quite reasonable.

Victor drove to Monkhams Lane and after leaving his lorry near the park entrance, walked along the road looking for obvious signs of an empty flat. Unable to identify which property it was, he went into an ironmonger's. "I'm sorry sir," the owner said, "you're the third person who's asked today. Is it just for yourself? I have a couple of rooms upstairs if you're interested." He turned to his assistant, "Sue, keep an eye on the place while I show this gent upstairs. This way, sir. It's got its own front door."

It was quite a nice flat with two bedrooms, neatly furnished with a living room overlooking the park, not spacious, but adequate for what Victor wanted. "Who lived here?" Victor asked.

"Sue did," came the answer. "We were married in June this year, but she couldn't move in with me while my mother was alive. They didn't see eye to eye. Anyway there's me blathering about me. What do you think?"

"What's the rent?"

"Hmm, how does two quid sound?"

"What, a week?"

"No, a month; that's cheap for a furnished flat, oh, and four weeks' rent deposit." Victor reached into his wallet, two five pound notes changed hands. "We'll sort out the agreement and rent book downstairs. Welcome to 12A, Monkhams Lane. Oh, I haven't told you my name, Martin Starling, and you?"

"Bradburn," he replied," Victor Bradburn." The two men shook hands.

***

"I don't like having babies," Delilah said, "Just look at me, I'm enormous," she moaned. "I won't be attractive any more."

"You'll be all right if you watch what you eat and keep up your exercises after you've had your baby," replied Em.

"I suppose I'll have to wear a corset."

"I doubt it," answered Em. "I've had a family and I don't wear one."

"But you're in your thirties, old women don't need them. I didn't mean you," Delilah quickly retracted what she was saying. "Auntie wears one," she added laughing.

Em laughed too. "I suppose when I was your age I thought thirty was old," she said. "Now just rest, I'll bring your afternoon tea in about an hour."

Em quietly opened the nursery door, at first she didn't see anyone; then in the half light she could just make out the figure of Rebecca, lying on the chaise longue with Annabel snuggled up against her. Em smiled.

"She wouldn't settle," Rebecca whispered. "I tried a couple of times until I held her like this, then she fell asleep within minutes."

Em gently picked her daughter up and laid her in her cot. "Go and get your afternoon tea, then bring me one up, please," she said.

"Is it all right if I bring both our teas up?" Rebecca asked.

"Of course, dear," Em replied.

Just the two of them having afternoon tea together meant they were able to have a really good long chat. No, Rebecca hadn't wanted to work as a maid, she'd had a grammar school education and her sights had been on teaching and the possibility of foreign travel, maybe working as a nanny, but her family could not afford for her to go to college and therefore she had to take whatever job she could get.

"What about work as a nanny?" asked Em.

"Agencies only employ those they train, and that costs far too much. By the time I'd paid off my loan, I'd be working for two or three years for nothing."

"Then how about here?" suggested Em.

"You mean... you'd...?"

"Yes," replied Em. "Obviously I will need her ladyship's approval – and you'd need to go to her orphanage for formal training about childhood ailments and things."

"Oh, Em," cried Rebecca, throwing her arms around Em's neck.

"Steady on, I'll have to ask her first."

***

"Did James explain about yesterday?" Agnes asked as she came in through the office door.

"Yes, thank you," answered Em, "Would you clean through the Tudor and Stuart suites today? I know James is very careful but I want to be sure they're clean enough for the guests."

"But what about—"

"I'll have one of the girls look after the nursery today, thank you."

"But—"

"Was there something more?" asked Em.

Agnes shook her head. "No, I don't think so," she murmured.

"In that case, please tell Rebecca I'd like a word with her."

Em turned from her desk, and while waiting for Agnes to leave the kitchen, asked Rebecca to sit down. "I've had a word as I promised. Tomorrow while Agnes is looking after the nursery, we will go and see what her ladyship has decided and can arrange. I want you up there today, but please make sure that Annabel rests in her cot. That hour or two would be a good opportunity for you to study. You can take a copy of Mrs Beeton up with you to read when she is asleep. I think it would be best if you read about childhood ailments."

"Thank you!" said Rebecca.

Clang clang, clang clang, before the third sequence of clang clang Em had seen the indicator board showed Delilah had tugged on her bell pull. "Ruth, if I give three rings send James for the midwife, please," Em said as she disappeared up the service stairs.

"Ah, there you are," said Delilah, "has the *Picture Post* arrived yet? It should have been here yesterday."

"No, it has not, and you know I told you only to ring the bell three times when it is really urgent."

"But it is. I think it is!"

At that moment Lady Jane appeared at the door. "I thought I heard three bells…"

"I'm afraid it was a false alarm, madam," apologised Em.

"Why, what happened?"

"I want my magazine."

"Em, would you leave us, please," said her ladyship, "I want a word with my daughter-in-law."

"But Auntie…"

"Don't you Auntie me…" Em heard Lady Jane saying as she closed the door behind herself.

Fifteen minutes later Em was summoned upstairs to Delilah's room. "What were you going to say to our housekeeper?" her ladyship prompted.

"I'm sorry, Em," Delilah meekly whispered.

"Apology accepted," replied Em, smiling.

"I trust there will be no more of this nonsense," Lady Jane said as she turned to leave the room, almost colliding with Esther who had arrived carrying the said magazine.

"Sorry, ma'am" as she stepped back leaving the doorway clear.

"What is that? The *Picture Post*… I haven't seen one of these since before the war," said her ladyship. "I'd like a quick look through this. I'll send it back in about half an hour." She was heading towards her room as she spoke. The expression on Delilah's face said plenty.

The morning in Moore Hall passed in its tranquil state of normality, Lady Jane had sent the precious *Picture Post* back to Delilah with the message that she would like the opportunity to read it sometime. Lunch cleared, residents and staff sat down to enjoy the aroma and taste of coffee that still remained of what the Americans had left behind. A sixth sense made Em put her cup on the table, the abrupt suddenness of the clang clang made Ruth jump, spilling her coffee; clang clang. Em was already halfway up the stairs; clang clang, James who had left a painting touch-up job and joined them for coffee, checked his pocket for the car keys.

Em, trying to appear unrushed, entered Delilah's room. "What did you say? Water's broken?" Em looked, then reached for the bell pull.

Chapter Thirty-one

Liz looked at Victor. Have you really lost it? she wondered. Here we are out walking in a strong cold north wind, while there's a nice warm front room at home.

Victor stopped in front of Martin's ironmongers shop. "Here we are," he said, as he reached in his pocket and took out a key. "Let's go up and have a look."

What's he up to? Liz wondered as she crossed the threshold and climbed the stairs.

"Nice and compact," he said.

"I'll give you that," she replied. "Compact, nice, but who lives here?"

"Er, well, I do."

"You've bought it? Furnished?"

"Furnished, yes. Bought it, no, I've rented it."

Liz looked out towards the park, lit by the moon through the occasional break in the cloud.

"Liz darling," Victor said. She turned and saw him kneeling on one knee. "Will you marry me?"

"Of course I will, darling," she answered, "of course I will. Get up, idiot, the curtains are open, someone might see you."

"Come down here, then," Victor replied, "You'll be out of sight. Or better still, let me show you the bedroom," he added, as he stood up.

"Cheeky," Liz replied as they went through to the back of the flat.

***

The baby lay in his mother's arms. Delilah, now asleep with a smile on her lips, was exhausted; it had been a long day for all of them. Beth the midwife was busy clearing up, helped by Esther who had volunteered to do any running around needed to assist Em and Beth during the night. "Go on girl, it's two a.m," said Em, "off to bed, and I don't want to see you downstairs in the morning."

The sound of the front door bell echoed through the hall; Em wiped her hands as she hurried down the stairs. Who on earth can that be at this time of night? she was saying to herself as she withdrew the bolts, unlocked the heavy door and pulled it open.

"How is my wife?" Charles asked as he entered.

"She is sleeping," Em answered. "Congratulations, sir, you have a son."

"Can I see him?" he asked as he headed towards the stairs.

"Of course, sir, but quietly please, they are both asleep, but I think the midwife is still with them."

"Nothing wrong, I hope?"

"No sir, your son arrived a little late, about an hour ago. Is Alfred...?"

"No, I drove myself up."

***

For Gillian, the move to Nottingham should have been a great new adventure, but this was probably what the missionaries must have felt like when they found themselves in new countries. Don't be stupid, she told herself, you're a grown woman with two children in a strange city and no friends, feeling lost and lonely, now momentarily missing her family. Maybe the local church has a Young Wives Group, she thought; she had seen a church somewhere as she had been walking round. Feeling cold and slightly depressed she headed back indoors in the warm, but having first picked up some reading matter in the paper shop, including a local paper.

When she had been living in the Red Lion, she had never felt as lonely as she did now. Maybe she could get an evening job as a barmaid, well, not while she was breast feeding Molly, she'd have to wean her onto the same food as Malcolm was eating, and he was a year old before she'd got him off breast milk. Maybe Mavis might like to come and stay for a while, if she wasn't working. I'll get some letter paper tomorrow and drop her a line. she was a bit of a flirt and we had some good laughs together, Gillian decided.

Gillian checked the children were asleep, went downstairs, drew the living room curtains to close the cold, dark night out, and poked the fire. Picking up her magazine, she started turning the pages. That looks nice,' she thought when she saw a knitted twin-set, I've got some knitting needles somewhere, the pattern doesn't look difficult. A short story caught her eye. *The Mystery of the Laird's Ghost*, by Mary Campbell, and she settled down to read: 'The snow was deep and still falling as Jeanette made her way to her grandmother's house high up on the Scottish moor.'

***

"Struth," exclaimed Victor. "It's ten thirty. I think we ought to get you home to your parents before your dad comes looking for you."

"Couldn't we stay here tonight?" asked Liz. "I am twenty-one."

"Well, I suppose we could, but I haven't bought any food yet, and your dad would go bonkers if I didn't take you home. Anyway I'll be round in the morning," he said. Taking a last look around the room in case they had left anything behind, they went out into the night and headed towards Seventeen Northend Road.

"Ah, the wanderers return," said Mr Norman. "If he's staying here tonight," he added, "no shenanigans."

"Here we go again," Liz replied. "I am twenty-one, and if I wanted shenanigans, I'd have it, whatever it is." Both her mother and father burst into peals of laughter.

"What's so funny?" Liz asked.

Victor, trying hard to contain himself, answered, "Shenanigans is naughties."

"Oops," Liz murmured, looking a little embarrassed before joining in the laughter.

"You will stay tonight, please, darling. Can I tell them?"

"What's this 'darling' business?" Mr Norman asked.

"Victor has asked me to marry him."

"You're not pregnant, are you?" Liz's father demanded, jumping in with both feet.

"Of course not, Daddy, we don't do shenanigans."

"That's wonderful," her mother said, "let me congratulate you. Get the drinks out, Father, we've something to celebrate."

"What's all the noise, you don't expect me to sleep through that, do you?" Liz's sister Dinah was saying as she came through the door, wearing a scant two-sizes-too-short nightdress.

"Cover yourself up, girl," her father shouted, "we've got a visitor."

"He's not a visitor," she replied. "He's her fella."

"Go and put your mac' on over your nightdress," said her mother, "then you can come back and we'll tell you what it's about."

***

"Do I have to? Do I look as if I've got gallons of milk? You did say…"

"As you wish, dear, we'll put your baby on baby formula," answered Beth.

"I'll go down and get a bottle made up," Em said, turning to leave the room just as Charles entered, closely followed by his mother.

"What's this I hear?" asked her ladyship. "I suppose you want someone else to bring up your son?"

"But I thought…"

"No, child," Lady Jane answered, "no grandson of mine will go into an orphanage. If you're not going to accept your responsibilities, he will stay here until you do." Her ladyship turned and walked out of the room.

"I think you have upset Mother," remarked Charles. "I hope you like the taste of humble pie." He turned to Em. "Do you think you could have a word with Mother, please, Em?"

"I'll try, sir, but it might be better coming from you."

"I know," he replied, "but I don't fancy getting an ear-bashing."

Em knocked on the drawing room door, opened it and pushed the trolley into the room.

"Is that the time already?" asked Lady Jane. "The young people of today don't seem to want to accept responsibility. You were there. Do you think I was a bit heavy handed?"

"I am hardly the right person to judge, thinking of Brenda," Em replied.

"But that was different dear, you were on your own, Charles and Delilah aren't."

"I think there might have been a slight misunderstanding, ma'am. As I said the other day, Rebecca will make a very good nanny."

"Ah, Charles," Lady Jane said as he came through the door, "Em was just telling me that we already have a good nanny on the staff."

"I came to apologise for Delilah."

"Accepted, it was just a little misunderstanding on my part. By the way, have the pair of you come to any agreement over names yet?"

"Not yet, Mother, she is still calling him 'it' but I somehow don't think that'll be among the final choices," he said, trying to introduce a touch of humour.

***

"Can I be a bridesmaid? Will it be a white wedding? Will I—"

"Give over, Dinah, "said her mother, "nothing's been arranged as yet, and anyway that's up to your sister to decide, I'm sure she'll let us know in good time, so get on with your breakfast, and don't pester Liz or she might say no."

"I can't buy much in here," Victor said as they walked into the Maypole store, "I haven't got my ration book with me."

"Men," Liz said shaking her head, "I don't know how you would manage without a good woman behind you. Hullo, Mark, is your father handy?"

"Hullo, Liz, is this Trev?"

"No, silly, it's Victor."

"Hullo Victor," Mark's father said, "pleased to meet you, I'm Harry."

"Are you still wanting that old shed moved?" Liz asked.

"Yes," came the reply, "it's dismantled, in about seven or eight pieces."

"You'll move them for him, won't you, darling?"

"Higgins quoted twenty quid, I thought that was a bit, well, you know, it's only a small shed. Have a look, round the back."

"I'll only be a minute," Victor said as he went to fetch his lorry.

With Harry's help the shed was soon taken to its new home and in a little while they were back at the shop. Harry insisted on giving Victor three white five-pound notes. Victor put two in his pocket and handed one back. "That's plenty, thanks," he said.

"Are you sure?"

"I'm sure," Victor replied.

As they entered the shop Liz was about to pay for her shopping, "Put it on the slate." Harry said.

"But you don't have a slate," said Liz.

"I know," Harry replied.

***

"What's this about wanting to call him Douglas?" asked Delilah. "There's no one with that name in my family, and as far as I know, not in yours either. Why can't we call him Ernest Charles?"

"There's never been an Ernest in either family as far as I know."

"Maybe not, but I like the name and it's famous."

"What Ernest is famous?"

"Hemingway, he wrote *A Farewell to Arms* and *For whom the Bell Tolls*."

"All right, you can have Ernest and I'll have Douglas," said Charles.

"After who?" asked his wife.

"Bader, Douglas Bader."

"Oh," she murmured. "Ernest Charles Douglas. Haha," she cried, "it hardly needs a surname."

"Right," Charles said, "Ernest Charles Douglas Bucklow it is."

"Mother, we, Delilah and I have decided to call our boy Ernest Charles Douglas Bucklow."

A tear rolled down Lady Jane's cheek. "What is it, Mother?" Charles asked.

"Ernest, I never told you but Ernest was your father's middle name."

"Don't you usually get one of the others to do the bedrooms, Em?" asked Delilah, as she watched Em from her easy chair.

"Yes, miss... oh, listen to me, in my mind you're still Miss Delilah, I must try to call you ma'am."

"Oh, that's okay when there's just two of us. Have you heard of someone called Douglas Bader?"

"Oh, yes, miss, Douglas Bader, he lost a leg in an aeroplane crash but was a fighter pilot during the war, even though he had an artificial leg, a real hero and inspiration to his squadron. Charles would be able to tell you more about him than I can."

Chapter Thirty-two

It had been a tiring and stressful weekend, Victor had lost count of how many of Liz's relatives they called on and how many times and to whom Liz had shown her ring, fetching comments like 'beautiful', 'worth a fortune' and 'is it real'. Victor was glad to be back on the open road, with a bit of a mixed load though this time, a couple of bales of blankets each for Chester Infirmary and Walton Hospital in Liverpool, plus an assortment of packages to David Jones and Co, a wholesale grocery warehouse in Strand Street Liverpool, then hopefully arriving home to Gillian and the kids before their bedtime.

Driving across London was one thing, but the kerfuffle in Witney over the Chester bales had cost a lot of time and made him behind schedule, Maybe, he thought, if I drop the Chester bales off tonight, and perhaps I ought to offload the items for David Jones in Liverpool, packages the size of those are more likely to disappear than the bales, and then if I deliver the blankets tomorrow, that will give me two nights at home with the kids and the weekend back down south with Liz, that is if she's still not got a job.

***

With a chuff chuff chuff and an almighty great cloud of steam the engine came to a standstill. Gillian was standing as near to the barrier as the ticket collector would allow. "Keep the gateway clear," he shouted, "let the passengers through. Tickets please," he said to one passenger. "Wait over there, please, while I see to those with tickets," then another, very soon three or four travellers were waiting.

"Gillian."

"Mavis."

They shouted in unison, hugging as if it had been years since they had last seen each other. "Where are the children?" asked Mavis.

"My neighbour, Mrs Bonner, is minding them. It was much easier coming here without them. Anyway, how are you, putting on weight? Oh, don't tell me?"

"Yes, four months, and the problem is I'm not sure who's the father," Mavis replied, almost in tears. "But never mind me, what about you?"

"Oo no, thank you," Gillian replied. "I think two, one of each is enough, a nicely balanced family. How about a cuppa before we catch the bus?"

"They've been little angels," said Mrs Bonner when Gillian and Mavis arrived home. "I've given them their tea, so just a bath and bed I think."

"Er, thank you, Mrs Bonner," Gillian replied.

"Call me Jo, that's short for Josephine, 'Mrs' is a bit too formal for friends. Well I'll away, Goodnight," she said as she went out.

"Can I help with the bathing?" asked Mavis.

"Ooh, please Mummy can we have a bath?" begged Malcolm.

"Normally only on a Sunday," Gillian explained to Mavis, "but as a special treat."

Gillian was downstairs in the kitchen preparing an evening meal when Victor arrived home.

"Who's with the kids?" he asked when he heard the splashing.

"Why don't you go and see," prompted Gillian.

Victor ran up the stairs two at a time and entered the bathroom. "Mavis!" he said in surprise.

"Daddy," Malcolm was pointing at his sister and saying, "Molly hasn't got a—"

"Little girls don't," came the timely reply from Mavis.

"I'll leave you to it," Victor said as he turned to leave.

"No, don't go," said Mavis, "your son is ready to be dried, his towel is behind you."

The children had been tucked up in bed and were asleep, the three adults had finished supper and were sitting around a glowing fire, Mavis and Gillian in the two armchairs while Victor was spread out on the settee. Inevitably the conversation turned to the Red Lion and the new licensee and the proposed 'improvements'. Birkenhead Breweries had already spent a lot of money 'bringing the place up to date'. "Tarting it up," Mavis called it. If anything the number of customers had gone down; Colin was no longer the cellar man, so his father and Uncle 'Arry had taken their business elsewhere, not that they drank a lot, and as for old Chris, he was probably supping with 'Old Nick' down below. The old country pub atmosphere had gone, and Mavis said that once she had to stretch to reach the pumps, she would be going too.

The convivial company chatted well into the night before dealing with the question of who would sleep where. The children each had their own bedrooms and Gillian was quite adamant that they must not be disturbed, which only left the double bed in their room. "Before you suggest it," Gillian said to Victor, "three in a bed won't happen. In her state Mavis will not be using the settee, and," she went on, "neither will I, so don't even think it."

"I can't sleep on this old lumpy thing," he objected.

"It's a bed settee," said Gillian, "so see if you can open it out. You'll need it, 'cos Mavis doesn't go home until Saturday."

***

"I really must be going, darling," said Charles.

"But you've haven't been here more than a couple of days," whined Delilah. "I'm sure the Air Force can manage without you a bit longer… it's not as if there was a war on."

"I really must go," he reiterated, "the C.O. only said for a couple of days and I've been home a week already, my sweet." Charles gave his wife a bear hug and kissed her, then headed to the nursery to see his son before he left. On his way out, he popped into the drawing room to say farewell to his mother.

"You do look smart in your uniform, dear," she remarked. "Have a safe journey. You will be home for Christmas? Perhaps they might make you group captain by then, that would be nice."

That would be nice, hmm, some hopes, he thought, mimicking his mother, pigs can fly.

"I think we're in for a busy Christmas this year," Em was telling her staff. "We will know how busy as soon as her ladyship gives me her guest list. But first things first, Esther will you take the breakfast tray up to the nursery and then after breakfast keep watch while Ruth and I are in with her ladyship preparing the week's menus."

"But we've already made them out," said Ruth.

"Yes," Em replied, "but this is what we're suggesting. It is up to her ladyship to decide if she would like anything different."

Delilah walked into the nursery where Rebecca had just fed baby Ernest. "Let me hold him," she said, picking him up.

Rebecca quickly put a clean napkin on Delilah's shoulder.

"What's that for?" she asked.

"As a precaution," replied Rebecca. "Now hold him up to your shoulder, gently rub his back to—" Ernest burped and regurgitated all over the napkin. "Good boy," said Rebecca.

"I don't see what was good about being sick all over me," remarked his mother. "It's just as well you put that thing on my shoulder" she added as she gingerly removed the soiled item. "Can I change him?" she asked.

"I don't think you'll find it very pleasant at this age," answered Rebecca. "In fact, you might prefer to leave the room while I deal with it."

***

"Is that—" Victor asked quietly while Gillian was upstairs out of earshot.

"No, I was already, so you're quite safe, although I wish it was," answered Mavis. Then, hearing the stairs creak, "Perhaps you could run me back on Saturday."

"That would be a good idea," said Gillian, "it would save all the hanging around waiting for buses."

"If it's all right for you two, I've got work to do," Victor said as he headed for the door.

The late getaway didn't bother Victor. This time of year the road through Buxton wasn't usually busy. It was too cold up here in the foothills of the Pennines, even for hardy walkers. As he left Alfreton he wondered whether he should have taken the longer route through Derby, but that could put an extra twenty or so miles on the journey. Rain he could cope with, but mist in the narrow passes, well, that would be a different matter. Another two miles and he drove out into the sunshine, bright maybe, but the speed with which the clouds were scudding across the sky indicated a cold north wind.

The skid marks on the Buxton road meant the twists and turns of the road had caught out many unwary drivers. Victor was a cautious driver and had used this road many times. Even so, he had to be very careful; a change in the weather could make the road surface unpredictable, a challenge for anyone who used that route, especially in the winter.

Driving steadily, Victor followed the A615, turning sharp left at the road junction, then right through the village of Wessington. The rain came, then turned to hail, driven by the north wind and making it hard to see the road ahead. Victor stopped to wait for a break in the weather; as quickly as it had started, it stopped and he was about to drive on when a car slid sideways with the driver's side smashing into the signpost at the side of the road. Victor opened the passenger door. The female passenger, trying to run, slipped and fell. The driver tried without success to restart the engine. "The cow grabbed the wheel and pulled the hand brake," he was shouting.

Victor helped the distressed lady into the passenger seat of his lorry. "I was shopping in Buxton," she was saying in between her sobbing. "My husband was going to meet me off the bus at Doehole, the bus never arrived and Larry offered me a lift. As I knew him I thought it would be all right, but he drove fast right through Doehole and wouldn't stop to let me out."

"Where will your husband be now?" Victor asked.

"I don't know, he's probably driving to Buxton."

"Well, let's get you home. You'll have to tell me where to go," he said.

"Not far, first left."

A policeman was standing in the road signalling Victor to stop.

Victor wound the window down. "Is there a problem, officer?" he asked.

"Would you turn your engine off and step down a moment. We've had a complaint, sir, that you forced a vehicle of the road and also forced this lady—"

"I think you have been misinformed, Officer."

"If you will let me finish, sir—where was I up to—ah, yes, forced this lady to accompany you."

"Wrong," said Victor, "just ask the lady."

A car drew up and the driver jumped out. "My wife is all right, is she?"

"One thing at a time, please, sir."

The lady got out of the lorry. "What are the police doing? This man rescued me, Joseph."

"We've had a complaint that he caused Mr Parks to collide with a road sign."

"I made the car crash," she said, "arrest me." The policeman looked flustered. "I crashed his car because Larry Parks was trying to hijack me."

"I'll kill him."

"There'll be no killing on my patch, Jo, and I'll pretend I didn't hear that. If your good lady is prepared to lodge a complaint, we'll get a warrant for his arrest." The policeman wrote a few details in his notebook, and said to Victor, "If you would give my colleague a few details, name and address, you will be free to leave."

"You will come to the Highwayman and let me buy you a drink?" asked the lady's husband.

"Thank you sir," replied Victor, "but I still have deliveries to make in Chester."

"I'm sorry, sir, the road beyond Buxton is closed, there's been a landslip."

Victor thought for a moment, "Okay, Jo, I will join you for that drink."

Victor sat looking at his map. It was printed in the thirties and showed A roads and a few B roads, but the hills around Buxton showed as a dark mass, with no alternative road from where he was, unless he backtracked and took the more southerly route, then goodness knows what time he'd be back in Carlton. I suppose I'll have to head back home and go by way of Derby tomorrow. It's going to mean that I won't get back down to Chingford until very late, or even Sunday if I run into trouble again.

I wouldn't want to get stuck with Mavis on board, he thought, hmm, I don't know though, that could be interesting.

Chapter Thirty-three

"Agnes's daughter has invited her and me to stay with them in Lincoln for a few days," said James, "but I've told her that I can't be away in case her ladyship needs me."

"Why don't you go, I'm sure Harris would be available to drive."

"He wouldn't look after the motors, and I wouldn't want him messing around with them," James quickly replied, interrupting Em, "and anyway, I don't really want to go. I don't get on with the daughter's husband, and apparently Jimmy Cleghorne has offered to drive her."

"When is she going?"

"I think she'd like to go later today."

Hmm, thought Em, it's hardly worth travelling that far for less than a week, any longer and we'll be into preparing for Christmas guests. "Did she say how long for? I'll give her time to come and tell me before I have a word with her ladyship," Em said to James. "I'll probably need to get someone else in to cover for her."

Ruth studied the recipe in Em's handwriting, trying to visualise putting all the ingredients into the big mixing bowl, then mixing them by hand, quite a job, still if Em could do it, so could she, at least she was going to give it a go. Em was watching her from the office. Only a slip of a girl, but then I suppose I was too at that age, she thought, nice girl, should do well.

"Right, now I expect you've remembered it all," she said. Ruth looked horrified. Em laughed. "Don't look so worried, dear, that's why it's all written down, so that you don't have to remember everything. But first things first. Let's put the kettle on for a cup of tea, I'll take Lady Jane's tea while you take a tray up to the nursery for Rebecca and Esther. I should think Rebecca feels cut off from the rest of us, so the two of them can have their tea together."

"I'd just got to my back gate when I saw them leave," James said, "Jimmy's got an old First World War bread van. It looked like something out of Keystone Cops." He shook his head and laughed. "I don't know how long it will take them, or even whether they'll get there, but I watched them go."

"Well, she certainly hasn't been to see me," replied Em. "Pour yourself a cup of tea, after that we will both go and have a word with her ladyship."

"Ah, James, would you bring the Rolls around to the front, I wish to go into Chester to buy an outfit to show off my new slim waist." Delilah's voice seemed to echo down the hall as Em and James were coming out of the drawing room. Delilah was coming down the stairs, dressed in a hat and coat that probably came from a Paris salon, and would turn a few heads in Chester.

"Delilah, why do you need the Rolls?" Lady Jane's voice carried from the drawing room, as Em held the door open.

"To go shopping, Auntie."

"On a Thursday? You do realise that Davidson's are closed on Thursdays?"

"Oh, fiddlesticks, I thought today was Wednesday."

"And to go dressed like that would double, or they might even treble, the prices you were quoted," added her ladyship.

"Fiddlesticks, oh, fiddlesticks," Delilah was heard to mumble as she climbed the stairs.

"What are you two laughing about?" Ruth asked as they entered the kitchen.

The aroma of fruit cakes in the oven filled the kitchen. Em and James were sitting in the office enjoying a mid-afternoon cup of tea. "I think I'll wait until next week before I advertise for a cleaner, that will fit in nicely with taking on seasonal staff for Christmas and New Year," Em was saying. "I think we might have a full house this year." The bell rang, Em looked at the indicator board, Lady Jane, although it might have been Delilah feeling her feet. Em made her way to the drawing room, "Yes, ma'am?" She addressed herself to the most senior personage present.

Delilah, sitting quite upright, pointed to the tea trolley. "Take the trolley away," she said.

"Please be a little more respectful of my staff," said Jady Jane.

"They're employed to do as they are told," came the sulky reply.

"If you want to keep good staff, you treat them as equals. Oh, Em, the guest list, see if you think anyone has been forgotten."

"Thank you, ma'am," Em said to Lady Jane, and "Thank you, miss," to Delilah. Her ladyship was watching her daughter-in-law's reaction with amusement.

***

Not that the drive back was tiring, but disappointment at things not going to plan was frustrating. Upon entering the lounge and finding both armchairs were occupied, Victor threw himself down on the settee, about to ask who was going to make him a drink, when the memory of his mother's reply all those years ago made him get up: "Anyone for a cuppa?" he asked.

The two women looked at each other in surprise, then answered in unison, "Yes please!"

"Sit down, love," said Mavis, with a slip of the tongue that seemed to go unnoticed. "I'll make it."

Victor sat down again. "Daddy!" cried Malcolm as he ran and threw himself at his father.

"Have a good day, love?" asked Gillian as she put her knitting down and picked up the pattern, hardly expecting an answer and not paying much attention as she tried to fathom out what the designer meant by 'k.12, sl.2bk, k.2, k.2 sl., k.2, sl.2f., k.2, k.2sl., k to end'. "Struth, and this is supposed to be an easy pattern," she mumbled.

"Let me see it," said Victor.

"You won't be able to…"

"It's straightforward," he answered. "Knit 12, slip 2 on to cable needle at back, knit 2, knit 2 slip stitches, knit 2, slip 2 to front, knit 2, knit 2 slip stitches, knit to end," he said. "It's quite simple." He handed the pattern back.

"Ooh I do hate clever dicks," Gillian replied, "why don't you do it then?"

"My daddy is cleverer than my mummy," Malcolm said, and Victor and Gillian laughed.

"What are you two finding so funny?" Mavis asked as she carried in the tea tray.

***

Em quickly ran her eyes down the list of overnight guests knowing that overnight would be likely to mean a week or more. Hardly surprising that Harry Rock is top of the list, Cynthia and Nigel (if he has returned from Canada), Lady Jane's friends Brenda Pilkington and Wilfred; Marjorie Dawes and her friends Alice and Malcolm Cooper (I can't recall that name), Charlton Hawthorne, I certainly hope he keeps his distance, then lastly Ernest and Nicole Bombridge. Quite an assorted bunch, and of course not forgetting Alfred Higginbottom, Charles's batman.

As for which suites she would allocate the guests, with six named suites, but requiring accommodation for seven parties, Em decided to put Charlton in one of the seldom used rooms in the west wing, well away from the female servants' quarters and their back stairs. That wing had originally housed the less favoured guests and male servants; during the war it had been occupied by the American nursing staff. Including the room that Charlton would be occupying, opening the west wing meant six more, though less spacious, rooms being available.

"James, would you be kind enough to take this card to Mrs Grant in the general store, perhaps she would put it in the window."

James looked at the card. "Three staff?" he asked.

"Yes," replied Em, "just in case I need someone to replace Agnes."

"And what if she gets back in time?"

"It'll make it easier for the others, and provide extra help in the nursery."

An hour later James was back. "Guess what? Cleghorne's back in the village, but there's no sign of Agnes. The blighter crossed over the road when he saw me. I've had a word with Constable Biggens, he's going to make a few enquiries, he said he'll let me know at the end of the week."

***

If Victor thought he could get an early start, he was very much mistaken. "Wait a moment while I get… Ooh, while I think of it…" whatever it might be, and "Oh, I forgot to tell you…" took best part of half an hour. Why couldn't she have put it in a letter? he thought. He wasn't taking chances, as soon as Mavis was in her seat, and almost before she had shut the door, the lorry was moving and hardly slowed as it turned into the Carlton High Street.

"Oh, I meant to tell Gillian—"

"Put it in a letter, we haven't time to turn back now," he said as he drove past Chilwell Barracks and headed out of Nottingham and on towards Derby.

"I'll need a loo stop soon," Mavis said.

"You'll have to wait while I look for a gorse bush," he joked.

"You're 'orrible," she replied, laughing.

"Will this do?" Victor asked as he slowed and stopped outside The Rose and Crown.

"I'll have a gin and it," she said, as he helped her down.

This is starting to get expensive, he thought, both in time and money. As they left elevenses behind them, still it is a nice day and there's little on the road, he thought, as he gently pressed his right foot further down on the pedal, well the road sign did indicate 'unrestricted'.

As Uttoxeter, Blythe Bridge and Sandbach diminished in the rear view mirror, Victor was starting to feel more relaxed. "How soon will we be at the Red Lion?" Mavis asked.

"I don't know," Victor replied. "I need to make my deliveries first, or I'll be stuck with them all weekend, and I'm due to pick up another load in Oxfordshire Monday morning." Chester was almost deserted, and after making a quick stop at the infirmary, they headed north for the Mersey Tunnel and Walton Hospital.

"I need a—" she didn't need to say more as he stopped at the King's Head, just off the East Lancs road, a couple of miles north of Warrington.

"I know," he said, "mother's ruin."

"I've ordered some sandwiches, and a room," Mavis said.

"But—"

"No buts," she interrupted.

"But you'll be back twenty to thirty minutes from here," Victor expostulated.

"I know," Mavis answered.

It was almost dark when Victor drove away from the Red Lion. He didn't relish driving a hundred miles or more in the dark, and regretted a late start in the morning, but at least the roads were almost empty. The possibility of running into army convoys on a Saturday night was virtually zero. Military personnel were usually either in the NAAFI, a local hostelry, or at home with the missus. I certainly hope so tonight, he thought.

Driving steadily, not too fast, not too slow, squeezing every mile he could from the diesel, there'd be no garages open tonight if he ran short. Passing Walsall on the right, the glare from the street lights tended to make it difficult as he drove on into the night, and ahead he could see the glow in the clouds that heralded his approach to Birmingham. Worming his way through A and B roads, he avoided the street lights of the metropolis by using the sparsely lit country roads.

On the A45 heading into Coventry, Victor remembered the devastation there had been last time he was there. New buildings had replaced many that had been flattened that night in 1941. A mile south of the city centre he saw a pinpoint of light waving in the darkness, he slowed and stopped, having seen two figures in his headlights, and lowered his window.

"Are you going to London?" a voice called out.

"Okay, get in," he said, and as soon as they were seated drove on.

Further south, the skies were clearer and the countryside was lit by the full moon; it was already cold, and the absence of cloud carried the promise of a frost. Occasionally Victor glanced across at his passengers. When he asked them what part of London, Eddy, the taller of the two, explained that he was taking Shirley, his lady friend, to meet his parents living in Hackney, and Victor realised that the companion was a female. Military uniform, in the dark, can so easily hide a person's gender, and in the moonlight through the windscreen he could only just see the RAF uniforms.

In the warmth of the cab, Victor's passengers had dozed off. They had been driving along the A5 for some time, passed Luton and were driving through Barnet when they stirred. "Where are we?" asked Shirley in a melodious Welsh voice.

"Barnet," answered Victor.

"Can we stop for a drink, please?" that charming voice once more.

Victor stopped outside The Jolly Fiddler. "Mine's a bitter. Better hurry," he said, "it's getting late."

Eddie had just ordered when the barman rang the bell. "Last orders, please."

"Where's Shirley?" Victor asked.

"Gone to powder her nose," answered Eddy. "Keep an eye," he said as he dashed off. Shirley was still missing when Eddy returned. He looked around. "I didn't think her nose was that big," he murmured, then, "Don't tell her I said that."

Victor delivered the young couple to Hackney, for which he received a kiss from Shirley. "Don't you dare," he told Eddy. "Kisses from lovely young ladies are always welcome, from fellows, never," he said laughing. "All the best," he called out as he drove away.

It was close to midnight as he arrived in Monksham Lane. Turning off the engine he coasted to a standstill across the road from the flat. Quietly climbing the stairs, he peeped into the bedroom and saw the still form in the bed.

Quickly and quietly he stripped. Slipping between the sheets, he snuggled up to the figure. "Hmm…" the figure murmured.

Chapter Thirty-four

It was seldom that Constable Biggens had any reason to call at Moore Hall, in fact the last time he had called there had been back in 1939, checking to see if the air raid siren could be heard that far away from the village. Today, just as then, he found riding his bicycle along the gravel driveway was so difficult that he had had to walk, pushing it; leaving it by the gate would risk it being stolen. His predecessor had had that happen, and been made to pay for the replacement out of his own pocket.

He gave the bell pull such a hefty wrench he wondered if he might have broken it. "Constable," said Delilah, being in the hall when the bell rang, "would you kindly go round the back to the tradesmen's entrance." She closed the door in his face.

Hardly a wise thing to do to a member of the Constabulary, thought Em, he'll be watching out for her.

"Sit down please, officer, James will be with us in a minute. Tea or coffee? Thank you, Ruth. Milk? Sugar? Do have a biscuit, freshly made, two if you like. Ah, James, Inspector, no, sorry, Constable Biggens would like a word. Of course, as her ladyship's representative I will need to know the outcome of your enquiries."

The constable got out his notebook, turning a few pages until he found the one he was looking for. "On Monday the—"

"You don't need all that formality," interrupted James, "just the basic facts, otherwise your coffee will be cold."

"All right," he replied. "According to Mr Cleghorne, he took Mrs Jones to Warrington, she caught the sixteen hundred hours, yes, four o'clock train, three hours after Mr Jones—you, James—said you saw them leave. I inspected his old van, there were one or two defects I told him to get sorted. What did you say, sir? Yes, there is or was a mattress. I also told him to remove it as the vehicle was not registered as a caravan.

Where was I?" After studying his notes he continued. "The Lincoln police confirmed that Mrs Jones is safely at the address you gave, which is her daughter's house. When she spoke to the officer, she said she expected to be staying with her daughter until after the New Year, the grand-daughter's first birthday being January the third. Was there anything more, sir? Madam? Then if you will forgive me, oh, and thank you for the coffee and biscuits, a real treat. I'll let myself out. Good afternoon."

"Well, what do you make of that?" asked James. "I bet she wasn't waiting all that long at the station."

"You could do with making a few enquiries. Someone may have seen where they were all that time; try the station goods office," suggested Em. "That old van would be very conspicuous," she continued. "Take the Wolseley, and call in at the general store and see if they've had any anyone showing interest in the advert."

"I won't be long," James called out as he went out of the door.

***

"I'm going to need your room for my sixteen-year-old boy Clarence," said Mrs Carter, wife of the new licensee at the Red Lion. "He'll be arriving at the weekend. I've had a word with Mrs Grace at number eight, she can put you up for a modest rent."

"Just how modest is modest?" asked Mavis. "Remember, the money I get is *after* the cost of my room had been deducted."

"Oh, I don't know about that," countered Mrs Carter.

"Okay," replied Mavis, "give me my money for yesterday and I'll go now. I'm paid daily."

"But you can't leave me without a barmaid."

"I can," answered Mavis, opening the till. "Day rate is four shillings," she said, taking the right money out and signing the till receipt.

"But I don't know where anything is," Mrs Carter answered, almost in tears.

"Hey, Bill," Mavis called out, "is your taxi available? Good, ready in ten minutes, okay?" She turned to leave and almost bumped into Mr Carter.

"What's going on?" he asked.

"Ask the missus," replied Mavis as she disappeared through the doorway.

When Mavis reappeared, carrying her case and a bag containing all her clothes and knick knacks, Mr Carter was waiting for her. "I want you to stay."

"It'll cost ya."

Mr Carter inwardly groaned. "How much?"

"A coupla' quid extra and I'll stay the week."

"A couple of quid extra and you stay two weeks and you teach your replacement."

"And my room?"

Mr Carter paused. "Okay, agreed," he said.

"Now."

"What?" he asked.

"The coupla' quid."

"Okay, but tonight, you're a tough nut," he said, "and I like that." As they shook hands, he added, "Tomorrow I'd like you to start teaching my wife."

It was a furious Mrs Carter who disappeared out through the doorway.

**

"Firstly," said James, "there are several people interested in earning a few quid over Christmas and the New Year, and two who it seems are looking for a more permanent job, so I put up a card to say I would collect them on Thursday morning at nine o'clock. I hope that was okay."

"Yes, that's fine," replied Em. "What happened at the station?"

"Well, apparently he occasionally pulls into the yard, there's always a lady in the passenger seat, but no one gets out, and it's usually there for a couple of squeaky hours then drives off. Jo Collins, the station master, reckons the van needs some oil on the springs to stop them squeaking 'cos the passengers waiting for their trains keep commenting. Yes, the van was there on that day for about two and a half hours and they were seen getting out of the van together. I quote 'the van was squeaking for nearly two hours before they got out'. He drove off about a quarter of an hour before the train that she got on arrived. They didn't need to make it public," James said, "it makes me look such a fool."

"You're not a fool, James," replied Em, "just a lovely, honest, trusting husband married to a dishonest unfaithful wife. You deserve someone better. It's her who's the fool."

"Someone like you... maybe?"

"Maybe," answered Em. "Only time will tell."

"How about some muscle relaxing massage tonight, about seven?" he asked.

"Shush, not so loud, I don't want the others to hear. Make it eight."

"If anyone wants me, I'll be moving my stuff into the flat over the garage," James said, as he turned to leave Em's office.

"You'd better put the heating on right now. It hasn't been used since the Americans left," replied Em. "You'll need fresh sheets and blankets, there're some clean sheets and thingmies, er, pillow cases in the airing cupboard. On second thoughts leave them there until later, then they'll be nice and warm, and new blankets in the store."

There's nowt like being looked after by a good woman, James thought, smiling to himself. "Thanks, Em," he answered, as he headed for the garage.

***

After a late start, and a cooked breakfast prepared by Liz, she and Victor strolled through the park. Considering the time of the year, it was warm in the sunshine, particularly if you kept out of the cool breeze blowing from the south east, although even then they were glad of their coats. Victor looked up at the clock on the church tower, "Half past eleven," he murmured. It seemed so peaceful, almost a different world away from his everyday life.

"Half past?" Liz asked. "Mummy is expecting us for lunch, we'd better head back."

Victor put his spoon down in the empty dish. "There's only one thing a man can say to a woman who can cook like that," he said.

"What's that?" asked Liz's mum.

"Will you marry me!" Victor answered.

"You're too late," she said, laughing, "I'm already married. Anyway you've already asked Liz."

"Tell me," he asked, "where did you find the recipe for Ambrosia?"

"That wasn't Ambrosia," said Dinah, "that was bread pudding." She was frowning as she looked around the table wondering why everyone was laughing. Victor reached down to rub the spot on his leg where Liz had kicked him.

"Fancy a beer, lad?" asked Mr Norman. "Go on, have a Guinness, get some—"

Seeing Dinah sitting in the room, he stopped in mid-sentence. "Get some what, Dad?" she asked.

"Beer in your belly," suggested Victor.

"Thank you, Victor," Liz's mother said. He can be so embarrassing at times, she thought, shaking her head, one of these days he'll just blurt out something inappropriate, without realising who's in the room.

With Mr Norman at one side of the fireplace and Victor at the other, a half filled glass of light ale on the book case beside him, Victor relaxed. He was watching Mrs Norman and her two daughters sitting on the floor playing snakes and ladders. He could see where Liz got her good looks from; for someone in her early twenties Liz had a really good figure, but for some one probably twice Liz's age, Mrs Norman was, well, what could one say? Victor's gaze then rested on the youngest one of the group; but for a little puppy fat, for a girl of fourteen she was already quite well developed and had the makings of a figure to match those of her mother and sister.

"Have another," said Mr Norman, distracting Victor from his musing.

"Er, no, thank you," he replied, "I haven't finished this one."

"Home!" shouted Dinah.

"How many games is that?" asked Victor.

"Eight," answered Dinah, "and I've won five."

"Seven," corrected Liz, "and you've won four."

"Five," insisted Dinah, "you won two and Mummy won one and, oh, yes, that's four I won," she conceded. "Let's play something else. Do you want a game, Victor? No? All you men are the same," she said.

"You just sit down on the settee and read a book," Mrs Norman said, "while Liz and I do the tea."

As they walked back to their cosy little flat in Monksham Lane, Victor was explaining to Liz how with an early start in the morning he should be able to deliver a load up north, stop somewhere overnight, pick up another load and be back on Tuesday. "That's fine, dear," she said, and sure enough with a breakfast of fried egg on toast, saying, "But I wanted to be up to see you off, dear," Victor, with a kiss, was on his way shortly before six.

It was inevitable that the mills that had been churning out blankets for so long would occasionally need some repairs, and so it was that weekend that the wheels of industry had come to a grinding halt. Well, not quite, the mills were still rolling, but the machine in the packing department had seized up, and it was back to making up bales by hand, while they waited for a part no longer available from the makers to be made and fitted by a local engineering works.

The expected load for the Midlands would be ready tomorrow, they promised, but would he like to take a load to Southampton Docks? Better than nothing, Victor thought, and soon he was heading down the A3. However, his arrival at the docks was delayed by a lorry that had shed its load, and then having to join a long queue at the dockside gates, all waiting while the SS Camberley, which had docked a day behind schedule, finished unloading, before access could be gained for Victor to offload in the warehouse.

Leaving the docks at five in the afternoon meant he ran into the busiest traffic as many offices and factories closed, and driving through the crowded roads, even for someone of Victor's experience, was hazardous and slow. However, back on the A3 there was very little to trouble him, and taking the South Circular Road he was able to avoid the traffic in the centre of London. The twisting and turning driving around through the suburbs of this great metropolis at times was slow anyway, but as the evening drew on it started to rain, making it harder to see and the traffic slower. Never mind, he thought, not much further. Once he had crossed the Thames it would be as easy as falling off a horse, he would then be in familiar territory.

London Bridge, City Road, Islington, it's going well, I don't want to speak too soon, through Highbury, fairly close to the Arsenal football ground, somewhere down one of the side turnings, down the hill to Finsbury Park and turn right with the park on the left, not far now, it's a pity the park is closed, I could have used their loo. Never mind, somewhere here I turn left for Haringey, ah, what's that, a public toilet, I should be able to stop here for a couple of minutes.

Angel Road and he was back in Chingford. Late, but never mind, he glided the lorry to a stop and parked it for the night. Quietly opening the door, he put his coat on the hook and climbed the stairs. Liz was ready for bed. She jumped up as he entered the room. "I wasn't expect—" A sound behind him made him look round as Dinah, coming from the bathroom, shrieked and tried unsuccessfully to cover her nakedness as she tripped over her towel.

"It's okay, I'll sleep in the lounge," he said as he passed Liz's sister in the doorway.

"I wasn't expecting you," Liz was saying as she followed him.

"I know," he said, "there was trouble at the mill. I've just got back from Southampton."

Chapter Thirty-five

Ruth watched Em plucking the pheasant. She had seen them hanging from hooks in the butcher's shop in Warrington. Since the end of hostilities she had seen sides of pork and beef there, even ducks and geese, but she had never before seen anyone removing feathers. Plucking, she called it.

"Okay," said Em, "you've watched me do it, now I want you to give it a try." Inwardly Ruth squirmed, she wasn't sure she could do it. "Hold it firmly, gently but firmly, try not to break the skin, nor the feather. Take out the broken piece, that's right, you've got it. Carry on with this one while I do the next."

I'm not sure I like this, but I suppose I'll get used to it, thought Ruth.

"Good morning, Em," said James, as he came through the door, followed by three girls and a boy. "Let me see if I've got it right. Sarah, sorry, no, you're Catherine, Sarah, Monica and Ralph."

"Ruth," Em called, "take a break from that for a moment and make us all a brew. I take it you all drink tea? Help yourselves to milk and sugar. Oh, Ruth, where did you put... thank you dear, you've got them... do help yourselves... Ruth made the shortcakes yesterday.

"Well, now that you're all a little more relaxed, I am basically looking for staff to do cleaning and for chambermaids, but don't despair, Ralph, I'm sure I can find something for you. I'll see you each individually in my office. In the meantime, if someone would be kind enough to help Ruth in the scullery with these few cups." Em drew James to one side as Ruth gathered the cups and plates and put them on the tray. Monica picked up the tray and followed Ruth into the scullery.

"When I saw there was a young lad among the group," Em was saying as they walked into the office, "what do you think? We'll have him in first."

"Sit down and relax, Ralph. Don't mind James, he's only here as an ornament. That's better, you can smile." Ralph looked at James, chuckled and looked back at Em. "This should only take a few minutes. First of all I'll take a few details: your name is Ralph Richardson. Was your dad in the army? The Royal Artillery? Your address? Your hobbies? Thank you, no, don't get up, at least not yet. Over to you, James."

"I would like you to stand up please, Ralph, at attention, that's it but relaxed, that's better. Head up but not stiff, good, you can sit down again now. Tell me, do you know anything about car engines? You help your dad in the garage, at home, I see. Can I take him outside for a few minutes? Thank you, Em. Ralph, come along with me," James said, and headed towards the door.

"Sarah, join me please, I'll have Catherine next and finally Monica."

Half an hour later, she said, "We'll wait a little while for James to reappear with Ralph. Ah, here they come now." Em looked at the four expectant faces. "Firstly, I cannot promise permanent employment. If I have given anyone that impression, I apologise, the end is likely to be some undecided date in January 1947, is that clear? Right, starting on Monday," she looked at the paper in her hand, "Monica, working in the kitchen with Ruth. Sarah and Catherine will be under Esther, doing cleaning and assisting her as chambermaids. Any of you will sometimes be required to wait at table. I will probably swap you round from time to time. Now, please wait while I have a word with her ladyship."

"You think so? And the boy? Very well, I'll see them."

The nervous group entered the drawing room. The three girls gave a slight curtsey, and Ralph a bow. Em introduced them, then the girls were asked to wait in the hall. Ralph was standing at attention. "Relax, boy," said Lady Jane. "stand upright but relaxed," she said. "That's better. Now bring me the plate of biscuits from the tray."

Ralph carried the plate to her ladyship, and with a slight bow proffered the plate, saying, "Madam." After she took a biscuit and gave a slight wave away Ralph took one step back, as he had been shown earlier, then turned and returned the plate to the trolley.

"Hmm, yes, he has the makings," she said.

"Thank you, ma'am," said Em, and they joined the others in the hall.

"Good lad," said James, "you did well."

***

Victor could not believe his eyes. "I thought I'd—"

"You did."

"And?"

"They said they needed my room for their son."

"But they've got lots of rooms."

"I know, but the workmen are using those. It looks like someone is too tight to pay for the workmen to stay elsewhere."

"Logical, I suppose, but they can't work on those rooms while they're sleeping in them. And by 'eck, they needed doing up," he said. "But what are you doing here?"

"Don't panic," said Gillian, "we've moved the children into the back room and Mavis will be in the box room."

"I always knew I'd finish up in a box," Mavis commented smiling.

"All together now: 'Ahh.'" Victor said, "and while I think of it, I'm not having you paying anything towards the rent, the council might class it as subletting."

Gillian looked puzzled. "Of course not, what are you suggesting?" she asked.

"Subletting is against the rules, dear. They could evict us if we did," Victor replied.

"What do you suggest then, payment in kind?"

"It never crossed my mind, dearest."

"Nor mine," Mavis quickly added.

"Maybe they would give us a bigger house," suggested Gillian. "After all, Mavis is now homeless."

"Have you ever seen a pig fly?" asked Victor.

***

"You know how I feel about you sleeping with someone before you're married," said Mr Norman.

"I know, Daddy," answered Liz, "that's why we need a bed. Can we borrow the folding bed, please."

"I suppose so, but what about the settee in the flat?" he asked.

"You won't catch me sleeping on that thing," said Dinah. Liz glared at her sister.

"You're not sleeping anywhere but in your own bed here," growled her father.

"But Daddy," pleaded Dinah.

"You heard me," he said.

"Mummy?"

"You're not dragging me into this," her mother answered.

"But…"

"You heard what Daddy said," she replied.

"Thank you, Daddy," Liz answered, "I'll get Victor to collect it."

"It's all right," her father said, "I'll take it round, I'm dying to see this love nest."

***

"Try these on," said Em. "Use the room across the way… Now that looks really smart. Comfortable? Try these others, there's more room where it matters. That's better, what do you think, James? Hmm, I think you'd look better in one of these jackets. Yes, perfect for when you're answering the door, or serving the ladies their tea in the drawing room. It's all right, we'll teach you what to do. Now change back, then James will run you home with the girls. In the meantime, I'll sort out a couple more outfits and get them cleaned, although they were done before they were put away, you won't want to smell of mothballs, of that I'm sure. See you on Monday, Ralph. Such a lot to get one's tongue around, can we call you Alf, or better still, Alfie, no offence meant, but Alfie sounds so much more homely."

"Yes, miss," he replied.

"And you can call me Em, except when Lady Jane and Lady Delilah or any of the guests are around."

"Yes, miss, I mean Em."

Em smiled. Nice lad, should do well.

"James," said Em, "with Charlton sleeping in the west wing, I want all the girls' rooms in the east wing, so would you give me a hand moving my stuff into the west wing… and while I think of it, make sure the yale lock on the door at the top of the staff staircase is working so that one needs a key to use it." With Charlton there, she thought, and two spare rooms in case they're needed, myself opposite the stairs, then Alfie and Alfred, that will leave the six rooms in the east wing for the girls, and come to think of it, gives easy indoor access to the flat over the garage.

***

"I'd like to come as well to see this little, what did your father call it, a 'love nest'?"

"That's fine by me," answered Liz. "I don't know where he got that idea from." It's a good job Dad was wrapped up in the football on the wireless last night, she thought, it gave me the chance to get round and tidy up. As Liz turned the key in the door to the flat, Mr Norman pushed past her.

"Pardon me," said Liz as he rushed up the stairs. He wasn't going to let anyone interfere with the evidence. Upon entering the living room he stood and surveyed the scene, there were a couple of magazines on the coffee table, and a pair of men's pyjamas strewn on a pillow at one end of the settee and a blanket half lying on the floor. The bedroom similarly showed signs of respectability, someone having slept in the middle of the bed, the bedding thrown open from the side and lady's night apparel lying on top.

"Apologise to your daughter," Mrs Norman demanded.

"But it could have—"

"If that's what you think of me, I'll—" Liz started to say.

"I'm sorry," said Mr Norman, "but, well, you hear about—"

"Yes, in the scandal-mongering *News of the World*, so don't tar every decent girl with the same brush, even less so your own daughter."

***

With guests due to arrive within the next two or three weeks the training started in earnest, at times amid great frivolity. The six girls and Alfie, as he had become known, all took turns in the waiting and being waited on, for Em had no intention of leaving anyone out, and they all took to it as if their lives depended on it. Well, their livelihoods did. It would be fair to say that Em and James did a good job bringing them up to quite an acceptable standard in the short time available, especially Alfie, who was seeking to memorise as much as he could about the wines and spirits that were stocked in the cellars.

Smartly dressed, Alfie was standing near the bottom of the stairs, unseen as Em answered the door. "Good afternoon, sir, madam welcome to Moore Hall, I hope you had a pleasant journey." A brief raising of Em's hand brought Alfie into life. "I've put you in the Edwardian suite," then half turning to Alfie, she said, "Please take Mr and Mrs Ashburton's luggage up to the Edwardian suite, thank you."

"Oh," said Cynthia, "I didn't see him there."

James appeared from the kitchen. "I'll give Alfie a hand, before I move the car," he said, seeing the lad struggling with the large number of cases Cynthia usually travelled with.

Harry Rock was the next to arrive. He took one look at Alfie and quipped, "One's not enough, you should have bought the pair." Upon seeing Alfie smile, he added, "Oh, it smiles. Take no notice of me, son, I'm just a silly old fool."

"Not so old. Silly? I'll pass on that," said Em.

"Are you his grandmother?" Harry asked, making Alfie chuckle. "What kennel am I in tonight?"

"Tudor suite, Harry," Em answered.

"What, 'Enery the Eight not invited?"

"May I help you with your bag, sir?" asked Alfie.

"Goodness, it talks, what will they think of next?"

Most of the other guests had settled in before the blue RAF car arrived, bringing Wing Commander Charles Bucklow, driven by Alfred his batman. As Charles mounted the steps, Alfred drove the car round to the back entrance, unloaded and took the luggage upstairs.

"Good afternoon, sir, your mother and lady wife are in the drawing room."

"Thank you," he said. "Would you knock up a sandwich or two for me, we didn't stop so I haven't eaten since brekkie, there's an angel, you know what I like, something meaty. Ooh, and something for Alfred, he must be famished."

"Ham, chicken or pheasant, sir?"

"Yes, please, and some of that splendid pickle."

Alfie knocked on the door to the drawing room, counting to twenty, that was what Em had said was a good guide to save the embarrassment of walking in on something private, whatever that might be she did not say. Opening the door, he pushed the trolley to the centre of the room. "Would you like me to serve, ma'am?" he asked, but was dismissed by a movement of Lady Jane's hand.

A slight bow and Alfie turned, about to leave when Delilah called, "No, stop, let us see him serve." Confused, Alfie turned back to see what her ladyship instructed; Lady Jane once more waved her hand in dismissal.

"He is not a toy for your entertainment, so leave him alone and let him carry on with his work."

"But he is employed to serve," she insisted.

Lady Jane replied, "I said no." As Alfie closed the door behind him, she continued, "Now, Delilah, would you serve the tea, please."

Chapter Thirty-six

Alice and Malcolm had started out early to avoid the worst of the traffic, only to find that Marjorie was not ready when they reached Batch House, her home in Wincanton. Consequently they lost all the advantage of getting up at five and leaving home in Ramsden shortly after six a.m.

Malcolm was eager to show off his newly purchased car. He had seen the Armstrong Siddeley Hurricane, a drophead coupé, in the showroom and had fallen in love with the style. The run from Ramsden to Wincanton had shown how good she was—to Malcolm all cars came under the category of 'she'—with a fine burst of speed and modest fuel consumption, according to the salesman, of as many as twenty miles per gallon, very economical for a two litre motor.

As the two ladies were seated together in the back, Malcolm hoped their chatter would not distract him, especially with comments about his driving. At Taunton he joined the A38 and headed north to Bristol, then on up to Birmingham where he joined the A5. At this time of the year there was very little traffic on the road, mainly slow moving lorries; the Hurricane had no trouble overtaking those.

"Will we get to Lady Jane's before lunch, dear? No? Then can we find a place to stop for something to eat?" asked Alice.

"All right, dear," Malcolm replied. Slowing down as they crossed the River Severn, he pulled up outside a likely looking eating house. Malcolm looked at his map. "Hmm, I reckon we've another two, maybe three hours' drive, so come, ladies," he said as he folded his driver's seat forward to allow them to alight, "I suggest we try here for lunch."

"Cherry Tree Café," read Marjorie, "sounds like my kind of place."

***

"Not a bad estimate," said Malcolm as the car turned into the driveway of Moore Hall.

"You said two, maybe three hours," Alice reminded him. "It was more like four."

"That was going to be after we'd stopped an hour for lunch," he countered, trying to defend his estimate.

The ladies laughed. "Men," murmured Alice, "men."

"Good afternoon, ladies," said Em, "welcome, I hope you had a pleasant journey."

Alfie was on the move almost before Em raised her arm. "Let me assist you, sir," he said as he reached the bottom step, his hand held out ready to take hold of a case.

"You new here?" asked Malcolm. "I don't remember seeing you last time I came."

Alfie had stopped for a moment as he looked at the car. "Nice car, sir," he said, "really nice car."

James was coming down the steps. "Good afternoon, sir." Hmm, Armstrong Siddeley? This deserves a place in the garage, he thought, as he drove it around to the back of the house.

"Why wasn't James at Warrington to meet me?" asked Charlton.

"Did you ring from the station, sir?" asked Em.

"No, of course not," he replied. "I wasn't able to, I'd given my last change to the ticket collector on the railway."

Probably because you hadn't bought a ticket, thought Em. "I thought you used to have a car."

"We won't talk about that," he answered.

It was probably on hire purchase, she reflected. "You should have come through Chester, it's only a tuppenny bus ride away. I've put you in the west wing, room one, you should get a good view of the sunset from your room, sir."

"What about...?"

"Sorry sir, the other rooms are all in use. Alfie will take your bag up for you."

Em inspected her 'troop', the same as she did every time lunch or dinner was being formally served in the dining hall. The girls wore black dresses with white aprons. Alfie's outfit was normally a smart black suit with a short jacket, white shirt and bow tie, and a grey housecoat when he was assisting downstairs. When serving in the dining hall at lunchtime he wore the suit with a short jacket, but in the evenings and for special occasions, he changed into an even smarter suit with tails.

Tonight was to be the first night that all the guests would be joining the host family at dinner. Em, standing discreetly in the background, had positioned James and Alfie by the door. As each guest entered, James checked the list, giving Alfie the place number, or numbers. It was his job to escort each party to their place, assist the lady to sit down, and draw the gentleman's chair from the table. Lady Jane's place was at the head, with Charles at the other end and Delilah seated on his right.

"I have a headache," Delilah said, hoping to be excused from attending dinner.

"You must forgive an old lady," answered her ladyship, "but I wish you wouldn't mutter, girl," and feigning slight deafness, said "Did you say have or am? Whatever it was you said, they are *our* guests and we will *all* be there." As Lady Jane and her family entered the dining hall, she was pleased to see all guests were in their places. James was assisting her ladyship with her chair, while Alfie, having gone to assist Delilah, was treated to the wave away, for which she received a stern look from her mother-in-law.

While the soup was being served, James, assisted by Alfie, started to serve the drinks. Initially, Em had told them that James would start at the head of the table working right while Alfie would start with Charles, also going in the same direction, but, in view of Delilah's behaviour with Alfie and the chair, told them to change ends. Delilah had obviously decided to take things into her own hands and placed her hand over her glass, rejecting James's offer of wine, but while trying to beckon to Alfie, wasn't aware that Em had filled the glass, much to the delight of the guests seated near her.

"I do not know what got into you this evening, young lady, but I would not expect such behaviour from a guest, and certainly not from a member of *my* family. Even though you are now a member of the family, you are here upon my invitation, *not* by some divine right, otherwise, well, I will say no more on the matter, but remember good staff are hard to come by, and can be hard to keep, so leave the young lad alone."

"But Auntie, Mama, I only—"

"You heard."

"You did well, Alfie. Don't feel bad about Lady Delilah, from the looks she was getting I feel sure her ladyship will have a few words with her. Don't forget, we're with you, let me know if you have any more trouble with her, but always be respectful."

"But Em, I am—"

"I know, so don't let someone who thinks they're God's gift get you down. You did a good job tonight, we are proud of you, and as for you girls, you all did me proud, just one or two slight mishaps, but nothing to worry about. Is dinner ready, Ruth? Will you say grace, please, James? Tuck in, everyone. Sit down, Alfie. Oh, all right then, white wine for me, thank you. Hmm, this is delicious."

***

"How much? Complete with the mattress? Hmm, I don't know, I'll have to think about that." Victor wasn't one to be rushed into something like paying out for a brand new bed at that price when he could get a perfectly good serviceable one at old Eli's second hand shop for thirty bob, complete with mattress. He'd have to collect it but then he owned a lorry. Maybe it could lead to the odd delivery at the weekends. Why not, it was worth a try.

Mavis didn't mind sleeping just one more night on the old fold down bed settee; in her dreams she was back in the lounge at the Red Lion, the last night before the new landlord took over. Suddenly she was awake, she could hear the wind outside banging someone's gate, she felt cold. The fire was little more than a glow, but a few pieces of wood, two or three lumps of coal and a couple of puffs got the fire going. I could do with a hot drink, she thought as she made her way into the kitchen. Just enough water in the kettle. Now where are the matches? She lit the gas and put the kettle on to boil.

"Make one for me while you're at it." The voice behind her made her jump. It was Gillian. Victor's snoring had woken her and as she lay there she had heard the sound of running water, and guessing that Mavis was probably making herself a drink, decided she would also like one.

As the two cousins were sitting talking in the warmth and the flickering light of the fire, their thoughts turned to Christmas, just a week or so away. It would be so nice to make it special for the sake of the children. "I've no idea what Victor has in mind," said Gillian. "If you can keep them occupied tomorrow, I'll ask him."

Mavis looked at the clock on the mantelpiece, "Tomorrow, it's already today," she said, "It's ten past three in the morning, we should try to get some more shut-eye."

"I can still hear him snoring like a pig," replied Gillian. "If you've no objection, I'll climb in with you."

***

The Springfield boys were about to get up from the breakfast table. "We must be ready to be on the coach by two o'clock," Sister Millicent said, "so you need to have your Saturday jobs finished in good time. Lunch will be at twelve sharp, so off you go. Philip, would you help Sister Hannah in the kitchen today please." There was a scraping of chairs as the boys stood up. Will they never learn to get up from the table quietly? she wondered. I've told them enough times.

Breakfast dishes being washed, dusters dusting, brushes sweeping, bumpers—those weighty things holding cloths down in contact with the floor—gliding over the highly polished parquet floor in the hall, even the ornately carved figures on the banister were getting their weekly polish. In the bathroom the floor tiles, which were mopped on bath nights and scrubbed with a disinfectant twice a month, were being done with a great deal of vigour. Anthracite was collected from the boiler room in the cellar and carried up the stairs to keep the big hungry Aga cooker in the kitchen fed.

Everywhere all spick and span, everybody clean and tidy, thirty boys and four staff climbed into the red coach, the younger boys full of excitement at something new, the older boys not necessarily looking forward to the concert, but were on the ride for the beanfeast that followed. The staff were there to make certain that the younger ones were treated fairly by the big boys and to meet and talk with some of the church members. A half hour journey saw them arrive at the Hucknall Methodist Church, where they were shown into the church for a short concert of community singing, three numbers by the choir—the home boys were the choir—a thank you to the choir for singing from the minister, the Reverend Laurence Parker, and thank you on behalf of the boys by Peter Baronowitz, one of the youngest in the group.

Downstairs, under the main body of the church, as usual in the design of most Methodist churches, was the large hall, with a platform at one end, and facilities including a kitchen, storeroom and toilets. Sister Hannah made the boys stand behind their chairs until after Reverend Parker had said grace; there was another great scraping of chairs, some boys stretched out across the table to grab a sandwich, or in some cases two, even before they were seated. There were plenty of sandwiches for everyone, fish paste, meat paste, corned beef, tinned cooked pork and even jam sandwiches, and when those were almost finished, dishes of jelly and trifle were brought out from the kitchen, followed by mince pies and cup cakes coated with icing and hundreds-and-thousands. To the youngest, it was a feast worthy of a story book, to some of the older boys, a chance to keep on eating until you could eat no more. All this was accompanied by fizzy drinks: lemonade, cherryade, and the most popular among the older lads, dandelion and burdock.

As they were heading out to the coach through the darkened passageway, they had to pass Father Christmas, who asked each boy his name and age. Then he would put his hand into one of the two sacks and pull out a present hopefully suitable for the boy's age and interest; maybe a colouring book and crayons, a story book or for some a cut-out, or rather press-out, book to make a model galleon or aeroplane. The red coach arrived back at Springfield half an hour after the younger boys' bed time, and about an hour before it was time for the older boys to head for bed. Sister Hannah took the box of leftovers into the staff room for their supper.

This ritual of sing for your supper would follow three or four more times into the New Year, only this year it had started later than usual. There would also be a couple of pantomimes to fit into the rather tight schedule of events before the season was finished.

Chapter Thirty-seven

Presents for Gillian, Malcolm and Molly were far from Victor's mind; what to get Liz's family? He hadn't given them a thought. How to be in two places over a hundred miles apart was the problem. It might be easy when in Chingford to blame a breakdown and being stuck as a reason for not getting to Carlton in Nottingham, but to give the same excuse for not getting to Chingford when Liz knew he had a car... he'd need to think of something else. Just a few more miles and he could unload the timber he had collected from Tilbury. There was something else that was bothering Victor, but it had to wait while he unloaded at Grantham sawmills, only part of a bill of lading. If he dropped in and gave Gillian ten pounds to cover presents and whatever she needed over Christmas, he reasoned he could be back in Chingford that evening and in Tilbury again in the morning. It seemed that transporting timber paid well.

"Much as I'd love to, darling, I must get back to Tilbury," said Victor. "There's a good sized load they want shifting, and if I'm not there first thing tomorrow, they could give it to someone else."

"He's got a girlfriend down there," joked Mavis.

"As if I would," answered Victor. Mavis frowned. "I'm hoping to have it all shifted by Christmas, I expect to be back before then." With that he kissed his wife and the two children and disappeared round the corner at the end of the road as he turned left onto Carlton Road, heading towards the city and beyond.

***

Life for the guests at Moore Hall once more fell into a regular relaxed routine. Breakfast was usually buffet style any time between eight and ten a.m. and anyone wanting a hot breakfast would have it prepared according to their preference. At eleven there was usually a snack and hot drink, again self-service. Lunch and dinner were normally at set times, although they were often quite casual, unless Lady Jane elected to dine with her guests.

Instead of the usual four staff plus Agnes (who had previously dealt with the laundry) of previous years, this year there were seven, due partly to Agnes being absent, partly to the practicality of having the girls working in a rota, pairs in the bedrooms and taking it in turns in the laundry. The chart on the wall of Em's office might have looked complicated, but it worked efficiently. Alfie was available to assist when and where needed. The staffing level meant that usually two and sometimes three staff were able to have the afternoon and, quite often, the evening off. Rebecca seldom took any time off. She was quite happy looking after Ernest, or playing with Annabel, or Annie, as she called her. Whenever Em visited the nursery, which was most days, Annabel was helping with Ernest, playing with 'Becca' or having an afternoon nap. After the evening meal had been cleared and everything cleaned, either Em or Ruth would remain on duty, assisted by one other person, listed on the rota, in order to attend to the guests, but there were normally two or three others who stayed too, rather than retire to their room.

On the evening when Ruth was left in charge, once or sometimes twice in the week Em would be above the garage, practicing her massage skills under the guidance of, and on, James, her mentor, or feeling the pleasure of relaxation when James used his skills on her, a towel draped over her body giving her privacy, although she seldom seemed to notice when it slipped down onto the floor. After washing any traces of oil from her body, Em would return to her room, so relaxed that she never had any trouble going to sleep.

***

After a long, uneventful journey, Victor parked his lorry across from Martin's ironmongers. Being as quiet as possible, he opened the door. The flat was in darkness. Taking his boots off he went up the stairs in his socks and into the bedroom. He could see from the movement of the blankets that Liz was asleep, so he went into the other bedroom; that bed was occupied too. That can't be Dinah, he thought. She's not that tall, and her hair... Victor headed back into the living room. After that long drive he didn't bother to open the bed settee or even get undressed, he just stretched out full length on the settee and within minutes was snoring.

"Who the hell? Shut up, you're snoring loud enough to wake the dead," Shirley said, pushing his foot, and causing him to roll onto the floor.

"What the..." he murmured before he was once more fast asleep.

"Wake up, sleepy head."

Victor opened his eyes: what am I doing on the floor? "Oh hullo, love," he said, "I suppose I must have rolled off the settee. What time is it?"

"Nine," Liz answered. "You remember Shirley, don't you, she's dropped in on her way to Dover, she was in the spare room last night. Breakfast in five minutes, then we'll go round to see Mummy, so get a move on." Victor headed for the bathroom. Apart from anything else, he wanted to freshen up.

"Good morning, Shirley," said Liz, "sleep well?"

"Well yes," she said, "until I got woken by snoring loud enough to wake the dead."

"Ooh, I hope I didn't—"

"No, not you, 'im," replied Shirley, just as Victor walked into the room.

"I think you owe Shirley an apology, love," said Liz.

"Who, me? What have I done now?"

"Your snoring woke her," replied Liz.

"Me snore? No way."

The two friends looked at each other and shrugged. "Men," they said in unison.

"Come on," Liz said as she put the plates and knives on the table, "toast is ready. The butter and marmalade are in the larder. Would you get them please love, while I make the tea."

***

"I ain't seen your Agnes around lately, what you done wiv 'er?" asked Bernie, (Bernie, or Bernard Cribbins, was the head groundsman-cum-gamekeeper).

"Nothing," answered James, "she's visiting her daughter in Lincoln. She should be back in a couple'a weeks, 'n I'm staying up at the hall."

"Oh, I see," said Bernie. "Well, if the cottage's goin' to be empty like…"

"Why, what's wrong with your place?"

"It ain't got no barf room. It's a hovel agin your place."

"You should have a word."

"Nah, I w'dn't waste ma bref."

James let himself into the cottage. Bernie was certainly right, he had seen Bernie's hovel as he called it. Against Bernie's place, this certainly is a palace, he ruminated. Mind you, he had to admit that without Agnes's woman's touch it could have been very different.

As James was making his way back to the hall, through the woods and along the path by the edge of the field, he was feeling more alive, whether it was due to Agnes's absence, or the relief from muscular tension in receiving as well as giving massages, or maybe, just maybe the feeling of being in love, real love.

"That kid certainly knows his stuff," Alfred was saying to Em. "he was telling me details about the staff car that I didn't even know."

"His dad has the garage in Shurlach, he was in the MT section in Larkhill in the thirties," replied Em.

"You were there?"

"Well, yes, I was supervisor in the NAAFI."

"They could do with you in our RAF Wittering."

"Maybe, but—" at that moment the door bell rang. "You will excuse me," Em said to Alfred as she headed towards the door.

"It's time you got it into your head, Nigel, you're not in Canada now," Cynthia was saying as they came through the door. "Oh, good afternoon, Em, we're not too late, are we?" she was asking as they entered the Dining Hall. "Damn, you arguing with that policeman has made us miss lunch. Would you send me something up to my room please, Em? You heard what that policeman said about driving on the left," she was saying as they were going up the stairs to their room.

It seems such a pity letting a Rolls get so dirty, James thought as he drove Cynthia's car round to the back of the house. It wouldn't get as much muck on it if… but of course, the Ashburtons boast a fine riding stable. Half an hour and the car was spick and span. If a job's worth doing, it's worth doing well, and that was a job well done, he thought with pride, as he backed the car into the garage. Next job, equally important, was to clean up the mud that James had removed from Cynthia's car. It would be very easy to slip on mud when wet, and apart from anything else, James always took great pride in a clean courtyard, and he was determined to leave it that way before the day was over.

***

It wasn't long now to Christmas. The tree was standing in the middle of the hall, with the fairy visible from the landing upstairs. The boys had spent happy hours making the streamers that decorated the rooms. This year the theme was swifts and swallows.

Today was the day for the Sunday school Christmas party at Sherwood Methodist Church. All the children from the church would be there, and probably a few others as well. Saturday jobs done; today Freddie had been peeling the potatoes, not as bad as it might sound when you had a machine to do it for you, although removing the eyes took a while. Lunch was meat pie and vegetables, followed by rice pudding, better than semolina, or sago, which stuck together just like frog spawn. Hmm, yes, rice was nice.

The boys would be wearing something tidy and warm, but suitable for games. Their mackintoshes, scarves and gloves, and the knee high socks they wore, were little protection from the cold north wind that was blowing. By five o'clock the boys, all carrying the presents they had received from Santa Claus, and some with cherished prizes from the games, had arrived back at Springfield, and in spite of having eaten plenty at the party, were quite ready to tuck into an evening meal of baked beans on toast.

***

Victor worked hard to get all the timber transported within the last few days before Christmas, from very early morning starts at Tilbury docks to unloading at Grantham mid-afternoon, then driving back to Chingford late into the night, tired but happy, a good job jobbed, a new customer satisfied, with the possibility of more work in the future, and a nice roll of white five pound notes.

"We've seen so little of you over the last few days, Mummy was wondering…" Liz was saying.

"I know, dear," said Victor, "but that was a golden opportunity to get my foot in at Tilbury docks for what could bring in more work locally. But I'm all yours for the next few days in a manner of speaking, I'm letting my lorry have a rest."

"Oh," replied Liz, a little disappointed. "Mummy was wondering if you could move some furniture for Auntie Hilda."

"That's different, love," he answered, "as long as it's not further than John o' Groats."

"No, just to Land's End, dear," she said laughing.

A long silence followed as they ate their breakfast. "Am I mistaken, or have you lost weight, love?"

Liz looked up at Victor nervously. "I think, I think."

"What is it, love?" asked Victor.

"Don't be cross, dear, but I think I might be pregnant," Liz answered. "I've missed two months."

"Are you sure?"

"Of course I'm sure, dear," she said.

"That's fantastic, darling, if it's a boy—"

"Daddy will go mad, you know what he's like."

"Oh," Victor said. "Yes, so we won't tell anyone, we'll get hitched. Perhaps when we've finished breakfast we could go round to the vicarage and fix a date?" Liz gazed at Victor. He looked thoughtful, but pleased.

"Hmm," murmured the Reverend Thomas Carlisle, vicar at St Michaels, as he turned the pages of his diary. "It is rather short notice. Hmm, three weeks for the banns, the best I can do is…" Turning another page, he shook his head. "No, I'm due at the bishop's that day." Then turning yet another page, "Ah, yes," he said, "how about the eighteenth of January? Shall we say eleven o'clock? Let me see, I assume you are both free to marry? Good, one must ask, you know. We'll say a short prayer then I'll let you go, you will have a lot to arrange."

After the prayer and blessing they stood up and shook hands. "Thank you, sir, have a happy Christmas," said Victor.

***

Christmas is coming, the geese are getting fat, please put a penny in the old man's hat. Well, it certainly wasn't going to be geese at nineteen Warwick Street, Carlton. The best Gillian could afford after buying presents for Malcolm and Molly, and a few extras, even with a little help from Mavis, was a rabbit, oven ready, and no penny left for the old man's hat.

Gillian and Mavis sat listening to the wireless long into the night. It was Christmas Eve and so far there was no sign of Victor. Surely he would be back for the sake of the children.

Chapter Thirty-eight

Em woke to the sound of a knock on her door. At her invitation, Ruth entered. Placing a cup of tea and a mince pie on the bedside cupboard, she said, "Merry Christmas, Em."

"Thank you, Ruth," answered Em, "and Merry Christmas to you," then glancing at her clock, "I'll be down in about half an hour."

"There's no hurry," replied Ruth, "everything is under control."

Em smiled. Ruth is a good girl, she thought. Given the opportunity, she should do well.

***

"Go away," said Walter, "that's my brother's sock." Freddie sat up just in time to see Maurice going back to his bed.

"I only wanted to look…"

"Yeh we know your look. You aren't called sticky fingers for nothing."

"That's not true," Maurice objected.

The bedroom door opened. Sister Hannah stood, looking around the room, all was quiet. "Why are you sitting up, Freddie?" she asked.

"I thought I heard someone say my name," he answered.

"You were probably dreaming," she said. "It's still early, lie down and go back to sleep." Sister Hannah stepped out onto the landing and gently closed the door.

***

Liz woke and looked at the figure of the man soon to be her husband, as he lay on his side. Trying not to disturb him, she slipped out of bed, put her dressing gown on and walked into the kitchen to make a pot of tea.

Victor had actually been awake quite a long time. He was thinking about the twins in the children's home, also about Gillian, Malcolm and Molly. He should be with them, and he was thinking about Liz. What could he do? He couldn't just leave her. Liz brought in a mug of tea. "Merry Christmas, darling," she said. Victor sat up, pulled her down onto his lap and kissed her.

"Merry Christmas, dear," he replied.

* * *

Em surveyed the dishes on the server in the Dining Hall, there was little evidence to suggest that many, if any had been down to breakfast, not unusual for Christmas day morning. Monica had been at the server, both to serve if required, and to keep a list, not to stop anyone having a second breakfast, but so that Em could see who had breakfasted. Em looked up as Charlton strode into the room. "Merry Christmas, Em," he said.

"Good morning sir," she replied. "I fear your dressing gown is revealing more than it should. Would you kindly go back upstairs and get more respectably dressed."

"I will not be spoken to like that. I shall complain to Lady Jane in person," Charlton snapped.

"Very well," Em replied, turning him round by his arm. "I believe she is free, I think it will be best to see her now, while your complaint is still fresh in your mind."

Just at that moment Charles and Delilah entered the room. "What's going on?" asked Charles. "Get some clothes on, man."

"Now I've seen everything," said Delilah, bursting out laughing.

"I hope not, dear," Charles said, "I shall have something to say about this to mother."

Charlton quickly disappeared through the door on his way upstairs.

Liz and Victor walked into the room. "Merry Christmas, everyone," they said together.

"What have you got for me?" asked Dinah.

"Dinah, stop it," said her mother, "it's rude to ask."

"But Mummy—"

"Enough, you heard your mother," Mr Norman said.

"After lunch, sis," Liz was heard to say.

"Right, lunch is ready, let's all sit down. Would you like to carve, Victor?" asked Mr Norman.

"No, Dad, he's not been cooked," answered Liz laughing,

"Thank you," replied Victor, "but that should be a job for the man of the house." Liz looked at Victor, proudly admiring his diplomacy.

Lunch over, they sat sipping their drinks and opening presents. The womenfolk had bought each other brooches and delicately embroidered handkerchiefs. The menfolk received fountain pens, large white handkerchiefs, tie pins, and cuff link and stud sets.

"Oh good," said Victor with a big grin, "I must go out and buy myself a tie."

"You don't need to do that," replied Mr Norman. "I've got more than I need."

"But dear, I gave them…" Mrs Norman protested.

"What do I need thirty-two ties for?" he asked.

Victor glanced at Liz who gave a slight nod of approval. "What about the eighteenth of January?" asked Victor, taking the bull by the horns.

"What's so special about the eighteenth?"

"We're getting married," Victor said. "We planned to tell you today. We'd like a quiet wedding," he said. "We don't want you to go to any great expense."

"Don't worry yourself about that," replied Mr Norman. "But first, have you spoken to the vicar?"

"Yes, Daddy," Liz answered. "Anyway, we can talk about that later, let's just enjoy today. Who wants a game of Ludo?" she asked.

"Me, please," said Dinah.

***

Christmas at Springfield started with breakfast of porridge followed by scrambled egg on toast, then after the breakfast things had been washed up, the boys and staff, apart from the two on duty in the kitchen, attended the morning service at Sherwood Methodist Church in Mansfield Road. Back in time for their special dinner of roast turkey (the turkey usually donated by a local farmer), and all the trimmings, followed by home made Christmas pudding, (that had been matured), and mince pies. After everything had been cleared away, the tradition was to listen to the king's speech, then everyone sat on the floor around the Christmas tree while the presents were handed out, at least two for each boy, whether they had received anything from their family or not.

Once everyone had their two or more presents, the boys went back into the lounge-cum-living room to unpack, put the wrapping paper in a pile and enjoy their games, books, puzzles and whatever else they had received until teatime, when there was a general scramble to put things away and sit up at the table. Just like dinner, the Christmas tea was enjoyed: sandwiches, jelly, mince pies and cup cakes, followed by Christmas cake, with lemonade and cherryade to drink.

After tea the table was cleared, the washing up done, all the boys and the staff including Mr Smith, the governor, gathered in the one room, leaving a large clear area at the end nearest to the scullery and hall doors, the boys sitting on the floor while the staff, well, most of them, sat on chairs.

The evening started with songs like *Old MacDonald had a Farm*, *Way Down Upon the Swannee River* and *The Quartermaster's Store*, *Run, Rabbit, Run*, and some of the popular Vera Lyn songs, like *Blue Birds over the White Cliffs of Dover*. But the part that everyone liked best was when Mr Smith stood up and, in a very broad north country accent, started reciting monologues. The most popular was the one starting 'It was Christmas day in the trenches, In Spain in Peninsular War. And Sam Small was cleaning his musket. A thing he'd ne'er done before': the story of *Old Sam's Christmas Pudding* and how the pudding was accidently used as a cannon ball. Each recital, and the accent Mr Smith used, made everyone laugh. After a prayer and blessing, the boys happily went up the stairs to bed.

***

Mavis lay awake next to the sleeping form of her cousin, listening to the steady sound of her breathing, and watching the rise and fall of the blankets with each breath. This had been the third night that Gillian had cried herself to sleep. Victor had failed to arrive home and had consequently missed the children's Christmas. He had given his wife money to buy presents for the children and presumably thought he had given her enough for all the shopping. There had been sufficient for either presents or necessities, but not for both, no matter how frugal she had been, and Gillian had proved she was a master at frugal shopping.

Christmas day should be full of joy and happiness, and for the children it had been. Malcolm was delighted with his Bayko set, and spent many hours building Mummy a new house, then taking it apart to build Auntie Mavis a house, or he sat with Molly listening while Auntie read from the beautiful new book of nursery rhymes. Molly loved her doggie on wheels, pulling it around on the end of its string, stroking it, or giving it a cuddle.

At the sound of a car engine, Gillian would rush to the window in the front room, hoping to see Victor's lorry park at the side of the road, then disappointed, return to the kitchen. She had never cooked a rabbit before. "Cook it the same as chicken," the butcher had said, so she had tied it up to resemble a chicken, or as near as she could bearing in mind that a chicken only has two legs. Should she set the table for four or five? He should be here... Gillian had set four places, the children had accepted their father's absence. She had saved some of the rabbit for

Victor to have in a sandwich if he'd arrived home; as he didn't, she shared it with Mavis, it tasted delicious.

Yes, thought Mavis as she got dressed as quietly as possible so as not to wake Gillian, in spite of Victor not being here, the children had quite a good couple of days, but it's a pity he missed it.

Gillian stirred. "Victor?" she murmured and drifted back to sleep.

Mavis watched her for a moment, then went downstairs to put the kettle on. Half an hour later Gillian came down to the kitchen. "Oh, Mavis," she said, "what am I going to do?"

"Stop worrying," Mavis replied, "I'm sure he would have been here if he could. Maybe the lorry broke down or ran out of diesel."

"Or he's has an accident," worried Gillian.

"Don't think like that, he'll probably turn up today," she said, more in hope of comforting her cousin than believing it herself.

"Sit down," said Gillian, "while I do some toast. We could do with some shopping, there's hardly anything in the larder."

"I'll nip out as soon as I've had a cuppa," Mavis offered. "It would be best if you're home when Victor gets back. There's bound to be somewhere open."

***

It hadn't been easy getting away from Chingford, but after a marvellous couple of days with Liz's family and managing to convince Mr Norman of the importance of being ready to pick up a load as soon as the mill opened after the Christmas break, Victor had been able to get away very early, and with almost empty roads on the way, he was back in Carlton unexpectedly soon. Stopping at a road junction to allow some pedestrians to cross the road, he saw a familiar face. "Hey, Mavis," he called, "where are you going?"

"Shopping," she replied.

"Hop in, there's a lot more shops open in Chilwell." As Mavis got in the passenger seat, Victor explained that he had run out of diesel just five miles north of Watford, and been stuck there until this morning.

Quite a few shops were open, and it didn't take Mavis long to purchase a good selection of fruit and vegetables while Victor was getting one or two extras for the children, and for Gillian and Mavis; after all, he hadn't left enough money for his wife to buy all that she needed.

"Look what I've got," Mavis said as she lifted her shopping bag onto the table.

Gillian got up off the floor. "Where did you get all that from?" she asked.

"Chilwell," came the reply.

"How did you get to Chilwell?" asked a bewildered Gillian.

"'Im," Mavis answered, pointing her thumb over her shoulder. Gillian spun round as Victor walked through the open door.

"Oh, darling," Gillian said as she threw her arms around him, "I've been so worried. What've you got?" she asked when she saw his bag. "You didn't need to, but gosh! How much did all that cost? You shouldn't have."

***

Em walked into the kitchen; Ruth was picking up a breakfast tray. "Who is that for?" she asked, then glancing at the note on the table, added "I will take that up. I don't want anyone else to take any trays up to that room. Mr Hawthorne has a tendency to cause embarrassment by walking about without adequate dress, and to pinch girls' bottoms, so only James or myself will be entering his room." Em took the tray up to Charlton's room where she knocked on the door.

"Come, dear," the voice said, "I've something for you." As Em entered, the tray held in one hand while she opened the door with the other, she collided with Charlton's arm as he reached forward, presumably to pinch her, and although the teapot stayed on the tray, the jug of hot water tipped and spilled down Charlton's front, just at the moment his dressing gown opened. "Ahhgh! You've scalded me!" he screamed.

"Quick, Sit in the cold water for fifteen minutes or so, to take the heat off," Em said. Pushing him into the bath, she turned the cold tap on full, douching him where the hot water had tipped.

"You scalded me," he repeated.

"No, Charlton, if you hadn't tried to grab me it would not have happened. Perhaps that might teach you a lesson. I will arrange for your meals to be brought up while you are indisposed, and I will, of course, have to inform her ladyship."

Chapter Thirty-nine

"Yes, Mother," said Charles, "there's nothing official yet, but I've put in for a transfer to a pilot training station, somewhere like Jurby, in the Isle of Man, to teach others to fly. At least it would reduce the likelihood of being sent to trouble spots like Malaya. Yes, I'd be able to take Delilah and... why not, it's not that far away... No, I haven't told her yet, can I leave them here until I know what's happening? You're an angel, Mother dear... I'll just go and... Yes, she's still in bed... Bye bye, Mother dear." Charles kissed his mother, then went upstairs to Delilah.

"Yes, dear... shh, you'll wake Ernest... Yes, I'll let you know." Thirty minutes later Em was standing at the front door, watching as Alfred and Charles drove away down the drive.

The guests had started leaving earlier than in previous years due to the forecast of a much colder spell for the New Year. Last to leave, on the second of January, were Marjorie with her two friends, Alice and Malcolm, and a still very sore Charlton whom James drove to Chester Railway Station in the Wolseley, before calling in at the cottage to collect the last of his personal belongings and check that all the locks had been changed.

As he left through the back door, he ran into Bernie. "Yon wife o' yorn aint arf mad," Bernie said. "She gon up the 'all spittin' blood, she 'as, you wanna keep yer 'ed da'n, she wern't 'appy abat not gettin' in the cottage."

"Thanks, Bernie," James replied, "owe yer one pal."

***

Agnes stormed into the kitchen. "What the hell is this all about?" she shouted. "Old Bernie wouldn't let me into my house, he told me to come and see you."

"Please sit down and quieten your tongue," said Em. "If you don't I shall call the police and have you removed."

Agnes sat down on the office chair with a heavy thump. "Okay, spit it out," she said.

"I would appreciate a civil tongue if you expect me to make any approach to her ladyship in your favour," Em remarked as she dried her hands. "You have to consider the position I was in last November when you decided to go off to your daughter's. Because you left without warning or agreement with your employer, you ceased to be an employee of Moore Hall, and I didn't have any option but to employ someone else to do your work. In effect you walked out of your job and… please have the courtesy to let me finish. As the cottage is a tied cottage, you also walked out of your home, therefore it has been made available to a member of the staff."

"But I am a member of the staff."

"No, Agnes, not since you walked off in November. Your belongings have been boxed up for you to arrange collection."

"And my furniture?"

"The furniture belongs in the cottage," Em replied.

Agnes began to cry. "It's been my home for more than twenty years," she mumbled.

"I have had an inventory carried out, anything not belonging in the house has been packed with your belongings," Em replied. "You may stay here tonight, but you will be required to leave tomorrow morning. You may leave your things for one month while you arrange collection. Dinner is at seven, and breakfast tomorrow finishes at eight. Esther will show you to your room. Esther, please show our 'visitor' to room six in the west wing."

"But what about—"

"The choice is yours; accept our hospitality and go along with Esther, or you leave through that door, right now."

***

Victor was worried, the New Year had hardly started and the London truck drivers were on strike for a forty-four hour week and a pay increase. It was spreading like the plague, even self-employed drivers frightened of their vehicles being sabotaged had stopped work. No work meant no pay, and for many that meant hardship for their families. At least down in Chingford Liz was now working, maybe not really what she was hoping for, but Martin's wife, Sue, had gone to look after her ailing mother in Ilford and Liz had readily stepped into the vacancy in the ironmongers. At least, she thought, I will be putting something into the housekeeping.

Meanwhile, at nineteen Warwick Street, Mavis was getting concerned. She knew that Gillian was very pleased to have her company, and she enjoyed being with her cousin, but Mavis was very conscious that having an extra mouth to feed was stretching the household budget, and she knew that it was unlikely that anyone would take her on in her condition. Gillian suggested that if Mavis wouldn't be able to work, but would be happy to look after the children, perhaps she could find something herself, such as bar work in the evenings.

The Fox and Hounds in Station Road, within walking distance, had been advertising for an experienced bar person for some time, so Gillian thought she might try there. "My father was the licensee at the Red Lion in Thornton Heath, so I grew up in a pub," might have seemed a bit far-fetched, but they were quite prepared to give her a trial, which as far as the licensee was concerned was satisfactory, and Gillian was taken on for three evenings each week, with the occasional weekend.

From Victor's point of view, and no doubt other self-employed truck drivers would agree, bringing in the military would only aggravate the situation. He had stopped making deliveries, not in sympathy, but in self-preservation; where would he be if his vehicle was vandalised or he was refused work because he had continued during the strike? He couldn't afford to take that risk.

Victor turned off the wireless and breathed a sigh of relief; the strike was over. "I must take the opportunity to get down to Witney and pick up a load in the morning," he said, picking up his overnight bag and kissing his wife, Gillian, who was sitting at the breakfast table. "Back soon," he called from the back door. The wind that morning was as cold as any north wind would be, but he hardly seemed to notice as he gave the engine a few quick turns, then put the starting handle away behind the driver's seat, being careful not to damage either the bag or his best suit, shirt and shoes which he had surreptitiously packed the night before.

He turned the ignition key and pressed the starter button; the engine turned over twice, then fired with a roar. He let it run for ten minutes to allow it to warm up and then he drove away. He was well beyond the outskirts of Nottingham before he felt the warmth rising from the heater. Driving steadily, he headed south down the A1, expecting to reach Potters Bar on the northern boundary of the great metropolis in about another four hours, then Waltham Abbey and drop down to Chingford.

London had always fascinated him with all its parks and green spaces. Even in this huge city, no one was far from open country, if you could call places like Berkeley Square and Lincolns Inn Fields open country, with all those big buildings around them. Then there were the canals and waterways and all the wild life, the pigeons, sparrows and thrushes. I wonder how many swans there are in London. When was it decreed that they all belong to the king? Steady on or I'll miss my turning.

***

Victor looked at himself in the mirror. He cut a fine figure in navy blue, with the silver grey tie he had borrowed from Mr Norman, Liz's father. Perhaps he should have bought a new white shirt, but Gillian had used the coupons on something. Never mind, too late to do anything about that now. A touch of Silvikrin rubbed into his hair and combed out gave it that slight sheen, oh, and a quick rub to his shoes with a duster, that should do nicely. Slipping on his Navy demob overcoat, he set out on foot to St Michael's Church to meet Harry Norman, Liz's cousin, the son of Auntie Hilda and Henry Norman, and brother of Edna, who was the chief bridesmaid. Harry had been asked to stand in as best man, as Victor had no friends or family near enough to attend the wedding. Being a stranger to the area, and having planned a quiet wedding, Victor was pleasantly surprised at the number of people already in the church, as were Liz and her father when they arrived.

Liz looked stunning as she stood in the living room of her parents' house, her trim figure in the white three quarter length silk dress with lace overlay, that her mother had worn more than twenty years before when she was wed. A headdress of finely woven silk flowers with a short silk veil that allowed her blond hair to show through, hung halfway down to her waist. "Come, my dear," Mr Norman said. "Your chariot awaits," proudly leading his daughter out to the car, accompanied by the applause of the waiting neighbours, to be met at the church by Liz's mother and Dinah, who was the second bridesmaid alongside her cousin Edna. Both girls wore simple light blue satin dresses with the puffed sleeves that were popular at that time.

As the organ played, the bride, on the arm of her father and escorted by her two bridesmaids, moved slowly up the aisle. Harry, who had turned to watch them approach, quietly uttered a, "Phew," when he saw his cousin, causing Victor to half turn and beam with pride at the sight of his beautiful bride.

"Dearly beloved," the vicar read out, "We are gathered together… 'in the sight of Almighty God …'

Victor was almost reciting the words in his mind. Yes… yes, get on with it… Hardly paying attention, he had heard it all before, ah, at last, here we go.

"Victor Thomas Bradburn, do you take this woman to be your lawful wedded wife, to honour…"

He could hardly wait to say, "I do."

"Elizabeth Miriam Julie Norman…"

Victor's mind was no longer on what the Reverend Carlisle was saying, he was just waiting to hear Liz say 'I will'. That was what he was here for, to Victor that was all that mattered.

Victor and his smiling bride hurried through the waiting crowd standing outside, and through the clouds of confetti, the strong cold wind blowing clouds of it towards the church doors. The reception was to be in the church hall, and the photographs would have to wait until they got indoors, it was much too cold and overcast outside. Victor was hoping that someone would think to collect his big overcoat, he certainly didn't want to lose that, it would be handy if it got any colder.

Liz and Victor had said they didn't want more than a dozen or so guests, but when it came to sending out the invitations, the list had come to more than twice that number, although some replied that they were already committed, some were maybes and some, like Liz's ATS colleagues, never even replied. Three of Liz's old school friends, Naomi, Sheila and Deborah, and neighbours, Roger and Karen, Archie and Alice, and Joe and Valerie, plus of course Rocky Lane, his brother, Anthony and sister, Cleopatra, who would be providing the music, with the bridal party making eighteen, plus the vicar, and the organist, David Hammond.

After the toasts and speeches, fortunately kept quite short, Anthony and Cleopatra, or rather Tony and Cleo, along with Rocky, their brother, and David Hammond on the piano, formed a small dance band and started to play. Prompted by the guests, Victor and Liz took to the floor, Liz attempting to move to the music with Victor trying to disguise their movements as a waltz, to the applause of those present. Once the music started, the rest of the afternoon went with a swing, with popular tunes like *Love's Old Sweet Song*, *Can't Help Singing*, *Always* and *Californ-i-ay*.

After the pressure of the wedding, and having decided to postpone their honeymoon until the warmer weather of June or July, they decided to enjoy a few days relaxing in their little love nest together as man and wife. Liz was no longer worried about being pregnant, as the doctor had explained that monthlies were likely to stop if she was below a particular weight, which she was, so once she had stopped worrying about her figure, and put on a little more weight, her monthly had returned in good time before the wedding, and they were able to relax more. On two days they took the opportunity of walks in the park, but life could be so frustrating; only a few days after the strike had ended and just three days after the wedding, the snow came. For several days they were not able to get out except for a quick dash to buy food, if you could dash through several inches of slippery snow; as quickly as you cleared a pathway the wind blew more down. Salt would melt it, but overnight it would freeze again, making it more dangerous, and salt had to be bought.

Eventually it stopped snowing and Victor reluctantly decided he had better do some work. Wind and rain he could cope with, even a certain amount of flooding, but snow? That had been a different matter. He was on his way from Helmshore Mill with a full load of yarn for the Witney blanket factory. As he drove out of Rossendale there were slight flurries of snow, but nothing to worry about, maybe drive a little slower and allow a bit more distance when stopping. The roads down through Warrington and past his old home, the Red Lion in Thornton Heath, were reasonably clear, and the A5 wasn't too bad, although below Birmingham the snowfall was a little heavier and the build up where the snow had settled was deeper.

As he drove on he could see snow piling into drifts on the road ahead as it was blown from the fields. He was happy to see the sign for Maids Moreton, a road he had used many times as he travelled to or from Witney, so at this point he turned off the A5. Driving along a road that almost headed west, Victor found the roads relatively clear of snow. Heading into the wind had the benefit that what snow had settled had been blown off the road. It was already dark when he stopped outside the Wheatsheaf; knowing he might get stuck anywhere along the way, he decided to enjoy the warmth and comfort of the country pub.

***

Moore Hall may have only been a couple of miles from the village, but as James said earlier that morning, it was unlikely that even using the big tractor he or anyone could get through the snowdrifts that had built up where the road dipped at Squire's Brook. Em thought it would be wiser for the three girls to stay overnight before James took them home now that they were no longer being employed by the hall, they were welcome to stay as guests, albeit downstairs. Alfie was being kept on, to learn all aspects of house management and butlership, occasionally assisting James with the maintenance of the cars, and being permitted to drive the Wolseley after qualifying for a licence.

Alfie turned out to be quite an asset to the household at Moore Hall, especially with the recurring spells of severe cold weather. He would be out before breakfast, clearing the snow and sprinkling salt on the steps, both at front and back of the house, and helping Em and the staff. Annabel took great delight when he sat and read to her. "I've got a little sister her age," he would say, with a gentleness that amazed everyone.

***

The winter of 1946 to 1947 was a harsh European winter. The cold weather played havoc up and down the length of the country, not just the once, but repeatedly. Large snowdrifts blocked roads and railway lines, there was massive disruption to electricity supplies due to coal deliveries not reaching the power stations, sheep and cattle froze or starved to death, and many businesses had to shut down temporarily. There were fears of a food shortage as supplies were cut off and vegetables were frozen into the ground.

Many schools were closed because of frozen and consequently burst pipes, not just in schools, but in offices and houses alike. Huntingdon Secondary School was one of those closed, and the boys at Springfield were being taught by Mrs Smith, the governor's wife. Even without access to the textbooks used in the school, she devised her own lessons. She had set out, quite successfully, to keep the boys' young minds active with puzzles, reading exercises and mathematical problems. The education of the boys at High Pavement Grammar School was not interrupted as their school did not suffer from burst pipes, and except for the very worst of the snowy weather, they would be seen going off in the morning.

Up and down the country there was great delight at the white stuff falling from the sky, fathers searching attics for long forgotten sledges, helping their children to make snowmen, and enjoying snowball fights.

The snow that had brought such chaos on roads and rail, and had grounded most aircraft, brought pleasure to many people. Walter and Freddie, along with the other Springfield boys, would go sliding down the steep slope in the big field on folded corrugated cardboard, trying to avoid crashing into the trees or wall at the bottom by rolling off into the snow. Get it wrong and you could finish up with a bloodied nose, or worse.

***

March brought warmer air which thawed the snow, causing severe flooding in many parts of the country as the meltwater ran into the rivers. Heavy rains aggravated the situation; in Nottingham large areas were flooded when the River Trent spilled over its banks. London, Yorkshire and East Anglia were among the worst affected areas, and over four million sheep were lost in Wales alone. One of the knock-on effects was the waiting for the land to dry out, leading to the late planting of crops and the consequential reduction in the size and quality of the harvest.

Chapter forty

Lady Jane Marbury sat in the drawing room in Moore Hall listening to the weather forecast on the wireless. The month of March was already halfway through and the prediction of more gales, heavy rain and snow appalled her. It would be of little comfort to those whose farms and houses had been flooded or damaged by the gales, trees blown down blocking not just the back roads, but arterial roads and railway lines across the country. Goodness knows what Delilah's crossing must be like, she would insist on going to join Charles in the Isle of Man by ferry just now, surely she could have waited for better weather, her ladyship was thinking, and talking of driving that absurd little car was ridiculous, they're passenger ferries. It's a good job James is taking her to the ferry with Rebecca and Ernest in the Rolls Royce, along with Delilah's luggage. At least Charles will be meeting them when they get to Douglas. I hope they have a comfortable journey and arrive safely.

Lady Jane pressed the bell push on her desk. A few moments passed and there was a knock on the door. Her ladyship counted two, three, four and the door opened. Em entered, "Yes, ma'am?"

"Ah Em, there will be no guest list this Easter, one or two may drop in, but I would not want anyone to feel obliged to drive here in this terrible weather with all the floods and things."

Rebecca had been sent to look after Ernest on the journey. It was suggested that if Delilah wanted to keep Rebecca as a nanny and personal maid, she should also employ a local girl for general housework, including cooking; otherwise, as she was still employed by her ladyship, Rebecca would return after a brief stay on the island.

"Don't forget, the best place for the least movement is halfway along the boat," James said, as he helped them on to the *Ben-my-Chree*, a member of the crew taking the luggage from him. "Have a safe journey m'lady, and you, Rebecca," he called.

Holding Ernest close to her, Rebecca half turned and waved. "Bye."

A short blast on the ship's whistle. "All ashore who're going ashore," was announced on the tannoy, resulting in a quick scurry of half a dozen people rushing onto the jetty, and the gangway and access doors closed. Very slowly the ship eased away from the pier head in Liverpool, out into the Mersey, then turning north headed towards the estuary and out to sea. James stood watching as the ship disappeared into the rain and the darkness. Envious of the opportunity to visit the island, but thankful he wasn't on the boat in this weather, James turned away and walked back to the car.

As the ship moved out from the estuary into the open sea it began to pitch and roll. Rebecca held Ernest close to her chest. She had already realised that the crossing was going to be long and rough, and she was terrified, not only for herself but for the safety of her charge. Taking a strap from one of the cases, she fastened the travel cradle that Ernest lay in to the fixed seat next to her, thereby allowing herself both hands available to hold on if necessary. Delilah had disappeared, looking for the restaurant as soon as they were on board, and didn't come back until they were well out to sea. She looked a little the worse for wear and was already wishing she had not insisted on travelling before the weather changed. It was going to be a long time before they were docking in Douglas.

***

After a couple of narrow squeaks when only his quick reaction, and enough space with no vehicle alongside, allowed him to manoeuvre against the strong gusts of wind that threatened to blow him over, Victor decided that during the bad weather he would have to reduce the size or rather the height of his load. It was an advantage taking a double load, but not at the risk of damaging his lorry and the cargo in the current weather conditions. It wasn't unusual for March to be windy, but so far

1947 looked like having the worst weather he could remember; some roads and fields were still flooded from the recent snow and heavy rain, and as he was nearing his destination, Canada Docks in Liverpool, a few snowflakes fell against his windscreen. I don't want to get stuck driving through Buxton, he thought. I could be there for days. A couple of quid in the foreman's hand and he was soon on his way. Maybe it wasn't quite cold enough for snow. Whatever the reason, he breathed a sigh of relief as he reached the outskirts of Derby without encountering any more, and headed home to Carlton, Gillian and the children. Well, Mavis and the children. Gillian was working at the Fox and Hounds.

"That's two light ales, and a... hey, Charlie, what're you 'avin'?... and a brown... bottled... You new 'ere?... I don't remember seein' you 'ere before, love... you married?"

"Ask 'im," Gillian said, pointing to the door. "That's my husband, just comin' in," she added, as she put the light ales on the bar. "Two light ales and a brown... thank you, sir." Then to Victor, "I'll be with you in a moment, love, after I've served." She turned to another customer. "Yes, sir?" Victor watched Gillian as he'd so often done in the Red Lion; quick, efficient and friendly, and still had a great figure.

***

"The *Ben-my-Chree* is a nice looking ship," said James, "but struth I wouldn't like to be on 'er in this weather."

"You look done in," said Em. "Go on up. I'll be up when I've taken her ladyship her Ovaltine. I'll give you a massage, that should help you relax."

As she entered his room twenty five to thirty minutes later she could see James, stripped and lying on his stomach. Em lightly oiled her hands and applied a small amount of oil to his body and started massaging his neck and shoulders. "Mmm..." James murmured. Em continued with a gentle but firm pressure as she massaged his shoulders and then his back. "James? James?" Em asked after a while; there was no answer. James was asleep. Em gently wiped the oil from his back and shoulders then covered him with his sheet and blankets. Slipping quietly from his room, she retired to her bed and lay thinking of the three of them, somewhere out at sea in a ship on this terrible night.

***

"I don't mind about Delilah, she's only got herself to blame," said Lady Jane. "She would insist on going yesterday instead of waiting for the finer weather. It's not that I don't care, I do, but Ernest and Rebecca…" Her ladyship looked a little distraught. "I couldn't very well say no, after all Ernest is her child. Thankfully Charles telephoned to say they had arrived safely this morning." Lady Jane looked up at Em. "I don't know how much you have taken in but you are a good listener, Em, but as for your idea of paying towards, please don't even think of it."

"Thank you," said Em.

"How is your protégé, Alfie, getting on?" asked her ladyship.

"James was supposed to be teaching him to drive, but I think he is teaching James about tuning and care of engines. I think he could be a great asset to the household."

"Where's Becca, Mummy?" Annabel asked as soon as Em entered the nursery.

"Becca is taking Ernest to be with his daddy," Em replied.

"When is she coming back?"

"Soon dear, soon. I will tell you when," Em answered. "Esther, I'll stay with Annabel while you go down and take a break with Ruth. I'll see you back up here in about half an hour. If you see James, would you ask him to come up, please."

After a little while James poked his head around the door. "Esther said—"

"Shh." Em was holding her finger to her mouth. "I've just settled Annabel for her afternoon sleep." Em quietly closed the nursery door. "You must have been tired, you were asleep almost as soon as I started last night," she said.

"Yes," he said, pausing when he thought he heard someone on the stairs.

Esther appeared. "I've settled Annabel," Em said. "You can tidy up and have a quiet read, just be there for when she wakes. I'll send Ruth up with the things for Annabel's tea, yours as well if you like."

"Yes, please, Em."

"All right, she'll be up about six."

James and Em went downstairs to the kitchen. "Ah, Ruth," said Em, "when you prepare Annabel's tea, would you take something up for Esther, and yourself if you like, then call it a day. I'll see to her ladyship's meal. Cup of tea, James? Perhaps you'd like to see what Alfie's doing and ask him to come and get his tea. Oh, there you are, Alfie," she said, as he came through from the scullery. "Wash your hands and join us for something to eat. I'll go up later to relieve the girls and settle Annabel. Tell me what you've been up to this afternoon."

"Oh," Alfie said as he washed his hands, "I've been having a look at the Riley Lynx car. It's fantastic, whose is it? I'd love one of those, did you know that it can do over eighty miles an hour. Wow, just think, eighty, that's fast."

"That car belongs to Lady Delilah," said James, "so please don't touch it unless you want to be hung, drawn and quartered."

"I was only looking," Alfie replied.

"Come and sit down," Em said. "James, will you say grace please."

"And I was hoping to get an apprenticeship in motor engineering but it would mean going and working in one of the big factories," Alfie was saying. "Anyway, Dad reckoned I'd be wasting my time, he said they wouldn't be able to teach me any more, he had shown me all I needed and he says I have a natural ability, a sixth sense when it comes to engines." Then, turning to James, he continued, "Maybe that's how I was able to tell what the Wolseley needed done to it."

"He certainly did," said James. "It didn't take him long. He had it running sweetly in no time at all, well, fifteen to twenty minutes maybe."

Em sat listening. Alfie was certainly a quick learner, he could remember fifty percent of a hundred or so wines already: their vintage, what grapes, the vineyards, what they best went with. Incredible, he just seemed to soak up information.

"It's getting late, leave everything Alfie, I'll see to it all. James can help me. Off you go. Goodnight, sleep well. Would you clear the table while I lock up, it shouldn't take long."

By the time Em got back the table was cleared and James had washed the dishes. "Leave them to drain, Em, they'll be dry by the morning," then looking round, he added, "I've loaded the Aga, so let's go up and you can practice your massage."

"That's right," he said as he lay on his stomach, "gentle but firm, mmm," he muttered in pleasure. "I'll turn over." There was no semblance of modesty. "Start at the feet, hee hee, I can't help being ticklish, now gradually work up to my chest. Now it's your turn, that's right, lie on your tummy." Em relaxed as James's hands worked miracles with her tired muscles, she hadn't realised just how tense they were. "Now turn over," he said. With no thought of shyness or modesty, Em did as she was bid, and marvelled at the softness and gentleness but firmness as his hands passed from her shoulders and down to her hips, then smoothing any tenseness out of her abdomen, back to her shoulders and chest, it was wonderful, then down to her feet up past her groin and down again, she was almost oblivious of his hands as they found their way around her body…

"Oh, James," she murmured as she wrapped her arms around him. "Oh, James, darling."

***

Liz woke and turned over. Victor's side of the bed was empty. Of course, he had gone off yesterday morning. It must have been early because the cup of tea he'd left her was stone cold by the time she had woken up. At least he had lit the fire before he went, but that was little consolation now. Yesterday she had felt fine, but not so good this morning. Feeling nauseous Liz quickly jumped out of bed and ran to the bathroom. I haven't eaten anything different, she was thinking. I can't remember ever feeling like this before. I hope I'll be okay for work today, I don't want to let Martin down, she thought, as she splashed her face with cold water and dried it on her towel.

Chapter Forty-one

"Good morning, Liz, isn't it? I'm Sue, Martin's wife. You don't need to worry, you won't be losing your job, I'm just in 'cause Martin's gone to the wholesalers. But first things first, I'll put the kettle on. D'you have milk? Sugar? Just a quick flick around with a duster an' we'll be ready to open up," she said.

I think we'll probably get on quite well together, thought Liz as she started flicking the duster around, well maybe a bit more than flick, dusty goods on display suggested laziness, a bad impression for someone as they entered the shop.

"Tea up," said Sue as she put the tray with two mugs of hot tea and a packet of biscuits on the counter. "Put that duster away, come and sit down and have your tea while it's hot, there'll be more than enough times it'll get cold when we're busy. Help yerself to biscuits, I could only get Rich Tea this time."

At that moment the shop door opened. "Oh, hello, Sue," said the customer, "I didn't think you'd be back, how is your mother?"

"Oh, she's back on her feet, thank you. Half or full gallon this time? The paraffin's out the back, I'll only be a little while. You've met Liz?" A few minutes later Sue was back and put the heavy can down by the door. "How's Dennis?" asked Sue. "I heard he'd hurt his back. Not a good thing for a coalman," she said.

"He's all right. He's always complaining about his back, but he won't give it up for something else. Did you hear about old Briggsy," then eyeing Liz, continued, "er, I'll tell yer another time, tarraa love," as she went out the door.

"It's your tea that'll be cold," remarked Liz, chuckling.

***

It had only been a couple of weeks, and already Delilah had Rebecca doing a lot more than she was supposed to. She was only meant to be Ernest's nanny and personal maid to Delilah, not a general skivvy. The first housemaid had only stayed three days. Eileen had been a nice pleasant girl. Rebecca had liked her, a good worker, polite, and had been recommended by the padre; as the sister of Ellen, his house girl, she had stood in when her sister was unwell. Rebecca never heard what it was about, but Delilah had flown into a rage about something, no doubt trivial, and there had been strong words. Eileen had fled in tears and not returned, not even to collect money due to her for the days she had worked.

The second one, Glynis, was a strong-willed girl who wouldn't take any nonsense from anyone. She had answered the advertisement in the local store in Jurby. Again Rebecca wasn't given to know what it was all about, but after telling Delilah what she thought of her she had walked out. Neither Delilah nor Glynis had been aware that Charles had entered during the upheaval. "If you can't get along with life here, you'd better go back to Moore Hall," he said.

"I'm not going back on that boat," Delilah retorted.

"Then be like Mother, she never has trouble with her staff," he said. "Let them get on with their work and they'll serve you well." Delilah wasn't pleased, Charles seemed to be siding with the staff and she didn't like that.

"Oh, and while I'm at it, the C.O. isn't too happy with you flaunting yourself in front of the young officers."

"Yes? And what about you with the WAAFs?" she parried.

"I prefer to treat them with respect, not shout at them, they appreciate that *and* carry out their duties," he answered.

In spite of the advertisement being in the general store for another two weeks, no one had applied for the job; word had obviously gone round the village as to how Delilah treated her staff. Rebecca had written to Em asking to be relieved of her duties. Lady Jane, much displeased, had telephoned the camp to speak to Charles, who was at that time in the air with a student pilot. Upon her insistence she was transferred to the

C.O., Group Captain Dart, who was not pleased to be involved in domestic problems.

Pilot Officer Kinsman lifted the steps and securely closed the door of the Avro Anson. "Yes, miss, that's right, then when you undo the straps, yes, that's the idea. You don't need to worry, I've made the travel cot secure. No, not like that, madam… let me show… good, you've got it… I have to remind you to keep the straps fastened until either the wing commander or myself tell you it is safe for you to release them, I hope you have a good flight." He disappeared into the cockpit and the aircraft moved forward.

Rebecca looked out of the round window, watching the aeroplane twist and turn as it moved across the airfield, then it stopped. Rebecca held her breath as it emitted a mighty roar, along with clouds of smoke from the engines, and started to roll forward; the passengers were pressed back in their seats as they gathered speed, bumping along, and then Rebecca was aware of the seat straightening up as the Anson's tail lifted. The bumping stopped and the ground sank away, they were airborne and as they turned the wing looked as if it was dropping. For a moment Rebecca was even more nervous, then the wing came up and she relaxed. She was fascinated with what she could see: the countryside below, the trail of steam as a miniature train moved slowly along its lines, a river winding its way to a seaside town complete with a harbour and what looked like a pier that stretched out into the sea, and in the distance the coast reaching out to the east, not that she could tell what direction they were heading. The plane continued to climb and suddenly it seemed they were flying through and then above cotton wool. The engines settled down to a quieter sound, and Rebecca dozed.

Maybe it was the tilt of her seat that woke her, they were flying through cloud with rain streaming past her window; then she could see below them as they circled, the glint of light reflected from greenhouses. Rebecca watched in amazement as the aeroplane wings appeared to change shape, blocking her view. She felt a sinking feeling and closed her eyes. A slight bump, and a second, then the feeling of being driven along a road; the engines had quietened, as she opened her eyes she could see the wings were going back into what to her was their normal shape. They were on the ground, but the bumping had woken Ernest, he was crying; Rebecca undid her seatbelt and crossed the aisle to him just as the plane lurched to a halt, throwing her off her feet and against the seat in front of the travel cot.

"I thought I told you, are you all right?"

"I think so, Ernest was crying."

"We can have you looked at…"

"No, I'll be all right, thank you," she said. "It'll only be a slight bruise."

"How about me," Delilah demanded. "How am I expected to get out of this confounded contraption?"

"Try pulling that," Charles quietly said to his wife, as he stepped down from the cockpit.

The Anson had come to a standstill on the far side of the airfield, well away from the main airport buildings. It was sometime before James had been allowed to drive round to meet them, and as they had a couple of hours drive home from the airfield he had got Em to pack a picnic lunch. Much to Charles's amusement, whereas the rest of them ate theirs inside the plane, Delilah insisted on having her picnic served by James while sitting in the Rolls.

***

"It was amazing," Rebecca was saying, "there we were looking down. It was beautiful… ouch."

"Keep still, girl," said Doctor Stephens. "How can I carry out an examination if you wriggle: Hmm, lucky for you it looks like you've only bruised the muscle closest to the bone. A break would have been really serious. I'll give Mrs Summers a liniment, apply it first thing in the morning and last thing at night. It'll probably be sore for two or three weeks, although it could ache in damp or cold weather. Now, where was this beautiful place?"

Rebecca looked at Em. "I think it's called the Isle of Man," she said. "It was just so different from here."

"Ah yes," replied the doctor, "it is said to be an island where there are more fairies than people."

***

Wing Commander Bucklow stepped out of the car. "Thank you, Alfred," he said, and closed the gate behind him as he walked along the path through the pretty garden. Almost before he reached the cottage, the door was opened; a homely looking lady stood in the doorway, Charles could make out the form of a man standing a little way behind her. "May I come in?" he asked.

The lady stepped to one side. "Let the gentleman past, Erik," she said, then trying to peer into the car, "Is she with you?"

"Who… oh, my wife; no, she's not with me," he answered. They showed him into a pleasant, warm living room.

A girl aged about eighteen, who was sitting knitting, looked up. "It's no good asking," she said. "I'm not going back to work for her."

"It's all right," replied Charles, "no one is going to ask you. First of all, I still owe you your pay for the days you worked," he said, handing her an envelope, to which she meekly thanked him. "I would like you— don't worry, she's gone back to England and won't be coming back—I would like you to come and work for me."

"Ooh, I don't know," she replied, looking up at her mother.

"Go on, Eileen," her mother replied, "give it a try. Like the gentleman says, as long as she's not coming back."

***

"I don't know," said Mavis, "it could be May if it was…" She appeared to be deep in thought. "Or… I just don't know," she said, almost in tears from frustration.

"Don't worry, love," Gillian said, putting her arm around her cousin's shoulder, "it's not that important. The baby will come when it's ready, not necessarily when it's due. For what it's worth my guess is June. How about you putting the kettle on while I settle the kids."

"Hello, anyone at home?" Victor called out as he came in the door.

"Of course we are, you daft hap'orth," replied Gillian. "Not so loud, I've settled the kids."

"How's my favourite lady? he asked jokingly.

"You mean you've got more?" asked Mavis.

"Sh, don't tell the missus," he replied.

"I heard that," answered Gillian, "and who are you calling your favourite lady, may I ask?"

"You of course, my beloved," putting his arms around her.

"Steady on, you'll make Mavis jealous, anyway what brings you here, apart from your lorry?"

"Cannot a loving husband—"

"Heh," she interrupted, "we haven't seen you for about a week."

"Fortnight," corrected Mavis.

"Well, I've been busy trying to make my fortune."

"We haven't seen any of that either," said Mavis.

"Didn't you see them?" asked Gillian. "A whole squadron of pigs just flew by."

"I'm just rustling up something for us to eat," said Mavis. "Are you going to join us?"

"What are you having?" he asked.

"Welsh Rarebit," Mavis replied. "The rare bit is the cheese. I can stretch it, if you don't mind more sauce than cheese. Even three people's cheese ration doesn't go far these days."

"You must know someone among your contacts," hinted Gillian.

Hmm, Victor was thinking, Jim and 'Arry are both serving time, while most of the others have gone to ground. "I'll give Joe Harvey a try, although I don't know what his line is lately," he replied.

The evening passed quite amicably as they sat chatting about life in general, the weather, films, wireless, the neighbours, anything and everything.

Eventually Mavis stood up. "I think I'll go up and get some beauty sleep," she said. "Goodnight."

Gillian waited a while before she spoke. "I can hardly ask Mavis for money. She's going to need what she has for her baby." Gillian paused for a moment while she considered what she was going to say. "Even with what I've been earning I'm finding it difficult to manage, and I can't work much longer with Mavis looking after the kids in her condition. Another couple of quid a week..."

"Surely she can give something," interrupted Victor.

"No," answered Gillian, "it could get back to the council, and they would say we were subletting and you know what that could mean."

"Okay, but two quid?"

"Thirty bob would be a bit tight, but I suppose..."

"All right," he said, taking out a roll of notes and peeling off two fivers, "that should cover the next month."

***

Betty Grable was going to be on in the Gaumont Cinema in *The Dolly Sisters*.

The buzz went round the older boys in the school. "Who?"

"Her with the *Million Dollar Legs*."

Freddie was not impressed, who would want to insure their legs for a million dollars anyway? Probably a publicity stunt but maybe a film star might want to insure their legs. However, the film was a musical and Freddie liked music, so that Saturday he was to be found sitting in the audience when the film was shown during the matinée; the basis was a typical Hollywood story of two pretty young girls who could dance and sing, but then all the female stars in Hollywood films were pretty and could dance and sing. A romance was inevitable, but what he remembered most was the tune and song, *I can't begin to tell you how much you mean to me.* The story? Soon forgotten. Betty Grable? Not impressed. But the picture Jimmy had shown him of Cyd Charisse, cor, she really was beautiful, even to a thirteen-year-old.

Chapter Forty-two

"She's been telling tales," Delilah said vehemently. Em looked at her ladyship.

"On the contrary," replied Lady Jane, "I have her letter here. When a good member of *my* staff resigns, it troubles me, so I rang Charles's commanding officer, Group Captain Dart. It was he that told me what was happening. If you want to blame anyone, blame yourself, *definitely* not Rebecca." Em was greatly relieved, but still had doubts about whether Delilah would accept what her ladyship had said until Delilah was given the letter to read for herself.

"I don't wish to be disrespectful, ma'am, but I have been told that I must only take instructions given directly by her ladyship or Mrs Summers," Rebecca said. "They said that while I am in here, I am only to attend to things relating to the children and the nursery."

"But what about, oh, never mind," Delilah grumbled as she turned and walked out, slamming the door as she left, waking her son and making him cry.

"It's not fair," Delilah moaned as she threw herself down in the chair. "I just wanted Rebecca to rinse a few things and she said she's been told she can't."

"If it's what I think it is, I would think you should be proud enough to prefer to do them yourself. A little hot water, soap and elbow grease."

"But, Auntie—"

"Otherwise put them in the laundry basket."

"But it will be days before they're back."

"The choice is yours. Now pick up a book or something and let me finish these letters."

"Laundry goes on Mondays, and takes a week," said Em.

"But I need them."

"The girls all hand wash their own, so I might suggest—"

"But Em!"

"Sorry, dear, I can't, nor would I ask them to. As I said, if you can wait, the laundry goes on Monday."

Delilah was furious. What's the good of employing servants, she thought, if you have to do something as mundane as hand washing? I wouldn't want to risk sending my delicate Paris fashions to the common laundry, they might get spoilt, or stolen.

"Where's Mrs Summers?" asked Alfie as he walked into the kitchen.

"She in with her ladyship," Ruth replied. "Is it urgent?"

"Well no, and yes," he answered looking round to see if they were on their own. "Would you like to come with me to the Odeon tonight? There's a super film on, *The Odd Man Out* starring James Mason," he told her.

Ruth looked Alfie up and down. He seems a nice lad, she thought, not brash like the others in the village… well… maybe.

"Please."

"All right," she answered, "if Em lets me off, but it will have to be early. The buses don't run after nine-thirty and the films don't finish until ten," she reminded him.

"Oh, Ruth," Em said as she entered the kitchen, "would you prepare her ladyship's tea trolley please, and set it to include Lady Delilah."

"Can you spare a minute please, Mrs Summers?" asked Alfie.

"Oh! Mrs Summers is it, Alfie? What are you after?"

"I wonder if," he was saying, ignoring Ruth's glare, "Ruth could finish early today?"

"What's this about, Ruth?"

Ruth looked a little embarrassed. "Alfie's asked me out," she replied.

"Please," pleaded Alfie, with a sheepish look on his handsome face.

"And where, Prince Charming, do you plan to take Cinders?" Em asked joking.

"To the Odeon," he answered, "there's a super film on, but we'll need to go early and we'll have to leave before the feature film finishes or we'll miss the last bus."

"I'll have a word with James," said Em. "He's picking up guests for her ladyship and will be dropping them in town later. I'll ask him to drop you at the Odeon, and also pick you up, so you can watch the film right through. It spoils it if you see the finish before the beginning."

"Oh, Em," Alfie said, "I could kiss you."

"Don't you dare, save any kisses for Cinders."

"You just wait 'til I get you later," whispered Ruth to Alfie.

***

Walter and Freddie stood outside the office door waiting for the governor; Walter looked at Freddie who shrugged his shoulders, he couldn't think why either, they would just have to wait.

"Come in," Mr Smith said, standing by the open door. The twins entered and stood in front of the desk. Freddie had been there several times before for various misdemeanours and felt the same feeling of apprehension, especially when he saw the punishment book on the desk in front of him. Mr Smith closed the door, sat down and looked at the two boys. "What have you two been up to?" he asked. The twins looked at him not knowing what to say, in case they admitted something Mr Smith had not been aware of. "Okay then," he said, "what were you doing in King Street, lunch time on Thursday?" Still no answer. "All right then, I'll tell you," he continued, "you were standing at the window of the Government Surplus Shop looking at wirelesses and such things. I was driving down King Street and I saw you. Are you interested in that sort of thing?"

"Yes, sir," two voices answered as one.

"Well, you both know full well that you are not supposed to leave the school premises when you stay for school dinners."

"Yes, sir."

"Don't let me see you there again."

"No, sir."

"Now run along."

***

Mr Pilcher, the commissionaire, was standing at the top of the steps as the Rolls Royce glided smoothly to a standstill outside the Odeon. He watched as the chauffeur came round the back and opened the door to the young couple who stepped out and stopped for a few words, before ascending the steps towards him. He had recognised James, the chauffeur to her ladyship, Lady Marbury, and saluted the couple, obviously two of her guests. "Good evening, sir, good evening, madam, this way if you please," he said, leading in through the door and up to two empty seats on the circle. "Have a pleasant evening," he said, and returned to his place outside on the top step. Alfie was puzzled. Maybe Em or James had organised a treat for them? Ruth was impressed, thinking Alfie had arranged it all. Whoever or whatever, they were going to enjoy the evening.

The programme started with the usual advertisements: furniture from Collins in Lower Bridge Street; taxis for hire from Acme Cars; Cooks Accompanied Tours, Paris fashions and then the trailer for next week. Oh no, not another American war film, thought Alfie. Anyone would think they were the ones who won the war. Another short break to sell more ice creams, Alfie slipped out of his seat and returned with two choc ices, sitting down just as the lights were dimmed and the feature film began. With ice creams finished, in the darkness while they watched the film, Alfie surreptitiously slipped his arm around Ruth's shoulders, smiling as he felt her head rest on his own shoulder. All too soon the film ended and along with most other patrons, they stood up for the national anthem, while some couldn't wait to leave. The commissionaire escorted them down the steps to the waiting Rolls, opened the car door and saluted as they got in. Once James had driven well away from the cinema, they erupted into delighted laughter. Upon their arrival back at the hall, Ruth bade Alfie good night, kissed him, quickly jumped out of the car, ran indoors, up the stairs and threw herself onto her bed. She was ecstatic.

***

"Come in. You'll catch you death o' cold. Yes, it's just there, pick up the handset and ask… That's right… I don't know but the operator should be able to connect… The midwife?… You go and be with your friend, I'll call the midwife then I'll be along… Fred," Mrs Hodges, Gillian's neighbour called out, "when Carol comes, I'll be next door at Gillian's… Oh, hello, can you come quickly to Mrs Bradburn's, I think the baby is on the way… I think so… I'll tell her… Fifteen minutes… thank you."

"He's lovely," said Mrs Hodges as the doorbell rang. "Oh, that'll be Mrs Miller, the midwife," she said, "sooner than she thought, she'll probably want to make certain everything is all right, though it was all over by the time she arrived. Have you thought of a name yet? Never mind, there'll be plenty of time for that. Stay here with Mavis, I'll go down and make a cup of tea. Do you?… All right… two teas… no sugar… Don't worry, I'll keep an eye on the little 'uns."

"That's right, dear," said the midwife, "the little fella's certainly taken well to the breast. I'll be round in the morning to see how you're both doing. I'll let myself out." With that Mrs Miller headed to her next call.

"I was wondering—" Mavis stopped in mid-sentence.

"What?" asked Gillian.

"If Victor had a second name," replied Mavis, already aware of the answer but wanting to hide the fact from her cousin.

"Yes," said Gillian, "Thomas, why?"

"Well, you two have been so kind, letting me stay with you, I wondered if you would mind me calling the baby Thomas."

"I think Victor will be quite pleased, ask him when he gets back, he should be home over the weekend."

***

"Well?" asked Em the next morning, as she and Ruth sat down to a cup of tea, before preparing the breakfast.

"Thank you, Em," blushing slightly as she looked up, "it was lovely. We got to the Odeon, and the man at the door—"

"The commissionaire," said Em.

"Well, getting out of the Rolls, he must have thought we were toffs, 'cos he escorted us to the best seats in the balcony. He didn't ask us to pay… oh, sorry I forgot, thank you for paying for us."

"I didn't pay, and I don't think James did," Em said.

"Oh! Well, maybe, anyway, it was so romantic. Alfie put his arm round my shoulder. I didn't see much of the film. Not that we did anything," she hastened to add, "but it was lovely."

"I'm pleased you had a nice evening, now if you will… Oh, hullo, good morning, Alfie, good film last night? I was just saying, Ruth, please prepare the breakfast while I take up the things for the nursery."

"I haven't said anything," Ruth said. "Well, not much. You do still love me?" she asked.

"Of course I do," he answered. "I've fancied you since junior school."

"You never said."

"You were always with a group of your friends."

"Hush, there's someone coming."

"Where did you two get to last night?" asked Esther as she entered the kitchen. "I was going to suggest we went to the Odeon, so I went by myself. The bus was late leaving Chester last night, if I had known it was going to be late, I could have watched the end of the film." Alfie smiled as he looked at Ruth.

***

Victor had been very busy cramming in as many shorter more local deliveries as he could while based in Chingford, and with longer daylight and better weather, trying to make up for the loss of business during the strike and then snow and ice in the early months of the year. As a result, he had not been back to Nottingham for several weeks. He was going to need to dig deeper into his pocket with Liz expecting an infant in the autumn. She wouldn't be able to work much longer. She'd probably need to move back with her parents in Northend Road for the last month or so before the baby was due. He looked at his lovely wife lying there in the semi-darkness. He felt an overwhelming affection for the beautiful, sleeping form; he didn't want to leave, but there was work to be done. "I'll be back soon, very soon, my love," he whispered as he turned and went out to his lorry.

It was as if the traffic lights had conspired against him. Most mornings there were one or two at red when he reached them; today they all seemed to sense his approach and turn to red at the crucial moment, and the traffic was the heaviest he had experienced in a long time. Consequently he arrived at Witney an hour later than planned and had to join a queue of lorries waiting for loads. There was just one load of blankets, for Irvine Johnsons, a wholesaler in Derby. Never mind, he thought, at least that gets me most of the way back to Nottingham and Gillian.

By slipping the gears into neutral and turning off the ignition, the lorry was able to quietly coast along the road with the minimum possible sound, stopping outside nineteen Warwick Street. Turning the key in the door, he entered and walked into the lounge. "Hullo, ladies, I'm home." He saw Gillian sitting facing him as he appeared, the top of Mavis's head visible above the back of the chair facing away from him.

"Stay there, Mavis," said Gillian, as she stood up. "His lordship can have my chair tonight. Fried egg on toast, dear?" she asked Victor. "Sit down and I'll get you a beer." As he sat down, he saw that Mavis was feeding a baby. For a brief moment he remembered the silhouette in the copper, the night he left the Red Lion. Today the form was very much fuller, but then Gillian had a fuller figure when she was feeding an infant.

"How old?" he asked. Mavis looked up.

"Two days," she replied.

"Wha…? But I thought…" Victor was trying to calculate dates from memory.

"I got it wrong."

"You mean it could be—"

Mavis shrugged. "Who knows, much as I'd love it to be, there's no need to worry."

"What are you two talking about?" Gillian asked as she entered the room.

"We were talking about choosing a name, I was going to ask Victor if I can call him Thomas, you told me it's his second name," Mavis answered, "because you both have been so good to me."

Victor looked distinctly hesitant....

"Tuck in, love," said Gillian, as she put the tray of food down on her husband's lap, "half an hour earlier and you would've seen the little'ns."

Gillian stretched herself out on the settee. "Isn't he gorgeous," she said. "I wonder if he looks like his dad," causing Victor to choke.

"It's all right, dear," he quickly said, "I think a piece of toast got stuck in my throat."

"Do be careful, dear, they say that for everyone that passes on another child is born, and we don't want another baby just yet."

"What d'you mean 'just yet'?" he asked. "I hope you're not feelin' broody." The girls looked at each other and grinned.

Victor sat back in the chair, subconsciously counting his offspring, three with Em, two with Gillian, possibly one with Mavis and one on the way with Liz, chuckling to himself, just four more for a football team. Then his mood changed, he really missed the twins, maybe he could think of some way of seeing them from time to time.

"A penny for them," said Gillian.

"Naw," he replied, "you wouldn't want to know."

Chapter Forty-three

Mother and baby were doing well. Thomas was gaining weight as babies do, and Mavis was subject to mood swings, but she put that down to worrying about her parents' reaction when she took him home, or more likely to hormone changes. Victor had agreed to take Mavis and Thomas to her home at the end of the month, if the weather permitted, so with mother and baby in the front seat of the Hornet, Victor set off early enough so that in the event of rejection, there would be sufficient time for them to return to Nottingham.

It was a pleasant journey with adequate comfort stops. The sun was shining, driving up through Buxton, a favourite route for Victor, beautiful countryside, and stopping places with stunning views. Most drivers tended to be in a hurry and preferred the faster roads, but today time was not the priority. Sitting on a large rock at the side of the road, feeding Thomas, Mavis looked up at Victor. "Wouldn't it be nice to be a gypsy, sitting like this while admiring the view." Victor didn't reply. He thought of the lumbering horse drawn caravans holding up the traffic, the motorists and lorry drivers blasting their horns and shouting abuse. A gypsy life might sound romantic, but not for him; a houseboat rocking gently on the river, now that would be heaven.

***

Ruth was enjoying life. The week was almost over. Em had made her housekeeper for the week to see how well she would do. She had been advised that a good housekeeper treated all staff the same, in other words there could be no favourites; it had been hard, but she had a good mentor, and she hoped the others understood. Following Em's example, she had phrased instructions such as, 'today I would like', instead of 'today you will', and it had worked a treat. Standing in the corridor, she knocked on Em's door. There was no reply. She knocked again. There was still no reply. Gingerly she opened the door, the room was empty, the bed had been slept in but—she heard a sound behind her. Em had emerged from the bathroom. "Are you all right, Em?" she asked.

Em looked at Ruth. "Thank you dear," she answered. "I'll be all right, I'll be down in a few minutes," she said as she sat down on the side of her bed.

The talking stopped as Em walked into the kitchen, and a low undertone started up when she entered her office. Ruth brought her in a cup of coffee. "Thank you, Ruth," Em said, "if you can spare a few minutes." She pointed to a chair. "I've been watching how you've dealt with responsibility over the last week. This afternoon I'd like you to lead the discussion with her ladyship about next week's menus. Lady Delilah is likely to be there. Whatever you do, let her be the only one to be discourteous, try to avoid any, I repeat, any flying off the handle. If she is offensive, say nothing, just *look* towards Lady Marbury and await her reaction. Given time, she will respond. Now shall we go and get our breakfast?"

"Ah, Em," said James, "can you spare Alfie for a couple of hours please, Lady Jane has asked for Lady Delilah's car to be got ready for Delilah to drive down to her place in Wiltshire."

"You will need to ask Ruth," replied Em. "I'm training her to be housekeeper for when I eventually leave, so today she is housekeeper."

"You're leaving?" he asked. "I thought perhaps—"

"We can't talk about that here," she answered. "Tonight, dear, I mustn't keep Ruth waiting."

***

The car came to a standstill outside the gate to the farm house. Victor went round to the passenger door, opened it and helped Mavis as she stepped out carrying the baby. Mrs Woodstock, Mavis's mother, opened the gate. She wrapped her arms around her daughter and grandson.

"Hello darling," she said, tears in her eyes. "Take no notice of your father, the silly old fool shouldn't have turned you out. Oh, he's so sweet. What's his name?" she asked.

"Thomas James," Mavis answered. "You wouldn't want two James's in the house, so I've given him dad's name as his second name."

"That's clever of you," Mrs Woodstock said, "they'll both have the same names, only the other way round. Come along, let's get inside, you two must be ready for something to eat, and I daresay Thomas will be too."

"If you're settin' the table fer 'er, I'll 'ave mine in the kitch'n," Mr Woodstock said. "I ain't eat'n wiv 'er. She brought shame on the fam'ly."

"Please yerself then, yer silly old fool, now look what yer've done."

Mavis was in tears. "I can't stay here, Mum, it's not fair on you. He'll only take it out on you if I stay. Sorry, Mum, come on Victor, let's get away from here."

"Yes, Victor," shouted Mavis's father, "and take your son with you."

"He's not Victor's baby," Mavis shouted to her father.

"It's not fair," Mavis said through her tears, "he's a bloomin' hypocrite. He condemns me, yet he must have made Mummy pregnant long before they married…" Victor was straining his ears to hear Mavis above the sound of the motor. "I was twelve when they celebrated their tenth wedding anniversary. He's a two faced…" The sound of a lorry passing from the other direction drowned out Mavis's voice. "It's all right for you men, you can have your fun and walk away." She was muttering in her tears. "But us women have to live with the consequences. It ain't fair."

Victor pulled in at the side of the road. "I know you shouldn't when you're feeding," he said, handing Mavis a hipflask, "just a little sip, dear."

Mavis took a deep swig of the contents. "What the…? Phew… What was that?" she choked.

"Scotch whisky," he answered, "the real stuff."

"Are you trying to get me drunk?"

"No, dear; I did say just a little sip! I thought you needed a pick-me-up," Victor said, looking over his shoulder to check it was safe to drive off. Mavis looked at Victor; he might be her cousin's husband, but, well, maybe.

Gillian watched as the occupants of the car headed towards her front door. Mavis was carrying the baby and her handbag, the bag she had given her on her fifteenth birthday—it had worn well—and Victor carrying Mavis's luggage and, in case it would have been needed, the overnight bag that he carried in his lorry. Gillian hadn't expected to see Mavis back, nor Victor that evening. Either they had run into trouble with the car, or Mavis hadn't got the welcome she had hoped for. Whichever, she was pleased to see them. Mavis had been good company, and although she had only been gone a little under twelve hours, Gillian hadn't realised how much she would miss her and was greatly relieved to see her and Victor come back.

***

It was past eight in the evening when James walked into the kitchen. "I thought…"

"I know dear, but Ruth had scheduled me for the evening shift," Em replied, smiling.

"But I thought you were *her* boss."

"I am, but *she* is the housekeeper for today. It would have been wrong to change it to suit myself, it's all part of what I've taught her. Anyway, we can talk, but first things first; cuppa tea, love?"

"Yes, please," he answered, "but don't get up, I'll see to the tea. Refill for you, dear?"

"Have you heard anything at all from Agnes?" asked Em.

"No," James replied, "but it seems Jimmy Cleghorne has done a disappearing trick. It is rumoured around the village that he's probably gone to join Agnes in Lincoln. Apparently their jiggery-pokey was known and talked about in the village and had been going on a long time before I knew," James went on. "Good riddance to the both of them, they deserve each other," he said vehemently.

"I don't know what you'll think about it but—"

"You move in with me? That would be fantastic," James said, interrupting Em.

"No, silly, although it would be lovely, just let me finish. It's a little early so I can't be sure, but I think I might be pregnant."

"That's great!" he answered. "Oh, but what about your job. Is that why—"

"I'm teaching Ruth because I can see she's got potential, but anyway, if I am I can hardly stay here."

"We could get married."

"We'd both need to get divorces, it would cost a fortune, and even if we could afford it, we'd probably both be out of work, and homeless. Anyway, why are we talking as if it's happened? Let's wait and see if I really am pregnant."

"And then?" asked James.

"I'll be up as soon as I've finished tonight," Em replied smiling.

***

Dinah rang the doorbell to the flat and waited, but there was no reply. How annoying, she thought; she rang it a second time, holding her finger on the button longer than she had the first time; still no reply. I'll try the shop, they might have seen her. Ding went the bell on the shop door, bing went the bell on the counter when she brought her hand down on it.

"Just a minute," came the voice from somewhere out the back. "Good afternoon, miss," said Sue as she came through from the backroom, "can I help you?"

"I wondered, would you know if the lady from the flat is in, she was expecting me but there's no reply, I know I'm a little early but—"

"You are?"

"Oh, I'm her sister, Dinah," she said.

Sue brought her hand down on the bell.

Liz emerged from the back room. "Hello, Dinah, you're early. You've met Mrs Martin, my boss." Then, to Sue, "This is the girl I mentioned."

Dinah looked puzzled. Me? she wondered.

"Would you like a job?" Sue asked her.

Dinah couldn't believe her ears. She had already applied for several jobs without success. There were too many young women returning from the services and the Land Army snapping up the jobs. "Er, yes please," she replied.

"Come through to the back while I take a few details. Keep an eye on the shop, please, Liz, ring the bell if it gets busy," then glancing at the clock, "We won't be long" as she, followed by Dinah, went through to the back room. They emerged half an hour later, Dinah wearing an overall coat and a broad grin as Sue told her, "The shop closes in just under an hour, so pick up a duster and look round the shelves. If anyone comes in, look busy dusting, preferably behind the taller displays."

"You mean?" asked Liz.

"Dinah's on a month's trial starting tomorrow. It'll give her a chance to learn the job," answered Sue, "and if she learns as quickly as you did, I think she will be just the kind of person I'm looking for."

Dinah looked at her sister and mouthed a 'thank you', picked a duster from a shelf under the counter and disappeared behind the tall display of garden tools and accessories. Fascinated by the number of drawers on the wall, she started opening and peering inside: there were tap washers, rubber washers, and metal washers of all different sizes, there were screws of all different metals, for all purposes, shapes and sizes; thick ones, thin ones, long screws and short ones...

"It's all right, you won't be expected to know what they're all for," Liz said reassuringly, "just to have some idea where to find them, and that will in time become second nature."

***

"Take over please, Susan," Em said as she put the letter in her pocket. "Let Ruth do any of the lifting. I need to go up to my room for a moment." With the house guests having left, Ruth was helping in the kitchen while Esther and Rebecca were finishing the cleaning of the bedroom suites.

Em sat on the bed and opened the letter, her eyes quickly passed over the first short paragraph, and caught the next words. "I hate him," she read. "I'm a nurse and I would have understood, I knew she wasn't well, but mother wasn't one of the healthiest people," the letter from her sister Flo went on, "but I realise now just how ill she was, they should have had her in hospital, but she wouldn't have agreed to go. She thought hospitals were where you went to die. As she died at home, there has to be an inquest, so the funeral can't be arranged for several weeks. I'll let you know when."

The letter slipped from Em's hands as she reached for a hanky.

***

Em is faced with having to make decisions that affect her dream of having her family around her. Volume Three will reveal whether her determination is rewarded, and whether her wayward husband's overtures will bring about a reconciliation.